"This addictively readable thriller marries a breakneck pace to a complex, multilayered plot. . . . A roller coaster ride of adrenaline-inducing plot twists leads to a riveting and highly satisfying conclusion. Exceptional characterization and an intricate, flawlessly crafted story line make this an absolute must read for thriller fans."
—*Publishers Weekly* (starred review)

NO MERCY

"*No Mercy* grabs hold of you on page one and doesn't let go. Gilstrap's new series is terrific. It will leave you breathless. I can't wait to see what Jonathan Grave is up to next."
—**Harlan Coben**

"John Gilstrap is one of the finest thriller writers on the planet. *No Mercy* showcases his work at its finest—taut, action-packed, and impossible to put down!"
—**Tess Gerritsen**

"A great hero, a pulse-pounding story—and the launch of a really exciting series."
—**Joseph Finder**

"An entertaining, fast-paced tale of violence and revenge."
—*Publishers Weekly*

"No other writer is better able to combine in a single novel both rocket-paced suspense and heartfelt looks at family and the human spirit. And what a pleasure to meet Jonathan Grave, a hero for our time . . . and for all time."
—**Jeffery Deaver**

JOHN GILSTRAP

HELLFIRE

A Jonathan Grave Thriller

PINNACLE BOOKS
Kensington Publishing Corp.
www.kensingtonbooks.com

PINNACLE BOOKS are published by

Kensington Publishing Corp.
119 West 40th Street
New York, NY 10018

All Kensington titles, imprints, and distributed lines are available at special quantity discounts for bulk purchases for sales promotions, premiums, fund-raising, educational, or institutional use. Special book excerpts or customized printings can also be created to fit specific needs. For details, write or phone the office of the Kensington sales manager: Kensington Publishing Corp., 119 West 40th Street, New York, NY 10018, attn: Sales Department; phone 1-800-221-2647.

This book is a work of fiction. Names, characters, businesses, organizations, places, events, and incidents either are the product of the author's imagination or are used fictitiously. Any resemblance to actual persons, living or dead, events, or locales is entirely coincidental.

First printing: July 2020

10 9 8 7 6 5 4 3 2 1

ISBN-13: 978-0-7860-4552-5
ISBN-10: 0-7860-4552-3

Printed in the United States of America

Electronic edition:

ISBN-13: 978-0-7860-4553-2 (e-book)
ISBN-10: 0-7860-4553-1 (e-book)

*To Joy, my best friend
and my bride of thirty-five years.*

Chapter One

Ryder Kendall had heard every word spoken from the front seat. They thought he was asleep, and like every other adult, they believed that just because a kid's eyes were closed late at night, he'd been struck deaf. He should be so lucky. He hadn't slept more than a few minutes in the past three days. Not since the FBI crashed their house and tore his world apart.

Now, everything was ruined. He and his brother, Geoff, were being driven to some kind of orphanage by a lady driver, who he figured had to be a cop, and a priest named Father Tim. Both were nice enough to their faces, but the quiet conversations revealed their true thoughts. They pitied him and his brother. They felt *sorry* for them.

When the lady driver wondered how *the boys* would ever get past *this kind of trauma*, Father Tim shushed her, said that such things ought not be discussed within earshot. As if Ryder hadn't already wondered a thousand times how much his life was going to suck from now on.

Dad had warned him that that trouble was coming.

Ryder didn't understand the details, but he wasn't completely surprised when the cops kicked in their door. Okay, he was *terrified* when the SWAT team pulled him out of bed and onto the floor at three in the morning. And the handcuffs hurt. But only for ten or fifteen minutes, until they figured that a thirteen-year-old and his eleven-year-old brother didn't pose any real hazard. After that, the cops let him get dressed, but not without a lady cop with a rifle watching the whole time. She seemed as uncomfortable as he did. After that, they walked him and Geoff straight out to a car that whisked them off to a stranger's house.

He never got a chance to say goodbye to his parents.

Mom and Dad weren't specific about why they'd done the things that got them sideways with the FBI— those were the words Dad used, *got sideways*—but Ryder was smart enough to know that pissing off the FBI was a big deal. That meant that his parents had committed a federal crime, not a state crime. Everybody knew that federal crimes were the worst.

And man, oh man, were there a lot of FBI windbreakers among the cops that invaded his house.

"You're going to hear a lot of bad things about me and your mom," Dad had told him just hours before the invasion. "I wish I could tell you that they'll be false, but they're not. I've done bad things."

"I don't understand," Ryder had said. "What did you do?"

"You don't want to know the details," Mom had said.

Ryder had taken that as his cue to shut up. Questions never changed bad news, they only slowed it down.

Dad had continued, "Of course, when this happens,

it will have a huge effect on you and your brother."
He'd said it as if they were planning a family trip. "I
can't tell you how sorry I am."

Sorry? Ryder thought. *What happens to Geoff and me?*

It turned out that the answer came in several parts.
Part one: You get shipped to a house of well-meaning
but deeply weird people who smelled like hot dogs and
old socks and the family stared at you all the time.
Then you get shipped to another place, where they
punted Ryder and Geoff to the cop lady and the priest.

And now they were on their way to an orphanage
called Resurrection House, even though he and Geoff
weren't exactly orphans.

They were only half-orphans.

Tears pressed behind his eyes as he remembered the
sound of his dad rushing out of his bedroom after the cops
crashed through the front door. The sound of the gun-
shots. The stillness of Dad's body as he lay there in the
hall. The redness of the blood in the carpet.

Ryder had no idea what this Resurrection House thing
was all about, but for now, he figured that the Resurrection place had to be better than that first douchebag
house.

Ryder had always possessed an uncanny ability to
read people. Not their minds—not like one of the
Legilimens from the Harry Potter stories—but he was
great at reading their intentions, their state of ease. It
was like what they called *stranger danger* in school
and what Dad used to call *situational awareness* at
home. Right now, Ryder knew that the grownups in the
car were upset about something. They leaned close to
each other and talked quietly.

The driver lady kept glancing up into the rearview

mirror, as if she saw something that made her nervous. She had spiky white hair, but not the kind of white that comes with age. In the mirror, lit up by the lights of the car behind them, the brown eyes that had looked so friendly before now looked wrinkled and scared.

Ryder eased his seatbelt open and rose from his captain's chair to turn around and look out the back window. The one other car on the road was driving way too close, the way Mom would drive when she was getting ready to pass.

"Please get back in your seat," Father Tim said. He was completely different from what Ryder expected a priest to be. He seemed too young, and he smiled more than church people normally did.

"Are they trying to pass us?" Ryder asked.

The lady driver—her name was Pam—said, "If they were, they've had plenty of time to do it."

The priest repeated, "Ryder, I really want you in your seat."

Ryder opened his mouth to argue, but he decided to comply, instead. This didn't feel right to him.

He'd just turned to face front when the follow car's high beams lit up the back window and blue strobe lights painted wild shadows all over their van's interior.

Geoff jumped awake in the captain's chair to Ryder's right. "What's happening?"

"Shut up," Ryder snapped. He didn't want to be mean, but if little dickhead was talking, he wouldn't be able to hear what was being said up front.

"I don't like this," Pam said. "I'm not doing anything wrong. There's no legit reason for us to be pulled over."

"Well, we can't just ignore them," Father Tim said.

The cop behind them popped his siren, as if to cast his vote on what they should do.

Pam pushed the button on the dash to turn on the hazard flashers. "I'm slowing down to thirty-five," she said. "Call nine-one-one to see—"

"Tell me what's happening!" Geoff insisted, blocking out the rest of Pam's command.

Ryder would have been happy to call 911 for them, but the FBI had taken their phones. And their computers. Hell, they'd taken everything. He and Geoff weren't allowed to take anything with them but underwear, clothes, shoes, and a jacket.

As the van navigated a curve, another wall of blue lights erupted out front. Another police car, parked at an angle across the road.

"I guess that decides that," the priest said.

The driver stomped hard on the brakes, making Ryder feel better about his decision to sit back down and belt himself in.

"I'm scared," Geoff whined.

"Shut up," Ryder said. "We're all scared. Saying it doesn't help."

Very little about this pickup and delivery had felt right to Tim, and now this traffic stop was icing on the cake. He fumbled with his phone as he extracted it from his pocket.

"What do we do now?" he asked.

"We sit," Pam replied. A retired cop, she'd chosen social work as her second career. The same customer base, she'd explained, but nobody wants to shoot the lady with the clipboard and the smile. "Put the phone back in your pocket. You don't want to have anything in your hands. They'll tell us everything we need to know."

Out front, in the wash of the van's headlights, the cop's door opened, and a uniformed officer took a position behind his engine block, his hands full of pistol. "Holy shit!" Tim exclaimed out of reflex. It came out much louder than he wanted.

Pam seemed less unnerved. "What the hell?"

Behind them, Ryder and Geoff almost bumped heads as they leaned into the center space to see out the front windshield.

"Oh, my God," Geoff blurted. "Are they going to shoot us?"

"Stay in your seats, boys," Tim said.

An electronic loudspeaker popped from behind. "Driver, turn off your engine and drop the keys out the window."

"Remember," Pam said in a clipped tone as she turned the engine off. "You want your hands to be empty."

"What the hell is going on?" Tim asked.

"Ask me again in five minutes," Pam replied. "Do everything they say. Move slowly and keep your hands visible at all times." She made a show of dangling her keys out the window before dropping them to the pavement.

The cop on the loudspeaker said, "Driver, open your door and step out of the car. Keep your hands visible at all times."

"I told you," Pam said. She moved carefully. With her left hand extended out her window, she reached across her body with her right hand to pull the handle that opened the door. When it was unlatched, she used her foot to push it all the way open.

"Driver, step out, hands visible, fingers splayed, and sidestep two steps to your left. Leave the door open."

Pam gave Tim a look he wasn't sure how to interpret and went about the business of following directions. She slid off her seat, her feet found the ground, and then she stepped off to the side. She stood with her arms out to her sides, cruciform, in a posture that impressed Tim as one that would quickly become exhausting.

"I'm really scared," said the younger brother. *Geoff.* Tim owed it to them to remember their names.

"This will all be over in a few minutes," Tim assured.

"Front seat passenger," the guy on the loudspeaker said. "Same drill. Open your door, keep your hands visible . . ." The instructions were pretty much the same as before.

Tim turned so he could see both of their faces. Adolescents look so much younger when they are frightened. "Ryder and Geoff, listen to me," he said. "There's been some kind of misunderstanding. I'm sure everything will be fine. After I get out, I want you both to listen carefully and do exactly what the officer tells you to do."

"Are we in trouble?" Ryder asked. His voice trembled.

"I don't know," Tim said. "But if you do what they say, everything will be fine."

Father Tim slid out of the passenger side door and then moved away from the van.

"Hands farther out to the side," the cop commanded.

Tim raised his hands higher, splayed his fingers farther out. Could they not see his white collar?

"Stay cool, officers," Tim said. "I'm a priest, and my driver is a retired police officer."

For a second or two, nothing happened. Maybe longer. This was wrong. All of it seemed unreal. Unearned.

The kids.

Tim turned to look back at the boys, and that's when he heard the gunshot. Pam fell, and then something kicked Tim hard in the chest. As he fell to the street, he wondered how anything could feel so hot and not set him on fire.

He thought, *Please, God, forgive me.* Everything went dark.

The spatter from Pam's exploding head painted the window just inches from Ryder's face. He jumped and screamed something even he didn't understand. Another shot followed, and Father Tim dropped from view.

"No!" Geoff yelled. "Oh my God, they killed them!"

Ryder didn't say anything. His mouth wouldn't work. Through the smear of gore, he watched the cop from the front racing toward the van. His flashlight beam bounced as he ran. Ryder's stomach churned. He thought he might puke.

Except he didn't have time.

The cop pulled his sliding door open at the same time the other cop opened the slider on Geoff's side. They opened them hard, causing the panels to rebound halfway closed again.

"Get out," the closest cop said.

"What did you do?" Ryder shouted. "You killed them!"

The cop pressed his pistol against Ryder's forehead. "Open that mouth of yours again if you want to join them." The cop's face looked like it had been bloodied, a red splotch covering part of his forehead and eye.

To Ryder's right, Geoff yelled, "Leave me alone! Ryder! Help!"

The other cop slapped Geoff across the forehead with the barrel of his pistol, and the boy collapsed.

"Jesus!" Ryder yelled. "Geoff! Goddammit, leave him alone!"

The last part of his words sounded clipped and garbled as the cop with the weird face shoved a rough sack over his head and tied it tight across his neck. Out of reflex, Ryder brought his hands to his throat and pulled at the cinch.

"No!" he yelled, and he punched blindly at his attacker. "Get this thing off—"

A light flashed behind his eyes, and there was nothing.

Tim hurt. His chest felt hot, hollow, and numb all at the same time. He thought his eyes were open, but the world was dark. He thought he could see the outline of trees across the black sky, but he couldn't be sure.

"I'm alive," he said aloud. It was a test of his voice. It didn't sound right, as if coming from someone else and far away. "But I'm dead soon." The words didn't frighten him, though maybe they should. What they did was *focus* him.

He needed help, but out here in the wee hours, he could go undiscovered for longer than it would take for him to bleed out.

Ancient Boy Scout first-aid training tried to form in his mind. Should he raise his legs to counter the onset of shock, or should he try to raise his torso to slow down the bleeding?

Tim winced against the anticipated pain as he finger-walked his left hand to his pants pocket, where he could find his phone. Moving an arm meant flexing a chest muscle, though, and that brought the fiery agony back in Technicolor.

"Awww, *dammit*!" he grunted as he brought the phone up to his face. He shut his eyes against the brightness of the screen. He pressed the voice command button and said, "Dial nine-one-one."

The phone replied, "Please say a command." The electronic lady's voice sounded even bitchier than usual.

"Call nine—"

"Hey, Kim!" a voice shouted. "This one's still alive."

Tim closed his eyes again.

Chapter Two

Jonathan Grave awoke as something heavy punched him in the chest. He jerked upright, ready to fight, but as he reached for the .45 on his nightstand, he heard the phone blasting "Onward Christian Soldiers" and the picture cleared for him, despite the darkness. JoeDog, the eighty-pound black lab who occasionally claimed Jonathan to be her master, hated phones. Jonathan must have missed a previous ring or two, and the beast was tired of the noise.

He lifted the covers away and padded naked across the master bedroom to lift his phone from its charger on the dresser. He'd learned a long time ago that calls that came in after bedtime—was it really only 3:15?— brought important news. The short walk ensured that he'd be at least awake enough to understand what was being said.

The ringtone told him that Father Dom D'Angelo would be on the other end. "Morning, Padre," Jonathan said. His voice sounded a little like he'd gargled with glass. "Working late or getting up early?"

"Hi, Dig. Come downstairs and let me in. It's cold out here, and we need to talk."

Jonathan had known Dom since college—long enough to recognize the urgency in his tone. "Hang tight," he said. "Two minutes, max."

With his phone still in his hand, he swatted the switch for the overhead light and walked six steps over to the leather chair in front of the window, where he stepped into his bug-out jeans. He always draped clothes nearby when he went to bed, a habit that stretched back to his days in the Unit. In any emergency, dressed was better than undressed, and speed mattered.

JoeDog, fully awake and ready to go, apparently expected something good in her future. Her swinging tail was forcing her hind legs into a jig.

"This isn't about you," Jonathan told her, but his voice just spun her up more. He opened the bedroom door, and she was off.

In its previous life, Jonathan's home had been a firehouse. As a boy, he would hang out there in his spare time, shining brass and playing poker with the firefighters. They'd called him their mascot, and he wore the title proudly. After he fell into a little money—okay, a *lot* of money—and the powers that be determined that Fire Station 14 would be better situated out on the highway, he bought the place and turned the first two floors of the sprawling structure into his home and the third floor into the offices for his company, Security Solutions. He spent lavishly on the renovation, converting the space into a warm oasis of leather, wood, collectible art, and oriental rugs. While the external architecture remained the same—including the big rollup doors, all but one of which had been permanently secured—he'd gutted the interior. The brass pole remained, but it led nowhere, merely a decoration.

The hardwood steps felt cold against his feet as he made his way down to the main level, where JoeDog had already figured out that someone was at the door. Out of habit and an abundance of caution, Jonathan opened the drawer in the table adjacent to the door to reveal the chambered Glock 19 pistol that always resided there. Had he not known that the visitor was a friend, the Glock would have been in his hand, shielded by his thigh.

Jonathan opened the door to reveal Father Dom standing a few feet back, his hands shoved into the pockets of a beige canvas ranch jacket and his expression dour.

"Hey, Dom. What's up?" Jonathan stepped aside to leave room for the priest to pass. "Come on in."

Dom tipped his chin as a thank you and stepped forward. "We have a serious problem," he said. He walked straight to the three-cushion leather sofa and helped himself to a seat. "I'm missing a couple of kids."

Something stirred in Jonathan's gut. Among the significant charitable causes Jonathan supported, the one of which he was most proud—and most anonymous—was his perpetual endowment of Resurrection House, a residential school for the children of incarcerated parents. RezHouse sat on Church Street, up the hill from Saint Katherine's Catholic Church, on the grounds of Jonathan's childhood mansion. He'd deeded the massive structure and its acres of property to the church for one dollar, on the condition that it be used in perpetuity as RezHouse. A security breach a while back had resulted in Jonathan hiring a full security team to keep the place safe.

"*Missing kids* is a scary phrase, Dom," Jonathan said. "What do you mean?"

"Father Timothy left this afternoon with that new social worker we hired at RezHouse—Pam Hastings— to escort two brothers from a foster home out past Lexington, but he hasn't come back yet. No phone call, nothing."

Jonathan sat on the opposite sofa, facing the priest. Jonathan had never met Pam Hastings, but he knew Father Tim to be assistant pastor—or some such, the title didn't matter—of Saint Kate's. Quiet and always friendly, he was known among the parishioners as Father Flash, having reduced the duration of his masses to just under an hour each. During Saturday confessions, his line was always the longest because he also had a reputation for easy penance. "That's a long drive. You talking Botetourt County, that area?"

"Right. A little town called Haverville. About five hours from here."

"Well, come on, Dom. That's a ten-hour round trip. Maybe he stopped."

"Maybe he did," Dom agreed. "But he would have called. Certainly, by this hour, he would have called. At least one of them would have called."

Jonathan wanted to find a way to talk him off the ledge, to find a way to conclude that this probably was nothing. But it truly was *very* late. "Have you called the place they were supposed to be picked up from? Did Father Tim ever arrive?"

Dom was leaning far forward, his elbows forming a tripod with his knees. "I don't know. I called, but no one answered. It could be because of the hour when I called. I just don't know."

Jonathan understood the concern, but he didn't know why Dom was here. "How can I help?"

Dom seemed to be stumped by the question, too. "I . . . I don't know, to be honest. I figured you had contacts you could reach out to. You seem to know everybody."

Jonathan watched his friend's eyes. There was real fear in them. Yes, there were people he could wake up, but at this hour, that was an aggressive move to make. On the other hand, this was Dom asking.

"I know just the guy," Jonathan said. He pulled his phone from the pocket of his jeans, scrolled through his contacts list, and pressed a button. When the line on the other end shifted to voice mail, he clicked off and punched the number again. The line rang again. "I can do this all night," Jonathan muttered.

On the fourth ring of the second go-round, the line connected, and the very angry voice of the Fisherman's Cove police chief said, "Honest to God, Digger, if there's not a dead body in your foyer—"

"Missing kids, Doug," Jonathan said, getting ahead of the idle threat. "On their way to RezHouse and they never showed up. Father Timothy, too, along with a social worker Dom's worried that—"

"Stop there," Doug Kramer said. "Where are you?"

"I'm at home."

"The padre there with you?"

"Yes."

"How long have they been missing?"

Jonathan relayed the question, then put his phone on speaker.

"I can't give you a hard number on the time," Dom

said. "Tim and Pam left this afternoon—no, yesterday afternoon, I guess—to go out to Haverville and come back with two kids. Two brothers, Ryder and Geoffrey Kendall. I haven't heard anything from any of them since."

"Where the hell is Haverville?"

"Botetourt County," Jonathan said.

"Okay, and where the hell is Botetourt County?"

"Way west," Dom said. "Closer to Tennessee than here, but Father Tim would have called me if there was a delay."

"Murphy rules the universe," Kramer said. "If they broke down, it would only happen where there's no cell service."

"The boys are eleven and thirteen," Dom said. "Their mom was just arrested, their dad is dead."

Silence on the other end.

"Come on, Doug," Jonathan coaxed. "Eleven and thirteen. Yeah, could be nothing, but . . ."

"Give me thirty minutes," Kramer said. "I'll get my head straight and pull on some clothes, then head over to your place. And you'd better have coffee brewing."

Twenty-eight minutes later, JoeDog jumped to life and scrabbled her way out from her sleeping perch under the coffee table that separated the two sofas. She had an uncanny way of knowing before the bell rang that someone was at the door.

It wasn't yet four in the morning, but Doug Kramer was showered, shaved, and fully clothed in a freshly pressed khaki uniform, complete with gleaming Sam Browne belt and polished gold badge.

Jonathan greeted him with a steaming mug of coffee. "Cream and four hundred sugars, just as you like it," he said.

"I wouldn't press my luck on the humor thing at this hour," Kramer said. He hooked the mug's ring with his forefinger and wrapped his other hand around the barrel for warmth. "Morning, Dom."

The priest was standing at the sofa. "I hope this turns out to be a big mistake," he said.

Kramer prepared himself with a deep breath and took a sip of coffee. "Let's all sit down."

From body language alone, Jonathan prepared himself for bad news. He let Doug take the spot he used to have on the sofa while he helped himself to the William and Mary rocker that normally was his favorite anyway, thanks to too many years of back-yanking parachute drops.

"I'm not getting a happy vibe out of you," Dom said. His face was drawn tight.

"That's because I have bad news," Kramer said. "While I was getting ready, I had our dispatcher do some checking. You know, to see if anything bad has happened on the roads or whatever." His face turned to stone as he cast a glance toward Jonathan and then returned his gaze to Father Dom. "There was a car found on a back road where Botetourt County meets Bedford County—between Salem and Lynchburg. Local sheriff's department says it looks like it might be a carjacking. There was blood on the ground, but no sign of people. A couple of shell casings, but that doesn't mean anything out in that part of the world. People shoot all the time."

"They do that here, too, Doug," Jonathan said. "What about the car? Who's that registered to?"

"It's a rental."

Dom's head drooped. "Tim used a rental car for the transfer. It was too far a drive in his own vehicle, and the RezHouse van is in for service."

"Do you know which company he used?"

"I could probably find out," Dom said. "Who leased the car they found?"

"It's only been a few minutes," Kramer said. "Not a lot of time for questions yet. It's a pretty sure thing that an abandoned car didn't jump to the top of their to-do list, even in a place like wherever-the-hell-that-place-is."

"No mention of the boys?" Jonathan asked.

"No mention of *anybody*. As far as they're concerned, there's nobody to mention."

Jonathan ran it all through his head. He flat-out didn't believe in coincidences. Building on Doug Kramer's commitment to Murphy's law, Jonathan was a disciple of the codicil that declared when two or more unpleasant events happened in short proximity of time or space, they were presumed to be related until proven otherwise. In this case, the blood, shell casings, and missing children told the story of a murder and a kidnapping.

"What do you know about the parents, Dom?"

"No more than I know about any of our students before they arrive. A name. And in this case, I know that their father was killed in the raid on their house and that their mother is in custody. The rest will be in the file that comes with them."

"Is she rich?" Kramer asked. He looked to Jonathan. "I presume you've jumped right to kidnapping."

"Yeah, pretty much."

"I have no idea," Dom said. "It's not like we do credit checks. Tuition at RezHouse is free."

"We've all three of us got internet machines in our pockets," Jonathan observed, retrieving his phone. "You've said their names twice, Dom, but refresh my memory."

"Geoffrey and Ryder Kendall," Dom said. "I don't remember the mother's name. I could go back to the rectory and get it."

"Kendall," the chief said. His eyebrows knitted together in a scowl. "Boy, that name rings a bell."

Jonathan entered the name into his phone and laughed. "Not exactly a unique name, is it?"

"Might her name be Constance?" Kramer asked.

"It could be," Dom said. "In fact, I think it is."

Jonathan entered the name into his search engine and got nothing. "What are you seeing that I'm not?" he asked Kramer.

"You can't search where I'm searching," Kramer said. "The Constance Kendall I'm seeing here has a federal warrant out on her. DEA and FBI both. It's a felony pick-up order, but that's all it shows."

"Is that unusual?" Jonathan asked. "I mean, that the warrant doesn't say what it's for?"

"Very."

"What does that mean?"

"I have no idea," Kramer said. "It's rare enough to qualify as unique."

"And does unique imply important enough to kill or kidnap children?" Jonathan asked.

Kramer laughed. "You like running down a single track, don't you?"

"Eleven and thirteen," Jonathan reminded yet again. "Whatever this is, that makes it worth tracking down."

"What does that mean?" Kramer asked.

"That means I'm going to do what I do best," Jonathan said. "I'm going to bring them back home."

Kramer stood. "And that's my cue to leave."

The suddenness of his move startled Jonathan. "Just like that?" He stood, too.

"Don't take it personally," Kramer said. "I've never really understood what exactly you do for a living, but I've always sensed, as an officer of the law and of the court, that I'm better off for my ignorance. Am I wrong?"

Jonathan smiled. "Thanks for coming by, Doug."

He walked the chief to the door. "Keep the coffee cup," Jonathan said. "I have lots more just like it."

Kramer pulled up short just as he crossed the threshold. His face showed worry. "We've known each other long enough to speak plainly, right?"

"I'm hurt that you would even ask," Jonathan said.

"Be careful," Kramer said. "Around here, you're a big deal and you get away with stuff. That shootout at the mansion, for example."

Jonathan waved it off. A terrorist cell had come far too close for comfort not too long ago, and the results had brought headlines that no town council ever wants to deal with.

Kramer continued, "Don't make like that's nothing. It's something. It's a *big* something. Anyway, I could keep your name out of it because I'm your friend, and I know you're coming from an honest place."

"You don't want me hurting strangers," Jonathan offered, cutting to the chase.

"Well, not you, so much," Kramer said. "But this deals with kids . . ." He left the rejoinder for Jonathan to fill in the blanks.

"Boxers," Jonathan said.

Kramer hiked his shoulders, a silent yes. Brian Van de Muelebroecke—aka Boxers—was one of Jonathan's closest friends. They'd worked together since forever. Nearly seven feet tall and topping the scales at a deeply classified number, Boxers—also aka Big Guy—lived in a world where subtlety didn't exist. He was simultaneously kind and lethal. Jonathan knew of no one more loyal and dedicated to bringing justice where it was needed. He also knew of no one who showed less remorse when justice required killing. He was the number one person you wanted on your team when life got shitty.

Boxers had a soft spot in his heart for kids and a very hard spot for those who harmed them.

Kramer explained, "I'm just saying I have no pull in that part of the state."

Jonathan smiled. "I appreciate the warning."

Kramer shifted his stance. "Have you had many dealings with the Virginia State Police?"

"Can't say that I have."

"Well, out in that part of the world, they're the law, and they take their laws really, really seriously."

Translation: Don't expect any breaks from them if you break the law even a little bit.

"I appreciate the warning, Doug. If you don't mind me asking, please keep an eye out on the wires. If any other details surface, please reach out and let me know."

Kramer hefted his mug as a toast. "Will do. Thanks for the coffee."

As the chief walked away, Jonathan closed the door and turned to Dom. "It's time to wake people up," he said.

Chapter Three

Housed on the third floor of the converted firehouse that was Jonathan's home, Security Solutions was a boutique private investigation company whose client list included some of the most prominent corporate names in the world. What set them apart was their access to cutting-edge surveillance techniques and their willingness to deploy them.

Jonathan Grave—and by extension, Security Solutions—believed in winning. He lived by a moral compass that drew bright ethical lines that could never be crossed, but he considered legal lines to be less defined. For example, in Maryland, it was illegal to record a conversation without both parties' permission, while in Virginia, only one party needed to know. South and west of the Potomac River, firearms could be carried nearly without limit, while north and east of the Potomac, having a firearm under any but the most extraordinary circumstances was a serious felony. Jonathan thought laws like that were silly, and he was willing to bend them for the sake of his clients—and, occasionally, for his own convenience.

Security Solutions investigators had good instincts on such things, and since they toiled on behalf of clients who always knew what the operations would be, they mostly basked in the shadow of plausible deniability.

But Security Solutions had a second side—some might say a darker side—the operational details of which were known to only a tiny handful of people, and most of them were currently gathered around a teak conference table in the high-tech room that they'd dubbed the War Room. Located in the Cave, the moniker given to the closed and guarded executive suite, the War Room rivaled the technological capabilities of similar facilities in police headquarters and government agencies around the world.

Venice (Ven-EE-chay) Alexander was the technological genius who made Security Solutions the powerhouse that it was. The odd pronunciation was a throwback to a teenage temper tantrum that grew legs. She lived up the hill from the firehouse in the mansion that had been Jonathan's childhood home, back when his last name was Gravenow, with her son, Roman, and her mother, Mama Alexander, who, a thousand years ago, had served as Jonathan's housekeeper and surrogate mom.

Jonathan liked to say that electrons feared Venice. She could cause ones and zeroes to do things against their will, and not always for the Forces of Good. Just before Jonathan hired her, Venice had come *this close* to being charged with a felony as a result of her hacking escapades.

Accessed by a separate entrance that led to a long flight of stairs, the office was guarded twenty-four seven by a team of security officers that Jonathan had handpicked from medically discharged Special Forces operators. The nature of his business was such that it occasionally left people on the other end of his team's investigative efforts angered to the point of violence.

Venice sat in the command chair in the War Room, at the short end opposite the 106-inch projected computer image. Jonathan sat at the long end on her right, next to Gail Bonneville, one of the smartest, most intrepid operators he had ever known. A lawyer, former member of the FBI's Hostage Rescue Team, and retired sheriff, Gail was the newest addition to the team, and she had sprung back in nearly full form from an injury at the hands of a bad guy. Her back wasn't everything it once was, but whose was, after a certain age?

Boxers hadn't arrived yet, but he was on his way. An urban dweller at heart, Big Guy preferred to live near the nightlife in Northwest Washington.

Jonathan didn't want to wait for him.

The screen at the end of the table showed the Skyped-in image of Sheriff's Deputy Thomas Goolsby, who believed that he was speaking to Special Agent Neil Bonner and his staff on a secure link from Washington, DC.

The deputy wore a walrus mustache that concealed the entirety of his upper lip. He looked many times more awake and refreshed than Jonathan felt. "I confess that I'm a bit confused by the involvement of the FBI," Goolsby said. "I mean, it was an abandoned car."

Venice kept their camera tight on Jonathan. "I understand there were bloodstains and shell casings," he said.

"Yes, there were. In fact, we're reasonably certain that it's a homicide scene. One of the windows on the van bore considerable blood spatter. And brain matter, too, I believe. But there was no bodies recovered."

"You said *bodies*," Jonathan said. "Plural."

"Yes, sir, that's right. We found some blood pooled in the dirt on the other side of the car—the passenger side—but again, no bodies."

"Did you search the area?"

Goolsby's expression darkened. "Why, no, Agent Bonner, that never occurred to us. You know, out here in the country, if there's signs of a murder but no body, why we just assume they was beamed up by aliens."

Jonathan knew he'd asked a stupid question the instant it passed his lips. "Forgive me for that, Deputy. This is not my normal work shift. I'm a little sleepy-headed."

Goolsby dialed it back. "Our initial search didn't turn up anything, and the chopper tried its best from the air. We'll go out and scour the area again after the sun comes up."

"Second set of tire tracks?" Jonathan asked.

"Gravel road," Goolsby replied. No more answer was required. "You still haven't told me why the Bureau is involved in this."

"Well, technically, we're not," Jonathan said. While the FBI director herself had issued Jonathan and his team ersatz credentials—to be used in pursuit of agendas that could not legally be pursued—Jonathan didn't want to get too far out ahead of his skis. Nothing good could come from asserting federal involvement in a case in which the feds were not, in fact, involved. "We suspect that the car you found also contained two kids. Brothers. Eleven and thirteen."

Goolsby scowled and picked up something from out of frame. Probably a pen. "What are their names?"

The question startled Jonathan, and it shouldn't have. Blame the hour. "I'd rather not mention the names at this point," he said. He was playing his gut here, and his gut told him to withhold the boys' identities. "Did you see any signs of them at the incident scene where you found the vehicle?"

Goolsby's head twitched from side to side. "No. In fact, the inside of the vehicle was pristine. I'd say unusually clean, even. Maybe that's because it was a rental. Do you guys know something that I should know?"

Jonathan offered up the smile that had opened many doors over the years. "Let's say that I don't know anything that I'm allowed to share with you." He didn't want to say anything that might screw up a real FBI investigation.

"Names and faces go a long way in finding lost people," Goolsby said.

Off to the side, out of Jonathan's frame, Gail and Venice were gesticulating wildly. *Tell him!*

"The children are Ryder and Geoffrey Kendall," Jonathan said. "Ryder thirteen, Geoffrey eleven. They were being transported to a place called Resurrection House in Fisherman's Cove, Virginia. Their escorts were Father Timothy Dolan and Pamela Hastings. Hastings is a retired cop, recently hired as a social worker at Resurrection House."

Goolsby showed shock, and then he started scribbling. "Jesus," he said under his breath. "Ex-cop? What jurisdiction?"

Jonathan scanned the room and watched Venice

mouth the name of a Northern Virginia county. "Braddock County," he said.

Goolsby wrote some more. "I wish I had known this earlier."

The comment annoyed Jonathan. It was only natural that cops looked after their own, but the notion that Goolsby was more spun up by a missing cop than missing kids and a priest offended him. He kept his thoughts to himself. Instead, he filled the cop in on more details.

"The whole reason the car was on the road was to transport two boys from a foster facility to Resurrection House."

"Why does that require a cop to come along?" Goolsby asked.

"I can't speak to the specifics," Jonathan said. "But have you ever heard of Resurrection House?"

"Can't say that I have. I'm assuming it's some kind of orphanage."

"Not exactly," Jonathan said. "The residents are all children of incarcerated parents."

"Didn't they have some kind of dustup there a while back?"

"Yes, they did." Jonathan was struggling with the third-person pronoun. "From that alone it became clear that sometimes a little extra security is in order." He shifted gears. "Getting back to the evidence in the car, surely, there's some paperwork in the glove box that explains—"

"There's nothing in the car," Goolsby said. "And I mean *nothing*. Glove box and center console are both empty. And there's no sign of the victims, whoever they might have been."

"I'm telling you who they are."

"You know this firsthand?" Goolsby pressed. "You saw them in the car?"

"Of course not," Jonathan said. "But this comes from a very reliable source."

Goolsby sat a little taller. He was growing annoyed. "Did your reliable source actually see them in the car?"

"Well, no. But given the ages of the kids and the nature of the transport—"

"Agent Bonner, I assure you that we want to find those occupants as much as you do. I mean, clearly there was violence at that scene. But we've searched. We've done what we can for tonight."

"Are the State Police involved yet?" Jonathan asked.

"No, but apparently the FBI is. How did this become a federal case?"

Jonathan felt as if he'd stepped into a trap that he'd set for himself. "I think it's clear that the boys were snatched."

"Agent Bonner," the trooper said, "all due respect, there—"

Jonathan continued to press. "You know how this works. A clock started ticking the instant those kids were grabbed, and it's unforgiving."

"Thank you, Agent Obvious," Goolsby said. "We'll continue to work the scene in the morning. Meanwhile, I'm sure you're going to work things from your end, so if you come up with something, let me know. I'm not blowing you off, Bonner. I promise we'll go at this full-bore. The evidence will take us where it takes us."

Jonathan was done with this guy. It made no sense

to beat him up anymore. "All right, Deputy. Thanks for your time." He nodded to Venice, and the screen went black as the call disconnected.

Jonathan looked at his assembled team. "Are we one hundred percent sure that those kids were in that car?"

"How could we be?" Gail asked. "All we can be sure of is that you *told* us they were in the car."

Venice added, "Dom would not lie to you, Dig."

Jonathan considered that. "No, he would not. But he could be mistaken. Ven, I need you to wake some people up. Definitely Dom—oh, hell, he's probably still wearing a hole in the floor. And maybe Mama. Find out the details of where Father Tim was supposed to be and when. Then find out if and when they got there."

Gail sat a little taller. "Oh, my God, I just thought of something. We're assuming that whatever happened, happened on the way back from the foster home. Maybe they never arrived and the Kendall boys are sound asleep in their beds."

Jonathan gaped. That twist had never occurred to him. He turned to Venice. "There you go," he said. "Makes your calls even more important."

Venice spun her chair away from the conference table and stood. "I'll get right on that," she said. "Can I ask a favor?"

Jonathan opened his arms wide. "Your wish is my command."

"Food and coffee," she said. She made a point of looking at the clock on the wall. "Four-fifteen A.M.. Jimmy's just opened. Scrambled eggs and a biscuit, please."

Gail grinned. "Ooh, that sounds good. As long as you're going . . ."

Jonathan chuckled. "I remember a time when I used to be in charge of the company I own."

"And please don't dawdle," Venice added. "Sir."

When Ryder Kendall awoke, he was aware of nothing but pain and movement. Hard surfaces. He smelled burlap and blood. And piss. He later found out that the piss was his. He couldn't see anything. He remembered the bag being shoved over his head, but nothing else.

No, wait. Shooting. There'd been shooting.

And blood. Blood all over the window.

And Father Tim.

He knew he should be scared, and maybe he was, but mostly he was confused. He didn't know where he was or why he was here. Didn't know why those cops shot up the car or why they'd hit him so hard.

A hard bump cleared his head. Now he could hear road sounds, the rumble of tires, and the rush of air. The *ga-lump, ga-lump* as the wheels ran over those lines in the road.

Everything was so black. He was sure his eyes were open, and, yeah, he knew there was a bag on his head, but this was really, *really* black. Couldn't see his hand—

His hands! He couldn't feel them, either. They were tied behind him. And his ankles were tied, too.

Now, the fear bloomed. It erupted. A million thoughts flooded his head, so fast and so many that they created a clot of information in his mind. His breathing picked up, and there wasn't enough air to breathe. He now knew

that he was in the trunk of a car. He was being kidnapped.

Oh, Jesus, they're going to kill me!

He'd heard stories of what perverts did to young
boys before they killed them.

His heart hammered. If he didn't get more air, he
was going to pass out. If he passed out, was the next
step to die? Here in the trunk of a car? He didn't
want—

"Ryder?" The familiar voice threw some water on
his fuse.

"Geoff?"

"I can't see," Geoff said in a voice that cracked. "I
can't breathe good, either." He started to cry in earnest.

"You're okay, Geoff," Ryder said. "We're both okay."

"I can't see!"

"Okay, listen to me," Ryder said. The fact that his
little brother was panicking snatched that option away
from Ryder. One of them had to be strong. Or, at least
pretend to be. "You have every right the be scared. I'm
scared, too, but we have to keep calm. Think back to
the last thing you remember. Can you do that?"

Geoff's sobs dialed down to snuffles. "We were in a
van."

"Right, and do you remember when the police attacked us?"

It took a few seconds. "Yeah. Oh, my God, was I
shot? Is that why I can't see?" The sobbing started
again.

"Geoffy, listen to me." Ryder hadn't used his brother's
baby name in a long time. "You haven't been shot, okay?
You can't see because they put a bag on your head.

That's why you feel like there's not enough air. There is enough, though. I promise. Just settle down a little."

Ryder forced himself to take a deep breath, hold it, and then let it out. He could feel his heart slowing down.

"You okay, Geoff?"

"I feel like I'm tied up."

"You are," Ryder said. There really wasn't a way to soft-pedal that one. "And I think we're in the trunk of a car."

"Oh, God!"

"C'mon, Geoffy. Keep calm. We can't do anything about it for now."

"It stinks like piss in here. And don't call me Geoffy. I hate that name."

"Are you hurt anywhere?" Ryder asked.

"Everywhere," Geoff said. "My head hurts really bad. My arms and legs and back and neck. Hell, *everywhere*."

Ryder smiled. "Me too."

A long time passed in silence. Neither one of them were very big talkers. "Ry?"

"Yeah?"

"Why?"

"I don't know."

"Are they gonna hurt us?"

Ryder pushed away the horrible images that were in his head. "No, I don't think so. No more than they already have, anyway."

"Why?"

Oh, for God's sake, I don't know. Ryder opted to say nothing. He didn't have any more answers than Geoff did. He had at least as many questions in his head—

probably more since he was older and knew more things.

"I don't want them to hurt me," Geoff said, and he started to cry again.

Ryder started to say something to settle him down, then decided not to. Maybe Geoff needed to cry. Maybe Ryder did, too, but he didn't have the luxury. He was in charge now. He was the man.

He tried his best to relax against the cramps that were building in his calves and thighs and ignore the hands and arms that felt as if they were buzzing with electricity.

Ryder thought his eyes were closed, but there really was no way to tell. He concentrated on taking big breaths and releasing them slowly. He'd learned from his shrink that that was the best way to control his anger, so maybe it would help with panic.

Jimmy's Tavern had been a part of the Fisherman's Cove waterfront for as long as Jonathan could remember. At this time of the morning, the place catered primarily to the fishermen and watermen who filled their bellies before setting out for the day. At the moment, though, Jonathan was the only customer. While he was waiting for the food and coffee, Jonathan saw Boxers arrive in the Batmobile, a heavily armored and well-provisioned Chevy Suburban that Jonathan had caused to be custom-built to replace the Hummer that was its predecessor and namesake. "Hey, Irma!" he called across the bar into the kitchen.

"What!"

"Boxers just arrived."

"Okey-dokey. Five-egg omelet do it for him?"

By the time the food was cooked, Gail had wandered over to give him a hand carrying it all.

Twenty-five minutes after they'd left the War Room, they were back in it, breakfasts and coffees distributed, each meal concealed behind the flap of its biodegradable lid.

"Have we learned anything we didn't already know?" Jonathan asked. "I know it hasn't yet been a half hour—"

"None of it's good," Venice said. "Dom deferred on the details to Mama, so yes, I had to wake her up. Let that settle in and start writing my commendation." Mama Alexander was known to everyone simply as Mama, and she'd nurtured a reputation for tolerating exactly zero bullshit from anyone. Even Boxers was afraid of her. "She gave me the name of the foster facility where Father Tim went to pick up the boys. It's a place called the Shenandoah Station, out past Lexington."

"Is that an orphanage? School?" Jonathan asked.

Venice made a face. "Like you said, we're only a half hour into the hunt. It does not appear to be a government facility. Could be a private one. I don't know yet. The good news here is they answer their phone at this ridiculous hour."

"The bad news?"

Venice took a sip of coffee. "There's no record of the boys ever being there."

Jonathan leaned into the table. "How can that be?"

"It can't," Venice said. "At least I don't know how a record could disappear."

"You're suggesting they were never there?" Gail said.

"I'm not suggesting anything," Venice said. "I'm reporting what I've been told. Before Shenandoah Station, though, they were with a family named Ballentine."

"That was their first stop after the raid on their home?" Boxers asked.

"Exactly."

"I presume you called them."

"I did," Venice said. "When I asked about the boys, they hung up."

"Just like that?" Jonathan asked. "Just *click*?"

"Yes. And then I dialed back. That time, they didn't answer at all."

The room fell silent as they all looked at each other for answers that didn't want to come.

Boxers broke the silence. "We have to assume that the boys have been kidnapped."

"I agree," Gail said.

"That means we need to gear up to go find them," Boxers said. Big Guy was hands-down the most lethal man that Jonathan had ever known. Not homicidal, not sociopathic, but decisive. He seemed happiest when he was bringing violence to people who'd earned it. But he had always held a soft spot for kids. Nowhere in his declaration that they needed to go out and get the Kendall boys was there a question or request for permission.

Jonathan rubbed his face, perhaps to spur better circulation and the clarity of thought that might come with it. "Right," he said. "We'll start with the Ballentines and follow in the boys' footsteps." He stood and the others stood with him. "Load the Batmobile for bear. I don't know what we're running into, but I want to be ready for it."

"What about Wolverine?" Venice asked. "Maybe she can stir some action in the Bureau to help with the hunt."

Wolverine was the code name given to Irene Rivers, the director of the FBI, whom Jonathan had known for years. Way back in the day, when the future director was merely a special agent and Digger and Boxers were still in the Army, Jonathan had used some extraordinary measures to retrieve Wolverine's kidnapped daughters and mete out punishment for the asshole who'd taken them. That event had formed a bond of trust between them.

"I think Wolfie should be our first stop after we hit the road," Jonathan said. He looked at his watch.

As if reading his thoughts, Boxers said, "The Batmobile is ready to go. I keep her mission-ready."

"How is that possible?" Jonathan asked with a grin. "Guns aren't legal in DC."

"And thank God for that," Big Guy said as he headed toward the door. "That must be why no one ever gets shot there."

Chapter Four

King's Park Shopping Center sat at the intersection of Braddock Road and Rolling Road in a part of Fairfax County, Virginia, that had been deformed and defined by urban sprawl. It anchored the western end of a '60s-era housing development that was named, obviously enough, King's Park.

Jonathan sat in the shotgun seat of the Batmobile, watching rats frolic around the Dumpsters behind the supermarket that anchored the strip mall. "I tell myself that just because those nasty bastards scamper round outside doesn't mean that they can actually get inside."

"I got a .22 in the safe if you want to do a little plinking," Boxers said from behind the wheel. "What do you say, Gunslinger? Ready for another breakfast?"

"Think of all the snakes they're keeping away," Gail said from the back. "And for those keeping track of such things, it's almost eight o'clock.."

"She'll be here," Jonathan insisted.

Boxers asked, "What's the home run here, Boss?"

"I figure if anyone has the ability to pull important strings, it will be her," Jonathan said. "A home run would be her opening up a federal manhunt for Ryder and Geoffrey Kendall."

As he spoke, white light bloomed on the far side of the grocery store and danced against the Dumpsters and the woods behind. As the light beams grew larger, they were joined by others until, finally, the first set of headlights made the right turn toward the Batmobile.

The approaching vehicle—a ubiquitous official black Suburban—lit up the blue lights in its grill. Two more Suburbans followed the first, forming a straight line, nose-to-tail, about twenty feet ahead and on the left.

"What happens next?" Gail asked.

"The director never walks to anyone," Jonathan said with a smile. "Supplicants all walk to her." He reached for the passenger side door.

"What do you want us to do?" Boxers asked.

"Unless you've got pressing business elsewhere, I'd like you to wait for me till I get back."

"I meant, do you want me to come along?"

Jonathan pulled the handle on his door and pushed it open. Despite the heavy armor and bulletproof windows, it moved as if it weighed nothing. "No, I want to do this one as a solo. Thanks for the offer, though."

Jonathan appreciated that Boxers never liked to break up the team, even for conversations such as this one, but Jonathan didn't want to argue. He climbed out and closed the door.

As he stepped out of the Batmobile, Jonathan pulled a gold FBI badge from the front pocket of his jeans and clipped it to his belt. As he crossed into the open, he kept his hands angled away from his sides and his fingers splayed. He paused at the left front fender and waited for instructions. Security details in general were a jumpy lot. Given recent events in which one of their kind betrayed Wolverine and paid a heavy price as a result, he thought that an extra layer of caution was not out of order.

After only a few seconds, the passenger in the lead car exited his vehicle and walked toward Jonathan. "What's your name, sir?"

"Special Agent Neil Bonner," Jonathan said. He produced a set of credentials from his back pocket and held them out to be examined. "I believe Director Rivers is here to see me. Or, maybe the other way around."

The security guy took the credentials and examined them closely. He shifted his eyes a couple of times from the creds to Jonathan's face to assess the match.

"Is there a problem?" Jonathan asked.

The guard snapped the creds case closed and handed it back, saying, "Follow me." He led the way to the back door of the second car, driver's side. He rapped twice and the electric locks clicked. As he pulled the door open, the guard peeked inside. "Agent Bonner to see you, ma'am."

Jonathan heard the familiar voice but couldn't quite pick out the words. The guard stepped aside, and there she was. Jonathan had always thought Irene Rivers to be a sexy, nice-looking woman, though television cameras hated her. Yes, she had a hard side to her, but she'd been a door-crasher for the Hostage Rescue Team during her days in the field, and now she ran the premier crime investigation agency on the planet. As far as Jonathan was concerned, all those action scars, both internal and external, only made her more attractive. This morning she was dressed for business in a gray-on-charcoal pantsuit. As always the case, she was surrounded by stacks of paper.

"Good morning, Director Rivers," Jonathan said.

"Good morning." She pulled her reading glasses away and pointed to the seat facing her kitty-corner, behind the driver. "Make yourself comfortable."

As Jonathan sat and the door closed, Irene's shoulders relaxed and she leaned forward. "What's with the new wheels?"

"We kind of broke the old one," Jonathan said. "She was getting sort of long in the tooth, anyway."

Irene chuckled. "That monstrous Hummer was a girl?"

Jonathan let it pass. He wasn't sure why, but all vehicles were females in his mind.

"And a Suburban?" Irene pressed, needling him further. "How very . . . Washington." She kicked his foot with hers. "Oh, come on, smile."

He did. The decision to let the old Batmobile go instead of paying for repairs had been a tough one. Then, once the decision was made in principle, sifting through the choices was a painful process. In the end, there were better choices for armored vehicles, but it was the ubiquity of the Suburban that drove the choice. Finding one of many black Chevys on the road was a hell of a lot harder than finding the one exotic alternative.

"On to business," Irene said. "After I spoke to Dom on the phone—"

Jonathan's hand shot up. This was not a venue for using real names.

Irene looked confused at first, but then got it. "No worries," she said. She pointed to the opaque screen behind Jonathan's head. "We're totally soundproofed back here now. I don't always learn my lessons quickly, but I do learn them well."

Irene had made the mistake of trusting her previous security detail with information that nearly got Jonathan and his team killed. Actually, she hadn't *trusted* them with the information so much as she had failed to safeguard it as aggressively as she should have.

"Dom told me that children were involved in that business on the roadway, but that now they are missing. A priest and a social worker, too, though it seems we're presuming the adults to be dead, due to physical evidence at the scene."

"Exactly," Jonathan said. "I was hoping you could—"

"I can't," she interrupted.

"Excuse me?"

"I can't launch an independent search for people whose status is born of rumor rather than evidence."

Jonathan recoiled. This was not what he'd expected. "Jesus, Irene, this is me you're talking to. I'm not some network reporter with a bag full of rumors."

"I understand that, Dig. But you have no legal standing in this."

"They were coming to Resurrection House! I *pay* for Resurrection House. That gives me legal standing."

"No, it doesn't. It gives you emotional standing, maybe, but that's it." Irene's posture, tone, and demeanor were the very definition of businesslike. One hundred percent emotionally disconnected.

Jonathan opened his mouth to object, but she wouldn't let him.

"Let me ask you this," she said. "Did you see those boys, either at the foster home or in the car?"

"Of course not. But—"

"Did anyone see any evidence at the scene that the boys were there?"

"Jesus, Irene, this isn't a courtroom."

"Answer the question."

"You know the answer to the question! No, I was not there. But we know—"

"We suspect."

Jonathan's jaw dropped. He didn't get this at all. She wasn't just being uncooperative, she was actively fighting him. "What's gotten into you?"

"Did you know that the people who allegedly had custody of the boys have no record of them ever being there?" Irene fired the question like a punch, and it hit the mark.

Jonathan gaped. "I-I don't understand."

"Dom told me that the first stop for young Ryder and Geoffrey was a foster family out near West Virginia."

"Right," Jonathan agreed. "They wouldn't answer their phone."

"They answered for my team," Irene said. "They told us they had no record of the boys ever arriving there."

"That's what the second place said, too," Jonathan remembered.

Irene crossed her legs, folded her hands on her knee. "Look at this from my point of view," she said. "You want me to find children who no one has seen on the presumption that they were kidnapped from a place they'd never been. There's not much here to work with."

"But you talked to Dom. He wouldn't make this stuff up."

Irene's shoulders drooped. "Come on, Scorpion. I don't have agents sitting around with nothing to do. Everyone is assigned to important tasks. When a jurisdiction asks for our help, we try to be there for them, but largely in a secondary role. When there is a hard suspicion of a federal crime, we're all over it, and the locals are secondary."

"Kidnapping is a federal crime," Jonathan reminded.

"Not when there's no kidnapping," Irene said. Her frustration was growing. "My people reached out to the locals and to the state police, and they were told that there was no suspicion of kidnapping. I'm sorry, Dig, but that's where it is." She broke eye contact and reached for a folder. The meeting was over.

Or so she thought.

"What was that?" Jonathan asked.

She scowled.

"You showed your tell," he said. "You have an eye tic when you're bluffing."

She *piffed* and gave a look that questioned his sanity.

"We've known each other a long time, Wolfie. I know what I see, and you know that I'm right."

"This isn't a card game, Digger."

"Life is a card game. What aren't you telling me?"

"We're done here, Dig."

"Why don't you want to find the Kendall kids?" He was playing a hunch here, pressing his suspicion as fact to get a reaction.

Irene rewarded him with another tic.

He moved before she could speak, holding up his hand to silence her. "Wait," he said. "I get that there's stuff going on in the world that I don't have a need to know. If this is one of those times, that's fine. Don't tell me what I don't have the right to know." He leaned forward to make this next point. "But do me the honor of not lying to me."

Irene's eyes flashed anger, but then her expression softened, and she put her reading glasses back on. "Have a good day, Agent Bonner. Feel free to submit your field reports directly to me—but through secure channels."

Jonathan hesitated. He knew that she'd just delivered a subliminal message to him, but he wasn't sure what he'd received.

"It's not complicated, Agent Bonner," she said. The second reference to his alias was not lost on him. "The field office SACs might get confused by your efforts."

"I understand, Madam Director," he said, and he reached out to shake her hand.

"I prefer Wolfie when there are no witnesses," she said.

"How'd it go?" Boxers asked as Jonathan settled in and fastened his seatbelt.

"We're off to the home of Judith and Henry Ballentine," Jonathan said. "You have the address?"

"Already programmed in," Boxers replied. "I figure about five and a half hours, but I thought I'd wait till Wolverine's motorcade left before I headed out. Are you ignoring my question?"

"Not ignoring it," Jonathan said. "Just trying to come up with an answer. Wolfie came up with a list of reasons why she couldn't start a search for the Kendall boys. Jurisdictional mumbo jumbo. I'm not buying it."

"What aren't you buying?" Gail asked.

"The rationale behind her decision not to look for them."

"Oh, come on, Dig," Boxers said. He pulled out onto Braddock Road, on his way to the Beltway and a long drive. "One house won't answer their phone, and the other one says the kids were never there. What do you want her to do? I'm as loyal to the cause as anyone can be, and it feels flimsy to me, too."

"There's something else in play," Jonathan said. "I don't know what it is, but I saw it in Wolfie's face. There's another reason why she's not looking for them."

"Why would she need another reason not to look for something that's not out there to be found?" Big Guy pressed.

"We're not talking about finding a lost pair of shoes!" Jonathan said, more loudly than he wanted. "These are two kids who have no one sticking up for them."

"Don't get mad at me, Boss," Boxers said. "We're going wherever you want us to go. But I get it if the FBI is hesitant to go along. Have you got a conspiracy theory baking somewhere in your brain?"

"There are no such things as coincidences," Jonathan said. He couldn't think of a more succinct way of putting it. "The car was shot up, and Father Tim, Pam Hastings, and the kids are all missing. Blood spatter indicates that the adults in the car were killed. Jesus, what more do people need?"

"Maybe they hadn't yet gotten to the children," Gail suggested. "Maybe this hit had nothing to do with Ryder and Geoffrey Kendall."

"A hit on Father Tim?" Boxers asked.

"The driver," Gail said. "What do we know about her? I've only met her once or twice and she seemed nice enough, but what ex-cop doesn't have enemies?"

"But they're *missing*," Jonathan said yet again. "Yeah, maybe the adults are dead—hell, maybe they're *all* dead—but until somebody finds bodies, they're just missing and they need to be found."

"And I'm not arguing with you," Gail said, returning the same tone of frustration. "I'm just saying that I understand where Irene is coming from. Her hands are tied."

Jonathan decided to stop sharing his concerns about Wolverine. Since he couldn't articulate exactly what he was thinking, it wasn't worth pursuing, anyway. "She did sort of unofficially deputize us," he said.

"Oh, God," Boxers groaned. "What does that mean?"

"I'm not sure. But when we were parting, she called me Agent Bonner and emphasized that I should report my field reports only to her."

"Those were her words?" Gail asked. "Report our *field reports*?"

"Her words," Jonathan confirmed. He didn't add that the phrasing only doubled down on his feelings that a conspiracy was in play.

After time passed, maybe a minute, Gail said, "There's got to be a record. I mean, we know that their mother was arrested, which means that someone knows where the children were taken as she was driven away."

"The Ballentines," Jonathan said. "We got that from Dom."

"Let's just put it out there," Boxers said. "Do you

think the point of the hit on Father Tim's car was to steal the kids?"

"Absolutely," Jonathan said.

"So stipulated," Gail said. "From here on out, we all agree that Ryder and Geoffrey Kendall were kidnapped. Who would do that, and why?"

"Colonel Mustard in the library with the candlestick," Boxers said. "How the hell are we supposed to know that?"

"Kidnappings only happen for a few reasons," Jonathan said, reciting information they already knew. "I think we can scratch sexual violence off the list. At least that's what I choose to do. That leaves only revenge, leverage, or ransom."

"Is ransom even in play?" Big Guy asked. "Who are they going to squeeze money from? Daddy's dead and Mommy's in jail."

"What was the mother charged with?" Gail asked.

"I don't know the exact charge," Jonathan admitted. "Something drug related." As he heard the words, he understood the stakes.

Boxers beat him to the punch line. "So, the kids were kidnapped to keep her quiet."

"Whoa," Gail said. "Let's not leap too far on conclusions. That's one motivation, but not necessarily *the* motivation."

"It walks like a duck and quacks like a duck," Jonathan said. "I'm not sure it matters if we're right or wrong. But if we're right, that could be good news for the boys. If they're being used for leverage against their mother, then they have to be kept alive."

"God only knows what condition they're in," Boxers said. "Or how they're being treated."

Chapter Five

Ryder had lost track of time. He was pretty sure they were still in the trunk of a car, but he sensed that they had stopped. He must have fallen asleep. He heard a click followed by a creaking sound, and then cool air rushed in over him.

"Are they dead?" a man's voice said. "In the name of God and country, please tell me we didn't kill the little bastards."

"I'm alive!" Geoff shouted. There was some shuffling.

"Good for you," a second voice said. "What about your brother?"

Ryder considered playing possum just to see what would happen, but that would scare Geoff. And maybe piss the cops off. "I'm here," he said.

"So you are. Welcome to your new home."

Ryder heard some more movement, and Geoff squeaked. Maybe it was pain, maybe something else. Before he had a chance to think too much about it, a strong hand clenched around the top of his right arm and pulled him to a sitting position. Two seconds later, a fist grabbed his T-shirt, an arm wrapped around his hips, and he was airborne, with something hard pressed into his gut. In his mind, the guy had him in a fireman's carry.

The man carrying him had a bounce in his step that made the hood pull away from Ryder's face a little. He blew onto it, as if to put out a birthday candle, and that pushed the fabric away a little more. If he craned his neck and looked down and to the right, he could see movement. The legs of the guy who was carrying him appeared and disappeared from his field of view. It was still nighttime, so what he saw were more *suggestions* of legs than actual ones.

He couldn't tell what the guy was walking on. Grass, maybe? He couldn't smell any grass, but he wasn't sure that he'd be able to smell anything past the shield of burlap stink, anyway.

When they transitioned to gravel, the bouncing on Ryder's middle eased.

He heard talking from somewhere, and he thought he recognized Geoff's voice, but he couldn't be sure. Knowing his little brother, he was probably asking where they were going. Stupid question when you consider that they're going to be there soon, anyway. And if he recalled correctly, the last time Geoff asked questions, he'd gotten them both brained.

Finally, there was a bit of light, just enough to reveal that the gravel he suspected was, in fact, real and that the man was wearing black boots. The gravel changed to some kind of white stone, and then there were steps. Made of wood, he thought, but he couldn't be sure.

Brighter light. Much brighter light. They'd arrived at a real place. This was the place where the men who pretended to be cops—real cops didn't dump people into the trunks of cars—would do to them whatever it was that they wanted to do. Ryder felt the sour bubble of panic beginning to rise again in his gut.

"Hey, Geoff," he said. "Are you there?"

"What's happening?"

Before Ryder could answer, the angle changed, and he felt for a second that he was being flung somewhere. Turned out he was, and when he landed on his left side, he was surprised there was no pain. Well, his wrists hurt a little more, but he'd pretty much gotten used to that. The man carrying him had plopped him onto what felt like a bed.

"All right, boys," one of the men said. Ryder's hood was yanked off, and he squinted against light that wasn't as bright as he'd anticipated. He smelled woodsmoke and candle wax. When he looked over to his brother, he had to stifle a laugh. Geoff's hair was standing straight out from his head.

"My name is Officer Al, and that is Officer Kim. We'll be taking care of you while you're here." Both men were dark skinned but not black, and they looked strong. Officer Kim had a Bruce Lee vibe to him. He was the one with the red mark on his face, the one who had hit Ryder. Both wore police uniforms.

"If you promise to behave, we'll free your wrists and feet," Officer Al continued.

Officer Kim added, "But if you give us any shit, you'll be back in cuffs, and that will be just the beginning of your punishment. Do you understand?"

Geoff started to cry.

"Does that make you feel big?" Ryder asked. "Making kids cry?"

Officer Kim pointed a threatening finger at him. "Watch your mouth," he said. He drew a stick out of his gun belt and shook it hard to make it extend out two feet.

Ryder's stomach flipped.

"Give them a break," Officer Al said. "He's got a point. Why be such a hard-ass?"

"Because I want them to know that I wouldn't even blink before killing them."

"Look at me, boys," Officer Al said. "You're not going to be troublemakers, are you?"

Geoff shook his head enthusiastically, but Ryder didn't want to give him the satisfaction. His headshake was subtle.

"That one's going to be trouble," Officer Kim said. "Maybe we should kill him now and be done with it."

Ryder felt himself tremble, but he hoped it didn't show. The logical side of his mind told him that if killing them were an option, they'd be dead by now. Mom and Dad had sort of talked about that.

There are a lot of bad people out there, Dad had said. *They'll treat you like shit just to make you bend to their will. To keep your self-respect, hold out till it hurts too much. Then, when you give in, be proud of your resistance, not ashamed of your compliance.* Ryder remembered being confused at the time, but now he got it. It didn't hurt enough yet.

"Which one are you?" Officer Al asked. "Ryan or Geoff?"

"I'm Ryder."

Officer Al scowled. "You shitting me?"

"No, that's really his name," Geoff said. His tone projected an urgent edge.

Officer Al shrugged. "All right, then, Ryder it is. You're not going to be a pain in the ass, are you? Because I tell you, we are not the people to mess with. I know I sound like the good cop and Officer Kim sounds like the bad cop, but believe me when I tell you we both have bad sides that you don't want to see."

He produced a tiny key from a pouch on his belt. "Lean forward and I'll get those cuffs off your wrists."

That answered one question. Ryder had suspected that his hands had been tied with handcuffs, but he couldn't be sure. Now that he was paying attention, he saw that his ankles had been cuffed, too. He didn't even know that ankle cuffs were a thing.

Thirty seconds later, his arms and legs were his again.

"Go ahead and stand," Officer Al said. "Work some of the stiffness out."

As he slid his butt off the bed and set his feet on the floor, Ryder looked over to his brother, who seemed to be moving too gently. "You okay?"

Geoff rubbed his wrists and sidestepped over to Ryder, who put his arm around him. Outside of a few formal family portraits, this was the only time he'd done that. "We'll be fine," Ryder said. He rubbed Geoff's shoulder the way Dad would do when he was comforting them.

They were in an old house. A log cabin maybe? The walls were mostly covered in Sheetrock, but the huge fireplace in the middle of the long wall was surrounded by horizontal stripes of wood and mortar. It was hard to tell if it looked like that on purpose or if the place was falling apart.

"This is your new home," Officer Al explained.

"Are we under arrest?" Ryder asked. They didn't have to know that he knew they weren't cops.

"Yes."

"But this isn't a jail."

"Do you *want* to be in jail?" Officer Kim asked. "There are a lot of bad hombres in jail."

"A-are you going to hurt us?" Geoff asked. Ryder was grateful that his brother had asked it.

"Not if you don't make us," Officer Al said. "Do what you're told, and everything will be fine."

Ryder took in the surroundings. The inside of the cabin was shaped like an *L*. The king-size bed they'd been dropped onto sat across from the roaring fireplace at the corner where the long leg of the *L* met the short leg. The bed was on the short part. The only light in the room came from the fireplace and from a few table lamps, including one on the nightstand next to the bed. He looked behind him, down the long side of the *L,* and he saw a shelf filled with books on the left. Beyond the shelves, at the very end, sat a water cooler—the kind you'd find in an office, with the big bottle of water sitting on top of it. The right-hand side of the long wall was taken up by another bookshelf, and then there was an area blocked off by a cloth screen he couldn't see through. In between, the empty space in front of the door was filled with what looked like a homemade dining table surrounded by two backless wooden benches.

"Tell them about the shoes and socks," Officer Kim said. He hadn't moved from his spot on the far side of the bed, and his expression hadn't softened.

Officer Al seemed uneasy. "Okay, this is going to sound weird, but I need you to take off your shoes and socks."

Ryder's gut clenched. "Why?"

"Please just do as I ask."

"Is that all you're going to make us take off?"

Officer Al laughed. "Relax, kid. You're not my type. This is not that kind of party."

Geoff looked to Ryder for confirmation. Ryder answered by sitting back on the edge of the bed and kicking off his Reeboks. "Why are we doing this?"

"All in good time," Officer Al said. "Thank you for cooperating."

Ryder and Geoff pulled their socks off next. "Now what?"

The cop held out his hands. "Give them to me."

The boys did as they were told. Once Officer Al had their stuff, Officer Kim crossed behind his partner to take them away and throw them in the fireplace.

Ryder leapt from the mattress. "Hey!"

Officer Al pushed him back with a shove on the chest. "You wanted to know, now I'll tell you. When you're barefoot, you'll be less apt to run away."

That's when it hit Ryder that they truly were prisoners. Tears pressed behind his eyes, and he knew they were turning red. He clenched his teeth and breathed heavily through his nose to will the emotion away.

"And if you try to run away, we'll shoot you," Officer Kim said, walking away from the hearth to join his partner.

Geoff pressed closer to Ryder, grabbed his hand. Ryder almost pulled away. Holding hands was a baby thing to do. But tonight, it was okay.

"Let me give you the big picture," Officer Al continued. "We are in the middle of nowhere, miles from the next anything. Gets colder up here this time of year than you're used to in Virginia, but it's not so bad. Fifties at night, seventies during the day. Got extra blankets over there in the drawers under the bookcases.

"Basically, this house is yours. There's no running water, but there's a compost toilet over there behind the screen and plenty of water in the jug. You'll find glasses and toilet paper and whatever else you need in the drawers."

"Why are you doing this?" Ryder asked.

"Can't answer that," Officer Al said. "Kim and I are here to keep you safe and fed."

"And to shoot us," Geoff said softly.

"And to shoot you," Officer Al acknowledged. "But that's only as a last resort. Follow the rules and you won't have to worry about that. Or any of the other terrible punishments we can come up with."

Ryder felt a chill. Officer Al's eyes stayed totally friendly as he said that.

"Want to spend a week or so with your hands and feet in those cuffs? We can do that. We can break your legs or gouge out your eyes. But shooting is only a last resort."

Ryder couldn't stop the tears this time. "But *why*?"

Officer Al rumpled Ryder's hair, but the boy pulled away. "I don't want to scare you more than I have to, little man. I just need you to know that serious infractions bring serious results. We'll lock the door at night but unlock it during the day. You can't see it now, but there's a fence around this place. You're welcome to walk around outside, but you should stay away from the fence. First of all, the razor wire will cut you down to the blue meat, and there are sensors on the fence that will tell us if someone is trying to climb it. That's when we'd have to shoot you."

"Where will you be?"

"We'll be around," Officer Kim said.

"We'll bring you food," Officer Al said. "You'll have plenty of water." He lowered his voice. "And if you don't mind me saying, you should use some of that water to wash your pants. You guys stink."

Ryder felt his face flush.

"There's soap and towels over there, too. And a dry sink. You'll figure it out."

Officer Al looked to his partner and then back at his prisoners. "That's about it. Breakfast comes when it comes, normally around seven thirty. If you have any questions, save them till then. Night, boys."

The boys did nothing but stare as the two cops headed out the door and into the night. A few seconds later, something metal slid into something solid, and they were alone.

"Oh, my God, Ry. What's happening?"

Ryder settled himself with a huge breath and then started working on the button on his jeans. "Officer Asshole is right about one thing. We stink." He padded back to the corner with the water jug and wondered how to wash the stink out.

If Connie Kendall kept her fingers laced behind her head as she lay flat on her back on her bunk, and if she kept her legs flexed just enough for her feet to rest flat against the thin mattress, she could ease the pain that shot down her left arm from the pinched nerve in her cervical spine. Under normal circumstances, strict adherence to a stretching regimen could keep the pain under control, but after the . . . *aggressiveness* of her arresting agents, the kinked muscles in her shoulder had turned to rock, and her left arm felt like it was on fire.

For good or ill, she was the sole occupant of her concrete holding cell. She figured the dimensions to be roughly eight by ten feet. She knew for a fact that the cell was precisely ten toe-to-heels from front wall to back wall, but a foot and a half shorter measuring side to side.

The small space was a monument to efficiency, providing enough space for two stacked cots, a combo toilet and sink, and a tilt-down plank that doubled as a dining table or desk, equally accessible from the toilet or the edge of the bed. It reminded her a little of the efficiency apartment she and Craig had rented in Paris a before the boys came along. The jail cell had the edge on seating comfort, but it couldn't touch the view.

Oh, Craig. Why did you have to get yourself killed?

Ah, the view. A solid steel wall defined the view of what would anywhere else be her front yard. With the hinges on the outside, the door from her perspective was a black rectangle that could have been drawn with a Sharpie. Another rectangle in the middle of the larger one marked the location of her food slot—the only element of the door that had opened since the whole thing closed on her three days ago.

At least she thought it was three days. Without a view to the outside and without access to a light switch, she was at the mercy of her captors when it came to her perception of time.

She noted with casual interest that the two corners where two walls met the ceiling showed nearly identical triangles of spalling. In both spots, rusted blobs of rebar emerged from the slate-colored concrete like tumors from weathered skin.

Connie had every reason to believe that her attorney, Rafael Iglesias, would disperse whatever fertilizer needed to be spread to get her out of here on bail, but at moments like this, when so much time had passed without seeing a soul, the demons were knocking at the door of her mind.

The government was playing its usual games. Her isolation was part of the same rule book that made them refuse to tell her anything about her boys. Infliction of psychological stress. As if the work she'd been doing with Craig for the past three years hadn't immunized her against stresses that were far more life altering than a few days in a locked room.

Connie was terrified that decades in a locked room lay ahead for her, but that was where Rafael came in. He and his bosses owned every politician who mattered. And every prosecutor, too—as if there were a difference. She told herself that the mere fact that she had been denied access to counsel for this much time was a building block in her ultimate defense.

The lock on her door turned, startling her. It was too soon for another meal. Maybe they'd finally found Rafael.

Or, more likely, Rafael had found her.

When the door opened, she saw three guards in SWAT gear surrounding the opening. One held a big shield, while the other two held what appeared to be the kind of pepper spray canisters you could buy for use against grizzlies when you visited Yellowstone. Connie swung her feet to the floor and prepared for the worst.

A guard stepped out from behind the assault team. This guy wore a white shirt and green pants and sported the kind of beard that was either stylish or reflected the fact that he forgot to shave this morning.

"Okay, Kendall," he said. "This is your moment to whine to your mouthpiece."

Connie stood from her cot. "It's *Mrs.* Kendall," she said.

"Actually, it's Four Oh Three Four Three," the guard corrected, invoking Connie's prisoner number. "I was being polite."

"Fair enough. So, do I refer to you as Screw, as they do in the movies?"

The guard took a menacing step forward. "Don't ever assume parity with us," he said. "You refer to me as *Lieutenant Hoffman* and my officers as *Officer*. You are the property of the United States government, and we are the *citizens* charged with maintaining the zoo. This is our first meeting, but trust me when I say that you do not want to try me on this point."

Connie saw Hoffman as predatory, a man not to be crossed. She'd seen the same fierceness in the eyes of the cartel leaders she'd dealt with. They emitted a disregard for humanity. Connie didn't doubt that the man in the white shirt—and perhaps his padded colleagues—considered her to occupy the same level on the evolutionary scale as a cockroach.

"Lieutenant Hoffman it shall be," Connie said. She knew what came next. She turned her back to the crew at her door, took two steps closer, and presented her hands behind her back for the cuffing and shackling that she'd been told upon arrival would be the norm for any movement outside of her block.

They did the wrists first and then the leg irons. The guards moved with a practiced efficiency that had her thoroughly trussed in under a minute. When they were done, the SWATed-out guards stepped back and Lieutenant Hoffman took charge.

"Walk at my pace," Hoffman said as he wrapped his hand around Connie's left biceps. "I won't push you faster than the shackles can handle." His tone seemed surprisingly kind.

Gentle pressure on her arm urged her forward, and she complied. In the blur that was the night of her arrest, the details of her place of confinement had apparently eluded her because much of the surroundings looked strange to her. She now saw that her cell was little more than a hole that had been carved into a concrete canyon. Hers was at the end of a hallway that appeared that it might at one time have been a tunnel into a mine. Mesh-covered fluorescent light tubes bathed the entire length of the place with orange light. Connie's sense of dread began to blossom.

Everything in this place was either steel or concrete.

"Until they lift your isolation order, you'll be on lockdown twenty-three hours a day," Hoffman explained, as if listening to Connie's thoughts. "Otherwise, in this block, it's twenty-two hours of lockdown."

That explained why all the other doors were closed. "Not a big believer in sunlight?" Connie asked.

"I didn't design the place," Hoffman said. "I just enforce the rules. And in case it wasn't expressed to you strongly enough, I enforce those rules . . . *strictly*."

The SWAT force escorted them to the end of the cellblock as far as a wall of steel bars. The wall slid open as they approached. At Hoffman's urging, Connie shuffled through the opening and forward about eight feet until she was facing another wall of bars. After Hoffman slipped in behind her, the first bars closed again, and the second wall opened.

"We call this a mantrap," Hoffman said. "And it's exactly what it sounds like."

Connie had seen similar setups in airports and certain banks, but not designed to this level of security.

A second mantrap followed, and then a steel door led to a twelve-by-twelve room with a line of four stools that might have been stolen from a dining hall, lining a thick plexiglass wall that featured a long beige Formica table sprouting vertical dividers between the stools. Well-worn, old-school, yellow-wired telephones hung at each divided station.

Connie and Hoffman were the only two people on this side of the plexiglass, but a corporate-looking lawyer sat on the other side, waiting for his client.

"I thought you told me my lawyer was here," Connie said.

"And there he is." Hoffman pointed to the man on the other side.

"That's not my lawyer."

"I don't pick the lawyers, either," Hoffman said. "I just—"

"Enforce the rules. Yeah, I get it. But he's still not my lawyer."

Hoffman peered around Connie to look again at the man in the suit. "He looks like a lawyer to me. And he says he's your lawyer."

Connie started to object.

"But," Hoffman continued, "I can't make you sit down and talk to anyone you don't want to. If you'd prefer the view inside your cell, I can take you back to lockdown. Your call."

Connie saw the smirk and realized how foolish she must seem. Any view other than poured concrete was a welcome relief. "Can I lose the chains while I'm in here?"

"'Fraid not. Well, I can give you a free hand, but the leg irons have to stay. They're awkward till you get used to them, but after a few weeks, some say they feel awkward without them." Hoffman pointed toward the glass bubbles recessed into the drop ceiling. "We'll be watching, but we can't hear. You've got a half hour or until your lawyer leaves. Or whoever the hell he is. So, are you staying?"

Connie answered by pivoting and shuffling toward the man behind the glass. When she stopped at the table, Hoffman undid the bracelet on her right wrist, then slipped it through a reinforced loop that was bolted to the table.

The suit watched, but his face remained blank. The expression reminded Connie of some of the surgeons she'd met over the years through Craig—men so impressed with their own magnificence that personality seemed unnecessary.

Since the stool was supported by a buttress in the wall, Connie could shuffle her shackled ankles under the seat and straddle it like a saddle.

The suit lifted a telephone handset from his side of the glass, brought it to his face, and waited while Connie settled in.

Connie used her free hand to lift her handset, and as she did she wondered how many unspeakable viruses resided on the mouthpiece. "Where's Rafael?"

"My name is James Abrenio," the suit said. "I'm your lawyer." If it weren't for the five-o'clock shadow, he'd have looked like a child. Soft features and bright eyes, with an engaging smile. Impeccably dressed in a tailored blue suit with a starched white shirt and a perfectly Windsor-knotted red tie, he'd clearly seen success.

"Like hell you are. Rafael Iglesias is my lawyer."

Abrenio shook his head. "The court has appointed me to serve as your lawyer."

"They can't do that!"

Abrenio's smile disappeared. "Facts in evidence indicate that they can. I know I'm not your first choice in legal representation, but I'm very good at what I do."

"So is Rafael Iglesias!" Connie heard the frustration rising in her voice, and she tamped it down. "This conversation has become circular. You're fired."

Abrenio seemed to have been expecting that. "You are certainly within your right to do that," he said. "And when you do, the U.S. attorney will appoint another. And then another, if you'd like. At no point, however, will you speak to Rafael Iglesias, Armand Cortez, or any other member of the C-Squared set."

Connie recognized "C-Squared" as the media's flippant shortcut for the Cortez Cartel.

"You've been working with murderers, Mrs. Kendall, and the government has built a strong case that you are also a murderer."

Connie's heart rate picked up as she felt her face flush. She'd been keeping it together in the knowledge that she would be sprung as soon as the Cortez machinery shifted into gear. "You sound more like a prosecutor than a defense attorney," Connie said.

Abrenio lightened his posture and folded his arms across his chest, but not before he ensured that his lapels would not bunch. "You couldn't be more wrong. I am a very good defense attorney. And one of the rules of a very good defense attorney is to make sure his client understands what the stakes are. Uncle Sam has picked you for a very special shit list. Your arraignment is tomorrow morning, and you will be attending via video chat. You're going to plead not guilty, and then you and I are going to build a case."

The door on Connie's side of the window—the door she'd just passed through—opened, and there was Lieutenant Hoffman again. This time, he had a well-primped woman with him. She was tall and attractive, and her face showed nothing but malice.

"This meeting is over," the woman said.

"Who are you?" Connie asked. She looked back through the glass, and Abrenio looked concerned. She asked him who the newcomer was, then she realized he couldn't hear her, brought the phone back to her face, and asked again.

Abrenio explained, "That's Sandra Grosvenor, the U.S. Attorney for the Eastern District of Virginia."

"I said this meeting is over," Grosvenor repeated. "Take that phone receiver from her hand."

Hoffman looked a little apologetic as he walked forward. Connie put the handset down before he could take it from her.

As Hoffman released Connie's left hand from the loop in the table, he grasped her biceps to help her stand, then refastened the cuffs behind her back. Connie looked toward Abrenio. Someone had entered his side of the glass, as well. Another suit, and the conversation they were having did not look pleasant.

"I don't understand," Connie said. "What is going on?"

Hoffman said nothing.

She turned her attention to Grosvenor. "What are you doing to me?"

The prosecutor said nothing. Instead, she jerked her head in a silent *Follow me.*

Hoffman guided Connie out of that interview room, through another mantrap, and then into a different, slightly more elegant version of the previous interview room. This time, she got to sit in a metal-backed chair that was bolted to the floor, and there were no heavy partitions or telephone handsets to speak into. It wasn't anything close to comfortable, but it was a hell of a lot better than the round stools from the first interview room.

"Lieutenant Hoffman," she said. "Can you tell me what's going on here?"

"I'll be honest with you," he replied. "The short answer is *no,* Even if I knew, I couldn't tell you. But in this case, I genuinely have no idea. You must be one hell of an important lady, ma'am, because we are turning ourselves inside out to accommodate you."

"What kind of accommodations?"

Hoffman cocked his head and gave her what might have been an attempt at a warm smile. "Just hang tight. Soon enough, you'll know everything you're allowed to know."

And then she was alone. Hoffman's parting words

haunted her. Did they really understand the magnitude of the things she'd done?

The door opened again, and this time Grosvenor and Abrenio entered together. That couldn't possibly be anything but a bad sign, could it? Abrenio took a chair next to Connie while the woman stood by the chair opposite her, on the other side of the table.

"If you haven't already figured it out, I am Sandra Grosvenor, United States attorney for the Eastern District of Virginia." She hadn't yet sat. In fact, she hadn't made eye contact. "You're looking at life in prison if you're lucky," she continued. "A needle if you're unlucky. We have you for the murder of Pavel Grigonovich, and we're *this close* to linking you with at least two others." She presented her thumb and forefinger only an eighth of an inch apart.

"I want my lawyer," Connie said. It was the only thing she could think of. She herself was a corporate lawyer, for crying out loud, not a defense attorney. In a situation like this, she was as reliant on cop show tropes as any other citizen.

"You have your lawyer," Grosvenor said.

"I'll try not to be offended," Abrenio said.

"No, I have the lawyer you chose for me," Connie insisted.

"The point is, you have a lawyer," Grosvenor said. "You have representation."

"I don't *want* him as my lawyer. I *have* a lawyer."

Grosvenor turned her attention to Abrenio. "For the record, Counselor, are you taking Mrs. Kendall on as a client?"

"I am."

"You are not!"

Abrenio leaned closer to Connie and touched her arm. She shook him off, and he retracted his hand as if hit with electricity. "I meant no harm," he said. "I think we need to talk privately. You can fire me afterward, if you'd like." He shifted his attention to Grosvenor, who was already rising from her seat.

"I'll leave you two to speak. Arraignment's at nine sharp tomorrow. I'll see you both then." Grosvenor leaned in close to Connie and drilled her with a hard look. "Get your head out of your ass, Mrs. Kendall. You know what you have done, and we know what you have done. It's rare under circumstances like these to receive second chances. Listen very carefully to what Mr. Abrenio has to say."

Connie and Abrenio sat in silence while Grosvenor made her way to the door and rapped on it. It opened and closed, and they were alone.

"Have you already spoken to her about my case?" Connie asked.

"Of course," he replied. "At least through tomorrow's arraignment, I'm your lawyer whether you like it or not. As such, it's a good idea to know—"

"I have nothing to say to you," Connie said. Sometimes it was best to get ahead of what you knew was coming.

"That's perfect," Abrenio said. "That means you won't interrupt when I explain what's going on. Cutting to the chase, Uncle Sam doesn't care about you. They want your boss."

Connie kept her features flat. Abrenio already knew everything about her, or else he wouldn't have been handpicked by the government to pretend to be her lawyer. She refused to give any reaction to anything he said. "And who would my boss be?"

Abrenio rubbed his face with his left hand, revealing the monogram on his cuff. "Really? Do we really have to play the whole game? Okay, fine. They want to know about Armand Cortez."

"How would I know anything about the leader of a drug cartel?"

"I never said anything about a cartel," Abrenio said. He flashed a gotcha grin.

"I read the newspapers," Connie said. "It's hard not to know about the Cortez Cartel. The media likes to call it the C-Squared, right?" She had practiced this particular lie so many times that it felt like the truth. She'd been very, very careful over the years. She wasn't yet entirely convinced that they weren't playing a bluff hand.

"The government has you, Connie," Abrenio said. "You can claim the opposite all you want, but I'm telling you that they know the truth. I don't know specifically what they know or *how* they know it—it's too early in the process for that—but they're clearly playing a very strong hand. At least in their own opinion."

"So, you want me just to plead guilty to something I haven't done?"

"No, I want you to listen so you can save your own life. The government is offering full immunity to you in return for testimony that will put Armand Cortez behind bars."

Connie recoiled in ersatz horror. "How could I do that if I don't know the man?"

Abrenio's jaw locked. He didn't want to play anymore.

Connie changed her tack. "You say you're a lawyer. For the sake of argument, I'll take you at your word. But I've been an attorney for a very long time in the DC area. While I can't claim to know every lawyer in the DMV, I'm pretty much sure I've heard of all the good ones." There was a test in there to see if he knew the current vernacular for the District, Maryland, and Virginia, formerly known as the Greater Washington Metropolitan Area. "Judging from your suit, you make good money. I am *certain* I've heard of all the lawyers who make good money."

Abrenio chuckled. "You just don't want to believe, do you?"

"Would you, if you were in my position?"

"Probably not. But then again, I would never find myself in your position. I am, in fact, from out of town. Holland, Michigan, a little burg about an hour from Detroit. They brought me in because they could count on me to be clean."

Connie considered floating a "clean of what?" but decided against it.

Abrenio wasn't done. "It might not seem like it to you, but my being here saves your life. If your boy Rafael Iglesias were here, what do you think he'd do with the immunity deal? Tell you what, don't answer. I'll answer for you. He'd tell you to turn it down, and then he'd run back to his *real* client, and you'd either spend the rest of your life in jail or you'd be dead."

Connie understood the stakes here. She didn't understand *how* the government knew what they thought they knew, but she was fully aware of the truth. By giving her immunity, they thought she would confess to anything she wanted to confess to, all by way of betraying the most terrifying, ruthless man she'd ever known. To speak would commit herself and her boys to whatever was the Mexican version of a fatwa. Armand Cortez would let none of them live if she turned on him. At least now, by keeping quiet, she could keep Ryder and Geoff safe.

"How are my children?" she asked.

"They are not my problem."

"Are they safe?"

Abrenio's expression showed total disinterest. "How could I possibly know that?"

"You're in a position to ask, and I am not," Connie said, and she realized that she'd stumbled on her perfect dodge. "Until I find out about them, I won't say a thing to you."

"Look, Connie, this is a good deal, and I don't know how long it will be on the table. Especially if you piss them off."

Connie took her time answering. "Without admitting anything, if they have the kind of leverage over me that they seem to think they have and they are squeezing me this hard for information, that means they don't have enough on the cartel to get a conviction without me. They'll wait."

"I'm not so sure," Abrenio insisted. He seemed agitated.

It took everything Connie had not to explode with anxiety as she said, "My children, Mr. Abrenio. What you're suggesting—if it were to apply to me, to *us*— would put us all in unspeakable danger. If you assure me that they're safe and that any potential deal would include them, then maybe we'll have something to talk about."

She'd nearly run out of breath as she spoke. Very little time remained before she broke down.

Abrenio leaned in. "Listen to me, Connie—"

"We're done," she said, and she turned her back on him.

Chapter Six

By the time James Abrenio was cleared for an audience with United States Attorney Sandra Grosvenor, he'd been forced to kill nearly ninety minutes in a cramped waiting room on a butt-killing wooden chair.

Abrenio hadn't seen her in close to ten years, but Grosvenor's reputation as a queen bitch had traveled all the way to Michigan, and apparently, every word was true. He'd agreed to take on this assignment as a favor to her to honor their friendship from law school, but he'd not signed on for being shown disrespect.

"What the hell, Sandra?" After this much time in the wings, he wanted his opener to be a showstopper. "You called *me*, remember?"

"Not for this," Grosvenor said. She remained focused on writing notes on a legal brief, a fast scrawl using a gilded black-and-white fountain pen.

Abrenio took a step closer. "Holland, Michigan, is a very nice place. I have a thriving practice there. I don't need this bullshit. When I say I need to see you, I *need to see you*."

"Yet you have time to squander on a pointless rant." She still had not looked up from her work.

Abrenio yanked one of the wooden guest chairs from the edge of her desk and dropped onto the seat. "The Kendall children are missing," he said. He fired the words like a punch.

Grosvenor's hand stopped writing, but she took a few seconds to look up. "How do you know?"

"I called Resurrection House. Their car was attacked on the way there, and the boys never arrived."

Grosvenor said, "Huh." Then she looked back down. "Anything else?"

Abrenio slapped the desk. "Look at me, goddammit. Why are you being so difficult?"

After a dramatic sigh and an even more dramatic sag of her shoulders, Grosvenor capped her fountain pen and placed it atop the legal brief she'd been editing. She adjusted it so that the barrel of the pen was precisely parallel to the edge of the paper. That done, she placed her folded hands on her desk.

"Is this better?" she asked.

"I could do without the patronizing bullshit, but yes, it's better." Abrenio leaned in closer. "They were *kidnapped*, Sandra. When were you going to tell me?"

"There is no evidence of a kidnapping."

"Their car was attacked, for God's sake. At least two people were shot. One of them used to be a cop!"

Grosvenor scowled as she parsed words in her head. "Yes," she said. "A car *was* attacked, and at least two people *might have been* shot, among them a social worker. The kidnapping part, as I understand it, is hearsay at best. There's no physical evidence."

"Two missing boys are not evidence?"

"Yes. They are evidence of two boys not being where we thought they were going to be. What do you want from me, James? The locals searched the area, found nothing. My money says it's some kind of administrative snafu. They got sent to a different facility, and the paperwork hasn't had a chance to catch up. In any case, it's not our problem."

Abrenio leaned in closer still, his midsection pressing against the front edge of her desk. "But it *is* our problem. Connie Kendall won't consider a word of what you're offering until she knows that her children are safe."

"Okay," Grosvenor said. "Tell her they're safe."

Abrenio recoiled into the seatback cushion. "No, Sandra. No. We can't do that. You know the stakes here as well as I do. The C-Squared took those kids and murdered a cop. Christ, they shot a priest!"

"Those are *not* federal crimes, James. Get with the program."

"Oh, come on, Sandra. You're asking me to lie to my client."

"It's not a lie, James." Her voice crescendoed. "You are *assuming* that harm has come to those boys. You are assuming facts not in evidence. The real lie would be for you to tell Mrs. Kendall that her children are in danger. I suppose you can honestly tell her that we've lost track of them, but what would be the point of that?"

"She's their mother!"

Grosvenor shouted, "She's my detainee! Eighty percent of prisoners all over the world are parents, James. If they wanted to be good ones, they wouldn't have become criminals. You say she won't accept a deal that will save her life unless she knows that the children are safe. Well, good for her. I don't care."

"How very prosecutorial of you," Abrenio said. "May I remind you that I am her *defense* lawyer?"

"And as such, you owe it to your client to save her life." Grosvenor was clearly tired of the pleasantries. "Full immunity, James. Deals like that don't come around very often."

"She saves herself from prison but condemns herself to a life on the run from the C-Squared."

"There won't be any C-Squared if she takes the deal and testifies. Why don't you see this?"

Abrenio threw his hands in the air. "And in the process, she has to testify against a group whose reputation for violent reprisal is second to none."

"You know how this game is played, James. You knew what you were getting into when you left your beautiful Holland, Michigan, to get involved in this. At this level, the game is a blood sport. And I think I am being positively generous in my offer for immunity."

"I can *not* lie to my client. I *will* not lie to my client."

"Fine. Don't. Tell her you don't know where they are. Or, if you'd prefer, tell her your theory that they were kidnapped. I don't care. All I care about is bringing down the C-Squared. All I care about is stopping the spread of their poison across our southern border and stanching the bloodshed."

Abrenio wanted to argue more, but he felt a cloud of defeat looming over him. He didn't know his client well—hell, hardly at all—but he'd seen her concern in her eyes when it came to her kids. "I don't think she'll take the deal if it means that her kids will be jeopardized."

Grosvenor scowled as she looked to the ceiling. "She'd rather they be in the care of strangers for the rest of their childhood? 'Cause that's where they'll be after she's on death row."

Abrenio didn't know what to say.

Grosvenor leaned in very close across her desk and lowered her voice to nearly a whisper. "And don't think for a minute that I won't pull every string I can find to make sure that her boys are split up into different institutions. Don't think for an instant that I will hesitate to make the children pay for the crimes of their parents."

Abrenio felt his jaw drop. Who was this monster who'd once been his friend?

Grosvenor pushed back to her erect posture and returned to her paperwork. "But you're her lawyer, counselor. You do what you think is best."

The Ballentine house was like every other house on its cul-de-sac. Built in the style of Levittown, with a focus on blandness, these one- and two-story houses near New Castle showed their age. The neighborhood was a hodgepodge of well-kept and decrepit, with chain-link fences dividing yards into precise squares. No one had a garage that Jonathan could see, but the Ballentines had erected a free-standing pole barn next to their ranch-style house to double as a carport. And that carport stood empty.

"Looks like nobody's home," Gail said from the backseat.

"It's going on noon," Jonathan said. "Everybody must be at work. Cars were sparse and no one was outside.

"What do you want me to do?" Boxers asked.

"We treat it as if it's occupied," Jonathan said. "No shortcuts."

"How do you want to take it?" Gail asked.

"Quietly," Jonathan said. "No knocking, no crashing. I say we pick the lock."

Boxers gave a dramatic sigh. "Boring, yet old school."

"Then what?" Gail asked. "If they're in, what do we say?"

"It's not about what we say," Jonathan said. "It's about what we get them to say. Who are they, and what did they do with the boys?"

Jonathan pointed to the empty carport, and Boxers eased the big Suburban into the slot, where he dropped the transmission into PARK. "Back door?"

"Certainly not the front," Jonathan said. "Let's arm up and get out of sight as soon as possible."

"This is why we're supposed to do this shit at night," Boxers grumbled.

"Yeah, well, it's noon," Jonathan grumbled back.

In designing the new Batmobile, Jonathan had spec'd out holsters of sorts beside each of the captain-style chairs. Jonathan lifted his Heckler & Koch MP7 from the holster on the left side of his seat and took it with him as he opened the shotgun seat door. Barely bigger than a large pistol, the MP7 was an amazing firearm. Its 4.6-millimeter bullet left the muzzle at 2,300 feet per second and could give meaningful love to a bad guy at two hundred yards. He shrugged the sling over his shoulder and let the weapon dangle by his right hip. If he wasn't careful, the MP7 would clack and rattle against the .45 caliber Colt 1911 on his hip. He settled the bud for his two-way radio into his ear canal and clipped the radio itself onto his belt, just behind the Colt.

As they kitted up and left the vehicle, Jonathan led the way to the shelter provided by the bushes near the left rear corner of the house—the green-black corner, as he thought of it. He scanned every compass point for looky-loos but found no one watching.

As Boxers and Gail approached, likewise armed with MP7s, Jonathan keyed his mic. "Everybody on the channel?"

"I'm here," Venice said from back home. Boxers and Gail said likewise as they donned black tactical gloves.

In the near distance, a dog let loose with some fierce barking, causing Jonathan to whirl, but he relaxed when he couldn't see it. The dog was just being a dog.

The house defined *unremarkable*. The grass was neither long nor short. The façade was entirely flat, made of vinyl siding that showed its age. Waist-high dents spoke to Jonathan of a football tackle that went wrong, a suspicion confirmed by an abandoned football that lay in the yard near the other end of the house. A girl's bicycle rested against the back wall. The structure itself lay in the middle of a long hill. A sliding glass door provided access on the nearside—the high side. On the low side at the far end of the structure, a concrete stairwell sloped down to what Jonathan imagined was a basement door. He verified his suspicion with a quick check. Leaves and other yard trash littered the bottom of the stairwell, where a glass-paneled wooden door gave a glimpse into a dark basement.

These were the times when Jonathan missed having a government-funded full-size team. In a perfect world, operators would cover the front and back doors while other operators concentrated on entry, but that luxury wasn't available to him.

"Gunslinger, cover the back door and try not to look too much like a burglar," Jonathan said. "I'll let you know when we go downstairs. And keep an eye out for nosey neighbors." He flipped a switch on his radio. "Go to VOX," he said. Voice-activated transmission meant that everyone could hear everything everyone else said without having to key a microphone.

At this hour, in the light of day, the smart move may well have been merely to knock on the front door and see who answered. The problem with that, though, was the next step. A knock would attract attention, so what would they do if no one came to the door? One way or another, they were going inside, so it would be best not to be seen.

So, they'd enter like the burglars that he supposed they were. He decided to make entry on the main level because if the Ballentines were home, they would likely be on the top floor, if only because the basement appeared to be dark.

It had been a while since he'd broken into a place quietly, and he was aware of his team's attention as he moved to the sliding glass doors. He started by pulling on the handle, in case the door was unlocked. Hey, you never knew. No such luck.

"Remember the technique?" Boxers asked.

Jonathan planted his gloved palms flat against the glass, pressed just hard enough to get traction, and then he wiggled the glass panel up and down in its tracks. He heard the click, and he knew he was in. That much clearance between the door and the track was enough to dislodge the spring-loaded lock.

He looked to Boxers. "Yes, I do." As he slid the door open, he lifted his MP7 to his shoulder. He entered what appeared to be a family room. Two sofas met at an *L,* focused on an old-school big-screen television in the corner. Five dirty dishes sat on the coffee table, but those were the only signs of current habitation. The television was off.

"Okay, team," he whispered. "Clear so far. Let's go to work."

Jonathan and Big Guy moved through the dimly-lit space with smooth and efficient grace. Onstage, it might have looked like a modern dance as they moved through the main level of the single-story structure, clearing room after room. As they advanced, they shifted roles, with one person covering the hallway while the other cleared the spaces.

In operations where the smart money said that no one was home, the temptation to cut corners on the details could be overwhelming. People got killed when they got lazy, and Jonathan was a tyrant about taking as few chances as possible. If nothing else, a milk run like this provided opportunities to practice moves that they had already performed hundreds, if not thousands, of times.

The kitchen hadn't been cleaned in quite some time. Dishes sat in an unsteady stack near the sink, with flatware scattered around the countertop. The dining room was a mismatched collection of cane-back chairs and a pair of plastic card tables. An array of magazines and mail littered the tabletop. The three bedrooms were a mess, with bunched blankets and sheets atop the mattresses, but there were no people. The closets in the secondary bedrooms were packed with an array of boys' and girls' clothing. A stairwell, protected by swirly wrought iron railings, descended from the middle of the living room floor down into what appeared to be a furnished basement.

Clearing the main level took less than five minutes.

"We'll want to put the mail in a bag and take it with us," Boxers said.

"Not till we clear the basement," Jonathan said. "Gunslinger, we're on our way downstairs. Take a peek through the door window and radio back to me what you find. When you're in place, Big Guy and I will descend from up here."

Jonathan turned to Boxers. "Any thoughts?"

"To me, it looks like people left in a hurry," he said. "I don't see any signs of a struggle, though."

"I'm not so sure," Jonathan said. While speaking with Boxers, he'd switched on the white beam at the MP7's muzzle to get a clear view to the bottom of the basement stairs. "Does that look like a hole in the wall to you?"

Boxers added his light to the spot. "Looks like somebody took a header off the stairs."

Gail's voice said, "I'm in place at the basement door. I don't have a view here. It looks like a mudroom on the other side. There are marks on the floor that may be blood."

"Can you make entry without alerting the neighborhood?"

"I think so," she said. Three seconds later, Jonathan heard the sound of breaking glass. "Door's open."

Jonathan smiled. "Big Guy and I are coming down the main stairs." Jonathan led the way.

He hated stairwells, especially open ones like this. They were perfect kill zones. Whether ascending or descending, you revealed yourself a little at a time, and a patient killer needed only to wait for the perfect sight picture then press the trigger. It was more unnerving going down than going up. Something about having his legs shot out from under him and then falling into a headshot. While ascending, at least you had a better chance of seeing the shooter and making a fight of it.

The basement was unusually dark given the time of day. The Venetian blinds were all down and spun shut. Jonathan almost wished he'd opted for night vision. He swept his muzzle light in a circle, taking in as much data as would register, all the while staying focused on the red dot of his sight. At his first chance, he squatted low and scanned to his left and right. He was relieved to see the glow of Gunslinger's flashlight bathing the room in intense white light from a different angle.

"You're clear to come down," Gail's voice whispered through his earbud.

"Roger that," Jonathan whispered back. When he got to the bottom of the stairs, in front of the divot that had been taken out of the wall, he dropped to one knee and added his light and firepower to Gail's. The space down here showed no more love than the rooms upstairs. A Ping-Pong table took up half the space, and an air hockey table took up the rest. Another old-school big-screen sat in the corner, with a couple of ratty up-holstered chairs scattered in front of it. From his position, he could see three interior doors, all of them open and dark.

"I'm down," Big Guy whispered in his earbud.

"Let's clear the rooms," Jonathan said.

Two minutes later, they were done. The house was officially empty.

"We're clear," Jonathan said. He returned his attention to the hole in the wall. Now that he had the time to look more closely, he saw that the divot was actually in two parts, a torso and a head. Somebody had hit this spot hard.

"Somebody definitely tried to fly," Boxers observed.

Jonathan pointed to the edge of the head divot. "That looks like blood to me," he said.

Big Guy shined his light on the floor at the bottom of the stairs. "Here's some more." There wasn't a lot of it, but someone had clearly been hurt here.

"Hey!" Gail called from the far side of the basement. "We missed a door."

Jonathan's heart skipped as he pivoted away from the stairs. "How did we do that?"

"This rolling clothes rack was in front of it," Gail said.

"God *damn* it," Jonathan spat. This was the kind of shit that got operators killed. You jump to conclusions and you miss stuff. The chance that the space behind the door might be occupied was still small, but now they'd lost any notion of surprise.

When the three of them were gathered at the door, weapons up, Jonathan nodded to Big Guy, who turned the knob and pushed the hollow-core panel open onto an unfinished part of the basement.

"Oh, God!" Gail exclaimed.

Boxers grumbled, "Ah, Christ." He slapped at the switch on the wall and brought the area into high relief. Blood splashes and spatters smeared every surface from the floor to the walls to the side of the washing machine.

"Good God," Jonathan said. "Looks like they killed pigs in here." He pulled his phone from his pocket and took a picture. This part of the basement looked as if maybe the owners considered making improvements, but then changed their minds. Storage shelves stretched from floor to ceiling, and they were packed with household crap, from lawn gear to Christmas ornaments. The blood was mostly concentrated near an unenclosed toilet and sink, and it still was wet, though sticky.

"Kill the lights and let's get out of here," Gail said. "This is a crime scene. We don't need our DNA to be part of the lab results."

Jonathan didn't worry about that, and Gail shouldn't have. Given the work they had done over the years on behalf of Uncle Sam, they had no official records.

"Keep the lights where they are," Jonathan said. "What do you think happened?"

"Somebody was killed here," Boxers said. "My money says it was the Ballentines."

"Where are the bodies?" Jonathan asked.

"Took them out," Boxers said.

"There are no blood trails across the floor out there," Gail said.

"You said there's blood inside the door, though," Boxers recalled. His tone had turned argumentative.

Gail scowled. "I saw this once at a murder scene," she said. "The killer wrapped his victim up in a carpet to get her out of the house, but when he put the carpet down to open the door, some of the blood leaked out."

"Was that a crime of passion?" Jonathan asked.

Gail made a puffing noise. "Anything but. He was a very organized serial killer."

"You arrested him, then," Boxers said.

"Ate a gun when we were pulling up his driveway."

"Better than a needle, I suppose," Jonathan said.

"But not nearly as satisfying," Boxers said.

Jonathan placed his hands on his hips and surveyed the gore. "This is a *lot* of blood," he said. "But I don't see the fountain spray of, say, a cut throat. Nor the spatter of a gunshot."

"You're thinking torture, aren't you?" Boxers asked.

"The thought occurred to me, yes."

"Hey, look here," Gail said. She'd wandered a bit, into a deeper, shadowy part of the storage area and focused her flashlight beam on a pair of cane-back chairs that looked a lot like the ones they saw around the dining room table upstairs. "They're covered in blood."

"Get a picture," Jonathan said. He was beginning to agree that maybe it was time to be someplace else.

"And there," Gail said, pointing.

Jonathan couldn't see what she was looking at, and there wasn't enough room for him to slide in next to her.

She snapped a picture with her phone. "Bloody duct tape," she said.

"These poor assholes were tortured," Boxers said. He pointed to a spot deeper into the space. "Is that a kid's bedroom slipper I see covered in blood?"

"Ah, Jesus," Jonathan moaned. "I think they killed the whole family and took the bodies away."

Gail said, "But why—" She cut her question short as the ceiling creaked.

Boxers slapped the room light off, and they all froze.

"Mother Hen," Jonathan whispered. "Are you on the channel?"

It took a few seconds for Venice to answer. In that time, Jonathan pulled a dental mirror from a pouch on his left sleeve and cracked open the door to the rest of the basement to look back at the stairs.

"Go ahead, Scorpion," Venice said.

Jonathan whispered, "We're not alone here. Have you been monitoring the local emergency channels?"

"As I always do," she said. "I've heard no dispatches to your location."

"Rog," Jonathan said. "Stay tuned." Monitoring emergency response and dispatching channels was becoming more complicated and less reliable as public safety nets moved toward encryption.

With his rifle up and ready, Jonathan killed his muzzle light and pushed the door open the rest of the way and sidestepped out into the playroom.

"I'll cover the stairway," Jonathan whispered. "We'll leave through the back door."

"They're gonna have the Batmobile covered," Boxers said. "We should engage in here."

"And I think we should get the hell out," Jonathan said. Without taking his eyes off the stairs, he motioned over his shoulder toward the back door. "Move."

"Moving," Boxers and Gail said together.

Jonathan saw a splash of white light against the base of the stairs, and then creaking as someone descended. "I've got movement on the stairs," Jonathan whispered. "White light." He dropped to a classic kneeling marksman position. He sat on his right heel while he locked his left elbow into his left knee to brace his aim. He welded his cheek to the stock and lined up behind his red-dot sight.

"I have movement outside the back door," Boxers said. These guys were coordinating their attack. They were demonstrating a disturbing level of sophistication.

As the light descended the stairs, a second one joined it.

Through his peripheral vision, Jonathan saw Gunslinger backing up a few paces, and he knew that she was taking a pivot position, from which she could cover either the back door or the stairwell.

Jonathan heard male voices from the steps speaking in a language he didn't understand. It sounded Eastern European to his ear.

"Did you hear that?" Jonathan whispered.

"They're stacking up in the back, too" Boxers said. "And yes, I heard it. We're shooting, right?"

"If they've got guns, we shoot," Jonathan said. "If they were cops, they'd send dogs." God, he hoped that was true.

The team on the stairs started their descent after what sounded like a countdown from three. It was the rhythm of the language.

"It's happening," Jonathan said. The attackers' muzzle lights bounced around the far wall.

Then, they surged forward, four of them streaming down to the base, where they split into two elements. Two buttonhooked left toward Jonathan. They crossed in front of Jonathan's red dot, and he dropped them both with one shot each to the ear.

To his left, out of sight at the back door, wood and glass splintered, and the area around the exit erupted in three quick bursts of suppressed gunfire.

Jonathan tuned that out and shifted his aim to the right, toward the other pair of muzzle lights. These two posed a real threat to Digger, who had neither cover nor concealment. If their sights acquired him, he'd be an easy kill. He thumbed his selector from single-fire to auto-fire and let loose with three five-round bursts. The flashlights dropped to the floor.

"Four down, maybe more," Jonathan said as he turned his muzzle light back on and advanced on his AOR—area of responsibility. If Boxers and Gail had lost on their side, he'd know soon enough, but he needed to make sure that the threat he'd just neutralized stayed that way.

"We've got three," Boxers said.

Gail added, "Big Guy and I are going outside to make sure there aren't more." After a beat, she added, "Oh, my God, they're police officers."

Jonathan's insides tensed. Could this be the shit show of all shit shows?

That was for later. Now, he had a job to finish.

He kept his attention focused on the guys in the shadows. He knew the first two he shot were dead, but these last guys could be playing possum. His goal wasn't to finish off any who were alive, but rather to disarm them and make sure that they could do no more harm.

There were only two on this side, and both were toast. And they wore the uniforms of police officers.

Shit.

Stay focused, Jonny-Boy.

Jonathan looked at the patch on their shoulders, but he didn't recognize the jurisdiction. He took thirty seconds to get pictures of their faces, badges, and patches, careful to stay out of the spreading gore.

"Hey, team, we need to get out of here," Jonathan said as he stooped to get a better angle on a dead man's face.

"We're clear outside," Boxers said.

"We're moving to the Batmobile." Gail said. "Oh, my God, what did we do?"

Jonathan pocketed his phone and headed for the door. "We didn't get murdered," he said. "Hey, Slinger, give me a hand." One of the attackers who'd stacked up at the door had fallen half outside, and Jonathan wanted to drag him all the way in so the door would close. As he grabbed the collar of the dead guy's shirt, he noted with interest that the corpse was not wearing body armor. That spoke to the level of threat they were expecting.

When the body's feet were clear of the door by fifteen inches or so, he let it drop on the tile floor.

Gail stared at the carnage, her eyes glistening.

"Come on, Gail," Jonathan whispered. "We need to not be here."

They moved without further words to the waiting vehicle and climbed inside.

Rubbing his eyes, Jonathan stretched his back, first left, then right. The one to the right launched a ripple of cracks that sounded like popcorn. "Hey, Big Guy," he said. "We need to plot a course to Shenandoah Station, the kids' next stop after here. I have no idea what all this is about, but it can't be good for the people there."

Chapter Seven

Connie studied James Abrenio's eyes as he spoke. Something about him had changed. He seemed subdued, less inclined to smile or meet her gaze. They'd reconvened in the same interview room as before, the more comfortable one. Abrenio seemed older somehow. He smiled as Connie sat, but it was all mouth, no eyes. Perhaps it was a wince.

"In case you haven't figured it out by now," Abrenio said, "Your arraignment has been postponed. And your children are safe."

Connie didn't hesitate. "I don't believe you." It was partly true, but she was also trolling for a reaction.

Abrenio gaped. "Excuse me?"

"If they're safe, where are they?"

"Not where anyone expected them to be. They were on their way to a place called Resurrection House, but the U.S. attorney changed her mind. She doesn't like you—a fact that you should keep foremost in your mind as you consider immunity deals. She thought it best that you not know where the boys are."

Connie felt her poker face break. Tears blurred her vision. "Why?"

Abrenio pursed his lips. "She said something about better security, but I think it's just meanness."

"You mean cruelty."

"White versus ecru," Abrenio said. "They're pressuring you into taking their deal. That's the only acceptable decision in their minds, and the pressure is only going to get more crushing."

Connie felt dizzy. She knew she'd been cornered, and she couldn't see a way out. "Why the children?" Her voice cracked. "They didn't do anything wrong."

"It's not about them," Abrenio explained. "It's about you and the fact that you love them."

The rush of emotion surprised her. For the first time, the forever-ness of her plight hit home. Perhaps a minute passed before she could trust her voice again. "Do *you* at least know where they are?"

Abrenio looked embarrassed. "I'm your lawyer," he said. "That means they don't trust me, either."

"Then how do you know they're safe?"

James Abrenio issued a massive sigh. "Because they told me so."

There. Right there. His expression faltered. What was that?

Abrenio continued. "I know this is not what you want to hear—especially under the circumstances— but sooner or later you have to trust someone. Uncle Sam plays hardball, but he's not in the business of harming children."

Connie took her time evaluating his words. Abrenio was holding something back. Call it intuition. Over the course of many interviews and depositions of her own, over the course of many years, she'd learned that lies more often than not resided in the words that were *not* spoken, and not in the words that were articulated. What was James Abrenic not saying?

"Listen to me, Connie. You love Ryder and Geoff. They are your life. They deserve you in their world. The one shot you have to keep them out of foster care is to take the immunity deal. The reunion won't happen right away, of course, but in eighteen months, two years on the outside, you can be a family again."

"Without Craig. Without a way to support ourselves, and with a price on my head that will only increase over time. What kind of life is that?"

"It's the life of a woman who will get away with murder." His words came hard and fast, like a punch. "And without Craig because he was stupid enough to take a shot at a police officer."

"He was trying to protect his family," Connie said. The horrible image of his throat being torn open by a bullet would not leave her head. Would not dim even a little.

"He was lucky not to get your children killed," Abrenio countered. "Suppose a bullet had gone through the wall?"

"Stop," Connie said. "Just please stop."

"This is the reality, Connie. This is what you need to address. I guaran-damn-tee you that one hundred percent of other murder suspects would love to trade places with you on the dealmaking."

"We'd never be able to stop running." The very thought was more than she could comprehend.

Abrenio's face flushed. "It's a binary choice, Connie. You take the deal and live with some level of stress, or you sentence your boys to a childhood of foster care because you'll be rotting away in prison. You won't see them walk down the aisle with their brides— or husbands, I suppose. You will never see your grandchildren in the sunshine."

That was the image that dissolved her. She saw her boys as men—little changed but for fuzzy facial hair. They had faceless wives and infant children who looked exactly like their fathers. The babies were dressed in the same baptismal gown that had been worn by every Kendall baby for five generations. North of seventy children.

She juxtaposed that image—a dream she'd cultivated since the days they were born—against the reality of this nightmare of peeling gray and smudged beige.

As if reading her thoughts, Abrenio said, "The clock is ticking for you, Connie."

She wasn't ready for this. "You say that so easily. As if there are no consequences."

"It's my job, Connie. Uncle Sam is giving you the keys to your cell. He's giving you the opportunity to be a mother to your children."

She didn't know what to say. Didn't know what to think.

"You murdered people, Connie."

Something snapped inside her. "I did no such thing! Perhaps Craig did, but he's—" Her voice cracked. "He's already paid for that."

"You were there," Abrenio pressed. "You were an accomplice."

"No." She slapped the stainless steel table. "That is not true. I was *not* there."

"Fine," Abrenio said. "What the hell? I'll stipulate to that, irrespective of mountains of evidence that show otherwise. If you choose to take this to trial, and if it goes all the way to the end, and if everything cuts our way, I give you a thirty percent chance of a hung jury. That keeps you in jail until there's a new trial."

When he paused, Connie rocked her head up from the undefined spot on the table where she was staring.

"Listen to me carefully, Connie. This is your attorney talking to you. I'm the guy who keeps your interests always in the foreground, and I'm willing to honor whichever decision you make. But in my professional opinion, there is not a chance in hell that twelve jurors will find you not guilty. And there is even less chance that the U.S. attorney's office will ever stop pushing for a conviction. They've got nothing but time and resources. If they have to go to trial ten times, what do they have to lose? Meanwhile, where will your kids be?"

Connie wanted to scream. *Do you know who Craig killed? Do you know what they did for a living? We did the world a favor!*

Again, James Abrenio was somehow channeling her thoughts. "Murder is murder, Connie. Unless it's in self-defense, motivation is irrelevant. If you brought Hitler back from 1945 and shot him in the face, the public might thank you. The history books might call you a hero. But the Justice Department would still prosecute you as a murderer. It's what they do."

"But I didn't kill anyone."

"They say their evidence proves that you were there. If that's the case and you didn't report it or do anything to stop it, you know how this works. You're an attorney. Under the accessory laws, you might as well have pulled the trigger."

Connie's mind swam in a swirl of confusion. Had she really been that awful? They'd only been doing the bidding of a madman for the sake of keeping themselves alive. Craig never intended to kill anyone. The procedures were designed to be painful, not deadly. He even cared for his patients during their recovery from their lessons. The procedures left the patients changed but never ruined. And her only involvement in any of it was to make the patients feel better. She was never the one to . . . *harm* them.

Craig was a doctor in trouble, not a homicidal monster like the one they called Kim. He was the animal they should have in custody. Kim was the one who lived to kill others.

"I don't know what more convincing you need," Abrenio said. "If you piss them off, Grosvenor will just walk away. If you *really* piss her off, given the nature of the charges, if they think they have the right jury and judge, they can push for the death penalty. Either way, if they prevail in court, you'll be lucky to get less than twenty years, and more likely life, behind bars. Can you really imagine this"—he made a sweeping movement with both arms—"as the only view you'll ever see?" He leaned in closer. "And if they *really* turn on you, there are facilities in the federal system that make this look like a resort."

She felt overwhelmed. She had trouble forming words.

Abrenio softened his tone. "I know it feels like I'm piling on, Connie, but your decision is really about Geoff and Ryder. You're looking at missing your kids' entire childhoods. The statistics say that as foster kids, they have an excellent chance of ending up in prison themselves."

Connie stomped her foot on the concrete floor. "Okay, I get it. You've made that point and made it again and again. I get it. I'm a bad mom. But if I testify against a drug cartel, that's just another form of death sentence."

"The government is amenable to WitSec for you and the boys."

Connie scoffed, "That's just another form of prison, but includes the boys, too."

Abrenio lifted an eyebrow.

Connie looked to the ceiling, perhaps to God beyond the ceiling, if any such being existed. She needed a third option, but it wasn't coming to her. "You said something about eighteen months to two years. If I start talking with you, Armand Cortez is going to find out, and he'll stop at nothing to keep me quiet. Will I be with my boys during that time?"

"No. The government will insist that you stay in custody."

"What about Ryder and Geoff?"

There it was again. It was a twitch in his right eye. "They'll be taken care of," Abrenio said.

"What does that mean?"

"It means they will stay safe."

"Where?"

"I don't know. Frankly, it didn't occur to me to ask."

"I want you to find out," Connie proclaimed. "And I want to know where they are now."

Abrenio's jaw flexed. He was losing his patience. "Connie, what gave you the impression that you have any leverage here? You're telling the prosecution that you won't let them save your life unless your conditions are met. That's not how it works. Do they want your testimony? Of course, they do. But if they have to trash your deal and put you away forever, they're perfectly fine with that."

"I need time." She was stalling.

"You don't have it. Deals can disappear as quickly as they appear. You don't want to push these people too hard."

This time, when Connie felt the tears coming, she knew she would not be able to stop them. Sadness and desperation welled up from deep inside and poured out as wracking sobs that shook her whole body.

How could it have come to this? How could she have let this happen?

Craig had never told her the entire story—and she'd never asked for details—but she knew that it had all started with oxycodone. He'd known Armand Cortez from back when they went to undergraduate school together. He'd attended the Kendalls' wedding, for crying out loud. When Armand reached out to his old friend for help obtaining oxy, it felt like a gift from above. Craig had just lost his malpractice insurance in the wake of a disastrous lawsuit, effectively ending his career, and he was staring down the bore of poverty and humiliation.

It was a crime, yes, but a victimless one. People who wanted drugs were going to find them. They didn't care where they came from, and since they were going to get them anyway, where was the harm in being a resource? They way that Connie saw it—the way that Craig presented it to her—this was God's way of rescuing them from the awful business of the lawsuit.

Besides, this was not some street dealer. This was Armand Cortez. He was a player. He knew how to protect his sources. And let's be honest, if the police came after Cortez, they weren't going to give a damn about a small scale, part-time supplier.

And the money! Good Lord, the money was huge. So huge, in fact, that Craig had suspected the scale of it to be a gift from Cortez to his old friend.

Then came that awful day nine months ago, when Craig visited Mexico and came back changed. Fundamentally changed. Now that his *friend* had proof of Craig's involvement in the drug trade, Cortez weaponized it. He explained to Craig how important it was for his enemies and competitors to be terrified of him. He wanted the skills of a surgeon who would do things that should never be done. To refuse would have been to be expose Craig as the drug dealer he was. And then there'd be the impact on his family.

Craig felt as though he had no choice but to sell his soul.

But it was never supposed to be murder. That's what they call it, though, when someone dies on the table in the middle of a procedure that was designed primarily as a form of torture.

And then there was the rest, the worst of it all. The things they did that no one even suspected.

"I need an answer now, Connie. Will you take the immunity deal or not?

She could barely form the words in her throat. "Yes. I'll take the deal."

* * *

"We crossed a line back there," Gail said from the backseat. They were only five minutes away from the scene, and Jonathan could tell that she was on the edge of cracking. "I mean, my God, we killed police officers!"

"Prefer to be dead, do you?" Boxers asked.

"Take it easy, Big Guy," Jonathan said. "Gail is right. If those guys really were cops, we're in deep shit."

"They came to *us*, Dig," Boxers objected. "We didn't pick that fight. And if they were real, what's with the foreign language?"

"We were where we didn't belong," Gail said. "We broke and entered. That is a felony. Anything that flows from that—"

"Easy, counselor," Jonathan said. "We don't need a lesson on the law."

Boxers declared, "I'm just sayin' that there is no quicker, more guaranteed way to die than trying to kill me."

"Just stop!" Jonathan commanded. "What's done is done. All those guys will still be dead a week from now. And, for the record, I don't think they were really cops. You've got the bizarre language to begin with, and then the patches and badges weren't right. From Frederick County, Maryland. Give me a break. What on earth would they be doing in New Castle, Virginia?"

"Mutual aid, maybe?" Boxers guessed.

"No," Gail said. "They'd have had New Castle PD with them. If not them, then the State Police."

"So, they were up to no good," Boxers said.

"Killing a cop is killing a cop," Gail said. "The Blue Line will always close around its own."

"So, why were they there?" Jonathan asked. "And if they were real officers, why didn't they have better tactical skills?"

"Because they wouldn't think that we had *any* tactical skills," Boxers said. "They got lazy. And given our performance down there in the basement, I'd be careful about going too far out on that limb."

"That's not the real issue," Gail said. "Like Digger said, why were they there in the first place? Whether real cops or fake ones, what were they there to do?"

"To kill us," Boxers said, as if it were the most obvious thing in the world.

"Are you sure?" Jonathan asked.

"They had guns, and they were moving in on us. Yeah, I'm sure."

"They were trying to kill *somebody*," Gail said. She was thinking like Jonathan now. "Maybe they were there to kill the Ballentines."

"They were a little late to the game," Boxers scoffed.

"But how would they even know we were there?" Jonathan asked.

Gail clapped her hands, startling the others. "I've got it," she declared. "They hadn't really left yet."

Jonathan pivoted in his seat to look at her while he waited for the rest.

Gail explained, "They'd just left when we got there. They saw us arrive."

"I don't know," Boxers said. "Wouldn't they have run if that was the case? Why come back?"

"Loose ends," Jonathan said. "We don't know who

these folks are yet, but if they are, in fact, fake cops and they'd just murdered some people and stolen the bodies, I can imagine that they'd be anxious to get rid of witnesses."

"The timing alone would unnerve them," Gail said.

"I could see that," Boxers said. "Though why take the bodies at all? It's not like they didn't leave a mess anyway."

"Maybe that's why they were still there," Jonathan said. "They were in the midst of cleaning up after themselves."

"I guess that would keep the stink down," Boxers said.

"And wash away evidence," Gail added. She thought for a few seconds. "Does that mean there's a vehicle somewhere near the house that's stacked with the bodies of the family?"

"That would be my guess," Jonathan said.

"Think we should go back?" Gail asked.

"Oh, hell no," Jonathan said. "That's not a picture we need anyone to see—us hanging around some falling-apart van where bodies are found. As it is, Big Guy, I need you to change out the license plates on the Batmobile, just in case."

"That's a damn good idea, Boss." As he agreed, Boxers pulled off the road into the parking lot of a self-storage park they were approaching on the right. "Won't take but a couple of minutes." He pulled around to the back of the complex, where they were not visible from the road, and threw the transmission into PARK.

"Hold off a second," Jonathan said. "Let me check something with Mother Hen." A sign on the front fence proudly announced THESE PREMISES PROTECTED

BY NORTH STAR SECURITY. He wanted to make sure that North Star was among the security companies that Venice had successfully hacked into. Being recorded by passive camera systems mattered less when you had the ability to reach into those systems electronically and wipe away incriminating footage.

"I've had access to their systems for over two years," Venice said after Jonathan inquired.

Jonathan gave Boxers a thumbs-up, and Big Guy slid out of the driver's seat. As a matter of course, the Batmobile carried seven registrations from seven states, all of them tied to fictional businesses that nonetheless paid property taxes, answered their phones, and collected their junk mail. If you had enough money and knew the right contacts, there were very few tracks that couldn't be covered in the covert world.

Venice lowered her voice to a conspiratorial whisper. "Do you need me to address the, uh, *mess*?"

Jonathan knew she was speaking of the bodies left behind at the Ballentine residence. There was a time when such talk on an open line would have infuriated him, but he'd been told by the master of electrons that these phones were encrypted. Still, it didn't sit well with him.

"We've got it contained," he said. "Let's leave it at that. Are you hearing any chatter about it?"

"Not a word. Apparently, no one's stumbled upon it yet. What's your next step?"

"I don't think we have a choice," Jonathan said. "We're going to follow everything back upstream and see what we can find."

"I don't know what that means."

"Shenandoah Station," Jonathan explained. "I need

you to dig up research on it as we head there. And listen, do me a favor and reach out to Wolverine. Let her know there's a mess to be cleaned up."

"I'll see what I can do." Venice had never become comfortable around Irene Rivers—Wolverine. Jonathan had never discussed the details, but it seemed sometimes that Mother Hen went out of her way to avoid interacting with Director Rivers.

"And keep your ear tuned to the appropriate nine-one-one jurisdictions," Jonathan said. "If the emergency nets start lighting up, let me know right away."

Chapter Eight

Khasan Kadyrov calmed his nerves by concentrating on the hissing of his self-contained breathing apparatus. He'd been told that the characteristic sound of an SCBA had inspired the SFX for Darth Vader. He believed it.

This was the kind of work that should be performed in a high-tech lab, not in this converted barn in Blanton, Tennessee, the middle of rural nowhere. The ventilation hood should be a carefully engineered machine purpose-built for handling such a deadly material, not this Frankenstein contraption that he'd slapped together from parts ordered online.

Yet, here he was, making the best of what was available. He forced himself to concentrate on the containers he was manipulating under the chemical hood.

The "special product" had arrived just a few days ago—after fifteen weeks of endless waiting—and now Timur Yamadayev was screaming for a fast turnaround. Wait, wait, wait, then hurry, hurry, hurry.

All while being ejected from their house by two little boys and the thugs who were protecting them. Something clearly had gone wrong, but the details were none of his concern—especially not now.

Shoulder to shoulder with his twin brother, Aslan, he went through the motions that they had practiced so many times that they seemed natural, drilled into muscle memory. Only now it was real, and the tiniest mistake could spell the worst kind of disaster. All of those practice runs had involved inert liquids—water, mostly—but now, they were playing for keeps.

He'd studied chemistry at the university, and he'd trained for high-hazard chemical storage and deployment at the training camp in Yemen, so he understood the risks. The tiniest drop on the skin or in the eyes, or even a few molecules in the lungs, would result in a painful, awful death. Some people would take longer to die than others, but except for those with the smallest exposures, death was 90 percent assured.

The special product—the VX—had arrived in the middle of the night via helicopter less than a week ago in containers that reminded Khasan of plastic beer kegs. They had received only three but had been expecting many more. How many, he didn't know, but they'd outfitted this barn to hold at least twenty containers this size.

Aslan's job was to control the flow of product from the shipping container while Khasan monitored the Nalgene bottles that they would use to deploy the agent when the time came. A time that was ticking down to just a day or two from now.

They wore identical blue Level-A protective suits—moon suits, in the parlance of the hazardous materials business. Khasan thought of them as body bags with windows. There could be no spillage.

He'd learned to deal with the lack of tactile input through three layers of gloves, and his brain had learned to make sense of the images he saw, distorted as they were, first by the suit's built-in mask and then by the mask of the breathing apparatus. The real concern for him right here, right now, was controlling the rush of knowing that this time the product was real.

Once the deployment containers were filled—there were three of them, each holding a liter of agent—they had to be fitted into the dispensers in a manner that ensured a flawless seal. Of the hundreds or perhaps thousands of people these devices were designed to kill, he did not want to number himself or his brother among them.

"Approaching the fill level," Khasan said into microphone of his radio set. "In three, two, one, stop."

Aslan cranked the valve closed, and the heavy dark-yellow liquid stopped flowing.

"Are you ready for me to purge the line?" Aslan asked.

"Stand by one," Khasan said. Moving with deliberate precision, he removed the tubing from the fill port on the deployment bottle and shifted it carefully to an empty Nalgene container that he'd fitted previously with a scrubbed and vented seal. "Yes, purge the line."

Aslan opened the cock on an elevated bottle of purging liquid—a mixture of denatured alcohol and liquid chlorine. The intent was to make sure that the trace amounts of agent remaining in the fill tubing would be purged and neutralized.

Meanwhile, Khasan finished the process of sealing the deployment vessels. That done, he transferred them one at a time to the other end of the long workbench, then placed them inside a large glass aquarium where Templeton the rat was scurrying about. When the containers were set, he pressed a cover over the top of the whole assembly. Templeton would be just fine if the containers were clean.

If they were not, well, Templeton was a barn rat, named by Aslan after one of his favorite cartoon characters—one of the few they had watched while growing up in Chechnya.

This entire apparatus, from the ventilated bench to the handling procedures to the use of Templeton for leak detection, had been Khasan's brainchild. He had built it to specs that mimicked what he'd read from Soviet Army field manuals, but they did not have the Kremlin's budget. In theory, everything should work.

In theory. Khasan was confident in his engineering abilities, but this was a game where failures stayed hidden until it was too late, and the penalties were unforgiving.

"Are you ready for decontamination?" Khasan asked over the radio.

"Yes, I am," Aslan replied. His voice carried a tone of relief.

These suits were hot. By the time the brothers were done, sweat had pooled in their gloves and boots. Underneath, what few clothes they wore were saturated with sweat.

Decontamination procedures—decon—consisted of little more than an organized, choreographed shower. They walked toward the only door to the outside and opened it to reveal an eight-foot by eight-foot anteroom that housed three metal lockers that were identical to what you'd find in a high school hallway. Opposite the lockers was a large, high-flow shower. This is where they'd scrub away contaminants that they had no reason to believe were there.

The zippers that encased them in their moon suits ran diagonally from their left hip to their right shoulder on the back side of the garment. The suits were heavy-duty things that required assistance to don or doff. Aslan would take first shower. The hardest part of this exercise was granting the full five minutes for the decon rinse. It felt like a long time when you were the one under the water stream, but it felt like forever when you were killing time waiting for your brother to finish.

When Aslan was done, Khasan wrestled his brother's zipper open to allow him to extricate himself from the garment, and then took his place under the water stream. Five minutes later, he turned the water off and stepped back into the locker room, where Aslan was waiting to open him up.

Khasan pulled his arms free from the gloves and sleeves, then quick-marched free of the boots and hung the dripping suit on the hanger next to the one Aslan had just hung up.

Now clothed only in his underwear and breathing apparatus, Khasan stepped out into the chilly sunshine. The chill against his flesh felt refreshing as he turned off his air bottle and pulled the mask off his face. The air smelled of autumn.

"Well, we did it," Aslan said. He sat in a green and white lattice-webbed folding garden chair, clad in tighty-whities and a wife beater.

"We did step one, anyway," Khasan agreed. He shrugged out of the SCBA harness and hung the rig in its designated plastic box on the outside wall of the converted barn. "Step two is still a big if." He laughed when he got the full view of his brother. "You look like shit."

"You should see a mirror."

The eldest of the pair by four minutes, Aslan was literally Khasan's mirror image. Left-handed instead of right, hair parted on the right instead of the left. They'd soon be twenty-six years old. The ladies seemed to find them attractive, though for the life of him, Khasan couldn't understand why. When he looked at his reflection—either a glass one or the living one—he couldn't see past the large ethnic Chechen nose and tangled hair. Today, right now, make that *matted* hair.

"Why is step two a big if? You mean the deployment?"

"The problem," Khasan explained in the patient tone that often pissed Aslan off as sounding condescending, "is that we've only tested it with water. Now that I know what the special product really is—VX—I realize that we've tested for the wrong viscosity. Water is only five centipoise, maximum. Maybe less. The special product is, like, ten centipoise."

The laboratory-slash-barn sat atop a hill behind the farmhouse from which they'd been banished—their home since they'd arrived in the United States. The eighty-acre spread gave them the privacy they needed to do the jobs they needed to do. In this part of Tennessee, no one questioned the regular gunfire on their private range. No one saw the assembled stacks of food and water, nor did anyone raise a stink when deliveries were made by helicopter during the darkest hours of moonless nights.

Aslan said, "If you want me to say you're smarter than me—again—I'm fine with that. Now, what the hell does all of that mean, and why do we care?"

"The VX is thicker," Khasan said. "More like kerosene than water. I don't know how that might affect the performance of the dispenser."

"Can it really make that much of a difference?"

"I don't know. That's the point. We get one shot for this thing to do the maximum possible damage, and we have no idea how it's going to perform." Khasan helped himself to a second folding lawn chair. His was blue and white.

"So, what's your solution?" Aslan asked.

It felt strange to articulate the thought that had been rattling in his head for the past couple of days. "We need to test it with the real product."

Aslan's jaw dropped. "With the VX?"

"We have to."

"But how? We don't have enough of it as it is."

Khasan dismissed the concern. "We have as much as we have," he said. "If the apparatus works, it will be plenty to make a big impact. I don't think it will make that big a difference if we kill a thousand people or two thousand. Either way, I think America will get the point."

"But how do you test nerve gas? I mean, who are you going to gas?"

"It's not who," Khasan said. "It's what. Let's see how Templeton is doing."

Khasan rose from his folding chair and headed back toward the lab, pausing at the door to slip his feet into the tennis shoes he'd left there on his way in to get dressed. There was no need at this point to climb back into the moon suit.

Aslan got up, too. "How long are we going to be kicked out of our house, anyway?"

Khasan smiled. "First of all, it's not *our* house, unless you signed a deed I don't know about." He looked back and saw that his brother was likewise smiling. "We go back when Timur says we can go back. Welcome to life as a soldier."

When the kids arrived, the Kadyrov brothers had been pushed out to a smaller cabin that sat on the top of the same hill with the barn. It was furnished and it had a well, plus it also had electricity, thanks to its proximity to the lab.

"Why are they even here?" Aslan asked as they stepped into the locker area.

"Because Timur wants them here." Khasan worried sometimes about his brother's insistence on questioning everything.

"No air packs?" Aslan asked as they neared the inner door.

"I just need to get close enough to see if your pet rodent is still wandering around," Khasan replied. "If he is, we're good. If he's not, well, I'm not sure what we are."

Khasan kept his feet on the locker-room side of the door as he leaned in through the opening and waited for his eyes to adjust.

"What do you see?" Aslan asked from behind him.

"Movement," Khasan replied. "I'm going in to take a closer look."

"Are you sure you don't want to pack up?"

Again with the questions. "If Templeton is alive inside a closed container with the dispensers, then we should be fine out here."

Aslan hesitated at the door.

"We're not going to deploy these things wearing moon suits," Khasan said. "Now's as good a time as any to get used to handling them barehanded."

Khasan had no expectation that he would ever see Chechnya again. He accepted that he would likely die violently. But it would not be here in a barn, and it would not be on this first operation. When they deployed the dispensers, the event would be the first of its kind. No one would be expecting it. Complacency and soft targets were his dream.

Their second mission, whatever that might be, would be dicier because number two would establish a pattern, and then the third mission would likely be the one that would kill them. You could try to be careful, and you could be mindful of repeating patterns, but the police had resources at their disposal that he could only begin to imagine. Even if you didn't make a mistake, you couldn't guarantee that a fleck of dry skin might not slough off or that a hair wouldn't fall onto the crime scene.

After half an hour alone in the glass case, Templeton looked perfectly healthy, if a bit harried by his incarceration. Khasan walked the fifteen feet across the lab space to parole their furry friend. He lifted the rodent out of the aquarium and placed him on the worktable, where he could decide for himself where to go next.

"Are you ready, Aslan?"

His twin materialized on his left. "Ready for what?"

"We're going to take this one out and test it. See if it works."

"And how are we going to do that?"

"Cows," Khasan said. A three-foot-long roll of Bubble Wrap hung from the wall behind the table. He pulled off a two-foot length and cut it free with the box cutter that sat there for that purpose.

"Where are you going to find cows?"

"You're kidding, right? Where *can't* you find cows around here?" Khasan lifted the dispenser assembly out of the aquarium and set it atop the spread of Bubble Wrap. He lifted the wrap up and around the assembly and held it together while his brother sealed the edges with a strip of packing tape.

They were ready to go.

The prison house looked bigger from the front yard than it did from the inside. A black chain-link fence surrounded a small yard. Ryder wasn't good at judging distances, but to his eye it looked about fifty yards square, about the distance he had to run for gym class tests. The fence was tall—over twice as tall as Ryder, and he'd topped five-five this year. It looked kind of like chain-link, but the wire was much thicker, maybe a quarter inch in diameter. There'd be no cutting through this sucker à la *The Great Escape*.

The fence itself didn't wrap around the whole house, but rather around the back and side yards, like you'd build to keep a nasty dog away from visitors when they approached the front door. The wire along the top—what they'd been told was razor wire—was good old barbed wire, just like every other fence along every other road. And if there were sensors, he didn't see any wires for them. He hadn't walked the entire fence line yet, but he'd get to it. It wasn't like there was a lot else to do.

Officer Al told them that they needed some exercise and then announced that he had to take off for a while. That would leave them alone with Officer Kim, and Ryder was more than happy to be as far away from that psycho as he could be. The guy stared at them all the time. He barely even blinked. It was creepy, made creepier still by that big red splotch that covered his left eye. A port wine stain. Jimmy Grady at school had one of those, only his didn't make him look crazy.

Ryder watched as Officer Al exited the front door and walked to the old Ford pickup that was parked sideways in the front yard, on the other side of the fence. It was smaller than most pickups and was painted the color of moss.

"He's not wearing his uniform," Geoff said. Captain Obvious strikes again.

"That's because he's not really a cop," Ryder said.

Officer Al opened the truck's door and slipped in behind the steering wheel. He tipped down the visor with his right hand, and with his left, he caught the keys that dropped down.

"I didn't think so. They're too mean."

The engine turned and caught. Officer Al slung an arm over the seat, backed out ten feet, then ground the transmission into gear before driving down the gravel driveway ahead of a gray cloud of dust.

"Who are they, then?" Geoff asked. He held a filthy soccer ball in both hands—the focus of their forced recreation.

"I don't know. Kidnappers, I think."

Geoff's face lost all expression. "We've been *kidnapped?*"

"They put us in the trunk of a friggin' car, doofus." Ryder took the ball away and walked toward the center of the yard. "Stay there. I'll pass it to you." He walked less than twenty feet, then turned and dropped the ball onto the grass. He tapped the pass, nothing aggressive.

Geoff trapped the ball and passed it back. "Is Dad dead?"

Ryder stayed focused on the ball. "I'm not sure," he said.

"You're lying."

"If you're so sure I'm lying then you must think you already know." Ryder didn't want to talk about this. The way the arrest had gone down the other night, Geoff had slept through the whole thing. If only Ryder could have been so lucky.

When the soccer ball came back to him, he chipped it into the air, setting up a header for Geoff.

"I think I heard shooting," Geoff said. "I know I smelled gunpowder. And Mom was crying." He let the ball bounce on the ground, then settled it with his chest before chipping it back to Ryder. "But the way they took me out, they didn't let me see anything."

So, Geoff hadn't slept through it, after all.

"They didn't let me see anything, either." *But goddammit, I wish I hadn't seen it on my own.* He let the ball bounce off the crown of his head, caught it with his thigh, then juggled it from knee to knee. Ryder had awakened at the sound of people moving around outside the house. When he peeked out his window, he saw men in black uniforms with their helmets and guns.

He bumped the ball high off his knee, then headed it back to Geoff.

When Geoff got the ball, he grounded it with his foot. "Is he dead?"

Ryder felt emotion rising. "Why don't you just let it go?"

"Why don't you just tell me? Stop being such an asshole?"

Sadness morphed to anger. There was too much shit in Ryder's life now to put up with Geoff talking to him that way. He took a menacing step toward his little brother—a move he'd made thousands of times over the years—but rather than backing away, Geoff took a step forward, daring him to engage.

"Are we really going to fight?" Geoff challenged. His fists were clenched.

Ryder was stunned. Yes, he thought. Yes, he wanted to fight. He wanted to hit someone. But no, this was not the way to vent.

And Geoff wasn't really the person he wanted to hit, anyway. "Yes," Ryder said. "I think Dad is dead." He watched his brother for a reaction and was surprised when he didn't get much of one.

Geoff's fists opened, and his shoulders sagged. "What about Mom?"

Ryder looked at the ground. "I don't know. I think she's still alive, but I don't know."

"Why did the police come in the first place?" Geoff walked to the soccer ball and tapped it back to his brother.

Ryder trapped it with the sole of his foot. "I don't know. I think it had something to do with drugs. After Dad stopped working. I think I heard them talking about . . . stuff."

He rolled the ball a few times on its axis with his toes. Then he kicked it as hard as he could out into the yard. "Shit!"

Tears erupted out of nowhere, and then he was even more pissed. He whirled away from Geoff and swiped at his eyes. Snot was dripping, too. God *damn* it!

He felt Geoff's hand on his back. "We'll be okay."

Ryder turned to face him. To hell with the tears. Let him see them. "No, we won't," he said. He lowered his voice and pulled Geoff farther away from the cabin. "None of this is right, Geoffy. These guys are killers. They killed a *priest* for Christ's sake. A *priest*. Instant ticket to hell. And the lady who was driving us. If they'll do that . . ." His voice trailed off because he didn't know how to complete the sentence.

"They're not going to hurt us," Geoff said. "Al said so. All we have to do is obey the rules—"

"And they'll still kill us. A *priest*, Geoff. A *priest*."

Geoff shot a nervous look back over his shoulder, toward the cabin. "That doesn't mean they'll hurt *us*."

Ryder tossed up his arms. Was Geoff really so stupid that he couldn't see it? Couldn't see that Al and Kim had no choice but to kill them? "We witnessed the murders," he whispered. "That's a death penalty offense. And you know what? So is kidnapping. We have to get away from here. Away from them."

Another panicked look back toward the cabin.

"Could you be more obvious?" Ryder snapped. "Quit doing that."

"There's no way," Geoff said. "If we try to get away, they'll kill us."

"They'll kill us, anyway."

Geoff's expression changed as he looked at something over Ryder's shoulder. He showed curiosity and humor. "Who are they?" He pointed.

At first, Ryder couldn't see what he was pointing at. Then when he did, he laughed. Two guys up on the crest of the hill were hanging out in their underwear. "How gay is that?"

"What are they doing?" Geoff asked.

"How the hell would I know? Comparing dick sizes?"

That made Geoff laugh. It was a good sound to hear.

"Hey!" a voice called from the cabin. It was Officer Kim, the psychopath. "What are you two talking about!"

"Nothing." They answered in unison.

"Bullshit. Get over here." Kim pointed to a spot at his feet.

"Don't say anything," Ryder instructed.

"About what?"

"About anything."

Kim shouted, "Now!"

The two boys walked together, stopped about ten feet short of Kim.

"Tell me what you were talking about," Kim said. When the boys stood silently, he said, "What, are you afraid of me?"

Yeah, Ryder was terrified of him, but he wasn't

going to give him the satisfaction of showing it. He locked his jaw.

"Big brother, tough little man, eh?" Kim baited. He took a step forward and leaned in until his face was level with Ryder's and only a foot or so away. He smelled like sweat and onions. "You want to do battle with me, kid? You want to take a shot at me? Throw a punch?"

Ryder forced himself not to blink. This day—these days—were shitty enough without adding any of this to the mix. He wasn't going to fight a man who no doubt could turn him inside out, but he wasn't going to back down, either. He was in too deep for that now.

"One way or the other, you're going to answer my question," Kim said.

"We were wondering whether or not our parents are dead," Geoff said. "We know our dad is, but we don't know about our mom."

Kim continued to glare at Ryder as he said, "And what did you decide?"

"We think that Mom is still alive," Geoff said. Then, after a beat, "Is she?"

"You better hope she is."

"Why do you say—"

"Shut up, Geoff," Ryder said. "He's enjoying it too much."

Ryder never saw the backhand coming. Looping in from his blindside, it hit him full on the cheek and pirouetted him down to the grass.

"*That*, I enjoyed," Kim said. "Talking, not so much."

Ryder sat up and brought one hand to his face while the other went to his nose to check for the blood that he could smell in his sinuses. He was surprised not to find any.

Kim moved his forefinger from one of their faces to the other, as if pivoting on a turret. "You behave yourselves, boys, or I swear to God I will hurt you." Then he turned on his heel and went back inside.

"Don't worry about him," Geoff said, stooping to help Ryder to his feet. "He's just a bully."

Ryder shook off the assistance. "I can get myself up." He rose first to his knees and then got his feet under him, brushing the grass and dirt from his backside.

"I'll go get the ball," Geoff said, and he jogged off in that direction.

"I don't want to play anymore," Ryder said. Geoff either didn't hear him or just chose to ignore him. Probably some of each.

They were getting away from here. Ryder didn't know much about a lot of things, but that was one thing he was one hundred percent sure of. And he had to take Geoff with him.

Chapter Nine

Jonathan was expecting Shenandoah Station to be a government facility, more akin to a prison complex—or maybe a hospital—than to an actual home. Resting on what must have been five or six acres, the place had a Kansas farmhouse vibe. Clearly built in the '40s or maybe early '50s, the single-story structure sported a wrap-around porch and even had a barn in the back. A split-rail fence surrounded the rolling perimeter, keeping the dozen or so head of cattle and an equal number of goats from wandering off.

"Quite the place," Gail commented as they rolled up.

"Nicer than the place I grew up in," Boxers added.

"Takes a lot of money to keep a place like this running," Jonathan said. "No wonder they charge so much for kids to stay here."

Venice had done the research. Shenandoah Station was less an orphanage than it was a drug and behavioral treatment center for the children of wealthy people. Specifically targeting boys under fifteen years of age, the home set patients on the straight and narrow by teaching them the value of hard manual labor by day while nourishing them with farm-to-table meals in the evening.

"Did we know the Kendall boys had drug issues?" Gail asked.

"I didn't," Jonathan said.

Boxers said, "Maybe we should have called ahead."

"Negative," Jonathan said. "This is where the chain of events started. I don't want to give anyone a chance to cover their tracks."

"What tracks would they cover?" Gail asked.

"Let's find out," Jonathan said.

As Boxers nosed the Batmobile to a stop off to the side of the drive, short of an *S*-shaped walkway to the front door, a team of golden retrievers trotted out from the shadow of the right side of the house, tails wagging hard enough to knock them off-balance. Both went to Jonathan's door as he opened it and slid to the ground. He stooped and rubbed their ears.

"Dogs just like you, don't they?" Gail observed.

"Not *everybody* can hate him," Boxers said and then blew an air kiss.

They'd left all weapons but their sidearms in the vehicle, but they were still tac'd out in black-on-black. "We look like cops," Jonathan observed. "I'm going to go ahead and badge them. The lady in charge of the place is named Lightwater. Soren Lightwater."

"Soren," Boxers mumbled under his breath. "Christ, I miss real names."

When they got to the porch, Boxers and Gail stayed at the base of the three steps while Jonathan walked to the door and rapped on the screen door with his middle knuckle. Then he stepped back and to the side to move out of the "cone of death"—the area likely to take the most damage if someone were to, say, blast a shotgun through the door.

After about ten seconds—long enough for Jonathan to wonder whether he should knock again—he heard footsteps on the other side, and the door pulled open to reveal a young man of about fourteen. He wore jeans and a T-shirt that was soaked around the collar. Rivulets of sweat cut tracks through the grime that had accumulated on his face. His hands looked like he might have been greasing an axle, though he was doing his best to wipe the grime away with a blackened towel.

"Hey," he said. "Can I help you?"

"Is Ms. Lightwater here?" Jonathan asked.

"May I ask who's asking? She'll want to know."

Jonathan held up a gold badge. "FBI."

"Oh, shit. Yeah, hang on."

As the kid turned to walk away, Jonathan stepped inside and beckoned for Gail to follow him. Boxers strolled around to the back of the house. Bad events had begun at this house. That meant the perpetrators of bad things might try to avoid a conversation with the FBI. If someone tried to bolt, Big Guy would be there to change their mind.

The kid stopped short and turned back to them as they crossed the threshold. The look that flashed in his eyes was hard to read. Whatever it was, *welcoming* wasn't it. Jonathan flashed him the kind of smile that was designed to make him even more uneasy. All lips, no eyes.

"What's your name, son?" Jonathan asked.

The boy considered not answering, then said, "Charlie."

"Nice to meet you, Charlie."

The boy said nothing more as he made his way toward the back door.

When they were alone, Jonathan said, "Agent Culp, stay here and greet them when they come back. I'm going to look around." A while ago, Irene Rivers had presented the Security Solutions team with almost-real FBI credentials. Gail's name of record was Gerarda Culp, Jonathan's was Neil Bonner, and Boxers drew Xavier Contata. That last bit was a deliberate effort to fry Big Guy's bacon a little, and it worked. Even Venice got a badge and a handle, though no one was sure why she would need it. Still, if anyone ran a background check on Constance DuBois or any of the others, they'd find totally false yet completely legitimate dossiers on each of them.

"Where are you going?" Gail asked.

"On a treasure hunt." Jonathan saw the disapproval in her eyes, but he ignored it. Gail's FBI credentials were once real, and when Jonathan first met her, she was the elected sheriff of a little burg in Indiana. Throw her law degree into the mix with all that experience enforcing the strictest interpretations of legal conduct, and she often had difficulty playing by Jonathan's rules.

The interior of the farmhouse was laid out like a cross. On the north-south arm, the shorter of the two, the foyer-slash-family room gave way to a dining table with fixed benches that might have been lifted from a public park. Beyond the dining area, a '70s-era kitchen, complete with harvest gold appliances, looked clean but was hard worn. While the counters and cabinets gleamed, Jonathan noted that years-old accumulations of dirt were caked in the hard-to-reach corners of the floor and ceiling.

Bedrooms took up the east and west wings. An en-suite master anchored the far eastern end. Five smaller bedrooms and a small bathroom made up the rest of the house. Each of the smaller rooms contained a twin bed and two stacked bunks, with identical five-drawer dressers somehow wedged in among them. Jonathan wasn't sure that it mattered, but he noted that none of the smaller rooms had closets.

As he moved from room to room, he opened the dresser drawers to peek inside. He had no idea what he was looking for. All of the garments he found were well-worn, but also well folded. Shoes were all placed in pairs at the foot of the beds, and where applicable, the laces were carefully aligned along the tongue on their respective shoes. Other than footwear, the floors were free of clutter.

Jonathan was in the bedroom at the far western tip of the cross when he heard a screen door screech open and clack shut. He headed back toward the family room.

"I'm Soren Lightwater," a voice said before Jonathan could see its owner. It had a scratchy, basso quality to it that nailed her as a smoker in his mind. Interesting, he thought, since he'd neither seen nor smelled evidence of tobacco. "Charlie said you were a man."

"No, ma'am," Jonathan said as he approached from her blind side. "Agent Culp is a woman. I'm Neil Bonner, and I'm the one Charlie spoke to."

"Can I help you?" Soren's tone dripped with displeasure. "You'd better tell me that you have a warrant. A child can't grant you permission to search my home."

"What did you do with the Kendall boys?" Jonathan fired the question like an arrow. He could see her now, and she puffed up like an angry chicken. Mid-forties and built like a farmer, she was more attractive than her voice.

"Who the hell—"

"I'm the FB-friggin'-I, ma'am, and you delivered two children you were responsible for into the hands of murderers. I'm not interested in your righteous indignation."

"Get out of my house."

"When I'm ready. Understand this, Soren. When I do leave, if I don't have the answers I want, I swear to you that I will burn this place down on my way out the door."

Soren looked as if she'd been slapped. Her mouth gaped, and her eyes showed confusion. Or maybe that was fear.

To sell his point, Jonathan pulled his creds case from his back pocket and displayed it for her, not five inches from her face.

"I'm calling the police," Soren said.

"The number is nine-one-one," Gail said. The addition of her voice to the conversation—and the addition of her credentials—seemed to startle Soren. Gail might not like playing the game by Digger's rules, but when she played, she played well. "But I don't think prison would agree with you."

"Prison! *Prison? For me?*

"A police officer has been shot and, we believe,

killed," Jonathan explained. "We believe the same to be true about a priest. And two children have been kidnapped. All because of you. Prison is the *best* you can hope for when I'm finished developing my case on you."

Soren looked to the back door, as if expecting reinforcements. "I want a lawyer."

"I'll bet you do," Jonathan said. "But you can't have one."

"We're in a hurry to find these boys, Soren," Gail said. "I'm afraid we need to put technicalities and niceties on hold today."

"When did my *rights* become a nicety?"

"Really, Soren?" Jonathan said. "We're trying to rescue children and the best you've got is a debate question?"

Something changed in Soren, and the change wasn't pretty. She took a step closer to Jonathan and locked her arms at her side. "I am sick to death of this horse twaddle," she said. They weren't nose-to-nose, but it was close.

Jonathan admired the passion.

"We're doing the Lord's work here, helping children who otherwise have no hope. We instill in them the intrinsic value of a rewarding day's work, and you agency types want to call that child abuse. Now you make up this story—"

"Stop!" Gail ordered, again startling Soren. "Were Ryder and Geoffrey Kendall here or not?"

"I don't recognize those names any better now than I did when people called about them earlier. When were they supposed to have been here?"

"Two days ago."

"Two *days*? Absolutely not. This is a care center, not a hotel. People don't just check in. In order for children to be admitted, they first need to—"

"Um, Mrs. L?"

They all turned to see Charlie half in and half out of the back door, his silhouette framed by the jamb.

"What is it, Charlie? Step inside, please. Let's leave the bugs out where they belong."

The kid looked unnerved. "There's a really big man in the backyard. He's just standing there."

"He's ours," Jonathan said. "He's just doing his job."

"Thank you, Charlie," Soren said. "Does your presence here mean that the chicken coop is now spotless?"

"Not yet."

"Then you know what you need to do."

Charlie clearly knew a dismissal when he heard it, but after he started to back out, he stopped. "Um, Mrs. L?"

This time, she planted her fists on her hips.

"Um, I kind of overheard what you've been talking about." He cast his eyes to the floor.

"Overheard? Really? From all the way out in the yard? What do we call that, young man?"

He got smaller. "Eavesdropping, ma'am."

"And what is that?"

"A sin."

Jonathan couldn't take it anymore. "Oh, for God's sake. Young man—Charlie—do you have something to share that we need to know?"

Charlie looked to Soren for permission. She nodded once. Jonathan would have throttled her if she hadn't.

Charlie cleared his throat. "Those two kids *were* here the other night. Ryan and Geoff, right?"

"Ryder," Gail corrected.

"That's right. I remember now it was a weird name. But I was close. You were out, ma'am. Mr. Zambrano took care of them."

Recognition dawned on Soren's face. "Monday night?"

Charlie looked at the ceiling while he did the math. "Yes, Monday."

"And when did they leave?" Gail asked.

"That same night. Well, next morning, I guess. Technically, anyway. It was really early. Dark."

"Who picked them up?" Jonathan asked.

The boy hunched his shoulders up to his ears.

"Don't be obtuse, Charlie," Soren scolded. "A shrug is a lazy answer. It's not an answer at all, in fact."

"I don't know!" A flash of adolescent angst. "They'd crashed in the extra bunks in my room, and then Mr. Z came in with a flashlight and woke them up."

"Did you say anything?" Jonathan asked. "Did they?"

"No, sir."

"What about their things?" Soren asked.

"They never unpacked."

This was apparently the most disturbing part of the story to Soren. "You're serious?"

"What am I missing?" Jonathan asked.

Soren explained, "It's one of our rules here. We believe that children need a sense of belonging. A sense of permanence. So, the very first thing we do when they arrive is help them unpack and place their things in a drawer that is theirs alone."

"So, it's a major break in tradition to do otherwise," Gail concluded.

"It's not tradition. It's policy."

"So, who's this Zambrano guy?" Jonathan asked.

Soren addressed the boy. "You're excused now, Charlie. Thank you for your input and assistance."

He beamed.

"Out!" Soren pointed out the back door.

Jonathan started to object, unsure that he was finished debriefing the kid, but he caught the glare from Gail and swallowed his words.

"It was nice meeting you, sir. Ma'am." And Charlie was gone.

Soren returned her attention to her visitors. "May we sit?"

The sudden change in demeanor startled Jonathan.

"Of course," Gail said.

Jonathan made sure to take the seat that afforded him the most unobstructed view of the room, with special emphasis on the front door.

Soren was still in the process of dropping herself into the worn leather recliner that anyone would recognize as the local throne of power when she said, "Bobby Zambrano is an exception to the rule here. He's not a counselor, and he's not trained in social work, but he's a very special man."

"So, why did Charlie have to leave the room before we could talk about him?" Gail asked. She'd taken a seat with a good view of the back door.

"Because I figure you guys already know about Bobby's past, and I don't think that Charlie needs to know of such things."

"Which part of the past are you referring to?" Gail asked. Considering that she was playing a bluff, Jonathan thought she pulled it off well.

"The drug conviction, of course. Why, is there something else I should know about?"

"Not necessarily," Gail said. "Tell us the rest of what you know."

Soren grew defensive again, reared back in her chair. "Let's get one thing straight. I believe in second chances. I've devoted my life to them. When a man has served his time, it's wrong to continue punishing—"

"We've got a runner!" It was Boxers from outside, and he sounded startled.

Soren gave a little yip as Jonathan bolted out of his chair and blasted through the screen door onto the front porch.

To his right, a skinny guy about thirty years old in worker's coveralls and soiled Wellington boots sprinted past from the back of the house toward the fence out front. Jonathan couldn't see Boxers, but he could hear the hammering of his size fourteens as he struggled to catch his prey. Big Guy was lighter on his feet than most men his size, but he had no chance of catching this runner.

Jonathan did. He exploded off the porch and tore after the man, sprinting faster than he had in a very long time. As he closed the distance on an angle, he was thankful that the runner was hampered by the awkward Wellies.

The running man cast a glance over his shoulder just in time to take Jonathan's linebacker tackle, which nearly cut the guy in half at the rib cage. Jonathan heard the grunt and the explosive exhalation, and then they were both on the ground.

Jonathan's shoulder hurt from the impact, but nowhere near as bad, he presumed, as the other guy's midsection hurt.

The runner was still trying to find his feet when Jonathan said, "Don't tell me—let me guess. You're Bobby Zambrano."

Chapter Ten

Zambrano tried to stand, but the best he could manage was an inverted *L*. He hugged his middle and struggled to get a good breath. "I think you broke my ribs, man."

"Be happy I didn't get to you first," Boxers said.

"You're okay so long as you're not spitting blood," Jonathan said. "Why were you running?"

"I didn't do nothing wrong."

"Again. Why were you running?"

"'Cause I heard that the FBI was here."

"Yet you did nothing wrong," Boxers said.

Zambrano coughed and moaned from the effort. "I need a doctor."

"Fine," Jonathan said. "Let's go back up to the house, and we can call one."

Zambrano looked from Jonathan to Boxers. A veil of fear darkened his face. Sometimes you needed to be next to Big Guy to truly understand his dimensions.

Boxers smiled at him. "It'd be easier for both of us if I didn't have to carry you up there."

Zambrano's shoulders sagged as the inevitability sank in. "All right," he said. "But don't push me."

"Don't make us, and we won't," Jonathan said.

The poor guy walked like an old man, listing to one side, taking tiny steps. Jonathan almost felt sorry for hitting him that hard. Almost. He did lend a helping hand as Zambrano climbed the stairs to the porch.

Soren and Gail flanked the doorway as Zambrano limped through and entered the house. He eyed the soft chairs of the living room with a look of dread. "I'll sit on one of the benches if that's okay."

Over the years, Jonathan had learned to gauge how hard he'd hit someone, and he recognized Zambrano's show as a delaying tactic, at least in part. All too often, those tactics resulted more in lies than truth. The truth didn't need delay. It came easily— quickly—and Jonathan heard the ticking of the clock more loudly with each passing second.

"You all right now?" Boxers asked, his voice sweet with irony. "Can we get you a blankey? A hot milk, maybe?"

Zambrano looked on the edge of accepting the offer before he understood it for what it was.

"Why were you running?" Jonathan asked. He and the others stood in a semicircle in front of the man.

"I didn't know I was doing anything wrong," Zambrano said.

Soren scolded, "So, that means now you *do* know you did *something*."

Jonathan felt a flash of anger. Interviewing people was a form of art that was built on an evolving strategy of questions and follow-ups, listening and reading the subtle clues of body language. If he needed help, he'd have asked for it. He saw Gail lean over to place a hand on Soren's arm and whisper in her ear.

Jonathan waited to hear more from Zambrano. Sometimes, silence drew more complete, honest answers.

"How could I have known that harm would come to those boys?" Zambrano blurted. "I would never do such a thing."

Jonathan saw his opening. "What harm are you talking about?"

"Charlie said that they been kidnapped, and that people died."

At least Charlie's a good listener, Jonathan thought. "What *did* you think would happen?"

Zambrano's jaw locked, and he looked to the floor.

"Answer his question!" Soren demanded.

Jonathan whirled on her and swallowed his tirade even as it was rising in his throat. "Please let me do this alone," he said.

She ignored him. "Did you plan this, Bobby? Was this intentional? Is that why you let me know that *Les Mis* was showing in Richmond?"

"Wait," Gail said, again placing her hand on Soren's arm. "What?"

"Bobby knows that *Les Misérables* is my favorite play, and he encouraged me to go to see it in Richmond on Monday night. Almost pushed me out the door."

Jonathan watched Zambrano's body language as Soren spoke. His head dipped lower. No sign of objection.

"What do you mean, he almost pushed you out the door?" Gail pressed.

"Tell them, Bobby," she said. "Tell them how you thought I needed a night away. How I needed to take in the show and then, while I was at it, stay in a hotel overnight. Tell them how you said you would take care of everything here to give me a night out." Soren lurched forward past Jonathan, then gripped the underside of Zambrano's face and tilted it up at her. She squeezed hard enough to dimple his cheeks and puff his lips. "Was all of that part of some terrible plan?"

Even with his face tilted up, Zambrano continued to look at the floor. At least he tried to.

"Please step away, Mrs. Lightwater," Jonathan said. He understood how personal this affront was to her and how hurt she must be. "Let us handle this."

"I took you in, Bobby. I trusted you. I gave you a home when no one else would. What have you done?"

Jonathan looked to Gail, and she nodded. "Come on, Soren," she said, gently pulling her back from Zambrano. Soren complied, but she didn't pull back far.

"I know you're sorry for what you have done," Jonathan said. "I don't know what that is yet, but it's clear that you are sorry. But what was done is not yet finished. Maybe there's still time to end this in a way that won't get any more people hurt."

"I want a lawyer."

Boxers took a menacing step forward—giant, and quick enough to startle Jonathan. Big Guy bunched the front of Zambrano's shirt in his fist and lurched him off his bench, lifting him till his toes were barely on the floor. The smaller man yelped in pain and tried to protect his ribs, but Boxers wouldn't let him.

"Agent Contata," Jonathan said, reaching out. He'd

seen this look on Big Guy's face a number of times over the years, and it usually ended in bloodshed. "He's no help to us if he's dead."

"From what I can tell, he's no good to us while he's alive," Big Guy growled. "Listen to me, *Bobby*. I don't give a shit about you, your criminal past, or the fact that you're sorry. Take that up with your priest, rabbi, or witch doctor. All I give a shit about is those two kids, and here are the three facts that I know to be one hundred percent true.

"One, those boys have been kidnapped and exposed to God only knows what kind of danger. Two, we don't know where they are, but you at least know how they got there." He shook the terrified man and pulled him even closer as he clicked open a folding blade. "Three— and you need to pay attention to this one—if you don't start working to help us help them, I'm going to give you a Colombian necktie. You know what that is?"

Zambrano looked confused.

"It's where I cut your throat and pull your tongue out through the slot. It's ugly as shit, and it will keep poor Charlie cleaning the walls and ceiling all night. So, give the next minute or two some careful thought." He dropped Zambrano back down on his bench, eliciting another groan of pain.

Jonathan knew that Big Guy was not bluffing, and he moved to tone things down. He straddled the bench just a couple of feet from Zambrano and leaned one arm on the table. "Come on, Bobby. It makes no sense to hold back now."

"You'll arrest me." Zambrano's voice was barely audible. "I can't go back to jail again."

"Look at me, Bobby," Jonathan said, nearly matching the other man's tone. When he had eye contact, he said, "I give you my word—I absolutely promise you—that we will not arrest you. I'm not even interested in arresting you. I just need to know what happened."

Zambrano dipped his chin till it was nearly touching his chest. "The lawyer paid me."

"I'm sorry, Bobby, you're going to have to speak louder."

"Rafael Iglesias. He paid me."

"Who is Rafael Iglesias?" Soren asked.

Jonathan shot a finger at her. "You need to be quiet, ma'am. Next words I hear from you, I'm having you taken outside." He returned his attention to Zambrano. "Who is that?"

"The family lawyer."

"Whose family?"

"The boys'. And mine."

"You shared an attorney?"

Zambrano nodded.

"What did Rafael Iglesias pay you to do?"

"I didn't think no harm would come from it. I swear I didn't. He said he'd be dropping two children off at the house, and then someone else would be coming for them." He cast a glance toward Soren. "When I told him that's not how we did things here, that Mrs. Lightwater would never allow that, he asked if there wasn't a way I could get her out of the house."

"How much did he pay you?" Soren demanded.

Gail put a hand on her arm but did not make her leave the room.

"A thousand dollars."

"Better than forty pieces of silver," Boxers said.

Zambrano continued, "When the people came to pick them up, one of them was a social worker lady and the other was a priest. He said he was from Resurrection House."

Soren gasped. "Oh, my God," she said. "The priest you mentioned. That was Father Dom?"

"Father Tim," Jonathan said. He hadn't realized that Dom was loved outside of the Northern Neck.

"They weren't gone but a few minutes—maybe a half hour—when the police arrived. When they found out that Ryder and Geoff were already gone, they were very angry. But what could I do? I thought maybe something changed in the plans."

Zambrano pressed his hands on the table and pushed himself to his feet. "Mrs. L, I am terribly sorry." Then he presented Jonathan with his wrists, ready to be cuffed. "I will go to jail peacefully."

Jonathan waved that off. "I already told you we're not here to arrest you. Sit back down."

Zambrano seemed confused, shifting his eyes from Jonathan to Soren and then to Gail. He seemed to be purposefully avoiding Boxers.

"Sit, sit, sit," Jonathan said. He knew they had to get past all the drama before they could get to the information he wanted, but his patience had thinned to see-through.

When Zambrano had planted his butt again, Jonathan asked, "Why do you think your lawyer wanted you to do this?"

"I don't know."

Jonathan smelled bullshit. "You didn't ask?"

Zambrano clammed up again.

"Don't play games with me, Bobby. Why did an attorney feel that he could lean on you to betray the lady who went out of her way to give you a break? That's not the kind of thing that someone would do if he didn't have full expectation of compliance. What leverage does he have?"

Another uncomfortable glance at Soren.

She said, "I am the least of your problems right now, Bobby. You tell them what they want to know."

He cleared his throat. "Mr. Iglesias, he has other businesses. Other than the law. I help with those sometimes."

Boxers said, "Honest to God, little man, one more riddle, and you're dead."

"Drugs!" Zambrano nearly shouted the word. "He buys and sells with some very scary people. I help him with the money sometimes."

"Help him how?" Jonathan asked.

"I deliver things sometimes. Money, packages, that sort of thing."

"Packages of *drugs*?" Soren gasped.

"I don't know." He spoke quickly. "I never look in the packages. I just deliver them and then take packages back to Mr. Iglesias."

"You've had *drugs* in my home?"

He showed both palms, as if surrendering. "No, no, no, never in here. I would never do that. Not around the children."

"What does this have to do with Geoff and Ryder Kendall?" Gail asked.

"I don't know. All I know is what I've told you. He said if I don't do this, he will report me to the police."

"Report him right back," Jonathan said.

Zambrano puffed out a bitter laugh. "He is a fancy

lawyer, and I am an ex-con. Who are the police going to believe?"

Jonathan had no argument for that. He turned to Soren. "I'm going to guess that you knew of none of this?"

She shook her head, her face a mask of bewilderment.

"How much advance notice did you get from Bobby to take off to the theater?"

"Less than a day," Soren said. "We discussed it three days ago. I went to Richmond that night, spent two nights in a hotel, and returned home this morning." Turning to Bobby, she asked, "Have you done this before when I've been gone and trusting you? Have you been handling children as if they were your *packages*?" She used finger quotes.

"No, ma'am. Just this once. And I am so ashamed."

"No shit," Boxers said.

Jonathan said, "Now think carefully on this, Bobby. The police officers who came after the priest and social worker left. Had you seen them before?"

Bobby answered with his eyes but seemed unable to form the words.

"Were they people you'd delivered packages to before?"

He nodded.

Jonathan felt his hopes sag. The boys had been kidnapped to keep their parents quiet. These weren't street dopers, they were no-shit cartel badasses, and they didn't give a whit who they tortured and killed. He'd seen what those monsters were capable of, and the Taliban and ISIS had nothing on their brutality.

Jonathan stood and untangled his legs from the fixed bench. "Y'all have anything else?" he asked his team.

"Not unless I can punch this shit stain's clock," Boxers said.

Gail had nothing.

"What about us?" Soren asked. "What's next for us? What are you going to do?"

"We're going to find those kids," Jonathan said.

"That's not what I mean," Soren said. "What happens to my license to operate?"

What little regard Jonathan had had for this woman evaporated. "*That's* your concern after what you just heard? Your employee is a drug mule, and two children who passed through here have been handed off to monsters, and you're worried about your little passion project? I don't give a shit."

He turned his back on Soren and led his team back outside, where they climbed into the Batmobile and started down the driveway.

"This is really bad," Gail said as Boxers piloted the Batmobile back toward the main road.

"Yeah," Jonathan said. "Only *really bad* doesn't touch it. Those kids are being used as pawns."

"What's the game?" Boxers asked.

"My money says drug lord chess," Jonathan said.

"Drug lords?" Gail said. "Where did that come from? Bobby talked about working with a lawyer who's got a drug connection. There's a big difference between a dealer and a lord, don't you think?"

"Look at the continuum," Jonathan said. "Remember that there are no such things as coincidences. Whoever took those Kendall boys—oh, shit, what are their names again?"

"Ryder and Geoffrey," Gail reminded.

"Right. Whoever took Ryder and Geoffrey had the resources to kill people and cover their tracks. That takes real coordination. It's the cartels. We've seen it before. The swiftness of it, the violence of it. The thoroughness."

Big Guy said, "Don't mean to be argumentative, Boss, but since when do the cartels hide their signatures? If they kill people, they want the whole friggin' world to know. It's their special thing."

It was not an insignificant point. Drug cartels, much like their terrorist counterparts in the Sandbox, thrived on their reputations for violence. Subtlety or covert actions were rarely part of their game plan. "Could be that they know they're on thinner ice working this far north of the Rio Grande. Could be they don't have the same support network this far north, and they want to stay quiet."

"Could be," Gail agreed. "But that's a long stretch from *must* be."

"I think we need to pay a visit to Rafael Iglesias," Boxers said. "Give him some serious shit to think about."

"I don't think it's time for that yet," Jonathan said.

"That's the only link we have," Gail said. "If we don't leverage him, we're dead in the water. We can't untie the knot if we don't have a string to pull."

"Unless Wolverine reconsiders and comes back in," Boxers said. "By the way, where am I going?"

"For now, we're just driving," Jonathan said. "Wolfie's already told me that she's out on this one."

"I really don't understand that," Gail said.

"It doesn't matter that we don't understand," Jonathan said. "But if we lean on Iglesias now and he doesn't break, then we're *really* dead in the water. You can't go into a critical interview blind."

"We're assuming that Zambrano is telling the truth," Boxers said. "I've never known an ex-con who doesn't play the angles pretty aggressively."

"You're saying we can't trust him?" Gail asked.

"How many trustworthy cons do you know?" Jonathan asked. "Most of them are so scared of having to go back in that they'll say whatever they think people will want to hear."

"So, what do you suggest?" Boxers asked. "We might have time, but those kids don't."

"It's not like they're going to kill them," Gail said. "If we assume that they're pawns as Dig suggests, then the only value they have lies in staying alive."

"Depending on the circumstances," Jonathan said. "Alive isn't the highest goal. If we could pluck them away right now, they'd never be the same again. Even without physical abuse, the psychological damage stacks up fast."

"You know, Boss, it's not like you to talk much about what we *can't* do," Boxers said. "I keep waiting for the sentence that begins, *so therefore . . .*"

Jonathan smiled. "So *therefore*, I've been thinking that with Wolfie out of the picture, we need to find our inside information elsewhere. This drug stuff is more a DEA thing, anyway." He paused for a beat. "Now we just need to think of someone we know in the DEA who might owe us a big favor."

He already knew his answer, but he waited for them to catch up.

"Harry Dawkins?" Gail asked.

"The one and only."

Boxers said, "Isn't he a field guy? And not a very good one at that?"

"Why do you say he's no good?" Gail asked. Her tone said that she was offended.

"Good agents don't get themselves captured and tortured by the cartels."

"Oh, come on, Box," Jonathan said. "He was set up. And he turned into a good fighter. I liked him."

A while back, Jonathan and his team had run an op to rescue Dawkins from his torturers, only to be betrayed by some duplicitous pukes in Washington. What followed was a shit show of major proportions, but they'd gotten out alive in no small part because of Harry Dawkins's willingness to fight his way out of trouble.

"But how's a field guy going to get us what we need?" Gail asked. "I hate to admit that Big Guy has a point, but he kinda does."

"Now you're talkin' sexy," Boxers said.

"Baby steps," Jonathan said. "The fact that he works for the right agency is a good start, and the fact that he owes us a major solid doesn't hurt, either."

"Do you even know that he's with the agency anymore?" Gail asked. "Have you kept in touch?"

"Of course not." Jonathan made a point of never staying in touch with precious cargo after they'd been rescued. The emotions made everything too awkward. "But I'll bet you a thousand dollars that Venice can find him in less than an hour."

No one would take so stupid a bet.

Chapter Eleven

Benny Ferguson enjoyed his time alone with the cows in the field. It wasn't something he could ever say out loud because people would think it was weird, but he didn't think of it as strange. It really wasn't about the cows. It was about being alone. About not being judged.

Benny thought that the biggest curse of growing up in a small town like Blanton, Tennessee, was the inability to escape anything you'd ever done in your life. He still got shit about the time in first grade when he didn't get the front of his T-shirt out of the way before he started pissing and soaked the fabric. Now, here he was two months into his high school experiment, and nothing had really changed.

And being out here really had nothing to do with the cows, per se. Though he had to admit that there was something pretty cool about them. They just ate, shat, and occasionally made baby cows. Not a bad life, really, unless you factor in that whole thing about becoming somebody's dinner one day.

He liked to sit in the root-crotch of a massive tree on

the edge of the field, where he'd write in his journal. Nothing fancy, just a yellow pad with blue lines and a substantial back that made it easy to write on. He smiled when he thought of it as the original laptop. He must have filled close to a hundred of these pads over the years. Sometimes, the journal entries were the personal crap that you thought about when you heard the word *diary*, but more and more the yellow pads were the place to write stories.

Benny had always been into stories, at least for as long as he could remember. He was pretty good on a computer, too, but there was something . . . *magical* about scrawling words onto sheets of paper. The advent of the gel pen made it even better. Bright blue ink against the dull yellow paper, with words bringing life to the thoughts in his head.

Presently, though, his notebook lay on his lap and his pen rested in his hand, so he wasn't doing any writing. The sun was at just the perfect angle to bathe him in warmth. The day had not turned out to be the shorts-and-flip-flops weather that his phone forecast had led him to believe. He wasn't cold, exactly, but he'd been on the feather edge of too chilly all day. The blast of pure sunshine felt terrific, if a bit too hot.

That's what autumn was all about, wasn't it? Neither hot nor cold, though a little of both, depending on the time of day.

Actually, he liked that turn of phrase. A little pretentious, maybe, but worth writing down for later. He opened his eyes and squared up in front of his pad.

Something was wrong.

He didn't know what it was, or even what he thought he saw, but something was different.

It was the movement of the cows. Herd beasts that they were—and stupid, at that—they were also curious. If one of them saw something that interested her, they would all wander in that direction, and so they were wandering right now, from right to left, maybe fifty yards away. Benny folded his feet under his thighs, Indian-style, and leaned forward for a better look downrange.

When he saw what the cows were looking at, he could see why they were interested. Two men were climbing the wood-and-wire fence. First one, who turned and accepted some kind of package from his buddy, and then the other. Benny shielded his eyes with his hands, as if holding a pair of invisible binoculars. He couldn't tell for sure, but they looked like twins.

They weren't naturals around cows. When they saw the herd approaching, they looked startled. There was some discussion between them that Benny imagined to be something along the lines of "let's get the hell out of here." He thought that was funny.

They swung wide to their left, away from Benny and around the gathering herd, which now seemed even more interested.

Whatever the guys were up to, Benny figured it was something they shouldn't be doing. It was the way they moved—not quickly, exactly, but with purpose—and the way one of them kept looking over his shoulder toward the road.

The two men stopped after a couple dozen steps. The one with the bag—Benny could see it was a backpack now—placed it on the grass and squatted next to it. While his brother watched—they were definitely related, maybe even twins—Backpack Man fiddled with it for a few seconds, then stood up. Together, they walked back toward the fence and the road beyond.

"What the hell?" Benny whispered.

He'd read a book recently that dealt with the poisoning of livestock. It was a fictional account of one rancher trying to run another one out of business, but it would be an easy enough thing to do. If not poison, what else would someone put down in the middle of a bunch of cattle?

This was Mr. Haverford's field, and these were his cows. Benny had always liked the Haverfords. Yeah, they were an older couple—probably in their seventies now—but they'd always been nice to Benny, allowed him to play with the animals even when he was really little. Now, Mrs. Haverford had cancer, and Benny's mom said that the prognosis was not good. Mr. Haverford had some awful times lying ahead for him.

He didn't need a dead herd to go on top of it.

So, what should Benny do?

Well, that was obvious, wasn't it? He should call the cops. But then what? Around here, the deputies could take forever to respond to anything, and by the time they got here, God only knew what might happen to the herd. They were already gathering around the backpack.

What if he called the police and it turned out to be nothing, just some abandoned homework or something? Yeah, that would be great, wouldn't it? He could hear the chatter in his head: "This is Benny Ferguson, the guy who pisses on his shirt and calls the police when he finds homework."

Um, no, thank you.

He didn't need the police for this. If it was poison, then all he had to do is pick it up and throw it away somewhere. If it was nothing, then he'd leave it alone.

He supposed it could be a bomb, but that thought made him laugh. Who'd want to blow up a bunch of cows?

He decided to give the brothers a few minutes to drive away before he stepped out from the cover of the tree. While he waited, he watched the cattle grow bored with the backpack. One of them nudged it a little, but she didn't try to eat it yet.

Benny approached the bag slowly, cautiously. He wasn't sure why, but by the time he closed the last few feet, he was walking sideways. The cows were gathering to say hi.

When Benny was nearly on top of the opened backpack, he craned his neck to look over into the opening. Even as he saw the contents, he wasn't sure what he was looking at. Some kind of motor sat on top of a round, flat-bottomed, clear plastic tank of some sort. If he had to guess, he'd say this was something from the lawn mower family, or maybe the outboard motor family.

Benny nearly jumped clear of his skin when the motor came alive. It clicked at first, and then it started to spin.

To hell with Mr. Haverford and his cows. He whirled and ran back toward the tree line, sprinting right out of his left flip-flop.

The whirring noise grew as whatever was spinning came up to speed, and then he heard a hissing sound. He threw a look over his shoulder and somehow overbalanced. He stumbled down to his hands and knees. By the time he got his balance again, he saw that a mist—nearly a cloud—had erupted from the opening, and in that instant, one of the cows fell. She just fell, her legs collapsing under her as if she'd been shot.

Oh, Christ. Benny didn't know what this was, but he knew that it was bad. This was serious shit.

As he passed his tree, he left the pad and the pen there in the root-crotch and grabbed the bicycle he'd left propped on the other side of the trunk. With both hands on the handlebars, he ran alongside the bike till it was up to speed, and then he hopped up onto the seat. A half mile from now, he'd be home and everything would be fine.

He'd almost made it to the street when a cramp hit his gut. It came out of nowhere and hit him like a punch. The front tire wobbled in his hands, but he willed himself to stay up and moving.

In five minutes, he'd be home, and everything would be okay.

Nan Ferguson turned off the spigot when she heard the front door open and shut. "Benny?" she called. He should have been home from school ages ago. She knew that he'd been unhappy and that he liked to hang out at some secret location to write his stories, but normally he called to say he was going to be late.

"Benny? Is that you? Where have you—"

A heavy thump from the foyer seemed to shake the whole house.

"Benny!" Nan snatched the dish towel from its rod on the back of the dishwasher and wiped her hands as she quick-stepped out of the kitchen and into the foyer. Her son was on the floor, propping himself on his hands and knees. Thick mucus dripped from his nose and mouth.

"Oh, my God, Benny! Oh, my God, what happened?" She dropped to her knees and draped her arms across his shoulders. "I've got you, baby," she said, and she helped him lie down on his back. He was soaked with sweat. She could feel his heart hammering through his arms.

"Mom?" His voice sounded an octave higher than usual. There was an edge of panic to it. "Mom, I can't see."

Nan looked at his eyes. They weren't right at all. His pupils had contracted to dots, and the whites were tinged with red. "Why, baby? Jesus, what happened?"

"I-I don't know," he said. "Two guys came into . . . into Mr. Haverford's field. Brothers, I think. Twins. I don't know. I-I can't breathe." His chest heaved at the effort to move air.

Placing one hand on his chest, over his heart, she stroked his cheek with the other. He'd sweated through everything. He couldn't have been wetter if he'd stepped into the shower.

"Try to relax, Benny. I'm calling an ambulance."

"I think I'm dying," he said.

"No, you're not! Don't even say that. I'll be right back." Nan pushed off from her legs to stand up, but when she was about half standing, she had to stop. Her knees didn't want to engage. They collapsed on her, driving her kneecaps into the carpet and causing a rug burn. She might have pitched over if she hadn't gotten her hands out, but as they made contact with the Berber weave, they collapsed, too.

Jesus God, what is happening?

She'd left her purse in the kitchen, on the table. Her phone was inside. In the zippered pocket. Nan didn't know that she'd be able to make it even that far.

But she had to. Her baby was dying. Now that she had whatever he had, she knew there was no doubt. They were dying.

Mustering everything she had, she dragged herself across the carpet and then onto the cold linoleum of the kitchen floor.

As her vision flared and then went away, the muscles in both of her thighs seized, followed immediately by her calves. She felt as if someone were breaking her legs, turning them slowly on a rack. She tried to scream, but her diaphragm had also seized. The only sound she could produce was a raspy wheeze.

That's the noise she made as she scaled the leg of the oak kitchen chair to reach the table. Thank God her purse was near the edge. She pulled it down to the floor, and everything spilled out. Everything but the phone because that was in the goddamn zippered pocket.

Her fingers had closed to gnarled fists. Her hands trembled as she pulled at the zipper with her knuckles. All but blind now, she had the phone. She didn't know how, but she had it, and she used her knotted fingers to dial 911.

"Blanton Emergency Dispatch. What is your emergency?"

Totally blind now, Nan tried to find the words to articulate the problem. In her mind, she said, "This is Nan Ferguson up on Feather Hollow Road. My son and I are dying."

In reality, she had no idea what she'd said.

Chapter Twelve

Armand Cortez didn't like guns. He'd seen too many of his family, friends, and colleagues lose their lives to gunfire. Yet, here he was, surrounded by them. When he'd first placed his order for this customized Cadillac Escalade, with its extended wheelbase and facing rear seats, he hadn't calculated properly for the cubic footage consumed by a five-man security detail that was armed for war.

Cortez cleared his throat to break the silence. "Lupo," he said.

The head of his detail looked up from whatever had consumed his focus on the floor. "Sir?"

Cortez pointed with his forehead to the muzzle of the stubby machine gun carried by the guard on Lupo's right. It was pointed at Cortez's belly.

"Fernando," Lupo snapped.

The young guard's head snapped around.

"Muzzle discipline, please."

Fernando seemed startled by his own loss of focus. "I'm very sorry, Mr. Cortez," he said. He shifted his grip on the weapon so that the buttstock was planted on his thigh and the muzzle was pointed at the head-liner.

Cortez leaned forward until his elbows were planted on his knees. "Fernando, is it?" he asked.

The young man could not have been thirty years old—perhaps not twenty-five—and fear clouded his face. "Yes, sir."

"Is that your real name?"

"Excuse me?"

"Fernando. Is that your real name?"

The young man looked uneasily at his comrades, all of whom refused eye contact. "Yes, sir, it is."

"Be careful not to lie to me," Cortez warned.

"I-I'm not lying," he said. "That is my real name."

"Is it the name you were born with?"

The other man hesitated.

"It is an easy question, Fernando. When you were a little boy and your mother wanted you for chores, what would she call you?"

Fernando shifted in his seat. "Simon," he said softly, almost inaudibly.

Cortez shifted to the man in charge. "Lupo, where do you find these men for my detail? Do they think that I would surround myself with people I didn't know about? People whose backgrounds I hadn't re-searched?"

Lupo didn't answer because he knew the question to be rhetorical.

"I think Simon is a strong name, Fernando," Cortez pressed. "Why did you feel the need to change it?"

The guard's discomfort was morphing into some-thing close to panic. He remained silent.

"Are you afraid of me, Fernando?" This question

was *not* rhetorical, and Cortez leaned in even closer as he waited for his answer. "Remember to be truthful."

Looking at his feet, Fernando dipped his chin a bit. "Perhaps a little," he said.

"There you go. Good for you. Now tell me why."

Fernando's eyes expanded to circles. "Why what, sir?"

"Why are you afraid of me? Have I ever hurt you?"

Fernando shook his head.

"I need to hear answers," Cortez said. "When I ask questions with my mouth, I expect to hear answers with my ears. Save your head motions for your drinking buddies."

"No, sir. You have never hurt *me*."

Cortez bristled at the emphasis on the pronoun. "It did not hurt you when I killed your uncle?"

Everyone in the vehicle tensed at those words.

When Fernando remained silent, Cortez pressed on. "I heard that you two were quite close. He was more like a brother than an uncle. Am I wrong?"

Fernando's jaw muscles tightened as his lips pressed into a tight line.

"Again, I must insist on an answer."

"Yes, Mr. Cortez, we were close."

"As close as brothers?"

"Yes, sir. As close as brothers."

The Cadillac hit a rut at the same time it swung a wide turn to the left. Cortez struggled to keep his posture steady without reaching for anything to hold on to. "Tell me why I killed him."

The look on Lupo's face begged Cortez to back off.

"They say he betrayed you," Fernando said, still without eye contact.

"*They* say? Who is *they*?"

"I don't remember," Fernando said. "That was a long time ago."

"Not that long," Cortez said. "What, six, seven years? That's just a blink."

The young guard shrugged. "Seems longer than that to me. I guess I forgot because I didn't want to remember."

"I see," Cortez said. "Yes, that makes sense." He pondered for a few seconds. "Who opened the box?"

"For God's sake, Armand," Lupo said.

Cortez shot out a finger. It was as harsh a warning as he knew to silence his old friend. "The box, Fernando. Who opened the box? Surely you remember that."

The muscles in the guard's jaw were trembling now, as were his lips.

"Tell your colleagues what was in the box."

Lupo shifted the grip on his own weapon, clearly waiting for Fernando to break and open fire.

"My Uncle Juan's head," Fernando said. His voice was barely working.

"I believe there was more than just a head," Cortez goaded.

"Armand, *stop*!" Lupo said. "This is not necess—"

"His penis and testicles," Fernando said. He sat straight up and looked directly at Cortez—*through* Cortez—as he spoke the words.

"Yes!" Cortez said. "Exactly that."

"And it was my grandmother who opened the box. She fainted and hit her head on the floor."

"See? You *do* remember. And your Uncle Juan didn't betray me, Fernando. He *tried* to betray me, and he failed. He tried to involve the American DEA in my business, and I needed to make it clear that the price for betrayal is very high." He gave the guard's knee a playful slap. "Did I make that point to you, *Simon*? Do you think you understand the price of betrayal?"

Fernando tried to hold his gaze, but he couldn't. "Yes, I understand," he said to the floor.

"Do you want to know why I think you changed your name?" Cortez asked. He didn't wait for an answer. "I think that you were afraid that I would find out my connection to your family. Now, there are only two reasons I can think of why that might be." He slapped the knee of another guard. "Miguel. Can you give me one of those reasons?"

Miguel had been part of Cortez's security detail for nearly three years and was a trusted insider. "The first one that comes to mind is that he wanted to get close to you so that he could kill you in retribution."

Tears rimmed Fernando's eyes now.

"That was my first thought, too," Cortez said. "But that would require him to think that I am an idiot. That would require him to think that I have not put orders in place that if anything happens to me—if I die from a bullet or from a lightning strike—I have plans in place that will pack boxes with parts from his grandmother and little brother and sister." He paused to let that sink in. He enjoyed watching the horror grow.

"But then I thought I was being too harsh," Cortez continued. "I realized that my *second* reason for Fernando's strange behavior is undoubtedly the true reason. Because he has pledged his loyalty to me, pledged to die for me if that becomes necessary, he wants to protect his family from reprisals by the police and the government. Perhaps even from my competitors in this ugly business we're in. Look at me, Fernando."

When Fernando looked up, his eyes were pleading and wet. His chin dimpled and quavered as he fought off tears.

The Cadillac was rolling to a stop. "Is that the reason you changed your name? Was it because you are deeply loyal to me and would die to protect me from harm?"

Hope returned to his eyes, and he nodded vigorously. "Yes, Mr. Cortez," he croaked. "I am loyal to you."

They jerked in their seats as the driver shoved the transmission into PARK. "That's good to hear," Cortez said. "And since we've already established that you will only tell me the truth, I will, of course, believe you."

"Thank you, Mr. Cortez."

Cortez bent his mouth into a smile. "Do your job well, Fernando." He gestured to the rest of his detail. "All of you, do your jobs well. If not for me, then for your families."

The driver and the shotgun guard flanked the Cadillac.

"It seems we're here," Cortez said. He knocked on the window to signal that he was ready, and then the door opened. He stepped out into the bright sunshine and stretched his face up into the light.

Shielded by his team and led by Serena Ramos, the proprietress of tonight's lodging, Cortez made the trip from the car to the hacienda's front door in only fifteen paces. Then he was inside with Lupo, and the rest of the team took up whatever positions they would man until morning.

"It's so nice to see you again, Mr. Cortez," Serena said when they were inside. She extended her hand.

Cortez took the hand gently in his own and bent to kiss it. "That's very nice for you to say," he said. "Even though we both know you are lying."

She smiled and did not argue. Cortez's presence at a place was not the result of a negotiation or a response to an invitation. It was obligatory compliance with a demand. Favors were never free in his world, and he had been most accommodating in sparing the lives of Serena's parents. This was their hacienda, but he controlled it tonight. His instructions had been clear. The parents were to be gone when he arrived, and Serena was to be left behind to serve him in so many ways.

"Can I get you something to drink?" Serena offered. "Either of you?"

Cortez smiled and strolled deeper into the living space. "If I recall correctly, your father is a fan of very good scotch. Bring me a bottle of his best, along with two glasses. Three, if you wish to drink with us."

Lupo held up both hands and smiled. "Just a Coca-Cola would be fine for me," he said.

Cortez's expression hardened. "He will have scotch," he said. "And Coca-Cola, too, I suppose." Cortez didn't even like scotch, but the liquor was not the point. It was all about control and value to the Ramos family.

Serena turned to leave.

"When is Miguel Martinez due to arrive?" Cortez asked. "I thought he would be here before me."

"I thought the same thing," Serena replied. "I will

be back very soon with your scotch, and maybe a little something to eat."

When she was gone, Lupo said, "You'll be lucky if she does not poison it."

Cortez chuckled. "I look at every day when I go to sleep alive as a gift. So, you'll understand why I expect you to take the first bite of everything."

Lupo checked his watch. "Perhaps the last-minute change of venue caught Miguel off guard."

"That is the very purpose of a last-minute change of venue, is it not?"

"I thought you trusted him."

"I trust him more than I trust anyone else who would profit so much from my death," Cortez replied. Miguel Martinez and Armand Cortez had been friends since childhood. In their preteen years, they grew to be an accomplished pickpocket duo—one distracting the mark while the other made his move—but as they got older and less *cute*, the marks became more aware and the business became too dangerous. That led to a long stint muling product for Fulo Gripando and his crew of drug smugglers.

Miguel dropped out of sight for six years when he was sent to prison, and by the time he'd gotten out, Cortez had already made his move on Gripando. With the old man dead, Cortez had taken things over after a brief war, but he could not afford to have so recent a parolee on his payroll.

Miguel had tried his hand at legitimate business, but he soon learned the secret that everyone already knew: legitimate businesses of any value no longer existed in the parts of the country where anyone wanted to live.

Everyone in power was on the take, and by the time you paid tribute to everyone from the local beat cop up through the politicians and the racket-runners, there was very little left for you and your family.

Want to work at one of the American automobile manufacturing plants? That's fine. Want to open a manufacturing plant of your own? Forget it.

Exactly one business model survived in Mexico for small entrepreneurs, and that was the business that employed Armand Cortez.

Miguel had grown as a lieutenant in the army of Santiago Lopez, Cortez's lead rival, either of whom would shoot the other on sight. In his trusted position, Miguel had grown to be most useful to both sides as a conduit for communication.

This particular meeting had been called by Lopez via Miguel, who said that the topic would be revealed when they were face-to-face. The original site for the parlay was set to be in a low-rise office park off of Highway 2, but just an hour ago, Cortez announced the change to this hacienda about twenty kilometers south, off of Highway 45.

He didn't expect an assassination attempt, but the unlikelihood became even stronger with a change. If it pissed Lopez off, then so be it. Cortez couldn't see how he had much to lose through the cancellation of a meeting whose subject he did not know.

As a city, Juarez was a dump. A disaster. A slum. Cortez spent as little time up here as possible, but like any other business, his required him to monitor activities from time to time. He had trusted lieutenants, of course, but all too often, they grew distracted and stupid, tempted by both the product they made and the flood of money that it brought in. Cortez paid his people well enough to buy their loyalty, and all of them knew the penalty for betrayal.

The Ramos family's decorating aesthetic seemed more Texan than Mexican, with the longhorn display over the fireplace and the furniture made of saddle leather. Francisco Ramos, the family patriarch, had earned his fortune in a different type of drug distribution business, serving as the general manager for one of America's biggest pharmaceutical companies. Cortez found the irony to be delicious. While the American government and its citizens grew rich watching their investment portfolios grow fat on the proceeds of *pharmaceuticals*, they dedicated billions of dollars to ruining Cortez's *drug cartel*.

The sound of vehicle tires crunching gravel drew his attention toward the front windows.

"It would seem that we're about to find out what the big emergency is," Cortez said. He rose and walked to the front door to greet the newcomers.

Commensurate with his rank within the Lopez organization, Miguel traveled with only a small security detail—a driver and a body man in a solo Chevrolet Suburban. A head taller than Cortez and twice as round, Miguel had the look of a man who was comfortable in his business. As he exited out into the sunshine, he shielded his eyes for a second, and then waved to his old friend.

Cortez walked out to meet him in the yard. "Miguel, my brother, how are you?" They embraced, and then Cortez stepped aside to allow Miguel to lead the way.

"You're welcome to bring your security man in with you if you'd like," Cortez offered.

"I arrived on the assumption that I would not need him," Miguel said with a wink. "And if I do, I will be woefully outgunned."

"If there is a fight, my friend, I will not have been the one to start it."

Once inside, Cortez took the lead. He helped himself to the thickest, plushest chair, the one that was positioned opposite the huge television screen. He gestured for Miguel to take a seat on the adjacent sofa. If each of them shifted about forty-five degrees in their seats, they could be eye-to-eye. Lupo made himself invisible behind his boss.

While they'd been distracted, a wooden serving tray had arrived, carrying glasses and a bottle of Laphroaig scotch along with a block of cheese and some bread. And a Coca-Cola. Serena had disappeared.

Cortez poured three scotches and passed out two, keeping the third for himself. He offered a silent toast to the room, took a sip, and sat back in his chair. "All right, Miguel, let's get to it. What is so secret and urgent that we need to meet in person like this?"

Miguel rolled his eyes. "Why do you think?"

"This is not a game I'm willing to play," Cortez said. The edge of annoyance in his tone was sharp and clear. "Just tell me what you want me to hear."

Miguel looked to Lupo for support, but Cortez didn't follow his gaze. Lupo's silence spoke his agreement with his boss. "The violence in America," Miguel said. "Mr. Lopez is upset that you are bringing too much attention to our businesses."

Cortez waited for more, but after a few seconds of silence, he said, "I don't know what you're talking about."

"Oh, please, Armand. You say you don't want to play games, and now—"

"I don't know what you're talking about." This time Cortez made his tone angry. "You can clarify your meaning, or you can turn around and leave."

Miguel held up his hands as if surrendering. "Okay, fine. In Virginia. The kidnappings and the murders. The two children. That is precisely the kind of violence that awakens the American media, and we don't need—"

"Stop," Cortez said. He twisted in his seat to look at Lupo. "Do you know what he is talking about?"

"I have no idea."

"Look, Armand. I understand that your business is yours and that neither Mr. Lopez nor I can change how you decide to run things. My mission is simply to express—"

"You don't understand, Miguel," Cortez interrupted. "I am not avoiding anything or dodging any question. I do not know what you are talking about."

"The Kendall children," Miguel said. "Or, excuse me. The children of Blue Bird."

The words startled Cortez. First of all, how did Santiago Lopez know about his team in America? And . . . kidnapping? "Those boys were not kidnapped," he said. "They were sent to a secure orphanage."

Miguel's expression changed. He cocked his head like a confused puppy. "Are you seriously telling me that you do not know what happened to them?"

"I have told you several times," Cortez said.

"*Those boys*, as you call them, never made it to the orphanage. Their car was stopped along the way. Their escorts were killed, and the boys were taken. How can you not know this?"

Cortez turned on Lupo. "How can we not know this?"

"How does he know it?" Lupo countered. "And how do we know he is telling the truth?"

"Why would I lie about such a thing?" Miguel asked.

"Why would I *do* such a thing?" Cortez shouted. "This is madness."

"To keep the parents quiet," Miguel said. "With their children in custody, they will not reveal the secrets of your organization."

"Don't be stupid," Cortez said. "Better yet, don't assume that I am stupid. What they know cannot hurt me. They are enforcers. There are other enforcers, as well. We all have them, and what they know is what everyone already knows. I don't need them to be silent, and if I did, I would have them killed. But seize the children? Absolutely not."

"And what about the family who kept them?"

"Who?"

"The family that kept the boys temporarily," Miguel explained. "Why did you kill them?"

"Again, I don't know what you're talking about. Where is all of this coming from?"

"We have our contacts, just as you do," Miguel said. "And you don't need to know who they are."

That was a fair answer. "Assuming what you tell me is true, Miguel, it is as I explained to you. I have nothing to do with it."

"The American Drug Enforcement Administration thinks that you do," Miguel said. "And that poses a problem for all of us. If they make their border tighter, that hurts all of us." He fired down the rest of his scotch and gasped against the burn.

Cortez stood to escort him to the door. "I will do what I can to get to the bottom of what's going on," he promised.

Miguel shook his old friend's hand. "It's not like you to lose control of your people, Armand."

"Nothing is out of control so long as I can bring it back under control," Cortez said with a smile. It was too easy to forget what a good friend Miguel had been for all those years.

Miguel held the handshake for a few seconds too long, raising concern. "Is something wrong?" Cortez asked.

"I don't know," Miguel said. "I hesitate to bring it up because if you thought the first part was outrageous, then this next rumor is truly absurd."

Cortez waited for it.

"I won't insult you by asking this as a question," Miguel said. "I'll make a statement, instead. I have spoken to people who think that you are smuggling chemical weapons into the United States to arm terrorists. If this is true, Mr. Lopez urges you in the most strident terms to stop doing so. This, he says, is nonnegotiable."

Chapter Thirteen

Venice didn't want to be here. She knew it was the right thing to do, but she'd give everything she had not to do what needed to be done.

The rectory for Saint Kate's Catholic Church looked just like the 1980s-era suburban house that it was, set well back from Church Street, situated between the church itself and the mansion that housed the administrative offices for RezHouse. Built of red brick and situated on about an acre of land, the two-story structure gleamed in the sunlight. The flowers that adorned the front bed and window boxes during spring and summer looked sad as the weather cooled.

Doug Kramer was waiting for her at the front gate. "Are you ready for this?"

"No, I'm not," Venice said. "It's been a tough year. Too much of this."

Kramer reached over the wrought iron spikes, disengaged the latch, and pushed the gate open. "Let's get it over with, then." He led the way down the mossy brick sidewalk, through the shadows of the two sprawling live oaks that adorned the yard.

The door opened as the chief was reaching for the knocker. No matter how many times she saw it, she could never get used to seeing Father Dom dressed in civilian attire. He was barefoot and wore a green William and Mary sweatshirt and gray sweatpants. His unshaven face looked grim. Venice didn't remember seeing the lines around his eyes before.

"Is this what I think it is?" Dom asked.

"Not out here," Kramer said. "Let's step inside and have a seat."

Dom heaved a deep breath, then stepped aside to make a path for his guests. He motioned with an outstretched arm for them to take a seat in the library. In any other house of its size and age, the book-lined room would be a living room, or maybe a TV room, but Father Dom was a bibliophile's bibliophile. There were, of course, the expected religious texts, but Dom was also an avid fan of mysteries and thrillers, and those commercial titles far outnumbered the inspirational ones.

Dom sat on one side of the sofa along the wall opposite the front window, and Venice sat on the cushion next to him, a little closer than she normally would have. Kramer helped himself to the reading chair in the corner, but occupied only the front few inches of the seat.

"I'm sorry to be the one bringing the news," Kramer said, "but it seems you're already ahead of me. The police found Father Tim's body a couple of hours ago. He'd been shot."

Dom's shoulders and chest seemed to deflate, literally as if the air had escaped from them. "Oh, shit," he said.

Venice and Kramer exchanged glances. It was also hard to get used to hearing priests cuss.

"You know," Dom said, "you try to talk yourself into believing that the obvious will somehow not transpire. You try to talk yourself into believing that sometimes being a good man could somehow shield you from the bad stuff that happens to other people." He gave a wry smile. "Jeez, Doug, how many times have we made this visit to people's homes?"

The question made Kramer look uncomfortable, unsure whether to smile.

Dom turned to Venice. "And in tonight's performance, the role of the caring shoulder will be played by Venice Alexander."

She caught the first hint of bourbon. "I'm so sorry you have to go through this, Dom."

"What about Pam Hastings?" Dom asked. "She'd only been with RezHouse for a few weeks."

Kramer's eyes answered ahead of his words. "Also dead," he said. "I'm so sorry, Padre. They'd been—" He cut himself off.

"Not my first dance," Dom reassured. "I don't bruise anymore."

Kramer cleared his throat, looked at Venice, then got over it. "Whoever killed them moved the bodies about a mile away and . . . placed them into a ravine."

"Oh, God," Venice moaned.

"I believe the word you're searching for is *dumped*, Chief," Dom said. His head sagged. "Any idea who did it?"

"If they do, the locals aren't talking yet," Kramer said. "I know this is the last thing you want to think about, but it won't be long until the press gets the story."

"No reporters for me," Dom said. He looked to Venice. "But Mama Alexander needs to be ready."

"With the bodies found," Kramer said, "and given the fact that they were handled, I'm thinking there's a good possibility for discovering physical evidence, trace evidence." His words seemed to embarrass him. "It's, uh, it's not much, but it's something."

Something about Kramer's delivery reminded Venice of Jonathan. Sail past the emotional parts as quickly as possible and drill down on the operational details.

"What about the boys?" Dom asked.

"Still no sign of them," Kramer said. "Sorry, I guess maybe I should have led with that. The inspector I spoke to told me that nothing inside or outside the car or in the ravine or along the route that leads to it points to those two boys ever being there."

"What would that look like?" Venice asked.

"Excuse me?"

"What evidence can prove the negative—than they were *not* there?"

Kramer shifted again. "No one is saying that there's evidence the boys *weren't* there in the car," he said. "They're only saying that there's no evidence indication that they were."

"So, what's the next step, Chief?" Dom asked. "Tim's family is from New England. Rhode Island."

"You know the drill," Kramer said. "For the time being, Father Tim's body is evidence. There'll be an autopsy, of course. After that, it will be up to the Virginia State Police. They have jurisdiction on this."

"What about alerting his family?" Dom asked.

"Right about now, give or take, police in Providence, Rhode Island, are having pretty much this conversation with Father Tim's family."

Dom looked at the floor with enough intensity that it drew Venice's gaze, as well. "You know," he said. "I feel like I'm out of ideas. Suddenly, I have no idea what to do or say."

Venice tapped his knee with her hand. "It's a lot to process."

Dom's head rocked up to look at Kramer, and then he stood. "Thank you for coming by, Doug," he said. "I know that this isn't easy for you, either." He extended his hand.

Kramer stood and shook it.

"Now, not to be rude—really, the last thing I want to do is be rude—but would you mind leaving Ven and me for some alone time?"

Kramer shot a concerned look to Venice, who gave a gentle shake of her head. She had no idea what was coming. There certainly was no threat. She watched as the priest escorted the chief to the door and let him out.

"What was that about?" she asked when they were alone.

Dom took his time answering. As he reentered the library, he crossed to his reading chair. "I've been doing a lot of thinking over the past thirty-six hours or so," he said. With his feet flat on the floor, he leaned his elbows on his knees. "What the hell are we doing here, Ven?"

She cocked her head, knowing better to answer a cryptic question during an emotional time. "I'm not sure I know what you mean."

"For years, I've pretended that what Digger does is something other than what it is. I've told myself that justice trumps the law and that the ends justify the means. All that death. All that killing. Sooner or later, it had to come here. Look at you. Look at Derek."

Venice hadn't expected the abrupt turn, and the swell of emotion at the mention of her deceased boyfriend's name startled her. Derek Halstrom might have been the one for her, the first man she'd loved in a long time. He'd been killed during a firefight at the mansion while trying to protect her from the attackers. "You've been drinking, Father," she said.

"Damn skippy, I've been drinking," Dom replied. "In fact, there's a very good chance that I will get quite drunk this evening. Been a long time since I've treated myself to a hangover."

Did she really want to wander down this path? Maybe it was better just to leave.

"You know I love Digger like he's a brother," Dom said. "Hell, I love him more than the guy who *is* my brother. I guess that secretly, I've expected the violence to hit close to home, and given all that's happened over the years, I'd understand if it came to me. I even think I could talk my way into Heaven. But I never thought it would come to the innocents."

Venice leaned back into the sofa cushion and crossed her legs. This might be a long one. "I've had this dialogue with myself more than once," she said.

Dom smiled. "That would make it a monologue."

"Really?" She laughed. "Yeah, okay, I've had this *monologue* with myself a number of times. I try not to think of it in terms of eternal glory or eternal damnation, but I think about it in terms of what's right and wrong."

She paused to gather her thoughts, to make sure that she was going to say exactly what she was thinking. "You know I've known Digger my whole life. Other than Mama and maybe Doug Kramer, I'm the only person you know who ever knew a boy named Jonathan Gravenow. He's a good man. Down to his heels and toes, he's a good man."

"No argument from me," Dom said. He stood and opened a cabinet door in the yew wood bookshelf along the perpendicular wall, revealing a wide selection of brown liquors. "Want one?"

"No, thank you," Venice said. She fought the urge to give him a lecture about drunk shepherds tending their flocks, but she let it go. Maybe he'd earned this one. She watched him pour three fingers into one of the crystal whiskey glasses Jonathan had given him for Christmas a few years ago, then waited until he returned to his chair.

"I'm sorry," he said. "I didn't mean to interrupt."

"It's been a bad couple of days, Father. You do what you need to do. No judgment from me." Again, she regrouped to gather her thoughts. "You know, up until a hundred, hundred fifty years ago, every city had a team of people who would take carts all around, from street to street, collecting dead animals. Somebody told me that in the late eighteen hundreds, in New York City, a hundred horses died every day. In nice neighborhoods, the carcasses were picked up. In not-so-nice neighborhoods, they were left to rot until the bones were light enough to be moved."

"The birth of the glue and dog food business," Dom quipped.

Venice ignored his comment. "We can agree that the men who collected those carcasses had the worst job in the city. And I would argue that they saved more lives than any doctor in the five boroughs. They endured stomach-churning awfulness to protect strangers from disease. Did you know that?"

"You'd likely be shocked at how little time I have dedicated to think about rotting horses," Dom said.

"What Digger does—what *we* do—is the modern-day equivalent of picking up horse carcasses. It's a stinky, awful job that no one in genteel circles wants to discuss, but it's still a job that needs to be done by *somebody*.

"Derek Halstrom understood that. He was excited by the prospect of joining our team. Pam Hastings and Father Tim were victims, pure and simple. The very nature of Resurrection House—the fact that every resident has incarcerated parents—bakes a certain element of danger into its cake. You knew that when you took the job, Father."

She'd said that last part about the job to be deliberately provocative.

As she spoke, Dom eased himself back into the leather cushion of his reading chair. He held the bourbon up before his eyes and swirled it, affecting the posture of Hamlet addressing Yorick's skull. He took a healthy pull and rested the glass on the arm of his chair. "You're a good friend, Venice Alexander." His earnest smile sold the words. "But I'm terrible at this end of the grieving curve."

Venice waited for the rest.

"For decades, it's been my job to ease the burden of grieving for other people," he said. "My job is always to sit where you're sitting and project strength. I am the rock upon which Peter built his church, and I am thus the rock upon which my parishioners can bare their deepest, most disturbing secrets."

Dom looked to the ceiling—maybe to God in Heaven—apparently contemplating the poetry of his words. Venice watched him in silence, gave him his space.

"Father Tim was a good priest," he said. "A good man. He deserved better."

Venice said nothing. Sometimes, the best thing for a friend to do is to just be there. She tried not to watch as Dom squinted against the tears he could not stop.

Chapter Fourteen

Venice hadn't just located Harry Dawkins, she'd also reached out and talked with him. Under the circumstances, he'd told her, he'd be delighted to meet with Jonathan, but the meeting would have to happen on his turf. He had time to talk, but he couldn't get back to Washington.

"So, I told him you'd be happy to come to him," Venice had explained to Jonathan five hours ago when she'd reported in. "You need to get to El Paso, Texas."

"Oh, Christ," Boxers grumped. "What is it about deserts and jungles? Why are we always traipsing off to deserts and jungles?"

"Gotta go where the clientele sends us," Jonathan said with a smile.

"Says the guy who doesn't have to fly the plane."

"Says the guy who bought you an airplane and allows you to fly it," Jonathan corrected. Not only had Jonathan paid for it—two of them, actually, both through fictional companies—he'd also allowed Boxers to pick out the models he wanted. Sometimes, Big

Guy was happiest when he was bitching about something.

The flight to ELP was uneventful, highlighted by perfect weather and direct routing. Once on the ground, Big Guy parked the Beechcraft Hawker 800 at the spot provided by Atlantic Aviation, the local fixed-base operator. Catering to private jet clientele (read: rich people), FBOs provided the kinds of amenities that regular air travelers would kill for. Showers, lounges, shuttle services, heated hangars, and gas pumps were yours—for a modest fee, of course.

Thanks to Venice's organizational skills, a rental black Suburban was waiting for them at the hangar. To bypass whatever security might lay ahead, Jonathan, Boxers, and Gail all wore their FBI regalia—badges and windbreakers—thus allowing them to remain armed without question.

The Customs and Border Protection Special Operations Group was headquartered at Fort Bliss, an Army post located a short ride from the airport. At the main gate, the MP took down the team's fake information, gave them a map of the post, and sent them on their way.

"God, I miss this shit," Boxers said as they drove deeper into the facility. Like every other U.S. military establishment, from GitMo to Fort Knox, Quantico to San Diego Naval Station, Fort Bliss had a community feel to it. The grass was green and impeccably cut, desert climate notwithstanding. Long stretches of houses could have been a suburb of any city, and the students in the elementary and high schools were more educated and better behaved than those at any civilian school in the country. On an Army post, neighbors might not know precisely what each other did with his or her workday, but all were united with the common goal of destroying America's enemies and coming home safely again. The friendships formed in military communities lasted forever—as did the enmities.

"It was great until it wasn't," Jonathan said.

Once inside Bliss's main gate, Boxers followed the map down Sergeant Major Boulevard to Randolph Street and finally to Staff Sergeant Sims Street, at the end of which lay what was left of Biggs Army Airfield. Jonathan had never been to this base before, but he was familiar with its history. From the mid-1940s to the mid-'60s, it was named Biggs Air Force Base. Sometime in the '70s, he believed, the facility changed hands to the Army. Now it was home of Joint Task Force North, a Defense Department omelet of various agencies dedicated to keeping bad guys from crossing America's southern border illegally.

They were very good at their job when they were allowed to do it.

The CBP Special Operations Group occupied a collection of high-end office trailers that might have been airdropped into the middle of nowhere. Jonathan had heard a lot of good things about the Border Patrol Tactical Unit (BORTAC), whose existence flew far under most radars. Gifted tactical operators with all the skills of the FBI's Hostage Rescue Team, BORTAC operators were the nation's very best trackers, able to follow just about anyone just about anywhere, using tactics as old as the Indians and as new as the latest technology.

"Park anywhere, I guess," Jonathan said as Boxers pulled the Suburban into a spot among randomly parked vehicles.

"I can't say I'm terribly impressed by the physical security," Gail observed from the backseat.

"They've got eyes in the sky, as far as I know," Jonathan replied.

Boxers added, "I don't see much, either, but I'll bet it's a mistake to rush the place."

"What are we supposed to do from here?" Gail asked. "How do we find Harry Dawkins?"

Jonathan pulled his phone from the pocket of his 5.11 Tactical cargo-style pants. They'd all selected a tacti-cool ensemble to sell the illusion of being Feebs. It helped that this was how Jonathan and Boxers dressed pretty much every day. On a normal day, Gail's style of dress was efficient yet feminine—more slacks than skirts and almost always with some kind of jacket to cover her Glock. Today, though, she was dressed like the boys.

Jonathan was halfway through punching the number Venice had given him into his phone when he saw a six-passenger golf cart approaching from behind the farthest office trailer. It was empty, except for the driver, and Jonathan recognized him right away.

"Here he comes," Boxers said, pointing.

"I guess that resolves the question of whether we're being appropriately watched," Gail said.

They all climbed out of the rental and formed a ragged line in front of the grill. The cart driver swung a wide circle as he approached, pulled to a stop, and set the brake.

"Well, I'll be damned," the driver said. "I hurt just looking at you guys."

"You clean up good," Jonathan said. He extended his hand. "Nice to see you again, Harry."

"And Big Guy," Dawkins said, craning his neck to look Boxers in the eye as they shook hands.

"Allow me to introduce another colleague," Jonathan said. "Harry Dawkins, this is Gail Bonneville, a member of my team. You may call her Special Agent Gerarda Culp of the FBI."

Dawkins coughed out a laugh. "Wow, now, that's a name." Then he added, "Harry Dawkins." They shook hands. "I know we haven't met, but weren't you on the other side of some radio traffic while your boss and I were wading out of Mexico?"

"I was one of several," Gail said. "I've heard a lot about you."

"What are you doing down in Buttscratch, Texas?" Boxers asked.

"TDY," Dawkins said. Temporary duty. "I'm attached to Task Force Five, keeping the revolving doors of justice spinning. Catch and release used to be a clever phrase until so many of our guys started getting hurt."

"Part of the price of being expendable," Jonathan said. "It's a shame your guys aren't snail darters or kitty cats. The Twitterverse would demand action."

"Makes you sick, doesn't it? We're guarding the walls, and the network news makes us the bad guys."

Dawkins clapped his hands together once, then planted his fists on his hips. "Mother Hen was a little short on details when she called. In fact, she gave me nothing. So, what can I do for you?"

"You're still DEA, right?" Jonathan asked.

"As far as I know. Unless you're bringing me bad news. By the way, are you a secret agent, too?"

"*Special* Agent," Jonathan corrected, knowing that

Dawkins had been joking. "Yes, I'm Neil Bonner, and Big Guy is—"

"Don't," Boxers said.

Jonathan laughed. "This one's good."

"I swear to God I'll kick your ass."

"Xavier Contata," Jonathan said.

Dawkins gaped for a second and then roared with laughter. "Perfect!"

"I liked you better when you were afraid of me," Boxers said.

"Oh, I'm still afraid of you," Dawkins said. "But as long as I've got witnesses, I figure I'm okay." He turned serious. Well, mostly. "So, do I introduce you as your aliases if we run into people?"

"Please," Jonathan said. "Is there a place where we can chat privately?"

"Sure." He gestured to the nearest trailer. "In there. The BORTAC guys are all out practicing their snake-eating techniques."

As they walked, Jonathan asked, "So, you said you're with JTF North. What's your role with them?"

"I can't talk about all of it," Dawkins said, "but you might have heard that there's a bit of a problem with drugs flowing across our southern border."

"No kidding," Gail said.

"Right? The best-known crisis that no one wants to talk about. So, that's what I'm here for. To help put a stop to that."

"Are the illegals bringing the drugs?" Gail asked.

"Hell, yes, they're bringing the drugs," Dawkins snapped. Then he looked sorry. "I'd say a solid twenty, twenty-five percent of the people we detain are muling drugs. The ones with kids are often the worst offenders because they understand the optics of detaining kids."

"Well, they *are* kids," Gail said.

"Yeah, but they're not the mules' kids. Half of them have either been kidnapped or sold and are being trafficked in plain sight. The very best thing we can do for them is pull them away from their *guardians*. Honest to God, it makes you sick if you think too hard about it."

"That or it makes you want to open fire on them," Boxers said.

"That, too. But we're pretty much hamstrung. That asshole in the White House won't let us detain but a few of them, and of those we do detain, we have to let them go after a minute and a half." They'd arrived at the base of the stairs to the trailer. "I mean, look at this place. Hundreds of millions of dollars pumped into a day care center with guns. It's insane."

The inside of the trailer looked like a collection of college classrooms, four individual classroom setups divided by electric-powered folding walls. In each classroom, rows of tables hosted ergonomic rolling chairs, all of which were oriented toward a front wall that was all erasable white board. The place smelled like new carpet.

"Nice digs," Jonathan said.

"They treat us well," Dawkins agreed. "They just don't let us do our jobs. Nobody wants to recognize the fact that roughly one hundred percent of the illegals who cross have paid the cartels for the right to do so. For goddamn certain sure, every coyote who smuggles them in has paid tribute to the cartels. Then the cartels turn around and take the money to fund mass murders against their rivals."

Jonathan waited him out.

Dawkins seemed primed for more, but then he raised his hands in surrender. "Sorry," he said. "This shit really frosts my flakes."

"I can tell," Jonathan said.

Dawkins gestured for everyone to help themselves to seats around the nearest table. Jonathan and Gail sat, but Boxers remained standing. "Okay, then, my fictional Feeb friends, what can I do for you?"

Jonathan leaned into the table. "Do the names Craig and Connie Kendall mean anything to you?"

Dawkins sat taller and reflexively shot looks over both shoulders. "Holy shit. That gets right to it, doesn't it?"

As Jonathan waited for the rest, he saw a cloud cross Dawkins's face.

"What do the names mean to *you*?" Dawkins countered.

"A lot of dead people and at least two missing children," Jonathan said. "All within the last three days."

"Missing children?"

"*Their* missing children," Gail said. "Ryder and Geoffrey Kendall."

"How did they go missing?"

"I was hoping you could tell me," Jonathan said. "All we know is that they were nabbed by people dressed as police officers, who, parenthetically, killed a real police officer and a priest."

"So, how did you come to be impersonating FBI agents?"

"Focus, Harry," Boxers said. "The common denominator in all of this is the Kendalls. Now it's your turn."

"I thought the Kendalls had been arrested," Dawkins said.

This wasn't going anywhere. Jonathan reset the conversation and caught Dawkins up to current knowledge.

"Wow," Dawkins said when Jonathan was done. "That's a lot of killing in just one day."

"So, what's the deal?" Jonathan asked. "What did the Kendalls know or do that makes everyone want to hurt their kids? It has to be more than just keeping mom and dad quiet. There's no exit plan for that."

"Yeah," Dawkins said. Something in his demeanor changed again. He would not have made the world's best poker player.

"What?" Gail said. Apparently, she saw it, too.

Dawkins's face went blank. "Give me a second for this," he said. "There's shit I'm not supposed to tell *you*, and then there's stuff that I'd need clearance to talk to *President Darmond* about. This is the latter."

For the first time since they'd arrived, Boxers became fully engaged. He folded himself into a chair and moved it in close to the table.

"First some background," Dawkins said.

"Ah, shit," Boxers said, and he pushed away again.

"Cut him some slack," Jonathan snapped. To Dawkins: "Go."

Dawkins cleared his throat. "This all goes back to the flow of shit and bad people across our border. I presume I don't have to mince my words with PC bullshit while I'm with you. You take a Muslim out of Syria, wrap him in a Juan Valdez outfit, and he looks a lot like a Central American. We've caught a few hundred of these assholes over the years—some of them two or three times—but we know that hundreds of others have gotten through. They're not officially my problem—not professionally—"

"They're everybody's problem," Gail said.

"Exactly. I've always wondered if they had anything to do with that business of shooting up the football fields and shit a while back."

It was Jonathan's turn to keep a poker face—a skill at which he was highly accomplished. Security Solutions had played a significant role in stopping that carnage. The world thought the FBI had taken the bad guys out. Thus, the faux credentials. He was relieved that Dawkins did not press for confirmation one way or the other.

"So, anyway, we've had this stream of bad guys who have established a conduit not just for drugs, but all kinds of other bad shit. Weapons, explosives . . . nerve agents."

He let that verbal turd float in the punch bowl until it registered with the others.

"Nerve agents?" Boxers repeated it as a question, perhaps wondering if his hearing had faltered.

"VX and GB that we know of," Dawkins said, his voice barely above a whisper. "Even back in the day, we chased the cheap labor market to make the most hazardous shit on the planet, and now it's coming back on us."

"We don't make chemical weapons anymore," Gail said. It was hard to tell from her tone if she was being ironic.

Jonathan assumed that she had to be. This wasn't their first dance with that shit. "Maybe that's why we sent the contracts down Mexico way," he said.

"Want to make your head explode?" Dawkins asked

with a chuckle. "Try to work out a flow chart that will make our geopolitical decision-making south of the Rio Grande make any sense at all."

"I'd settle for one that wasn't flat-out self-destructive," Boxers said.

"And you know what?" Gail asked. "None of it makes a difference."

"You're absolutely right," Jonathan agreed. "One of the aspects of my work that I've always appreciated is the purity that comes from dealing with things as they are. How they got that way isn't my expertise." To Dawkins: "How big a problem is it? The chemical weapons?"

"I don't even know how to approach that question," Dawkins said. "That's nasty shit. A little dab'll do ya."

"What I'm asking, I guess, is if this is a one-off, or is it a trend?"

"Call it a trend in the early stages," Dawkins said. "We've found canisters on three illegals. Assume that we catch twenty percent, that means we've got fifteen containers in circulation somewhere. Obviously, that's a guess."

"What kind of containers?" Gail asked. "How is it transported?"

Dawkins held his hands about twelve inches apart. "Most look like stainless steel coffee thermoses. In fact, that was their Achilles' heel. The stainless steel. What *refugee*"—he made finger quotes—"brings their coffee across in a hundred-dollar thermos?"

"They're not stupid," Jonathan said. "They'll adapt."

"We captured one big mother of a container, too," Dawkins said. "Think beer keg."

"Holy crap," Boxers said.

Jonathan asked, "What do the cartels plan to do with nerve agents? Are they opening up a new line in the terror business?"

"Another area where we're not sure," Dawkins said. "There's a lot of money to be made selling weapons to the Great Satan's enemies. We've got all kinds of suspected terror cells in the U.S. You know that. Hamas, Al Qaeda, ISIS, Chechens, Russians, MS-13, the whole nine yards. They're everywhere, but we're hamstrung against doing anything against them until they do something against us."

Boxers said, "So, the theory is that the cartels are the distribution network? Like a franchisor?"

"Essentially, yes."

"How does this involve the Kendalls?" Gail asked.

"It's in the chatter we've picked up," Dawkins explained. "You know that they were the big-dog enforcers for the C-Squared in the USA, right?"

"Tell me what that means to you," Jonathan said.

"They were the folks who made sure that distribution channels stayed effective and that disruptions were righted as soon as possible."

"Been workin' for the government for too long, Harry," Boxers said. "What the hell does that mean?"

"It means that they killed people and broke legs."

"Allegedly," Gail added. Again, Jonathan assumed the presence of irony.

"No, they pretty much did it," Dawkins said. "Yada, yada, jury, and all that, but Connie Kendall has no place to go."

"Were they killing people with VX agent?" Jonathan asked. "I'm not seeing the nexus between chem weps and two-bit enforcers."

Dawkins raised a finger. "Ah, be careful. Respect your adversary, remember? There was nothing two-bit about the Kendalls' operation. They were efficient and very smart. Some very tough dudes were scared shit-less of them."

"Weapons," Gail prompted.

"Yeah, the weapons. We don't have anything that connects them to that directly, but there's a lot of chatter that includes them. We believe their code name within the C-Squared is Blue Bird, and we've listened to some intercepts that use that handle in the same sentence with *the juice*, which we believe to mean the chem weps."

"This is the big secret?" Boxers asked. He seemed disappointed.

"That's the root of it," Dawkins said. "If the Kendalls are who we think they are, we can twist the remaining one to turn on Armand Cortez and expose the distribution network."

"For the drugs or the weapons?"

"All of it," Dawkins said. "That Blue Bird link to the juice is a really big deal."

"So, why is everybody who touched their kids being killed?" Gail asked.

"Maybe they know too much," Boxers said.

"Who, the kids?" Jonathan said. "No way. If that were the case, why not just kill them? They're being used as leverage."

"By us?" Gail asked "As in, the U.S.?"

Dawkins said nothing.

"Harry?" Jonathan pressed.

"I'd like to think that I lived in a world where that

sort of suggestion would be dead on arrival," Dawkins said.

"We *did* kidnap them?" Jonathan asked. Man, that was not where he thought this conversation would go.

"I have no way to say one way or the other," Dawkins said. "I'm DEA, not FBI. The chemical weapons end is all Feebs. And their history of staying in their ethical lanes is not all that stellar in recent years."

"Jesus," Boxers said.

"I'm not saying that's the case," Dawkins said. "But I can tell you this. The reason why this is all such a big secret is to keep the FBI from finding out about the Blue Bird connection and somehow throwing a stick into our spokes."

"Why would they do that?" Gail asked. She looked shocked.

"I'm not saying that they would. Just as I'm not saying that Uncle Sam had anything to do with kidnapping those boys. I'm just saying that I would be surprised if they did not."

"God *damn*," Jonathan said. He cocked his head as another thought arrived. "What do you know about Rafael Iglesias?"

Dawkins laughed. "Well, aren't you by God hitting homers today? He's a skank lawyer who works for a skank client."

"Cortez?" Boxers guessed.

"The one and only."

"Well, here's a little quid pro quo for you," Jonathan said. "A thank-you gift for tipping your hand to us. Iglesias is involved with all of this, too."

"Well, he's their lawyer—"

"More than that," Jonathan interrupted. "He arranged the boys' kidnapping. If the kidnapping is about chemical weapons, then that puts Iglesias squarely in the hot seat."

Dawkins stewed on that. "Have you paid him a visit yet?"

"We wanted to wait to hear what you had to say," Gail said.

"Then don't reach out to him," Dawkins said. "Not yet. If too many people get too spooked, everything just dries up."

"That's fine for you," Jonathan said. "You're trying to build a case and put people in jail. I'm trying to rescue a couple of scared kids and bring justice."

Dawkins laughed. "Have I heard that speech before? Side of the angels and all that?"

Jonathan felt his ears redden.

"You know our way is better, right, Harry?" Boxers asked. He leaned in closer. "Justice is a lot more satisfying than process."

Dawkins recoiled. Sort of. "Are you recruiting me?"

The thought hadn't occurred to Jonathan, but it wasn't a bad idea. "Are you recruitable?" He expected a hard no, so he was surprised to see the temptation in Dawkins's eyes.

"What's the offer?"

Jonathan laughed. "You've ridden in our rodeo before. More of the same. But this time in clothing that fits." Their last encounter had begun with Dawkins naked, later wrapped in the clothing of dead people.

Dawkins took his time answering, and Jonathan let him. The guy had already proven himself to be an honorable man and a fierce fighter. Jonathan couldn't imagine why he'd walk away from a solid job and a pension to wallow in the mud with the Security Solutions team on the wrong side of the law, but if he wanted a slot, Digger would make a slot happen.

"Ah, what the hell?" Dawkins said at last. "If I said no, you'd just burn up my phone lines with a lot of questions. Is this an all-or-nothing deal?"

"I don't know what that means."

"I've got a buttload of vacation coming, and I can't think of a better way to spend it than crushing C-Squared and seeing Armand Cortez either dead or in prison forever. When that's done, I might want to go back to the day job."

Jonathan looked to Gail and then to Boxers. "Any thoughts?"

"Give him the speech about what we're *not*," Boxers said.

The speech needed to be delivered, but it felt odd to get the request from Big Guy. Jonathan turned back to Dawkins. "When we were together last time, things got pretty violent and quite a few people died."

"I remember."

"Well, it's important for you to understand that that's not what we're about. We don't do revenge, and we don't do assassinations."

"You're not murderers," Dawkins said.

"Exactly right," Jonathan said. "If your mission in joining us is finding a short cut to fitting Armand Cortez for a coffin—"

"I get it."

"No, I need to say it, and you need to listen to me," Jonathan said. "We really *are* on the side of the angels. We do what needs to be done to accomplish our larger mission. Right now, that mission is to bring the Kendall boys to safety. All this that we have done here is merely about defining the source of their danger. If we bring Cortez down as a collateral effect, then that's fine. But we're not interested in doing DEA's or the FBI's job for them. You good with that?"

"Absolutely," Dawkins said. He looked sincere. "Now, are you okay with mine being a limited engagement?"

"You can't ask detailed questions about what we've done in the past or how we get behind-the-scenes stuff done now," Gail said. "A short-term engagement should mean a limited engagement, as well."

"Understood," Dawkins said.

"And about going back to the day job," Jonathan said. "You understand that if things go just a little bit wrong, you'll have no job to go back to."

"And possibly a jail cell with your name on it," Boxers added.

"How is that different from where we stand now?" Dawkins said. "Just telling you what I've said so far is a felony."

Another good point.

Jonathan polled his team. "Big Guy?"

"I'm good," Boxers said. "So long as I get to shoot him if he annoys me."

"Gunslinger?"

It took her a few seconds. "Sure."

Jonathan clapped his hands together. "Okay, then. Welcome aboard. When can you be ready?"

"When do you need me?"

"When can you be ready?" Jonathan asked.

"Ten minutes to send an email declaring myself to be on vacation, and another twenty to throw some personals in a bag."

"Thirty minutes, then," Jonathan said. "If you're not onboard in sixty, we take off without you."

Chapter Fifteen

Timur Yamadayev crossed his knife and fork on his plate and then pushed the remains of his dinner toward the center of the table. As he stood, he waved across the other tables in George's Roadside Café to get the eye of George's wife, Mary. He pointed to the bills in his hand, and then laid them under the edge of the plate. He was enough of a regular that he didn't need a check anymore.

"Thanks, Tom," Mary said. "Have a good night."

To the residents of Winston, West Virginia—and to everyone he knew in America—Timur was known as Tom Breen, purveyor of Breen's Body Shop. A dues-paying member of the Chamber of Commerce and the Rotary, he rode both fire and rescue with the WVFD. The Moose thing was a step too far, even for maintaining a solid cover. In three months, he'd celebrate his tenth anniversary in this godforsaken shithole. At least there finally was light for him at the end of the septic pipe.

The fact that his phone had buzzed a couple of minutes ago told him that relief might be even closer than he'd been hoping.

Stepping out onto the sidewalk, he inhaled the chilly air and let it go through pursed lips. A glance at the burner phone that so rarely buzzed revealed a simple message: "*Location six. Beagle.*"

In the newest version of the codebook circulated by Daud Masaev, the commander of all sixteen sleeper cells throughout the United States, *Beagle* meant 21:30 hours, and *Location Six*—one of eighteen locations throughout the local environs—meant a very dark culvert in the shadow of a crumbling bridge near the long-abandoned Mainline 17 mine. Countless such dormant mines cratered this part of West Virginia like so many massive mouths waiting to be fed again.

Perhaps the time truly had come. In one more week—two at the most—all the parts of the plan would be in place to blow a hole right through the heart of American self-righteousness.

And Timur would be able to start his long, circuitous journey home to Chechnya.

The site of the meeting was a solid thirty-five-minute drive away, the last ten or so on roads that only pretended to exist. Narrow and steeply pitched, those last couple of miles were nothing that his Ford F-150 couldn't handle on a night like this, but if there'd been an eighth of an inch of ice, it would have been a suicidal drive. Because there really was nowhere to go down here, there was zero risk of encountering oncoming traffic, so he switched his headlights off and donned night vision goggles. No sense attracting the attention of passing cops who might be curious.

Every time he engaged in one of these clandestine

meetups, his skin crawled with the possibility that it was a setup—that the FBI had turned someone and he'd been lured into a trap. Certainly, he'd been on high alert ever since he received word about the Blue Birds being caged. While he had no idea what the subject of this meeting was going to be, he thought the smart money pointed to that.

The Blue Birds—Timur knew their real names to be Craig and Connie Kendall—were the critical link that made the transfer of chemical agents across the border possible. They had recruited the mules on this side of the Rio Grande to accept shipments from the Jungle Tigers. It was unfortunate, what happened to the JTs when their leadership was killed, but somehow, the snake continued to live even without its head. A nasty bit of work named Quinto Alvarez was in charge of the JTs now, and he needed cash in a hurry to fight off the war they knew was coming to steal their business.

Timur's boss, Daud Masaev, had plenty of cash to bring to the table, but to get it, Alvarez would have to combine his drug business with Masaev's need to funnel special product into the United States.

As in any other business, success or failure in the cartel game hinged on effective distribution. In the weeks after the disaster that took out the JTs' leadership, before they could get their shit together again, their network of mules and coyotes disintegrated as they changed their loyalties to other cartels.

Through a chain of events that Timur hadn't entirely stitched together, either Masaev or Alvarez or maybe both of them together discovered discontentment within the leadership of the Cortez Cartel. Somebody wanted to make money on the side, and permission was granted to allow C-Squared mules to be used to transport special product along with their usual contraband. With their distribution network in place, the flow of special product was established.

The delicate trick was to make sure that Armand Cortez never got wind of what was happening under his nose. That would spell death for everyone in that supply chain. Not that Timur lost any sleep over it, but he did admire the cleanliness of the deception.

The Jungle Tigers needed only to get the special product to Juarez. From there, it would be handed off to handpicked mules who would ferry the stuff to El Paso, and from there, it flowed freely through the States. Timur worried that the smugglers might get arrested at the border—in fact, he knew of three cases where that had happened—but the Americans didn't seem to grasp the seriousness of what was happening. Of those three mules who had been arrested at the border, two had already returned to work in Mexico. Timur didn't know what had happened to the third.

The perfect storm of incompetence was making Timur's job ten times easier than it had any right to be.

The Blue Birds had made sure that the supply train through the United States stayed on its tracks, not just for C-Squared's drugs but also for Masaev's special product. The flow for the chemical agent was not as voluminous as that of the drugs, but it was becoming more regular. Last month, they'd moved seven canisters across the border, up from the three they'd been able to get through just five weeks ago.

Timur's job was to command the cells that received the special product. For now, that meant just sitting on them until the time came to make the attack. Just a few days ago, the cells were well positioned and well stocked, with fifteen canisters of special product distributed among the twelve cells throughout the various states.

When the Blue Birds got themselves arrested, Masaev ordered a massive change in the larger strategy, transferring much of the special product to a single location in Tennessee. Timur wasn't sure what the end game might be, but he imagined that he was about to find out.

The wait dragged on. Timur had arrived early to secure a good observation point, and now Masaev was late. The thermometer was in freefall, and the air smelled of snow, though the sky was clear enough to reveal the Milky Way. The silhouette of Baxter Bridge cut a sharp line across the sky. Below it, the high-flowing river danced with a million flashes of reflected starlight.

As much as Timur hated America, he would miss the West Virginia vistas.

At last, a large pickup truck with blinding LED headlights painted the final curve to make its way down the hill. It rolled to a stop directly under the bridge—a spot that made it visible and obvious to everyone who might be looking, except for those people driving directly overhead. Clearly, stealth did not come naturally to everyone.

The driver stepped out of the vehicle, put a cigarette between his lips, and lit it with a match. Without pausing, he dropped the cigarette onto the rocks without crushing it, then lit another. That was the signal.

Timur rose from his location behind a boulder on

the riverbank and walked toward the new arrival. He lit his own cigarette when he was still twenty-five yards away, helping to ensure that he wouldn't startle his contact and get himself shot.

"Is that you, Timur?" the other man called through the night.

"Around here I'm Tom," Timur replied. He would have to hide his surprise that his contact this evening would be Daud Masaev himself. Whatever was in play this evening was a serious matter.

Masaev made no effort to close the distance with Timur as he approached. Such was his rank that he didn't need to.

"*As-Salaam-Alaikum,*" Timur said when he was close enough for his voice to carry no more than a few feet over the sound of the rushing water. He never spoke his native tongue anymore, but to his ear, there was no English equivalent to the original greeting.

"*Wa-Alaikum-Salaam,*" Masaev replied.

"To what do I owe the honor?"

"The Kendall boys," Masaev said, getting right to it. "You took care of that?"

Rather than stubbing out his cigarette, Timur had kept his, and he took a drag. It had been too long since he'd felt the rush of the nicotine. Americans noticed people who smoked, or at least that's what someone had determined through whatever research protocols would make such a proclamation. Thus, it was a vice that needed to be refused, even as the consumption of alcohol had to be embraced. To be honest, he wasn't at all sure that that second vice would change. He'd come to enjoy the taste and effect of bourbon.

"We have the children isolated and under guard," Timur said.

"With much blood having been shed," Masaev said. His tone shimmered with disapproval.

"The Ballentines asked too many questions," Timur explained. "They seemed not to believe the story we told them. I could have ignored that and lived in worry, or I could solve the problem. I chose the latter."

"And you lost your entire Virginia team in the process."

Timur felt his stomach muscles tighten. Whatever Masaev was implying was a surprise to him. "I don't understand what you mean by that."

"Put out that cigarette," Masaev commanded. "That's a disgusting habit."

If he were not so much on edge, Timur would have objected to the order, but he dropped the Marlboro onto the rocks and crushed it under his foot.

"You need to watch the news," Masaev explained. "Seven bodies were found shot dead inside the Ballentines' house."

Timur pursed his lips. "The Ballentines numbered six. Two adults, four children."

"Aha," Masaev said, holding his finger in the air. "That was what I thought, too. As it turns out, the Ballentines' bodies were found inside a van parked down the street from their house. The bodies in the house remained unidentified, the reporter on television said, but one of them was later identified through his fingerprints to be Mansur Chichigov. Does this name ring a bell with you, as the Americans like to say?"

The tightening in his gut was beginning to turn into

a cramp. "He is the leader of our cell in Danville, Virginia."

"Was," Masaev said. "The operative word is *was*. Apparently, he is dead now, along with six others. By process of elimination, it shouldn't be too hard for you to determine who they will turn out to be."

This wasn't right at all. Why had he heard nothing? "How were they killed?"

"All I know is what I heard on the news. They were shot to death, and all of them were armed. The reporter quoted a police source as saying that they suspect a home invasion that went sideways."

Timur struggled to get the facts to align. "Who killed them if the Ballentines were already dead?"

Masaev paused for effect. "I think that's a very interesting question. I think you need to be very careful. Could it be that our friend in the cartel business is not as loyal as you wish he was? Could he be working the other side against you?"

"He is not *our* friend, Daud. He is *your* friend. What do your instincts tell you?"

"My instincts tell me that this is a bad time to be counting on my instincts. I'll do what I can to find out and get it to stop. Or, at the very least to make sure that you are adequately warned."

Timur nodded his thanks, then stood taller. "Wait. The bodies were found inside the home?"

"Yes."

"The Ballentines' home? Yet the Ballentines' bodies were elsewhere?"

"In a van down the street."

"How is that possible? If they'd already completed

their mission and had left the house, why would they go back?"

Masaev patted his arm. "It's a disturbing mystery, isn't it? But that is only part of the reason we are meeting."

"Uh-oh."

"It's not even the most disturbing part of the meeting," Masaev said. "Connie Kendall does not yet know that we have her children."

Timur closed his eyes and exhaled. He reached into his shirt pocket for another cigarette and fished the matchbook out of the pocket of his jeans. "Don't bother to object," he said as he peeled off a match and lit it.

Masaev said, "You got the word to their lawyer, did you not? The same lawyer who does the work for the Cortez cartel?"

"Yes. I already told you that."

"Well, the lawyer was not allowed to visit the surviving Blue Bird. She is being represented by counsel selected by the American government."

Timur savored the smoke. "Is that legal?"

"Apparently, it is. I suppose that Connie Kendall could challenge the legality in court, but not until the FBI has had many valuable hours to press details out of her. Weeks, probably."

Timur squinted up at the stars, fully aware that the chill he felt had little to do with the air temperature. "Shit."

"Indeed," Masaev said. "You need to get word to Connie Kendall that if she says a word to the officials about any of this, the next thing she will see of her precious children is their eyeballs stuffed into envelopes. Are we clear on this?"

"I'll get it done," Timur said. *How the hell am I supposed to get information to a prisoner?*

Even in the dark, he could see the flash of Masaev's teeth as he smiled. "Don't look so glum," he said. "You haven't had to do any real work for us in a long time. Just remember that all the clocks are ticking. Theirs as well as ours."

Chapter Sixteen

"**I** like the way you guys travel," Dawkins said as he settled into the beige leather swivel chair on the port side of the Beechcraft. They were on their way back to Virginia. "Is it safe to guess that our friends at a half dozen federal agencies would not be thrilled with the contents of the cargo hold?"

"Don't wear out your welcome until after we take off," Boxers said as he passed by on his way to the flight deck.

"We're prepared for most eventualities," Jonathan said. "Let's just leave it at that."

Ten minutes later, they were airborne, and ten minutes after that, they leveled out at their cruising altitude.

"We don't have flight attendant service," Jonathan said, "but help yourself to whatever you want. There's a bar up front. The lavatory is in the rear of this cabin. Beyond that is my personal cabin, and you're not allowed in there."

Dawkins made a show of spinning his chair on the swivel. "This really is pretty damn cool."

"You don't get to fly on Uncle Sam's executive jets?" Gail asked.

He laughed. "I haven't had the opportunity to fly on the big boys—Air Force One and its brothers—but the ones I *have* been on are what you might call *functional.* Better than commercial coach, but not a lot."

Dawkins rose from his chair and reached into the storage bin along the bulkhead to withdraw his briefcase. "Do you guys have A/V capabilities on this bird?"

Gail and Jonathan shared a smile. They were both recovering Luddites, almost entirely dependent on others for technology that was not mission specific. "Depends on what you're looking for," Jonathan said.

Dawkins pointed to the television screen on the bulkhead. "I have a video I want to share from my laptop."

Jonathan gave two thumbs up. "That we can do." He stood to help and led the two strides to the pulldown desk under the television screen. "All your hookups are there against the bulkhead. You've got power and whatever else you need. You know how to hook it up yourself?"

"I do."

Jonathan got out of his way and returned to his seat on the starboard side, opposite Gail. "What are we going to see?"

Dawkins concentrated on what he was doing as he answered. "I thought you'd like to know what kind of people the Kendalls are."

"On video?" Gail asked.

"Bizarre, isn't it?" Dawkins said. "We scooped this

up with a lot of other crap hauled out of a dealer's house in Port Arthur, Texas."

"What does it show?"

"You'll have to see it to believe it," Dawkins said. A minute later, he was ready to go. "Let me pull down the window shades."

"Don't bother," Jonathan said with a broad smile. He pushed a couple of buttons next to his captain's chair. The shades came down of their own accord, and the lights dimmed.

"Oh. My. God," Dawkins said. "You have the volume control over there, too?"

"Of course."

The screen blinked and danced, and then an image appeared.

"Is that in a hospital?" Gail asked. The setting looked like an operating room. A cruciform table dominated the foreground, with massive lights suspended above it. In the background, a skinny, filthy man in his twenties cowered against the wall, hugging an infant.

"We're not sure where this was filmed, but it looks like some kind of clinic. We also don't know who that guy is. You'll see Craig Kendall in the frame in a few seconds after I hit play. Y'all speak Spanish, right?"

Gail said, "Digger's fluent, I can read everything, understand most. Speaking, well, I'm told I have a distinctly gringo accent."

"Okay, then," Dawkins said as he tapped his keyboard and brought the video to life. "Pull your belts a little tighter and get ready for a helluva ride."

* * *

A door opens and closes somewhere off-screen. The man with the baby jumps at the sound and clutches the child closer.

"Hello, José," a voice says, still off-screen.

José says nothing, but his face shows utter terror.

"The image quality is terrific," Jonathan said. "This isn't security camera footage. That's what I was expecting."

"You ain't seen nothing yet," Dawkins said.

"Don't look so frightened," the voice says. He enters the frame clothed in surgical scrubs, complete with a cap and mask. No gloves. "I'm not going to kill you."

José tightens his hold on the child.

"And little Guillermo is safe, too," the doctor says.

"That's Craig Kendall?" Gail asked.

"That's what we think. Personally, I'm certain, but the prosecutor says he needs more. We're never going to see his face in this. And I don't know if you can tell, but the audio has been intentionally manipulated to alter the sound."

"Actually," Kendall says, "Guillermo's future is entirely in your hands. You know you have to be punished, right?"

"I promise I will never do it again," José says in a choked voice.

"And I believe you," Kendall says. His posture is easy, conversational. Nothing threatening at all. "That is why you and your family are still alive. Nevertheless, you did steal from Mr. Cortez. That comes with a price."

José sobs openly now. He's beyond terrified. "I am

a poor man," he says. "It was only a very small amount of money."

Kendall points a forefinger at him. "You should be quiet now, José. Words like that make me question your commitment to never steal again. The amount doesn't matter. It's about trust. Mr. Cortez trusted you, and you betrayed that trust in the most awful way."

José sags to the floor, sobbing.

"Don't do that," Kendall says. "Be a man. Be an example for your little boy. Come on, stand up." Kendall walks to the man and places his hand under his triceps. "You can do this, José. I know you can." He seems gentle. Caring, even.

José works to control his emotions as he stands. "I really am sorry. So very, very sorry."

When José is back on his feet, Kendall takes a step back. "Take a moment," he says. "Get yourself under control."

"What are you going to do to me?"

Kendall rubs his chin with some drama. "That depends on what you choose to do," he says. "Perhaps nothing."

A glimmer of hope blooms in José's face.

"Remember my promise to you," Kendall reminds him. "I will not kill you. I will not kill anyone today. But you understand that someone needs to be punished for your crime against Mr. Cortez, so here is your choice. I can punish you, or I can punish Guillermo. Which do you want?"

José looks stunned, as if he's been slapped. "What kind of choice is that?"

"An uncomfortable one, I'm sure. But it is the one you must make."

"W-what are you going to do?"

Kendall's shoulders sag, and he shakes his head. "Oh, José, you disappoint me. Is that really the question you want to ask? Is there a punishment you have earned that is better given to your infant son?"

José looks trapped. And ashamed. And horrified. "I meant, what will you do with Guillermo if I accept my punishment?" That clearly is a lie.

"He will go out to the waiting room. He'll be well cared for. You both will be able to go home together in just a few hours."

José considers that and nods. Then the horror returns. "Hours," he says, tasting the words.

"The surgery will last only thirty to forty minutes," Kendall says in a soothing tone that somehow deepens the horror.

José doesn't move for fifteen seconds, maybe more.

Kendall steps forward, reaches for the child. "The sooner we start, the sooner it will be over."

José's eyes dart around the room, as if hoping to find an exit. Then he kisses his boy on the top of his head and hands him over to Kendall. "You'll be nice to him?"

"I'll treat him as one of my own." Kendall takes the boy in his arms and gently chucks him under the chin. "You are a cute little one, aren't you? One day, your papa will tell you this story, and you will appreciate the sacrifice he made for you." He shifts his gaze to José. "I need you to take your clothes off, please. All of them." He points off-screen. "You can place them over there. You'll find some electric clippers over by the floor drain. Use them to shave away your pubic hair.

*When you're done with all that, climb up on the table
and wait. Some others will be here in a minute to help
you."*

*Kendall starts to exit, but then turns back. "Remem-
ber that Guillermo will be just on the other side of the
wall over there."*

*Alone in the operating room, José hesitates, then
takes off his clothes.*

"This is getting hard to watch," Jonathan said.
"Why don't you just cut to the chase?"

"Because you need to know what kind of animals
we're up against. I know you're focused on finding the
monsters' children, but you need to know how committed the monsters' enemies are to bring them down."

"Does this whole thing run in real time?" Gail
asked. "Watching a terrified young man take off his
clothes—"

"Gotcha," Dawkins said. "We can fast-forward to
the important parts."

He moved the cursor ahead three minutes and reen-
gaged the action with José naked and facing the far
wall. His body language said that he was shaving. Two
other players had joined the frame, a woman and man
with what might have been Asian eyes. Both wore surgical garb that hid their features, but the man had a dis-
tinct look nonetheless. A port wine stain dominated
much of the space between his mask and surgical cap.

Dawkins paused the action again. "We don't know
who these people are, either," he said, "but as the
recording goes on, you'll see that the male is also a
doctor, and maybe the woman is, too."

"Dear God," Gail said.

Dawkins continued, "I'll fast forward again, and here's what you're going to miss. José is going to voluntarily lie down on the table and allow himself to be strapped down and an IV inserted in his arm."

"I cannot imagine doing that," Jonathan said. "Allowing that to be done to me."

"They've got his kid," Dawkins reminded. He moved his cursor up to around the ten-minute mark. "You've got to see this." He clicked PLAY.

An IV line has been established, and Port Wine is tending to it. He attaches a syringe to a port and depresses the plunger. José's body seems to deflate.

"I know that's uncomfortable," Kendall says from the opposite side of the table. He nods to the other doctor, who moves to a spot near José's head. He lifts a laryngoscope and an endotracheal tube from a stainless steel tray. Hyperextending the patient's neck, the attendant pulls down on José's mandible, inserts the scope, and follows it with the endotracheal tube. He then hooks an Ambu bag to the end of the tube and starts squeezing.

"There you go," Kendall says. "That should ease things for you now that you can breathe again. Actually, we're breathing for you, through the tube." He stands close to José, looking down at his face, presumably so that they can see each other. "That drug I just gave you is called Succinylcholine, or Sux. It's a paralytic. That means that none of your muscles work anymore, so we have to breathe for you. What it doesn't do is anesthetize you. This is punishment, after all, and we want you to remember your transgressions."

Kendall leaves the man with the port wine stain at

*José's head to manage his breathing and moves toward
José's feet. He is met halfway by the female attendant,
who fits him with a pair of surgical gloves.*

*"You know, anesthesia is relatively new to the surgi-
cal theater. Maybe a hundred years or so. Until then,
all surgeries were performed on patients while they
were wide awake."*

*He speaks from a position on José's right side, at his
hips. To the attendant, he says, "Move the light here,
please."*

*The attendant reaches overhead and moves the light
to illuminate José's lower abdomen and genitals. The
area has been painted orange with antiseptic.*

*"Doctors in years past employed strong men whose
sole duty was to hold patients down so they wouldn't
buck around while sharp instruments were inside them."*

"I get it," Gail said, spinning her chair away from
the screen. "This is torture porn. Please turn it off."

*Kendall holds out his hand, and the attendant hands
him a scalpel. "The Sux that I gave you does the same
work as those strong men." He pulls the skin taut and
lowers his scalpel.*

Dawkins clicked his mouse, and the picture and
sound went away. "For the next thirty minutes, Kendall performs what's called an inguinal orchiectomy.
It's—"

"It's castration," Jonathan said. "Jesus."

"Only on one side," Dawkins said. "And he was
wide awake for all of it. Felt every cut, every tug, but
he couldn't move and couldn't make a sound."

"Stop!" Gail said. "For Christ's sake, just stop."

Jonathan was concerned by Gail's color. She looked

ill. He didn't blame her. This was as horrific as any of the many tortures he had observed over too many years.

"I'll give Kendall this, though," Dawkins said. "The man is true to his word. He let the poor bastard go after the surgery. He walked funny, but he could walk. Kendall even gave him some Tylenol and an ice pack to take home with him."

"Hell of a way to develop a badass reputation," Jonathan said. "When the penalty for an infraction is literally to have your nuts cut off, word will get around."

"Except they didn't depend on word of mouth," Dawkins said. "This video we just saw got distribution. Kendall's boss, Armand Cortez, wanted as many people as possible to see it."

"Maybe it will earn them a deeper hole in the dungeon," Jonathan said.

"There's not enough here to get him to the dungeon door," Gail said. "Unknown victim, unknown location—unknown *jurisdiction*—and a torturer without a face or a voice. There's no case."

As Dawkins made his way back to his seat, he explained, "We know through other sources that there's a medical enforcer in the C-Squared who's American, and he's known within the cartel as Blue Bird. We have reason to believe—but cannot yet prove—that there's a female half of Blue Bird, but we don't yet know what her role is."

"Bonnie to his Clyde?" Jonathan guessed.

"Maybe. We know she's out there because of a few eyewitnesses who would be out of their minds to testify."

Jonathan rose from his seat and made his way to the mahogany bar. He opened a cabinet door and retrieved a bottle of Lagavulin scotch and a cut-crystal Waterford tulip glass. He poured a finger of one into the other. "Anybody?"

"White wine," Gail said.

Dawkins waved off anything.

Now armed with two glasses, Jonathan made his way back to the others. He handed the wine to Gail and then sat back down in his command seat.

"So, help me piece this together," Jonathan said. "We'll stipulate that your guy is our guy. He mutilates drug mules who don't pay their bills. How does this tie to nerve agents being smuggled into the U.S.?"

Dawkins shrank a little into his chair. "That's where things get a little squishy. Call it intuition."

"Is that the same as a hunch?" Gail asked, drawing a smile.

"Some might see similarities," Dawkins conceded. "But my hunch comes complete with an educated guess. The guy we picked this video up from? He denies any ties with the C-Squared, and we can't find one, either. If anything, he might have ties with what's left of our friends the Jungle Tigers, but even that is soft."

"The JTs bounced back?" Jonathan asked, truly surprised. Last time he saw bits and pieces of that cartel, the leadership had been shot to bits and pieces.

"Not really," Dawkins said. "Not anything like they were. I think he does most of his muling for the Sinaloans or maybe Los Zetas."

Jonathan scowled. He looked to Gail, and she was

scowling, too. "I'm not seeing where you're taking me. You're still talking drugs. I'm talking VX."

"Blue Bird works for C-Squared," Dawkins said, as if it were obvious. "Exclusively. You don't stay alive in the business more than a few minutes if you scramble your loyalties."

Jonathan waited for him to realize he still hadn't said anything.

"Yet this is where we found the threatening video," Dawkins said. "With a mule who has no ties to C-Squared. If the guy on the screen is Blue Bird—and I'm betting my career that he is—and if he's not working for another cartel—which he wouldn't dare to do—then he must have another line of goods to trade."

"Coffee?" Gail asked, clearly being deliberately obtuse.

"I believe it was the man next to you who emphasized once to me that that which walks and quacks like a duck is likely not an ostrich," Dawkins said, dredging up one of Jonathan's favorite observations. "I'm the first to concede that I might be wrong, but I really don't think that I am. Blue Bird—Connie Kendall—is the link to the flow of chemical agents into the country."

This was all very interesting, Jonathan thought. Fascinating, even. "How does this get us closer to Ryder and Geoffrey? Again, if they were taken as retribution, then it would be easier just to kill them."

"Unless the other monsters torture in kind," Dawkins said.

"Oh, please," Gail said. "Don't even say that out loud."

"I think this is about either squeezing information out of Connie Kendall or about keeping her quiet," Jonathan said.

As they fell silent, Jonathan took a pull on the Lagavulin, savoring the velvety smokiness.

"I know what you guys think about this," Gail said after a minute. "But I think we need to go have a chat with Raphael Iglesias, after all."

Chapter Seventeen

The darkness inside the cabin wasn't all that dark at night. Lying on his back on the bed, Ryder stared at the gray-blue rectangle of the window. Shadows of tree limbs swayed in the wind, which itself was causing the fireplace to whistle. The cabin was noticeably colder than it had been earlier. Geoff kept invading Ryder's sleeping space, probably in search for warmth.

Ryder sensed that something had changed between Officer Al and Officer Kim. It wasn't that they weren't getting along anymore, but something wasn't right. They seemed stressed. Officer Kim seemed even meaner than usual. The look in his eyes scared Ryder in a way that he'd never been scared before.

He and Geoff needed to get out of here. If they didn't, there wasn't a doubt in Ryder's mind that they would die here. He had no idea where they'd go or how they'd get there, but anything was better than just sticking around here and waiting to get killed.

What if Geoff wouldn't go? He couldn't drag his brother against his will, but he couldn't leave him, either. Could he?

What would Kim do to Geoff if Ryder went off on his own? It would be awful, right? To leave him behind would be cowardly and mean. If they hurt him while Ryder was gone, Ryder would never be able to live with himself.

But he'd be able to live.

Or, maybe he'd be doing his little brother a favor by heading out on his own. Geoff would remain in the relative safety of the cabin while Ryder went to get help—wherever that help might be found. But where the hell were they? Where might help be? The thought of getting lost in the woods and dying of frostbite was worse than the thought of dying here. At least the cabin provided some warmth.

He supposed they could run to the creepy guys at the top of the hill and ask them for help, but that felt like a bad idea. He thought again about them maybe comparing dick sizes. Um, no. Besides, for all Ryder knew, those guys were buddies with Al and Kim. For sure, they were neighbors.

Wait. Why would he have to walk through the woods? Clearly, there were roads. They'd seen Officer Al drive away twice. And they'd been driven here in the first place!

"I can drive!" He proclaimed it aloud to the room, but at a whisper.

Geoff stirred beside him. "What?" The way he spoke made Ryder believe that his brother wasn't really awake.

That bullshit with the shoes and socks had been a good idea. They couldn't walk, but they could drive. Or ride.

Ride!

Was there a way to stow away in the back of one of the vehicles, the way people in movies and books stowed away on sailing ships?

No, there wasn't a way to do that. First of all, even if you could be that invisible, the timing would have to be perfect, climbing aboard just as the vehicle was leaving. All of that while no one noticed that you were missing.

An image materialized in his mind, and he shot up straight in the bed, pulling the covers with him. He remembered when Officer Al was getting into the piece of shit pickup truck. He pulled down the sun visor, and the keys dropped out.

He kept the keys inside the truck!

"No, really," Ryder said with a broadening smile. "I can really *drive*."

"What are you doing?" Geoff groaned. He pulled his knees to chest and rolled over to face away. "Go to sleep."

"Get up," Ryder commanded. He bladed his hand and poked his brother in the ribs, next to his spine. "Geoffy. Now. Get up."

When Geoff still didn't respond, Ryder grabbed the covers and pulled them all the way down to the base of the mattress.

"Hey!"

"*Shh*," Ryder hissed. "Are you awake?"

"No, I'm sleep-talking."

"Seriously, are you really awake?"

"Yes."

"Sit up."

"What are—"

"Dammit, Geoff, sit up. Please."

That time, he got through. Geoff pulled his feet under his butt and sat up. "What's wrong?"

"We're getting out of here."

Geoff pulled back. "What? No! They'll kill us."

"We've already talked about that," Ryder said. "Keep your voice down. You don't have to come with me if you don't want to. But I'm getting out of here."

Tears rimmed Geoff's eyes. "How?"

Ryder reminded him of the keys behind the visor.

"You don't know how to drive!" Geoff responded. His voice was growing squeaky with emotion. "You can't—"

"I'm leaving, Geoff." Ryder felt the muscles in his jaw straining as he clenched his teeth and ground them. "Come with me, or don't come with me, but I'm leaving. I'm trying, anyway."

"What am I supposed to do if I stay?" The bluish light of nighttime made Geoff look crazy with his big shiny eyes and wild sleep-mussed hair.

Ryder sat on the edge of the bed. "I don't know, Geoffy. I really don't know. What I really want is for you to come with me."

Geoff bounced a little on the bed as he thought about it. "When?"

"Now."

The tears started for real. "No. Tomorrow."

"Now, Geoff. It has to be now. The guards aren't here now. I don't know where they are, but they're not here."

"Where are they?"

"Someplace else. We don't know where they'll be

tomorrow. We don't know what they'll do to us tomorrow, either." He closed his hand around his brother's arm. "Come on, let's go."

Geoff didn't pull away, but he wasn't ready to come along yet, either. "Suppose they're just outside the door? They have to be somewhere."

"One problem at a time," Ryder said. They could talk this thing to death if they let themselves.

"What if we get caught?"

Ryder pulled a little harder. "We won't."

Geoff put his feet on the floor. Progress. "You don't know that."

"Then we'll try really hard not to. We need to keep quiet."

Geoff's resistance was melting, and Ryder felt suddenly terrified. Like the dog who'd caught the car he'd been chasing. They were really going to do this thing. They were really going to try to run away.

Jesus, what if he was wrong and Geoff was right? He could be getting them killed. He wondered if maybe he'd been counting on Geoffy talking him out of this crazy thing.

Too late now. Whatever was going to happen, they were on their way to it.

Geoff headed to the front door.

"No!" Ryder whispered. "They lock that door. They lock everything."

"Well, shit, Ry. How are we—"

"Follow me." Ryder had checked this out already. He noticed last night as he was cleaning up that they kept the window in the bathroom cracked a little, probably to vent the stink of the compost toilet. If a window was open a little, it could be opened all the way. Right?

He hadn't bothered to test it while he'd been in there. He didn't want to risk drawing the notice of Officers Al or Kim. What if it broke or squeaked?

"We're going to the bathroom?" Geoff asked. He seemed confused.

Ryder laughed. It felt good. "You'll see," he said.

Once inside the six-foot-square space, he closed the curtain behind them and pointed to the view of the sky. The window sat high, maybe four feet off the ground. It wasn't a regular size, a quarter of the size of a regular window, and it opened by sliding sideways.

"That's the way out?" Geoff asked. "We can't fit through there."

"Sure we can," Ryder said. He hoped the determination in his voice would somehow make the words true. In the dark, now that he was looking at it more closely, he wasn't so sure. "Let me give you a boost up. Stand on the toilet."

"Why don't you go first?"

"Because I'm bigger than you and don't need a boost."

Geoff looked like he wanted to argue but didn't know what to say. "What's on the other side?"

"Just the garden." Actually, it was a wannabe garden, a patch of dirt carved out of the grass at the base of the wall. "It'll be a drop of about five feet. Piece of cake."

Geoff didn't move as he stared at the opening.

"Come on, Geoffy. Stand on the toilet. I'll give you a boost from there."

"I'm supposed to go out headfirst?"

Ryder considered that. "Want to do feetfirst, instead?"

Apparently, he didn't want to do that, either. Ryder decided to play a bluff. At least he hoped it was a bluff. "Okay, get out of the way. I'm going. I'm getting out of here." He squeezed past Geoff and stepped up onto the seat of the open toilet. From there, he slid the window all the way open. It made way more noise than he'd intended it to.

"I thought you said I had to go first," Geoff said.

"Are you going to?" Ryder pressed. "You're just standing there."

"Okay, fine. Get down. I'll do it."

"Headfirst or feetfirst?"

"Which do you think is best?"

"Hell, Geoff, I don't know. I have no choice. I have to go headfirst. If you want to go the other way, I can hold your shoulders and you can walk up the wall till your feet are out the window.

Geoff stewed for another few seconds. "Screw it. If you're going headfirst, so can I."

Ryder stepped off the commode to change places with his brother. "Probably the best decision," he said through a smile. "The other way, if I lost my grip, your head would have landed in the toilet."

Geoff cast a glance between his feet at the pile of shit and toilet paper. "Gross. Whose is that, anyway? That's not all ours."

"Can we talk about that later?" Ryder moved to the other side of the toilet and pressed his back against the wall under the window. He made a stirrup with his hands. "Here."

Geoff braced his arms against the wall, then planted his bare foot in his brother's hands.

"Do you want to just press off, or do you want me to lift you some?"

"Lift me, but not till I tell you," Geoff instructed.

From this angle, Ryder couldn't see anything but the Geoff Kendall extreme close-up. He couldn't help any way other than listening and responding.

"Okay," Geoff said. "On three. One . . . two . . . *three*!" At the end of the count, Ryder tried to time his lift to the same instant when his brother pressed off.

It seemed too easy. Within two seconds, Ryder's hands were empty, and he could see the darkness on the other side of the bathroom. When he looked up, he saw Geoff's legs disappearing through the window and into the night. An instant later, he heard a thump and a groan.

Ryder thought about asking if Geoff was all right, then realized he'd find out soon enough. "My turn," he whispered.

As Ryder balanced himself on the rim of the toilet bowl, he wished he hadn't joked about falling into that disgusting mess.

The fence.

Oh, Jesus, the fence was topped with barbed wire. How had he forgotten about that? His whole plan rested on climbing over the chain-link. He never did see any of the monitoring crap they'd been told about. He didn't believe that the fence had any electrical anything attached to it. But the barbed wire was very real.

"Ryder!" Geoff whisper-shouted from the other side. "What are you doing?"

This was a problem. A really big one, too. He should have thought it through more thoroughly.

"Ry-Ry!"

"I'm right here," Ryder said. "Keep your voice down. I'll be out in a second."

There had to be a way to make this work.

The blanket.

There was his solution. The blanket from the bed. If he could fold that over on itself, he should be able to pad the barbed wire so that the points wouldn't tear them up.

"Ry-Ry!"

"Shut up! I need to get something."

It took thirty seconds for him to scurry back to the bed, grab the blanket, and return. He stood back atop the commode and scrunched the blanket into a ball in his hands. And stuffed it into the opening. He kept shoving until it disappeared into the night.

And now it was his turn. Reaching across to the window, he pushed his arms through the opening, but only as far as his elbows. *Oh, Christ*, he thought. *Am I going to need a boost, too?*

Stupid thought because it wasn't an option. "Okay," he told himself aloud. "If you're going to do this thing, do it."

Curling his toes over the outside edge of the bowl for additional grip, he pulled back a little from the window to bend his knees. With his arms outstretched the way he did when he played Superman as a toddler, he launched himself toward the opening.

His head and one arm went through clean while his shoulder impacted with the part of the frame that was still closed. Something snapped, but he was pretty sure it was part of the window and not part of him.

"God, Ry," Geoff whispered. "Why don't you make some noise?"

"Pound sand," Ryder grunted. With most of his body still inside the bathroom, he was losing his grip on the outside wall. He kicked out with his legs to get some momentum to roll over to the left so he could align the point of left shoulder with the angle of the window opening. "Grab my collar," he said to his brother. "Don't let me fall back in."

His shirt pulled tight as Geoff reached up, grabbed two handfuls of fabric, and pulled.

The window ledge dug into Ryder's ribs just below his armpits as he kicked out some more and bounced his way farther into the opening. After five or six kicks, his other arm and his shoulder were free, and the rest was easy. He pressed against the outer wall with his arms, and then his hips were free.

He fell straight down but was able to get his hands out to protect his head and turn the tumble into a somersault as Geoff overbalanced and backpedaled into the yard.

Something about the absurdity of it all struck them both funny, and they giggled through the pain. "You know, you're one of the great cat burglars, Marv," Geoff said in his best Joe Pesci, stealing from *Home Alone*, one of their favorite Christmas movies.

They were in the darkness of the moon shadow cast by the house, on exactly the opposite side from where the truck was parked.

"You okay?" Ryder asked.

"Yeah, I guess. You?"

"Sure." In reality, he felt as if the windowsill had stripped all the meat off his rib cage, and he'd landed funny on his right shoulder, but it was way too late to worry about that.

Ryder scooped up the blanket and led the way as they sneaked around the first corner and paused. He didn't see anybody, and he wasn't sure what he would do if he *did* see somebody. So far, so good.

"What's the blanket for?"

"You'll see."

Ryder sprinted down the length of the cabin to the other corner, where he stopped again.

"I don't see anything," Geoff said as he skidded to a stop behind him.

"*Shh.*" Ryder didn't see anything, either, and this was the moment of no return. He wanted to be really damn one hundred percent sure that nobody was there.

It didn't make sense that the guards would be gone. Could they just have disappeared? Maybe they'd just left, gotten tired of doing whatever this was all about. Like, *Seeya, kids—you'll figure it out sooner or later.*

Ryder didn't think so. They couldn't have gotten that lucky.

The nasty green pickup truck sat just where Officer Al had left it, parked crookedly on the other side of the fence.

Now came the *really* tricky part. Ryder took a huge breath and let it go.

"What's wrong?" Geoff asked.

Ryder shook his head. "Nothing. Let's do this."

"What about the fence?"

"We climb it."

"Suppose it's electrified?" Geoff asked. "Maybe that's why they left us alone."

"No, I checked it earlier today."

"Maybe they only turn it on at night."

Well, shit. Ryder hadn't thought of that. "I guess we'll find out." He took another deep breath. "I'll go first. You wait here."

"I'm not waiting anywhere," Geoff protested.

Bent low at the waist, Ryder sprinted the rest of the way and slid to a halt at the base of the fence. Geoff was with him step-by-step. When Ryder looked at him, Geoff said, "You can still go first."

Well, this was it. Why did Geoff have to ask about the damn electricity? Ryder extended his left hand—the one he figured he could most afford to lose—and then touched the metal with his knuckle. He jumped at the feel of the cold metal against his skin and pulled away, but that was nerves.

"Anything?" Geoff asked.

"No," Ryder said. "Help me fold this blanket. It's for the top, the barbed wire."

Geoff cranked his head to look up. "Huh," he said. He took the edge of the fabric that Ryder had given him and rose to a squat. He duckwalked backward until the fabric was taut, and then they matched the corners and folded the wool swatch lengthwise, and then over again on itself.

When they were done, they had a fairly neat rectangle that measured about three feet by four feet.

"Hand this to me after I'm climbing, okay?" Ryder asked. He heard the tremble in his voice, the fear.

Geoff didn't answer but Ryder could see his head bobbing in the moonlight.

Ryder took a huge breath and touched the fence one more time with the back of his hand. His shoulders sagged with relief. "We're good."

The metal diamonds of the chain-links hurt Ryder's toes as he stuck them through and used the openings as ladder rungs. His hands hurt, too, but not as much, so he tried to make them do most of the work.

He cringed against the noise. The sound of rattling chain-links was so distinctive that it could not be mistaken for anything else. If Officers Al and Kim were anywhere near, they'd know exactly what was going on. He was about halfway to the top of the ten-foot-plus climb when he looked back and saw Geoff on the ground, holding the folded blanket over his head.

Unsure whether he was quite high enough, Ryder climbed one more stride, then reached back and down. He clenched the near edge of the blanket into his fist, and then, using his whole arm, with the elbow locked, he slung it up so the middle of the fabric rectangle would drape over the line of wire.

It worked on the first try.

"That's good," Geoff whispered from below.

Ryder resumed his climb. As he got to the top, he gripped the blanket with both hands where it crossed over the wire and did a foot-assisted pull-up until he could press straight up to an elbow lock. It wasn't until he flung his leg over and was straddling the crossrail that he realized the vulnerability of his nut sack. He brought his second leg over without incident, and as he was on his way down the other side, he saw that Geoff had already started his climb. They passed face-to-face. "Try not to tear your dick off at the top."

Twenty seconds later, Ryder was on the ground, and ten seconds after that, his brother was with him.

"We can do this," Ryder said aloud. And he believed it—maybe for the first time. All they needed was for a couple more things to go right. If they could pull that off, they'd be on their way. To somewhere.

Where, exactly, was a problem for later.

"Hurry, Geoff," he whispered. It no longer made sense to move carefully or to be superquiet. What mattered now was to move fast.

He darted to the driver's door and nearly cheered when it pulled open. The dome light filled the interior with a dull yellow glow that somehow seemed brighter than noonday sun. He scooted onto the seat and closed the door harder than he wanted to.

"Shit! Get in quick, Geoffy."

The light popped on again as Geoff opened the other door. In the brief seconds that it was on, Ryder pulled on the sun visor. Just as he'd hoped—just as he'd prayed—a set of keys dropped toward his lap. He bobbled them once, then caught them.

Geoff's door closed as Ryder slipped a key into the slot on the right side of the steering column. He twisted the key.

Nothing moved.

"What's wrong?" Geoff asked.

Ryder tried again. Everything felt frozen. "I don't know."

"Are you sure it's the right key?"

He wasn't sure of anything. He withdrew that key and tried the second one on the ring, but that one wouldn't even go into the slot.

"Jesus, Ry, it has to work."

"No shit." He went back to the original key, slid it into the slot. Still nothing.

Geoff started to cry again. "Oh, Jesus, Ry. What's wrong. We have to leave *now*."

Ryder didn't answer. *Think*, he told himself. There has to be a way. A friggin' key is a friggin' key. There are only so many things that can go wrong.

"Maybe it needs to be in neutral," Ryder said. As if he really knew what that meant. Oh, and by the way, where the hell was the gearshifter? "Open your door again," he said.

Geoff whined, "The light will come back on."

"That's what I need. I can't see anything here."

"I thought you said you could drive."

"Really?" Ryder said. "Open the goddamn door."

The door clicked, and the light came on again. The gearshift was rooted in the middle of the floor, between their seats. It was marked PRND12. That meant it was an automatic transmission, which meant that it didn't have a clutch, and clutches were what new drivers always had difficulty with.

Another sign, just above the letter *P*, read DEPRESS BRAKE PEDAL TO SHIFT.

"Got it!" Ryder announced. No brake, no motor. He pressed the brake pedal and turned the key again. The engine turned and caught. "Yes!"

Geoff closed his door and searched for his seatbelt. Old habits. Ryder didn't give a flying shit about his seatbelt. With the brake pedal still down, he pulled the gearshift down to R and hit the gas. They spewed gravel and launched backward. With the wheel turned the way it was, the tailgate smashed into the fence.

Christ, now they might as well have been playing a trumpet to announce that they were escaping.

Pulling the shifter from P down to D, he hit the gas again, and they launched forward. Ryder thought he could see the outline of the driveway through the darkness, and he aimed for it, overcontrolling wildly from side to side.

"Turn on the lights," Geoff said.

"No! They'll see." He didn't bother to mention that he had no idea where the light switch was.

"You're going too fast."

Ryder hit the brakes again and slammed himself into the steering wheel. The pedals were way more sensitive than he'd imagined them to be. This time, when he pressed the pedal, he did it gently, and the truck eased forward.

The driveway—the road leading to the front of the cabin—wasn't paved, but rather covered with gravel. That gave Ryder a gray path to follow into the woods that seemed to swallow them whole.

"Do you think this is the way they brought us in?" Geoff asked.

"I think it would have to be," Ryder replied. "It's the only—"

"Oh, shit." Geoff spoke his words for him.

Ahead about twenty yards, a steel gate blocked the road. It looked to be constructed of stout metal, the same kind of chain-link as around the yard, but reinforced with thick crosspieces that formed an X on the far side. Ryder stood on the brakes to stop the truck.

"Oh, God, Ry, what do we do now?"

Before he could form an answer, Ryder's door jerked open. A dark stain of a man grabbed him by his shirt collar and his belt buckle and dragged him from behind the steering wheel.

For a second, he was airborne, then his back smashed into the trunk of a tree.

Chapter Eighteen

Sid Hoffman kept his eye on the gaggle of WVU football jocks as they sulked out of Patrick's Olde Tyme Saloon into the night air. He'd just finished a ninety-minute hustle with them at the pool table that had left them five hundred dollars poorer. On a different day, he might have taken it easier on them, but they'd arrived with so much testosterone and swagger that he couldn't help himself.

They'd sealed their fate when they called him "old man." He gave it even money that he'd see at least one of them one day as a resident at Murder Mountain.

When they hadn't doubled back after five minutes, Sid figured they were gone for good, and he bought a round for the house out of his winnings. The house had earned it, after all, more than a few doing their part to help him bait the trap and snare the kids' money.

Sid took a Maker's on the rocks for himself and wove his way back to the bar table in the corner where he'd been minding his own business when the hustle began. Most of the other customers were old buddies from way back, but one stranger caught his attention.

In his forties, the guy was dressed as a cowboy and sat at his own two-top. He'd been there for over an hour but hadn't done much other than sip and read. A whole hour on one drink. Yeah, it was odd, but a man's drinking habits were his own business.

As Sid passed, the guy stood and fell in behind him, causing Sid's radar to ping. There was nothing aggressive about the guy's move, but it was nonetheless alarming.

Sid made his way to his table, where the novel he'd been reading still lay spread open. He set his drink down, then turned to confront the stranger, who was still ten feet away. "Can I help you?"

The cowboy stopped and took a step back. "I mean no harm," he said.

"I don't, either. But you're the one following me."

The cowboy hunched his shoulders, palms up. "Yeah, I sort of am. But again, I mean no harm. Are you Sid Hoffman?"

The guy was showing his hands, but Sid worked hard not to draw the Baby Glock he kept tucked in a holster on his right hip. "Who's asking?"

The cowboy touched the brim of his hat. "Name's Tom. Tom Breem. I've from out Winston way, and I need to talk to you."

"It didn't end so well for the last process server who approached me," Sid warned.

Tom smiled. "After the way I saw you handle those kids, I can understand that. I'm here for good reasons, not bad." He gestured to Sid's table. "Can we sit a spell?" Then he gestured back toward his own two-top. "Or, we could do mine."

"Standing works for me," Sid said.

"Please relax, Mr. Hoffman. I just need to talk with you for a little bit. There's a lot good in it for you, I promise."

"If you're trying to sell me something, go ahead and quit right now."

"Please," Tom said. "Won't take ten minutes."

Sid never turned his back on the stranger as he settled into his seat and pointed to the other. "Sit and say your piece."

Tom sat, scooted his chair in close, and leaned his elbows on the table. This was an invitation to a clandestine conversation, but Sid wouldn't bite. Maybe he wanted to have witnesses hear what was about to be said.

Tom didn't press the point. "One more thing, just to make sure that you're the Sid Hoffman I need to speak to. You work up on Murder Mountain, right? The federal prison at Hazelton?"

Sid waited.

"You've been there a long time, right?" Tom continued. "You've got one hell of a service record, a steady line of promotions. Are you *that* Sid Hoffman?"

Sid crossed his arms as he leaned into the table. "That's a lot of research to do on a person you don't know. The time remaining for you to make your point is growing short."

"But there were problems along the way, weren't there?" Tom continued, as if not interrupted. "Nothing beyond what you'd expect, I suppose. People getting promoted to positions they didn't deserve because of where they were born or how they were born. A couple of accusations for conduct that nobody would have even cared about ten or fifteen years ago."

Sid felt anger begin to burn.

"Are you feeling me here, Sid? I'm not trying to be offensive, believe me. Far from it. It'd be stupid to piss you off right before I ask you a question."

Sid dropped his voice to a low growl. "You're about five seconds away from something bad happening to you."

"Look," Tom said. "I happen to know that you have financial issues."

Sid's heart rate skipped. Yeah, there were money issues, but nobody around here knew about those. It was nobody's business that his sister had cancer or that the oil rights he'd bought in Oklahoma never yielded anything.

Tom slapped the tabletop lightly with his palms. "Okay, enough of the mystery. My name isn't really Tom, but what my real name is, is of no concern to you. I wanted to impress upon you that I am . . . how do I want to say it? . . . *connected*. That's the right word, but not in the sense of the Mafia. Are you getting my drift?"

"No, I'm not," Sid replied. He'd found his conspiratorial tone at last.

"I'm probably not making myself clear." Tom leaned in very close this time. "What I'm about to present to you is illegal. I'm putting that right out front. And what I want you to know is that you are under no obligation to take on what I'm about to ask, but if you do, we expect performance. If you don't want to do it, then, well, we're done here. But if word ever leaks out that you revealed the offer, the price will be unimaginably high, and it won't stop with you." He lowered his tone even more. "If I'm really telling you the truth, the penalty won't even start with you. Watching others we love suffer is so much harder than suffering ourselves. Are you following me, Sid?"

Through the entire monologue, everything about this man exuded calm reasonableness. He might have been telling the story of an interesting conversation he'd overheard. Sid didn't scare easily, and it was that everyman demeanor that pushed him over.

"Get out of here. I don't even want to hear what you have to offer."

"Unfortunately, it's too late for that," Tom said. He reached around to his back pocket and produced an envelope. "How often do you come into contact with Connie Kendall?"

Sid tried to hide his surprise, but he didn't react in time. Only a handful of people knew that Connie Kendall was even at the prison.

"Please don't insult me by pretending you don't know who she is or that you've never heard of her," Tom warned. "As a supervisor, how often do you see her?"

Sid saw no upside to playing a bluff here. "We rotate shifts. Three days of day shift, three days of night shift, three days off. When I'm on, I see her at least twice a day."

"I didn't know there were women's facilities at the prison," Tom said.

"Well, as you clearly already know, there aren't. Whatever she did, Uncle Sam is jumping through hoops on special accommodations."

"Who else does she see on a regular basis?"

"No one, really. Her lawyer and the prosecutors.

That's who I'm told they are, anyway. Some things are beyond my pay grade."

"Why is she not allowed to see her regular lawyer?"

Sid chuckled, and he could hear the nervousness in it. "Look, Tom. Or whoever you are. I'm just the jailer. I make sure that the inmates get fed and that they don't kill each other. I'm not in anyone's inner circle."

Tom scowled. "Yeah, but you must hear things."

"You mentioned something about money," Sid replied.

The scowl turned to a grin. "There it is. There's always a place for greed in every man's heart." He put the envelope from his pocket on the table and slid it across to Sid. "Take a look inside."

Just from the dimensions, he knew it was cash, and from the heft there was quite a bit of it. All depended on the denominations. He spread the mouth of the envelope with his thumb and forefinger. A lot of hundreds.

"That's ten thousand dollars." Tom more mouthed the words than spoke them. "You can use that, right?"

Damn straight. "For this?" Sid asked. "For information?"

Tom's explosive laughed seemed real. "Oh, God, no." He dropped his tone. "The information is a sideline." He reached around to his other pocket and withdrew another envelope. This one was cream colored and seemed like higher quality paper. The flap was branded shut with an old-fashioned wax seal. He slid that over as well. "This is what you're getting paid for. You need to get this to Connie Kendall before noon tomorrow."

"I'm off tomorrow."

"Get back on."

Sid regretted even saying that. He was the one who did the schedules. And he worked most of his days off, anyway.

"Yeah, no problem."

"Now, listen to me very carefully," Tom said. "Because if you screw this part up, I will take a chainsaw to your kids in Fort Wayne. Are you listening?"

Sid nodded.

"And did you hear that part about the chainsaw? You wouldn't believe the violence I'm capable of."

The Maker's Mark had turned to something acidic and terrible in his stomach. "I heard you."

"If I don't hear from you before noon tomorrow, I will assume that you've done something stupid like handing this over to the FBI or to your supervisor."

It wasn't something he would do, anyway. He couldn't stand the pricks who ran Murder Mountain. "What am I supposed to tell you? Just that I delivered the letter?"

"No. When you give it to her, she'll tell you something in return. You'll need to repeat it exactly."

"Before noon."

"Yes, but remember that what she tells you is nuanced. You'll need to recite it back to me precisely. Pre-cise-ly. Do you understand?"

"I do."

"Remember, at twelve-oh-one, or if the response is wrong, it's Husqvarna time in Indiana."

Sid's hands were trembling.

"Pull it together now, friend," Tom said. "A lot of people are counting on you." He stood.

Sid stood with him. "Wait. How am I supposed to get in touch with you?"

Tom grinned and winked. "That's part of the response." He started to walk away, but then turned back. "I'll know if you try to warn your ex or your kids. Besides, I've got people watching them, anyway. Have a good night, Sid."

Chapter Nineteen

"**D**id you think we were *stupid*?"

The voice belonged to Officer Kim, and the question arrived with a brutal slap across Ryder's face. A kick to his gut brought a flash of light behind his eyes. It felt like his guts had burst, that the toe of Officer Kim's boot had gone all the way through his stomach into his backbone.

He couldn't breathe.

"I warned you," Kim said again. "I warned you what would happen if you did stupid shit like this."

A kick landed at the base of Ryder's spine, right at his tailbone, and that was the worst pain yet. A hand wrapped around the front of his throat, just under his jaw, and lifted him off the ground. He'd brought his legs up to protect himself, but now he had to lower them and open himself up to more body blows to keep himself from getting hanged by a hand.

"This is what I do for a living, *Ry-Ry*. I hurt people, and I like it. Did you think I was lying to you?"

He threw Ryder to the ground. The boy curled up again and covered his head, hoping to—

The next kick nailed his thigh and triggered a cramp, a charley horse. "Please!" he tried to say, but he couldn't produce much sound.

"Get on your feet," Officer Kim commanded. "Don't think for a second that I can't break every bone in your body while you're lying there. Get on your goddamn feet and get back to the cabin."

Ryder didn't know how long this abuse had been going on. It felt like just a few minutes, but it might have been an hour. He didn't know if he'd lost consciousness or not. Was he going to have permanent brain damage like all those football players in the news?

His hair pulled tight against his scalp, and he was being pulled up again.

"I said on your feet. Get back to the cabin."

The words startled Ryder. Gave him a flash of hope. Maybe he wasn't going to die here in the woods, after all.

"Where is Geoff?" He tried to spit a wad of blood but ended up drooling it, instead.

"You worry about you," Kim said, shaking him by his hair and slapping him again. "If I have to carry you, it'll be because your legs are broken." He let go, and Ryder stumbled.

Everything hurt. This was worse than the other night. Maybe because he went unconscious so fast then.

"Walk, kid," Officer Kim said. "Think of all the places that *don't* hurt. I swear to God I won't hesitate to take you apart piece by piece."

Ryder searched the darkness for his brother but couldn't see him. Couldn't hear him. "Is he still alive?"

"Not my table, kid."

This next kick was more of a shove with the sole of his shoe. Ryder lunged forward and stumbled, catching himself with his hands against the gravel of the road.

"All the way to the door," Kim directed. "Don't look back."

Ryder did as he was told. He limped against the gravel that ravaged his feet, but he didn't complain, and he tried not to make any moaning sounds. He didn't know what was coming next, but he knew it would be awful. All that hope from before was gone. Evaporated. Now, there was only pain.

His heart hammered so hard in his chest that it felt bruised. His whole body shook. He collapsed again but scrabbled right back to his feet. *Please don't kick me anymore.*

As tears streaked down his face, he heard the choking sound of a sob coming from his own throat. But he felt separated from all that. He felt as if he were maybe watching a movie of everything that was happening. A movie so awful and so real that he dreaded seeing the ending.

Because he knew what the ending had to be.

Where is Geoffy?

Ryder had talked him into this. Geoff wanted to stay behind, and Ryder thought he was a pussy for it. He played the big brother card, and this is where it ended up.

Though he couldn't see them to be sure, he was certain that the soles of his feet were bleeding by the time he got to the front porch. He climbed the two steps and waited, staring at the big padlock that dangled from the even bigger hasp.

"You know, I've been waiting for you to grow a set big enough to try and get away," Officer Kim said as he shoved Ryder out of the way and produced a key from his pocket. "That's why I've been leaving you alone. I can't believe it took you this long."

Ryder refocused his eyes to a spot back down the driveway, where he could see Geoff limping along in front of Officer Al. From posture alone, he knew his brother was crying, but he couldn't hear anything.

Kim pushed the door open and hurled Ryder again by his hair. He landed in a sprawl on the hard wooden floor. Expecting another kick, the boy scurried on all fours to get out of the way.

Officer Al arrived at the door with Geoff, who had a new bruise under his left eye and a bloody nose. He'd stopped crying, though.

"I was even on your side, boys," Al said as he pushed Geoff through the door and closed it behind him. "We fed you, gave you a place to shit and piss, and even gave you time out in the yard."

While Al spoke, Kim pulled up the corner of the rug in the middle of the floor to reveal a three-foot-square hatch.

"We even warned you that there'd be consequences if you didn't behave."

Kim turned a recessed latch and lifted the panel up. It folded itself over flat against the floor via a hinge that Ryder couldn't see.

"Go on," Kim said. "Both of you."

Ryder shared a panicked glance with his brother. "W-what is it?"

"I think they called it a root cellar a hundred years ago," Officer Al said. "But you can call it your new home."

Neither of the boys moved.

"It's going to be damned uncomfortable," Kim said. "But it'll be more uncomfortable with those broken legs we were talking about."

Officer Al moved first, urging Geoff along with a hand between his shoulder blades. Geoff cooperated until they were just a few feet away, and then he pulled back. "No!" he shouted. "Please! No, not down there! Please!"

Officer Kim took a step closer to the little brother, and Ryder yelled, "Stop! Officer Kim, stop! I'll do this."

Something passed between the two adults, something that Ryder didn't understand. Something they found amusing.

Ryder pushed past Kim and took his brother by the shoulders. "Geoffy, listen to me."

Panic had set Geoff's eyes afire. He was beyond panic, beyond being able to understand.

"Geoffy, come with me. I'm going, too. We'll be together. Come on, I'll go down first, and then you can follow."

"Just like you followed him before, *Geoffy*," Kim mocked. "How'd that work out for you?"

"Don't be an asshole," Officer Al said. That thing between them, whatever it was, turned unfunny.

Ryder peered down into the root cellar. It was dark, but there was enough of a wash of light from above to make out a dirt floor, maybe four feet down.

"Is there a ladder?" Ryder asked.

"Just jump," Officer Al said. "It's not far."

"What about a light?"

"Get used to the dark," Kim said.

Geoff made a keening sound with his throat. He was

desperate with fear. So was Ryder, but he couldn't show his.

Ryder went first. He sat on the floor at the edge of the opening, then slid down the rest of the way. With his feet on the dirt, his shoulders were still peeking through. He held out his arms for his brother. "C'mon, Geoff. We can do this."

"I don't want to."

"Neither do I. But we have to."

Officer Al used a coaxing, gentle push to move Geoff closer to the hatch. Ryder held his hands out, and Geoff took them.

"Sit on the edge like I did," Ryder explained. "And then just lean into me."

Still snuffling, eyes still unfocused, Geoff did exactly as he was told. A few seconds later, they were both in the root cellar.

"Watch your head!" Kim declared, and he flung the heavy wooden hatch up and over.

Ryder covered Geoff as if from a grenade in the movies, smothering him with his arms and pulling them both down into the dirt. He got a mouthful of it, and he spit out mud.

Now, the darkness was beyond black. It smelled wet down here, and it was cold. Not freezing cold, but blanket cold. Blankets they didn't have.

A wave of sorrow broke over Ryder and overwhelmed him. It welled up from someplace deep, and it churned his insides. In the blackness, he found his brother's shoulders and then his face. He moved in and hugged him close.

Ryder's sobs boiled up from a place he'd never visited before, driven by a pure, knife-sharp hopelessness and terror. "I'm sorry, Geoff," he choked. "I'm so, so sorry."

He only hoped that when they got around to killing them, Kim didn't really start by breaking all of his bones.

He hoped he'd die quickly.

Abbie Turner, the sally port guard, threw her hands in the air and gasped. "God in heaven and Sonny Jesus. What the hell is Sid Hoffman doing here at this hour?"

Sid smiled and tapped his temple with his forefinger. "It's called being crazy," he said. "I couldn't sleep, so I thought I'd come in and relieve Norm Syme. Let him get home in time to cook breakfast for his kids."

Abbie buzzed him in. "I don't like nobody enough to come to work at four in the mornin'."

"It's almost four-thirty," Sid joked. He ran his pocket junk and his jacket through the x-ray machine and walked through the magnetometer. He leaned in closer and winked. "Maybe he'll remember the favor when I want to party at home on New Year's Eve."

Abbie laughed, a big throaty guffaw. "I don't like nobody enough to do that, either."

Murder Mountain was one of the oldest United States penitentiaries in the system. Built in the early 1900s and designed to the same philosophical standards as Sing Sing and Alcatraz, this place was at least as much about punishment as it was penance. Back in the day—long before Sid's time—this was a place of heavy leg irons, years-long isolation, and bread-and-water diets. While incarceration philosophies had changed over the decades, the physical facility had remained more or less the same as it had always been. Because it had been incongruously named a historic landmark, every modernization to the exterior was required to perpetuate the incarceration nightmare theme.

The interior of the prison was the same monochrome white-turned-gray look that had become the standard for penitentiaries over the years. More modern prisons were built around central pods where inmates could gather in a place immediately outside of their cells, but Murder Mountain arranged their cells in tiered blocks. Twenty cells on a row, three tiers on a block, for a total of sixty inmates per each of the fifteen cellblocks that made up the prison.

Those were the design specifications. In reality, more than half of the cells that were designed for one prisoner, in fact, held two. An effort was made—or so Sid had been told by the makers of the rules—to match cellies by category of crimes committed (nonviolent drug offenders housed together, for example), but those same rule makers clearly didn't commit a lot of energy to the challenge. The cells were only six feet wide by eight feet long, and that space included two bunks, a toilet/sink combination and a fold-down writing desk. Occupied by two grown men. Every moment of every day was ripe for a fight, and in a place like Murder Mountain, fights were serious events, all too often fought until one of the combatants was dead.

Sid made his way to the command booth. He had to stop and be buzzed through three mantraps before he arrived, so there was certainly no surprise for Norman Syme, the officer on duty, when he did. Sid slid his I.D. into the reader, and Norman buzzed him in.

The command booth was a bulletproof steel-and-Lexan octagon packed with monitor screens and knobs and switches that controlled everything from the lights to the door locks to the air handlers. A countertop ringed the base of the monitors, forming a kind of continuous desk around the whole space. In the center of the octagon, there was enough room for three rolling office chairs, a minifridge, and a microwave. It wasn't much, but it was the space Sid Hoffman had worked an entire career to command.

From this spot, elevated to a level above the third tier of cells, they could see the length of each of the rows of cells that branched out like wheel spokes, but their view was limited by various levels of expanded metal screening and guard rails. Directly below them, similar octagons tracked the individual tiers.

"Mornin', Sid," Norman said. "Abbie said you were having a hard time sleeping."

"That Abbie," Sid said with rolled eyes. "She's a talker, isn't she?" He put down the black backpack that doubled as his briefcase and nudged it under the desk with his toe. He spun one of the chairs around and took a seat. "You're welcome to go home now, if you'd like."

"Not if it's gonna cost me my New Year's Eve at home." At twenty-eight, Norman still looked like a little kid. His hands and feet seemed too big for his body, his auburn hair was perpetually disheveled, and a patch of freckles littered the bridge of his nose and his cheeks.

"I was joking with her," Sid assured. Jesus, was there anything she didn't repeat? "Did she also tell you that I thought you might want to get home in time to fix breakfast for the family?"

Norman smiled and reared back in his chair. "Did you really say that?"

"I did."

Norman stood and grabbed his own backpack. "If you make that an order, I'm outta here."

"All right, then. That's an order."

Beaming, Norman swung his hand for a low five and headed for the door, where he waited for Sid to buzz him out. When the lock hummed, he hesitated, then turned. "Oh, are you going to take care—"

"Of your time card," Sid finished. "Yes, I'll take care of it."

"All right, then," Norman said as he pulled the door open. "Feel free to sleepwalk like this anytime you want."

As Norman disappeared into the maze of barred and locked passageways, Sid went to work. The regular morning shift would come on at seven, and when they arrived, they would be fresh and attentive and geared up for action the way that the outgoing night shift would not be. Like everywhere else in the world, the graveyard shift at Murder Mountain was where the staff could get the most rest while doing the least amount of work. For now, Sid was the most senior officer present in the facility—a fact that would change at seven. The graveyard crew wasn't used to seeing a lieutenant among their ranks, and they would be hesitant to question his actions.

As he walked out onto the catwalk and then down the stairs to Level One, he wondered how many officers' cell phones were igniting in their pockets. Lieutenant Hoffman was in early and on the loose. What the hell had someone done wrong?

Sid was headed for the CMU—the Communications Management Unit—an ugly child of the post-9/11 panic that created prison units specifically for those who were accused or convicted of terrorism. An advanced form of solitary confinement, the CMU was based on the theory that by keeping bad guys from speaking to other bad guys, ongoing conspiracies could be disrupted, and new ones would never form.

Originally designed as the storage facility for the prison back in the pre-refrigeration days, Q Block, as it was now called, was a dank corridor that had been blasted out of the bedrock beneath the prison. Using the firehose of Homeland Security money, the Federal Bureau of Prisons had employed huge drilling bits to expand the width and height of the cave and then outfitted it with twenty cells that would be dedicated to housing single occupants. The prisoners would be locked behind solid steel doors for twenty-three hours a day.

The CMU was a soul-stealing place, the ultimate psychological torture, Sid thought. It was so bad, in fact, that his correctional officers had to rotate on no longer than a three-week schedule in order to keep their sanity.

More recently, Q Block housed more drug kingpins than it did terrorists—though Sid could be talked into believing that folks who ran drug operations were terrorists. God knew they'd directly or indirectly taken at least as many lives as ISIS or the Taliban.

A few days ago, with exactly zero advance notice,

Sid and his counterparts on the other two shifts were directed to figure out a way to clear out Q Block to make room for a "special inmate."

The seventeen dudes who were so scary that they needed to be isolated from the world now needed to be moved someplace out among the general population. Seventeen of twenty cells in Q Block all needed to be cleared out so that *one* witness—not even a convicted criminal—could be housed by herself.

*Her*self. A woman. In a man's prison. What could possibly go wrong?

Connie Kendall had been placed in a Special Detention cell within the CMU. There were only two such cells, and they were located on opposite ends of the cellblock. Devoid of any furniture and equipped with nothing but a toilet/sink combination, the SDCs had irregular walls and ceilings and floors, and there were no right angles. What appeared to be concrete was actually lead-lined drywall covered with a heavy layer of rubberized epoxy paint. When the cell door was closed, the interior was nearly perfect, acoustically. Sound did not resonate. The inmate could make noise, of course, but the noise died against the nonreflective surfaces of the walls.

Connie Kendall was the only inmate on Q Block. She could be tortured in those cells, and the sound would die at the door. Only the shift supervisor interacted with special detainees, and then it was only to bring food or to escort them under heavy guard to meetings with prosecutors and lawyers.

And there had been more than a few meetings over these past couple of days.

As Sid turned the last corner to approach the command booth for Q Block, Officer Steiner was already on his feet, waiting just on the other side of the bulletproof Lexan. Sid slid his access card, and Steiner buzzed him in.

On the screens behind Steiner, Sid could see the images from low-light cameras showing the star inmate asleep in her bunk.

"What's up, Sid?"

"I need access to Kendall, Connie."

"At this hour? What the hell?"

"This shit just gets weirder and weirder." Sid was bluffing, now. Riffing, really. He needed to gain access to the detainee, and to do that, he had to create a reason. But the reason needed to be one that could not be verified.

"Who hauled you in at zero dark zip?"

Sid went for serious on this one. "You know how this works, Joel. Don't ask me questions I can't answer."

"What exactly do you need to do?"

"Was there something about *don't ask questions I can't answer* that eluded you? I need to get access to Kendall."

Steiner scowled and rubbed the back of his neck. "There's no protocol for this, Sid. You're asking me to break about a dozen rules. Where does your authorization come from?"

"My authorization comes from where it comes from," Sid said. He could hear the bullshit in his own words, and he tried to cover them with an even sterner tone. "Now, count the bars on your collar. You don't have any. I do. That means *your* authorization comes from me."

Steiner looked as if he'd been slapped. "Jesus, Sid."

Sid pulled back. "I'm sorry. It's early, I'm pissed that I have to be here, and I've got to get this thing done. If I could answer your questions, I swear to God I would."

"You know I'll have to put it in the logbook," Steiner said.

"No, you don't," Sid countered. "This is going to send you into orbit, but my orders are very clear. You are *not* to enter this meeting in the log, and you are to turn off the video cameras inside Kendall's cell."

"Oh, come on, Sid. Be reasonable. That's another dozen rules."

"Do you think I'm making this shit up?" Sid asked. "I mean, really. Do you think I'd haul my ass out of bed at this ridiculous hour just to make you break the rules? What, maybe I want your job? I'm a lieutenant, for heaven's sake. I don't want to be a CO again."

Steiner was only half sold.

"Nothing about this Kendall thing has been handled by the book," Sid pressed. This was the part of his plan that he thought could sell the scam. "We're not supposed to mix CMU inmates with GenPop, but that's what we've done. We're not supposed to do anything that disrupts the rhythm of this place, but we've put it on its ear, anyway. This is just another layer of shit that we're going to have to clean up later."

As he listened to Sid's words, Joel Steiner became agitated. He nodded aggressively. "What the hell do they think they're doing?" he asked.

"They don't care how all this crap affects us," Sid said. "I don't think this is Bureau of Prisons. This is

FBI or CIA. Their whole schtick is stirring shit. Why should they care what we have to clean up?"

More nodding from Steiner.

"So," Sid said, bringing the conversation back on point. "I need you to take the cameras offline in Kendall, Connie's cell, and buzz me in when I go down there."

"You're going into the cell by yourself?"

"I'll have my radio."

"That's not safe."

"She's a lady lawyer. I've beaten down friggin' monsters. I think I'll be okay."

Steiner clearly didn't want to do this. Sid could see the options to derail the plan steaming through the correctional officer's head. He could also see that he was pulling up blanks. "How long?"

"Jesus, Joel. As long as it takes, okay? I've got a radio, and I've got orders."

Steiner hung his head and shook it to make the point that he was deeply not happy, but he reached across the console and flipped the toggle switch that made Connie Kendall disappear from the monitors.

"Audio, too," Sid reminded.

"As a matter of course, I don't keep the mics active."

Sid glanced at the soundboard and verified that all the bars were at zero.

"All right, then. Here we go."

Steiner buzzed him into Q Block, and he was on his way.

Connie Kendall's left arm might as well have been ablaze. It burned that bad. For over a year, she'd known that the herniated disk between C5 and C6 in her neck was impinging on her spinal cord. The MRI never lied. But the pain came and went and was fairly well controlled through the use of a special pillow that kept her shoulders elevated, plus a generous prescription for gabapentin. The surgery necessary to relieve the pain permanently required the removal of the disks and the insertion of fusion material, all within millimeters of her spinal cord. It was the kind of procedure that was easy to put off.

But since her arrest, any pillow at all had been denied, and the powers that be had decided that gabapentin was some kind of gateway narcotic. The effect was nonstop agony when she lay down. There was some relief if she lay on her right side with her knees up and her right arm curled under her head, but it was a posture she could only hold for an hour or two at a time. She doubted that she'd had any ten-minute period of heavy REM sleep since she'd arrived here. Wherever *here* was.

The prison administration—is that even what it was called?—made sure that she was as unsettled as possible at all times. At any given point, she had no idea what time it was. Still, it seemed awfully early for the lock in her door to be turning.

Her neck and arm screamed as she rolled to her right side and then pushed herself up to a sitting position. Her heart hammered, and her hands shook. Nothing about what had transpired these past few days came close to being *right*, but this early morning invasion felt especially *wrong*.

After the last conversation with James Abrenio— after agreeing to the deal she had not yet signed that would ruin her family's future forever—any variation from the schedule felt like an imminent threat.

Relief washed over her as the opening door revealed Lieutenant Hoffman. "Inmate Kendall," he said. "I need you to wake up." He stepped inside and pulled the heavy door closed behind him.

"I'm awake," Connie said. "What time is it?"

"It's early," Hoffman said. "The exact hour doesn't matter."

"Is something wrong?"

"Are you awake enough to read and comprehend?"

The question did nothing to slow her heartbeat. "I don't understand."

"It's not complicated, Connie." Hoffman looked unnerved, frightened, maybe. "Do you need a moment to splash water on your face? Will that make it easier for you?"

"You seem angry," Connie said. "Have I done—"

"Answer the goddamn question, Connie. Read. Yes or no?"

She jumped at the outburst. "Y-yes," she stammered.

"Then here." Hoffman reached into a pocket somewhere beneath his uniform jacket and withdrew a plain number nine envelope. He handed it to her. It was unaddressed.

"What is this?" Connie withdrew into the unyielding wall. In her mind, the envelope was poisonous—the last thing she wanted to touch.

"I don't know," Hoffman said. "And I mean that. I have no idea what it contains, and I don't want to." He pulled the letter back and stepped closer. "Let me be crystal clear about this, Connie. I don't want to know anything about the contents. Truth be told, I don't think you're going to *want* me to know. Are we clear about this?"

Connie wanted to run. but there was no place to go. "No, we're not clear! I don't even know what we're talking about."

"Please don't make this any more difficult than it already is," Hoffman said. "Open it, digest it, and give it back to me. Then you're supposed to give me a message to take back." He thrust it out to her.

Connie didn't move. Neither did Hoffman. His hand and the letter hovered in space. His fingers trembled—not a lot, but she could see it. His grim features looked gray around his nose and mouth.

She took the letter from him. The sealed adhesive flap had been reinforced by Scotch tape with a dollop of wax at the point. No fancy crest or monogram in the seal, though. This one was purely utilitarian—a confirmation that she was the first to breach the envelope.

"I don't suppose you have a letter opener I can borrow?" she quipped. "Maybe a sharp knife?"

Hoffman attempted a smile, but it wasn't there.

It was useless to try to lift the flap. All edges were flush. Instead, she turned the rectangle vertical. Squeezing it, she tore the envelope along one of its short sides. She blew into the opening to puff it out, then slid out the trifolded 8½-by-11-inch sheet of white paper. She flattened it on her thigh to reveal what might have been a business letter. Ten-point Arial font, flush left, block paragraphs.

Dear Connie,
You've made promises to people. You have

obligations. You have responsibilities. And we have your boys. They were on their way to Fisherman's Cove, Virginia when we took them. I'm sorry to say that people died. Your boys are safe, though. For now.

Do you remember Kim? The Asian with the red spot on his face? Do you remember what he's capable of? He's in charge of your boys. Of Ryder and Jeff. No, it's Geoff, isn't it? How very pretentious.

I'd send pix if I could but that's not very practical. You have to trust me. Believe me. And believe this: if you speak of things you shouldn't we will take your children apart. We will disassemble them. Yes, they will die, but only days after they first start begging for death. Your husband was not a trailblazer in those areas, Connie. In the overall scheme he was a lightweight.

Kim is the expert. Think about this as you meet with your lawyer and the prosecutors. Whatever you do, we will know.

Have a nice day, Connie. Now, flush this letter down the commode and return the envelope to Lieutenant Hoffman with your fingerprint on it. Use dirt or blood for ink, but this will be our assurance that you received our letter. Tell Lieutenant Hoffman to meet me at 10am tomorrow at the place where he last spoke with Tom.

The letter was unsigned, but no signature was necessary. This was the work of Daud Masaev, and the brilliance of his plan could not have been held in higher relief. Anyone who might intercept this note would naturally—reflexively—assume that it came from Armand Cortez. Only she would know the truth, and she was uniquely disinclined to reveal it.

Her stomach churned and her hands trembled more violently as she tore the letter up into tiny pieces and floated them into the stainless steel toilet. "These are my instructions," she said, and she pressed the flush handle. As the paper swirled and disappeared, she stooped to the floor and rubbed her hands into the grime at the corner, and then pressed the tips of four fingers onto the face of the envelope.

She stood again and faced Hoffman. "He mentions you by name," she said. She threw the words as verbal rocks, and they made contact with as much force.

Hoffman grew paler still as his eyes grew wet and red. "I told you that I don't want to know."

"It says that if I sign a plea agreement, they will kill my children."

Hoffman lunged forward. With a sweeping arc of his left arm, he snatched the envelope from her hand. "Stop!"

"How did they know to mention you personally, Lieutenant Hoffman? What have you done? What have you done to *me*?"

Hoffman stood frozen in place. He looked as if he wanted to say something, but there was a disconnect between his brain and his tongue.

"You are to take the envelope back to him at ten o'clock where you met Tom." Does that mean anything to you?"

Hoffman turned on his heel and disappeared out the door.

The lock reset with a soft *thock*.

Chapter Twenty

Santa Fe, New Mexico, was a pitch-black town at 22:30 hours. While the GPS assured them that they were on track to find the house to which Rafael Iglesias had escaped, the instructions were perpetually one street too late.

Boxers was losing patience. "Goddammit, Dig, I need the name of the cross street before it's already behind us."

From the driver's side backseat, Harry Dawkins said, "You guys argue like you're married."

"It's a long walk home," Boxers said. "Even longer when your knees are broken."

"You've got to turn around, Box," Jonathan said. "At least we know where it is now."

They'd been halfway to Laredo to pay a visit to the lawyer shared by Connie Kendall and Bobby Zambrano when Venice had reached out to them in midflight. She'd been running through some standard verification protocols when she'd noticed that Iglesias's phone was no longer pinging off a tower in his hometown in Texas, but rather one in Santa Fe. By the time Boxers had put the plane down on the Santa Fe runway, Venice had been able to narrow his location down to a specific house on Johnson Lane, off Garcia Street.

Johnson Lane might have better been called Johnson Alley. It was barely wider than their rented Suburban. Once they'd made the turn, they were committed. "Here's where we pray that there's no oncoming traffic."

"I don't need to pray for anything," Boxers said. "That'll be the job for the guy in the oncoming car." A beat. "Call out house numbers if you can see them."

Johnson Lane was a canyon lined with red adobe walls. Each house sat off the road behind gated courtyards. The house numbers, if they were posted at all, were mounted wherever the hell the homeowner wanted to mount them.

"This is it," Jonathan said, pointing ahead through the windshield. "This is one-oh-eight."

"You see a house number?" Boxers challenged.

"No, but it has to be." Jonathan pointed behind and then ahead. "That one is one-oh-six, and that one is one-ten. This one in between has to be one-oh-eight."

"What does the GPS say?" Harry asked.

"It says it's confused," Gail replied. She'd been tracking progress on her phone.

Boxers said, "I'll do what you want me to do, Boss, but given the hour, it's important for us to be right."

"We're fine," Jonathan said. With a firm enough tone, even heavy doubt could be made to sound like a sure thing. "Park there, next to the Toyota."

The red walls of the canyon weren't straight, but rather presented a dentil pattern, with indentations between courtyard gates. A green Toyota had taken its share out of the middle of the space on their left. Boxers nosed the Suburban into what remained of the slot and threw the transmission into PARK. "Now what?"

"Now we find out what the lawyer knows," Jonathan said.

"And why he ran away to the other side of the country," Gail added.

Jonathan said, "Yeah, and that, too." He thought through his plan. Okay, *plan* was a generous word because he didn't have one. He was here to extract information, and there were any number of ways to do that. As far as he was concerned, with the Kendall kids in harm's way, none of those methods was off the table.

"Big Guy. I want you to cover the courtyard, both to prevent a break for it and to be instant reinforcement. Harry, find the backyard, wherever that might be, and tackle Iglesias if he tries to rabbit out a window."

Jonathan pivoted in his seat until he could see Gail full-on. "You and I are going to have a chat with the man."

"What does a homerun look like?" she asked.

"He's going to tell us where Ryder and Geoffrey Kendall are," Jonathan explained. "Call that a homerun if you want, but understand that there are no walks or singles in this game. No base hits. He either gives us what we want, or he walks funny for a long time." He let out a long, loud breath and settled his shoulders. "I hope it doesn't come to that—I really do. But I want you to be prepared."

"I won't abide torture," Gail declared.

"And I have no intention of inflicting it," Jonathan agreed. "But Rafael Iglesias doesn't know that."

He pulled the handle and opened his door. As he slid to the ground, Boxers said, "I'll get the irons."

Jonathan wasn't the least bit surprised to find that the heavy wooden door to the courtyard was locked—with a heavy-duty deadbolt, no less. Locks like these no doubt brought homeowners a sense of security, but in reality, they only slowed a dedicated team by less than ten seconds.

The "irons" kit was a standard element of Jonathan's load-out. The kit consisted of three main parts: a Halligan bar, a flat-head axe, and a K-tool. Together, they were specifically designed to gain quick yet noisy entry to denied areas. The K-tool was a block of steel with converging blades on the reverse side, which, when pounded into place with the flat head of the axe, would wedge itself between the door panel and the face of the lock cylinder. Once in place, a wrenching yank on the Halligan bar pulled the entire cylinder assembly free from the door.

Jonathan cringed against the cacophony of the steel lock parts clattering onto the stone pavers.

"*Shh,*" Boxers hissed, eliciting a laugh.

In his best Elmer Fudd, Harry added, "Be vewy, vewy quiet."

Once into the courtyard and out of view from the street, Jonathan opened the front of his jacket and extended the sling on his Heckler and Koch MP7. Over the past few years, the MP7 had evolved into his favorite PDW—personal defense weapon—for CQB, or close-quarters battle. It fired a wicked little 4.6-millimeter round at a muzzle velocity of 2,300 feet per second. The ammo weighed nothing, so he could carry a lot of it.

The MP7 wasn't as concealable as his Colt pistol, and it didn't leave as devastating a wound cavity as his 5.56-millimeter M27, but it filled an important gap.

Once inside the courtyard, Jonathan noted the oddness of the house's layout. The little *L*-shaped structure had two front doors. Dirt and leaves had accumulated around the base of the closest one, and it was bathed in darkness. To the left, past the dormant outdoor fireplace and the dining area with scattered wrought iron chairs, a Dutch door with glass on the top and wood on the bottom had been swept clear and was bathed in the light of a bright LED bulb in a wall-mounted fixture.

Jonathan pointed to the five-foot void space that separated the side wall of the house from the surrounding adobe wall. "Harry," he whispered. "Find a corner where you can see as much as you can." As Harry started to peel away, Jonathan grabbed his sleeve. "By the way, your radio handle is Thor."

"Do I get a big hammer?"

"Go to your station," Jonathan said. He turned to Boxers. "Big Guy, this right here is your chunk of real estate. Do your best to stay out of sight until we're inside."

"Roger that."

To Gail: "Ready?"

"As I'll ever be."

"Here we go." He moved the slung PDW to the rear, so it was concealed by his leg yet still accessible, and led the way to the door. A part of him wanted to disable the light, but he didn't want the lawyer's panic response to go completely off the charts.

"You do the knocking," Jonathan said to Gail. "Let

yours be the face he sees. I'll hold back until he opens the door."

Gail nodded and stepped up to the door. Standing off to the side—outside of the "cone of death" if Iglesias shot through the panel, which they had no reasonable expectation he would do—she rapped lightly on the glass with the knuckle of her middle finger.

Gail leaned in closer to the door and shielded her eyes as she peered through the glass. The move made Jonathan nervous. If Iglesias had been lying in wait on the other side, she'd have made herself a victim. "He's in there," she whispered. "At least somebody is." After thirty seconds or so, she tried again, a little more aggressively. "Rafael, this is the FBI," she announced in a tone that startled Jonathan and probably could have been heard by the neighbors.

Jonathan shot a look to Boxers, who shot a look down the void space toward Harry. No one had seen anything yet.

"Heads up, everybody," Gail said. "He's bolting." She took a giant step backward.

Reading the situation as an imminent threat, Jonathan shifted his feet to a wide, fighting stance and moved to bring his MP7 into play. He jumped when Gail used her new stance as leverage to fire a massive kick to the door panel, right at the spot where the lock met the jamb. Glass broke as the door exploded inward.

"Jesus!" Jonathan yelled. It was reflex.

Gail darted into the house through the opening she'd made and dissolved into the flickering light of the television. "Federal officer! Don't move!"

Boxers yelled, "Slinger!"

Jonathan held out his left hand—his free hand—to Boxers. "Hold the courtyard," he said.

Jonathan followed on Gail's heels, weapon up and ready, scanning for a target to shoot.

Rafael Iglesias stood frozen in a rounded archway at the far end of the living room, his hands braced against the wall. "Gunslinger, I've got your back," Jonathan said.

Gail hit the lawyer with the white glare of her muzzle light. He was barefoot, clad in baggy gray sweatpants and a faded T-shirt sporting the Mexican flag. His thick black hair was a mess, and a salt-and-pepper mustache drooped down both sides of his mouth.

"Don't shoot me," he said. "I'm not armed."

"Why are you running?" Gail nearly shouted the words. She was amped.

"You broke into my house," Iglesias said. "What would you expect me to do?"

From behind, Jonathan heard Boxers ask, "Everything okay, Boss?"

"Are you here alone?" Gail asked.

"Yes," Iglesias said. "No one else is here."

Jonathan said, "Big Guy?"

"I'll clear the other rooms," Boxers said. Over the radio, he added, "Hey, Thor. Get your butt in here and be useful."

"What is happening?" Iglesias asked.

"Just hang tight," Gail said, her tone now modulated.

"I told you I'm here alone," the lawyer repeated.

"Then you have nothing to worry about," Jonathan

said. He stepped forward to make a path big enough for Boxers and Dawkins to slip through.

As Dawkins squeezed behind, he whispered to Jonathan, "You might want to take a look at the coffee table."

Jonathan didn't want to distract his gaze from their detainee at gunpoint, but Gail really did have it under control. He looked down and to his left. An assortment of pills and capsules had been piled into a little dish like party candy. Half a dozen amber pill bottles littered the table next to the dish, and a bottle of Grey Goose vodka stood sentry over it all.

Making note, he approached Gail from behind, on his way to Iglesias. "Coming behind you, Gunslinger," he said. "Gonna pat him down."

Iglesias seemed to know what was coming. He stood a little taller and stretched his arms out farther.

"I'm not going to cut myself or get stabbed with anything when I search you, will I?" Jonathan asked as he pressed his hands against the side of the man's chest and squeezed.

"No, sir," Iglesias said. "I am not armed."

Within thirty seconds, Jonathan satisfied himself that Iglesias was telling the truth. "He's clean," Jonathan announced. A quick glance confirmed that Gail had broken her aim.

"House is empty, Boss!" Boxers shouted from another room.

"You can put your hands down," Jonathan said. "Please don't try to fight or run."

The lawyer lowered his arms, then rolled his shoulders against the stiffness. "I won't."

"Why are you here?" Jonathan asked. "In Santa Fe, I mean?"

"I might ask you the same question," Iglesias said.

Jonathan fixed him with a glare.

"I own the place," Iglesias said, looking away. "It's my desert getaway."

"What's with all the pills in the living room?"

Iglesias looked at the floor.

"Were you trying to kill yourself?" Gail asked. Now her tone was downright pleasant.

He didn't answer, yet the answer was obvious.

"You flew all the way out here from Laredo, and the first thing you did was try to take your own life? Why would you do that?"

"If you're here to find me then you must know," Iglesias said. "Can we sit down, please?"

Jonathan pointed to a dark arched opening a few feet away. "That the kitchen?"

Iglesias nodded.

"Let's go in there, then," Jonathan said. He turned to Boxers and Dawkins. "Big Guy, you stay inside. Thor, do you mind holding post out in the yard, just in case we get company?"

Dawkins spun on his heel and headed back out into the night.

The archway to the kitchen rose less than six feet above the floor. Houses in this part of Santa Fe stretched back several hundred years. Jonathan figured that they were crossing into the original part of the structure. As much as he wanted to watch Boxers navigate the archway and bust his balls over it, he opted not to. On the far side of the arch, the floor dropped two steps, allowing a ceiling height of eight feet or more.

As Gail led Iglesias to the four-seat kitchen table, Jonathan kept his eyes on the wooden block filled with kitchen knives. When they'd passed them, he grabbed the block and handed it to Boxers, who put it on the far end of the counter. That done, Big Guy went about the business of filling the Mr. Coffee carafe and building a brew.

Gail and Iglesias sat next to each other on the angle of the table. It was an intimate arrangement. Jonathan stayed standing, out of the way. Her approach appeared to be working. A third front door—a glass slider—lay on the other side of the table. Through it, Jonathan could see Dawkins holding his vigil. When he got the agent's attention, he motioned him to pull the slider open. The panel introduced a welcome burst of chilly air as it opened. If Iglesias noticed, he didn't show it.

"Okay, Rafael," Gail said. "May I call you Rafael?"

"Call me whatever you want."

"You need to explain what is happening. Why are you here? What happened at Shenandoah Station?"

Jonathan didn't understand why she wasn't asking about the Kendall boys, but this was her interview so far, so he decided to let her run.

Iglesias looked away. He didn't want to address the question.

Gail placed her hand on top of the lawyer's. "Tell you what," she said. "Maybe I should start, after all. Let me tell you some of what we know. Maybe that will take some of the edge off. We know, for example, that you are the attorney for Connie Kendall. Yes?"

Iglesias hesitated, but then nodded. Jonathan understood the approach she was taking. For some subjects, getting to the truth during an interrogation was a process. A flow. When you get the subject to say yes a few times, it's as if they get used to hearing the sound of the word, and they will slowly start to provide information you don't already know.

That was the theory, anyway. If it turned out not to work, there was plenty of time to work alternative strategies. By remaining quiet, Jonathan kept open the option of later becoming the bad cop.

"Why are you no longer her attorney of record?" Gail asked.

"They wouldn't let me."

"Who's *they*?"

"The police. FBI. U.S. attorney. Pick one. Any of them would probably be right."

"I see," Gail said, though Jonathan wasn't at all sure that she saw anything. "Do you also represent Bobby Zambrano?"

The question seemed to knock him off balance. "Who? Oh. Bobby. Yeah. How do you know him?"

"And what about Armand Cortez?"

"Of course." The matter-of-factness in his delivery startled Jonathan. "I'm confident that that relationship is why I have been frozen out of representing the Kendalls. Well, I've heard there's only one of them left. Is it true that Craig was killed by you folks?"

"Which folks do you mean?" Gail asked.

"The police, of course."

"I see," Gail said. She didn't elaborate.

"Closing me out was a stupid thing to do, you

know," Iglesias said. As he grew more secure in the discussion, he seemed to grow a stiffer backbone.

"Tell me why," Gail said.

Iglesias scowled as he cocked his head. It was the body language of a teacher confronting a dim student. "How many reasons exist to keep an attorney away from his client?"

Gail answered with an exaggerated shrug. One of the most basic tenets of interrogation demanded that information flow exclusively in one direction. Questions were a common tactic for diverting that flow.

"A plea deal!" Iglesias nearly shouted it. "They want to offer Connie Kendall a deal to testify against Armand Cortez, and they wanted me to be nowhere near it. It's the *only* reason. It was a stupid, stupid thing for the government to do. Especially before the rest of the family was secure."

"The boys," Gail said.

Jonathan's peripheral vision caught Boxers' posture stiffening.

"The boys," Iglesias confirmed. "What were they thinking?"

"Says the man who arranged for them to be kidnapped," Jonathan said from the lawyer's blind side. He just couldn't stand quietly anymore. He stepped around to be more clearly seen.

"Bullshit," Iglesias said. "I didn't—" His eyes grew large as his lips parted. "Wait. Did you say *kidnapped*?"

Jonathan said nothing, just glared as Boxers moved in closer to the table.

Iglesias looked at Gail. "Are you telling me that Ryder and Geoffrey Kendall have been kidnapped?"

"Don't even try," Gail said. "Don't. Even. Try. We've already been out to Shenandoah Station. We've spoken to Soren Lightwater and Bobby Zambrano."

Iglesias's face showed a puzzle piece falling into place. "That's why you brought up Bobby Z. But if you've spoken to him, then you know—"

"We know that you use him as a mule for drug distribution," Jonathan said.

Iglesias looked at the table. "I used him to handle packages," he corrected. "I never asked what was in them, and neither did he."

"I'm sorry," Boxers said. "Who do you work for again?"

"I'm not saying I didn't have my suspicions," Iglesias said. He wiped his palm across his mustache. "But suspecting and knowing are two different things."

"Plausible deniability," Jonathan said. His tone dripped disdain, as if the words were poisonous.

"Elements of the law," Iglesias corrected. "We can argue the nuances, but let's do that later. If you spoke to Bobby Z, then you know that I took care of the boys. I even arranged to have them sent to a very special shelter in eastern Virginia. It's known to have lots of security. I can only hope that it's strong enough, under the circumstances."

"Wait," Gail said, beating Jonathan to the same command. "*You* arranged for the boys to be sent to Resurrection House?"

"Resurrection House! Yes, that's the name. You've heard of it?"

"I believe I have, yes," Gail said. She touched his hand again. "Tell me what you did for Ryder and Geoff."

A cloud of suspicion fell like a curtain over the lawyer's face. "You said they were kidnapped."

"They never made it to Resurrection House," Jonathan said.

Iglesias brought a hand to his forehead. "Oh, shit. Oh, no. Jesus, what happened?"

"Their car was attacked," Gail explained. "All we know is that there was blood on the ground and the boys are missing. Their escorts are dead."

Iglesias leaned back hard in his chair. "The priest, too? Father Tim? And Pamela Hastings? All of them are gone?"

"For being shocked, you seem awfully familiar with their names," Boxers said.

"Of course, I know their names. I'm the one who brought them into all of this." He started to stand, but Gail urged him to stay put by shifting her hand to his forearm.

Jonathan stood straighter. "Wait. What?"

"What about the Ballentines?" Boxers asked.

Jonathan held up his hand to keep Big Guy from saying any more. A scenario was forming in his head, and he didn't want to blow it. He helped himself to another chair at the table and rested heavily on his elbows.

"Please tell us what you know."

"I want a lawyer," Iglesias said.

Jonathan sighed and looked to Gail. She answered with raised eyebrows.

"Okay, here it is, Rafael," Jonathan began. "No, we are not cops. We're private investigators who've been hired to find the Kendall boys. You don't need a lawyer to talk to us."

Iglesias cocked his head. He wasn't convinced.

"They're children, Rafael," Jonathan said. "I know a lawyer needs to be loyal to his client, but your loyalty to Armand Cortez can't possibly be more important than—"

"Armand Cortez wouldn't kidnap those boys," Iglesias declared. "No way in hell. If they've been taken, it hasn't been by Mr. Cortez. He and Craig Kendall were lifelong friends. Those boys were like family."

"*If* they were taken?" Gail asked. "You yourself said that it was triggered by a pending plea deal."

"Mr. Cortez would not do such a thing."

"Then who else?"

"Quinto Alvarez." Iglesias dropped the name easily, without hesitation. "And if not him, then most certainly Daud Masaev."

Jonathan reared back in his chair. Why did those names sound familiar? *Masaev. That's a Chechen name. Where—*

"Oh, shit!" Jonathan said, startling everyone in the room. He spun out of his chair and stepped to the sliding glass door that separated Harry Dawkins from the rest. "Hey!" he yelled. "Get in here."

With Dawkins inside, the kitchen felt very small. "What do you need?" he asked.

Jonathan said, "What do Quinto Alvarez or Daud Masaev mean to you?"

Dawkins's eyebrows combined as he thought. "Alvarez is the new leader, such as he is, for the Jungle Tiger cartel. You know who they are."

"And Masaev?" Jonathan asked.

Dawkins looked to the ceiling. "No, not really. It's a

pretty common Chechen—" His eyes turned round. "Holy shit."

"Yeah," Jonathan said. To Iglesias, he asked, "Is this about chemical weapons?"

The lawyer looked startled. He bolted upright in his chair. A twitch of his head confirmed it. "How did you know?"

Jonathan ignored the question. "Where are they coming from and where they going? The weapons, I mean."

"I have no idea," Iglesias said.

"More plausible deniability?" Gail asked.

"No, I really don't know. Craig Kendall was Masaev's point man on that in the U.S. That's why, when Connie was taken into custody and I was shut out, I knew that I had to protect their sons."

Being the new guy on the conversation, Dawkins recoiled at that. "*Protect* them?"

Iglesias held up both hands, as if to slow everything down. "Just stop for a second, okay? Just stop." He brought his hands to the sides of his face and pressed. He shivered, and then he seemed settled. "Okay, here's what happened. As soon as I knew the truth about Craig and Connie, I had to move quickly. Immediately after the arrest, the authorities sent the boys to one of the foster homes in their regular stable. Somewhere out in the western part of Virginia."

That would be the Ballentines, Jonathan thought.

"I knew they wouldn't have the right levels of security. I checked around and found this Resurrection House. Made some calls, and it looked like I'd be able to make the transfer."

"How were you going to work that out with the FBI?" Gail asked.

Iglesias scoffed. "Feebs don't give a shit about that stuff. They punt that to the locals, and truth be told, the locals don't give much of a shit, either. As long as they're in the custody of *somebody*, everybody's happy."

"Who else did you tell?" Boxers asked.

"No one I couldn't trust," Iglesias said. "Remember how you said you understood loyalty to my clients? Well, the Kendalls were my clients, too. It was in no one's best interest for those boys to come into harm's way."

"So, why did it go wrong?" Jonathan asked.

"I don't know. I didn't know that anything *had* gone wrong until you told me just a couple of minutes ago. What I *do* know is that word leaked to Masaev about where the kids were."

"How do you know that?" Gail asked.

That seemed to take some of the wind out of his sails. "Do you want to hear this story or not? I *found out*. Let's leave it at that. I had reason to believe that a team was coming to get the boys to hurt them, so I had a friend pull some strings to get them moved to a halfway house of sorts where they could await transfer to Resurrection House."

Jonathan said, "That was Shenandoah Station? And Bobby Zambrano?"

"Yes, exactly."

"Did the Ballentines know you were sending them to Shenandoah Station?"

Iglesias turned nervous again, as if worried he might say the wrong thing. "I had to," he said. "The Ballentines wouldn't let them go without me giving them that information. They are good people."

"Were," Jonathan said.

"Excuse me?"

"They *were* good people. They're dead. Murdered."

Color drained from Iglesias's features. "Oh, my God, no."

"Tortured to death," Boxers added.

"Oh, God. Oh, shit." Iglesias rocked his eyes up to meet Gail's glare. "That had to be how they found out about Shenandoah Station."

"How did you know that the Chechen knew the boys' location?" Jonathan said. When Iglesias resisted, he added, "At this point, secrecy only puts them in greater danger."

Iglesias issued a huge sigh. "I need to stand," he said. It wasn't a request. As he pushed his chair out and rose to his feet, Boxers circled around from behind Jonathan to get closer. If the lawyer did something stupid, the penalty would be swift and ugly.

He looked at Dawkins, as if seeing him for the first time. "Who are you?"

"Call me Thor," Dawkins replied without dropping a beat.

Iglesias appeared satisfied by the reply. He patted the air as if to settle himself. "Does the name Hector Alameda mean anything to you?"

He'd directed the question to Jonathan, but Dawkins answered. "He's Cortez's right hand. He calls himself the Wolf. *Lupo.*"

"Yes, exactly," Iglesias said. "When Mr. Cortez wants something done, he turns to Lupo and it happens."

Jonathan felt the clock ticking, and he was losing patience. "What does this have to do—"

"Let me get through this, will you?" Iglesias snapped. "Good God, just let me get through it." He paused, actually awaiting a response, it seemed.

"Get through it, then," Jonathan said.

"Okay, there are three major moving parts here. You've got the Jungle Tigers, you've got Daud Masaev, and you've got the C-Squared. The JTs used to be run by a man named Alejandro Azul."

"He was killed," Jonathan said, moving the story ahead. He didn't mention that he and his team had been players in Azul's demise.

"As were many others in the command structure of the cartel," Iglesias continued. "Quinto Alvarez, however, was still around. He was pretty much a nobody under Azul, but with all the others dead, he was left holding the pieces, and he's been looking for a way to get back in. Are you with me so far?"

"What are the barriers to entry in the cartel business?" Gail asked.

Iglesias seemed more comfortable speaking while standing. He looked professorial. Jonathan could imagine him going a good job in a courtroom.

"If it were a normal business, we'd call it working capital and sales infrastructure. Remember we're talking Mexico, right? Everything and everyone is for sale, but the prices can get steep."

"You just can't buy politicians as cheaply as you used to," Boxers said.

"Meanwhile, C-Squared and Armand Cortez are thriving, but there's discontentment in the ranks. Lupo, in particular, is looking to step out on his boss. Cortez is a badass son of a bitch, but there are lines he won't cross."

"Like kidnapping children," Jonathan said.

"That and terrorism," Iglesias said. "There's big money in shuttling weapons and jihadis across the border. Nobody comes across through illegal means without paying tribute to one of the cartels, but Mr. Cortez doesn't believe that the reward justifies the risk."

"Does Lupo feel differently?" Dawkins asked.

"Yes," Iglesias said. "And he feels frustrated that his voice is not being heard. In his mind, that translates to disrespect."

"What's he doing about it?" Jonathan asked.

"Originally, he was doing nothing more than complaining. Then Quinto Alvarez approached him with a business proposition. Quinto would pay Lupo dearly—I don't know the exact amounts, but it had to be quite a lot—if Lupo would hook him up with trusted members of Armand Cortez's distribution team."

"You mean mules," Boxers interrupted. "You make it sound like he was selling washing machines, not street poison."

Iglesias kept going as if not interrupted. "Lupo told him no way. It would be suicide to compete directly with Mr. Cortez. But then Quinto revealed the rest: He didn't want the mules for the usual product. He wanted them for *special products*."

"VX," Jonathan said.

"Is that what it is?" Iglesias asked. "I never knew the real name for it. Anyway, Mr. Cortez never would have gone along with it, so Lupo took it on as his personal project."

"And the *special product* was coming from Daud Masaev?" Gail asked.

"At least indirectly," Iglesias said. "I tried to know as little about any of that as possible. That man is sick. Brutal."

"How do you know about all of this?" Dawkins asked. "I mean, if you tried to ignore it, then how did you come to know so much?"

"I learned it all from Craig Kendall."

"Oh, for God's sake," Boxers said. "How many players are there in this saga?"

"Exactly as many as Lupo decided it would take," Iglesias said. His temper was fraying. "Kendall talked to me about it because he was concerned about getting crosswise with Mr. Cortez. I told him it was a bad idea, but he decided to do it, anyway. Kendall was the main router of special product on this side of the Rio Grande. Mr. Cortez's people could get it into the country, but Masaev didn't want even Lupo to know where it went once in the United States."

"Where did he take it after he had it?" Gail asked.

"I don't know. I told him I didn't want to know."

"Yeah," Boxers said, taking a giant step closer. "When you have the capability of killing thousands with a single sniff, it could keep you up nights if you knew where it might be used."

Iglesias thrust a finger at Boxers. "Back off, asshole," he said. "You might be huge, but I've faced down tougher people than you."

Jonathan rocketed out of his chair and stepped between them. "Hey!" He saw a look in Big Guy's eyes that he'd seen countless times, and historically, it was followed by a lot of blood. "Counselor, look at me," Jonathan said. "Seriously, look at me."

Iglesias took his time, but ultimately, he shifted his gaze to meet Jonathan's.

"If Big Guy decides to kill you, I won't be able to stop him," Jonathan said. "I'm not even sure how motivated I would be to try. But trust me when I tell you that he is exactly the last person to challenge to a fight. Are you hearing me? And I don't care who you've dealt with in the past. You've never met a soul you should be more afraid of."

Iglesias kept his features flat. He was without doubt the least wimpy lawyer Jonathan had ever encountered. He might even have admired the guy a little. If only he didn't run cover for mass murderers.

Iglesias turned his body perpendicular to Big Guy and addressed Dawkins. "When Lupo found out that Craig had been killed and Connie was arrested, he knew that everything was over. If the kids were targeted, Mr. Cortez would be furious. It would be simple to connect the dots back to Lupo, and through Lupo, to me. My job was to get the kids to safety. Which I did."

Jonathan cast a final look to Boxers and decided that Big Guy's urge to murder had passed. He decided to sit back down as he processed all that he'd just heard. Iglesias sat back down, too.

"So, why the suicide plan?" Jonathan asked.

Iglesias looked at the table. He said nothing, but Jonathan thought he understood, to the degree that he could understand anyone giving up on life. Sure, hard times were hard—duh!—but the hardest times were the ones in which you lived most intensely. Jonathan figured that Iglesias wanted to die on his own terms. If what he'd been told about Armand Cortez was even half right, death at his hands was a thing to be avoided at all costs.

"Are you going to do it again?" Boxers asked.

"The hell kind of question is that to ask?" Iglesias said.

Boxers drew his HK45 pistol and shifted his grip so the gun was butt-first. "A two-hundred-thirty-grain bullet through the brain pan is a helluva lot more efficient than that poison shit. Want to borrow this?"

Iglesias seemed surprised by the offer. He shifted his eyes from Big Guy to Jonathan and back again.

"He's got a point," Jonathan said. "If you want it to end fast, seems to me a bullet is the best way."

Iglesias's expression morphed from indignation to horror.

"Tell you what," Boxers said. He spun his grip again so that the muzzle was pointed at the lawyer's right eye. He thumbed the safety off. "I'm even willing to do the hard part for you."

Turned out that Iglesias wasn't that anxious to die after all.

His whole body jumped when Boxers clicked the safety back on.

Chapter Twenty-one

Timur Yamadayev chose to meet at Location Six again mostly out of laziness. Daud Masaev already knew where it was, and it seemed simpler to retrace steps and embrace the inherent security risks than to hope that Masaev wouldn't get lost on the back roads of West Virginia. The sky had turned gray overnight, and the air felt heavy with moisture. He wondered if it might rain. Another fifteen degrees colder and he'd be worried about snow. In a reversal of their previous meeting, Masaev's pickup was already parked at the mine. Timur pulled up to be nose-to-nose, then opened his door and stepped out.

He noted with interest that Masaev merely rolled down his window, choosing to stay behind the wheel. To Timur's left, the river seemed unusually violent this morning. "*As-Salaam-Alaikum,*" Timur said.

"*Wa-Alaikum-Salaam,*" Masaev replied. "Good morning. I have news."

"As do I," Timur said. "Your message has been delivered. By now, Connie Kendall is fully aware of her children's status. She knows not to say anything."

"That's fine," Masaev said. "But I have decided to go another way. With the Danville cell all dead, I've ordered the Blanton cell to move forward with their mission, and then we will all pack our tents and regroup. I have accepted the fact that we have been compromised. The damage cannot be undone."

Timur said nothing for a few seconds, perhaps waiting for Masaev to change his mind after hearing his words being spoken aloud. "You're being shortsighted, Daud. We've invested nearly two years of work in this plan. I have no idea how much money."

"I know exactly how much money," Masaev said. "And it's a staggering amount. Sometimes the best way to protect an investment is to accept what is and turn away from what might be."

In the distant reaches of his mind, Timur knew that he should be embracing this as good news—an acceleration of the time when he could leave this hellhole and return home to his family and lifelong friends—but it hit him as a failure. The plan from the beginning had been to hit multiple transportation hubs around the country simultaneously. As many as six. "So, how many sites will we be able to attack?"

"Step back for me, please," Masaev said. "I want to get out of the vehicle."

Timur stepped back, and as he did, he pressed his elbow against the Smithy .44 magnum that was holstered on his right hip. He had no reason to expect violence from his old friend, but one never knew.

Once out of the pickup, Masaev wandered down toward the rushing water. He stopped when he was close enough for water to splash the toes of his pointy cowboy boots. Timur followed.

"Forgive me," Masaev said. "I feel more comfortable with the background noise."

"I understand completely. I was asking—"

"I heard you," Masaev said. "We will attack only one location. Washington."

"Washington!" Timur had shouted the word before he could stop it. "Are you out of your mind? There is no harder target in the country. My God, why not Charleston or Dallas?"

"Because our cells there do not yet have special product, and we do not have time to get it to them. That distribution died when Craig Kendall died."

"Then we'll take our time and rebuild."

"We don't have time," Masaev said. "Have you been watching the news? Did you hear about the cow incident?"

Timur had not.

"It seems that the Kadyrov brothers enjoy more passion than sense."

Timur didn't know the twins well, but he had crossed paths with them. "They seem intelligent enough to me. What did they do?"

"They tested the distribution system with actual product in a pasture filled with cows."

From Masaev's attitude alone, he knew that something had gone wrong. "Did it work?"

"Oh, it worked," Masaev said with a chuckle. "It killed the cattle, and the self-destructor on the machine worked great."

"So, what went wrong?"

"A kid," Masaev said. "A fourteen-year-old boy wandered up to the device just as it was going off. He made it home before he died."

"Oh, God," Timur moaned. They'd lost a key element of surprise. Security officials would now be wary of an attack.

"Oh, it's way more than a simple *oh, God*. He had residue on him, and the residue killed his mother, too. Plus, a volunteer firefighter who arrived to help. Finally, somebody decided to stop people from traipsing through it all and closed the house down."

"Do the police know what they're dealing with?"

"If they do, they haven't told reporters. And that's as much of a concern to me as anything else. When the authorities stop talking to the press, it means they know they're on to something big."

Timur thought through the options that lay ahead for them. "VX is easily identified," he said. "It's almost impossible to believe that they don't know."

"All they have to do is close the link to Connie Kendall," Masaev said. "She will talk. You know that she'll talk. Anybody will talk over time. Our clock has ticked to zero. We need to go with what we have."

Timur saw it now. They truly had no choice but to push forward and then turn away. "Okay," he said. "When and where do we move on Washington?"

"I've given the twins a window," Masaev said. "Sometime within the next three days."

"And the specific target?"

"I'm leaving that to them, as well. I've found that the more you try to micromanage these things, the larger the problems you create for the operators on the ground. I would certainly stay off the subway system for the next few days."

They shared a laugh, but Timur mourned the lost opportunity. Numbers mattered when killing people to make a political point. Worst case, if the twins did the job they'd been trained to do, there'd be at least a hundred immediate fatalities, at least three hundred poisoned, of whom a high percentage would likely die. Then there'd be the people crushed in the panic, and then the secondary and tertiary exposures in ambulances and in hospitals. The only effective antidote for VX was atropine sulphate, and he imagined that there had to be limited supplies of that hanging around, even in a big city hospital. By the time they got the necessary supplies from neighboring jurisdictions, they'd be injecting corpses-in-waiting.

"What about the cells in the other states?" Timur asked. "Are you disbanding them, as well?"

"The ones on the coasts, yes," Masaev said. "I think life will get very intense for them. And any that were on the list for special product will certainly be disbanded because we have to assume that they are compromised."

"What about the operators?"

"In the short term, they will join their brothers in the Midwest and stay undercover until the right time presents itself again."

"It will be some time," Timur said. "The heat that will be generated by a chemical agent attack will be—"

"Unbearable, yes," Masaev said, completing the sentence for him. "And, of course, our friends in Mexico will have to be eliminated."

A list of potential names flooded Timur's head. "Which friends do you mean?"

"All of them," Masaev said. "Quinto Alvarez, of course, and that idiot Lupo. Others, as you see fit."

Timur sensed that Masaev would prefer to be cryptic, but he had to ask the next question: "Armand Cortez?"

Masaev tossed another rock into the rushing water, a lob, really—underhand swing, high, lofting arc. "My gut tells me yes, we should kill Cortez as well. But my brain tells me not to start a war I'm not equipped to finish." He shifted his eyes around to Timur and fixed him with a hard look. "But the first order of business is the Kendall boys."

"What about them?" Here again, Timur wanted no doubt as to what his mission was.

"Kill them both. Make it colorful and dramatic. Make a recording and send it to me."

As Boxers taxied across the tarmac at Manassas Regional Airport toward the hangar that Jonathan had rented on a twenty-five-year lease, Gail pointed out the tiny window. "Looks like Venice is here," she said. She and Jonathan were alone in the cabin because Dawkins had decided to ride in the right-hand seat on the flight deck, in part to keep Boxers company—something that Big Guy had never once in his entire life requested—but mostly for the view.

"I asked her to meet us," Jonathan said. "I'm not sure we have the time to waste driving back and forth to the Cave."

"Just to recap?"

"I've had her doing some research while we've been in transit," Jonathan said. "I feel that things are coming to a head. Problem is, I don't know when, where, or how."

The engines were still spooling down when Big

Guy dropped the stairs. After depending for years on aircraft borrowed from friends and clients, Jonathan had decided a short time ago to purchase his own fleet of two executive jets—one short-range and one long-range—and now he wondered how he ever did his job without them. Yes, they were expensive to staff, house, and maintain, but the convenience was worth every penny. The members of his ground crew were all former Special Forces operators of one ilk or another, and they knew not to ask questions about the materiel they were sure to stumble across as they performed their maintenance chores. Lesser maintenance crews might get freaked out by the stores of explosives, detonators, firearms, and ammunition.

Jonathan, Gail, and Dawkins headed straight to the conference room inside their hangar while Boxers chatted with the ground crew.

Jonathan's hangar, guarded twenty-four seven, was equal parts offices, meeting space, armory, and clubhouse. Each of the offices contained a bed, bathroom, and shower stall. Still a work in progress, the nonarmory parts were mostly built out in the tones of leather and intricate wood paneling that had always been Jonathan's favorites. The walls, floors, and ceiling concealed the latest in technology, built to Venice's specifications and providing her with nearly all the resources that were available to her in Fisherman's Cove.

The hangar conference room was a smaller-scale version of the War Room at the office. A ninety-six-inch LED monitor hung on the far wall instead of the larger projection screen, and the table sat six comfortably instead of twelve, but the creature comforts were all there. In walnut instead of teak.

Venice was waiting for them as they entered the conference room. She sat at her command console and had already brought up an article from the internet.

"Have a seat, everybody," she said. "I have news."

"Of the good variety or the bad?" Jonathan asked.

"I'll call it interesting, and you can take it from there," Venice said. "Should we wait for Big Guy?"

"I'm here!" Boxers yelled as he entered the room. "Don't wait for me."

Dawkins waited until everyone else was seated before choosing the spot next to Boxers on the opposite side of the table from Jonathan and Gail.

"Okay," Venice said. "I did some research on the heels of your discussion with the lawyer in Santa Fe. Iglesias, right?"

"Right," Jonathan said.

"Well, he's all over the internet because of his lawyering. Pretty controversial character, but I didn't come up with anything that indicates he's a criminal himself. He represents them. Vigorously. He's seen a couple of professional confrontations with the bar, but he's not been censured or punished, as far as I can tell."

"Why do we care about that?" Dawkins asked.

"Because it goes to his trustworthiness," Gail replied. "Whether we can believe what he tells us."

"He didn't print on me as a liar," Jonathan said.

Boxers agreed.

"Now, look at the screen," Venice continued. "This is an article about an incident in Blanton, Tennessee, a couple of days ago. You can read it if you want, but the bottom line of it is a bunch of cows were killed in a field. Just dropped dead, from what it looks like. Or *would* have looked like if a kid hadn't been in the wrong place at the wrong time."

"A kid?" Jonathan asked.

"Tell me you're talking about a baby goat," Boxers said.

"Fourteen-year-old boy," Venice said. "Benny Ferguson. I'm not sure why or how he got there, but he was exposed to what police are suspecting was a chemical agent of some sort."

"VX?" Gail asked.

"Some sort of chemical agent. That's all I've got. He lived nearby and was able to get himself home. He must have had some of the chemical on him or on his clothes because when his mother tried to help, she got exposed, too. She was able to make a nine-one-one call, but by the time the ambulance got there, she was already dead. The boy died soon after. According to a report I picked up from ICIS, Mom told the nine-one-one call taker that the boy mentioned something about twins."

"Something about?" Jonathan prodded.

"That's what the report says. The police are working on the assumption that a pair of twins had something to do with planting whatever they planted."

"What was it?" Boxers asked.

"Again, this is from ICIS." The Interstate Crime Information System was an outgrowth of the 9/11 attacks that allowed jurisdictions across the country to detail elements of ongoing investigations in real time. "The dispensing device they used in the field was rigged to self-destruct. There's nothing left except a pile of melted plastic and metal."

"That's smart," Dawkins said. "Leaves no trace evidence. But why would they want to kill a bunch of cows?"

"Practice run," Jonathan said. "Now all we have to do is find the right pair of twins in Buttscratch, Tennessee."

"Blanton," Venice corrected. "A couple of the state police crime scene techs got sick when they were going over the area, too, and a volunteer firefighter died from his exposure."

"VX is nasty shit," Jonathan said. "It sticks around. Unlike sarin and some of the others, VX is an area-denial weapon. It's supposed to kill bad guys and keep other bad guys from taking their place. If they deploy that in an urban area, I don't even want to think about the consequences."

"And I know who the twins are," Venice said. Her smile showed that she'd dropped her bomb with appropriate drama and timing.

"Of course, you do," Boxers said. "And God forbid you share it with the rest of us."

Venice explained, "While you were jetting back, I did some poking around the various security camera feeds in Blanton, Tennessee. To be honest, there aren't very many, but it was a place to start. There are two banks, one grocery store, and a half a dozen gas stations."

"You just sat and watched video feeds?" Dawkins asked. He looked horrified.

"Mother Hen has her ways of streamlining," Gail said.

"I didn't have to look all that long. On a whim, I tied

the video feeds with some of the specialized facial recognition software we got access to from Derek Halstrom."

"Who is Derek Halstrom?" Dawkins asked.

"He was part of the team for a while," Jonathan said. He watched Venice's face—her eyes, in particular—as she mentioned Derek's name. Jonathan almost wished that she showed more emotion, but maybe she really had fully processed the reality of his death. He hoped that was the case. She hadn't discussed it with him, and he'd be lying if he said he was disappointed by that. He supposed she had Father Dom and Gail as confidants if she needed them. "Let's just leave it at that," he said.

"I lucked out and got a hit within the first few minutes," Venice went on. "In the grocery store."

"You were looking for twins?" Boxers asked.

"No, I was looking for faces that triggered a warning through the facial recognition. You'd be surprised how many there are. But one that jumped out at me was this one." She pressed a button on her computer, and the screen displayed the image of a twenty-something man with unwieldy dark hair and a prominent nose. Jonathan pegged him as an Arab, but that didn't seem quite right. The picture was taken from an elevated angle and featured automatic glass doors in the background.

While they watched, Venice clicked another key, and a second picture crowded the first one over to the left. The new image appeared to be the same young man, but it looked more like a passport photo.

"This is Aslan Kadyrov," Venice said. "The image on the left is from the grocery store in Blanton. The one on the right comes from the Department of Homeland Security terror watch list. He's a Chechen national—"

Dawkins shifted in his seat.

"—and he is not supposed to be here in the United States." She clicked another key, and the same face appeared. "This is Aslan's twin brother, Khasan, also on the DHS list. Now, I'm sure there are a thousand legitimate reasons for these boys to be in Blanton, Tennessee—"

"I can't think of a single one," Jonathan interrupted. "Those are our guys. At least that's how we're going to treat them."

"Our guys?" Boxers said. "How are they *our guys*? I thought our guys were eleven and thirteen years old."

"We can't just ignore an imminent chemical weapons threat," Jonathan said.

"Then we'll tell the cops," Boxers said. "In fact, we've got one right here." He pivoted his head toward Dawkins. "Agent Dawkins, there appears to be an imminent chemical weapons threat that you should take care of." Back to Jonathan: "See? Done and done."

Dawkins looked okay with that. "Okay, fine. I'll see what I can do."

"No, you won't," Venice said.

Dawkins looked startled.

Gail explained, "How are you going to explain your methods for obtaining the information you bring to your supervisors?"

"Fruit from the poisonous tree," Jonathan explained. "You can't get officially involved without causing a lot of trouble for Security Solutions."

"There's got to be some way," Dawkins objected. "I

mean, this is huge. We could be talking about thousands of lives. Uncle Sam has a lot more resources—"

"They certainly do," Gail interrupted. "They have more operational *and* investigative resources than we do. We're not using any information that they can't dig up on their own."

"And if they don't?"

"Then they're not very good at their jobs," Jonathan said. "There were only a couple of rules in bringing you into the inner sanctum, as it were. One of them had everything to do with your skills as a keeper of secrets."

Dawkins looked offended. "I'm not going to betray you," he said. "Your team always comes first. But there's got to be something we can do. Sure, I get that we've got to get those kids away from the bad guys, but the two missions—the kids and the terrorists—are not mutually exclusive, are they?"

"No, they're not," Gail said. "In fact, I think they're complementary." She turned to Venice. "Ven, we need to talk to Connie Kendall."

The room erupted in laughter. "Good luck with that," Big Guy said through a guffaw.

"For what?" Venice asked.

"We need to know who her husband's contacts were for this distribution network for the VX."

"What will that give us?" Jonathan asked.

"Let me see if I understand all the moving parts," Gail thought aloud. "And we'll have to assume that everyone is telling the truth. Otherwise, we've got nothing at all."

"Agreed," Jonathan said.

"I concur," Boxers said. "But I'm not comfortable with it."

"For now, we have to assume that Armand Cortez—the entire C-Squared, for that matter—is just a distraction from what's going on. It's his right-hand man—" She looked to Dawkins.

"Lupo," he said. "Hector Alameda."

"Right Lupo is the only tie to the cartel for this, and only insofar as he's leveraging the mule network."

"Where are you going with this?" Venice asked.

"I don't know yet. Just stick with me as I connect the dots. The VX is everything. That's the reason for the panic south of the border, and it's the reason why the Kendall boys were kidnapped." Back to Dawkins: "How smart is this Lupo guy?"

"I don't know how to answer that. He doesn't impress me as stupid, but I'm pretty sure you won't find a Phi Beta Kappa key in his pocket. What are you thinking?"

Gail continued thinking aloud. "Let's assume he's not sophisticated, electronics-wise. Let's assume that he doesn't cover his cybertracks as well as he should." She bored her gaze into Venice, as if hoping that Mother Hen would figure out where she was going without having to articulate the details.

"Lupo is the pivot point," Venice said, her eyes growing wide with the realization. "If we can reconstruct his communications lines—"

"We can find the kidnappers," Jonathan said, completing the circuit. "Right?"

"Yes," Venice said. "Well, indirectly, but that's the bottom line."

"How can you do that?" Boxers asked. "You're going to get the chatter between him and the Chechen guy from Mexico. It doesn't take a Phi Beta Kappa key to know that it's stupid to deal directly with the people in the field. That's way too solid a line back to yourself."

"But we can find the go-between," Jonathan said. "At least we'll have a good shot at it."

"Don't forget that terrorism is a business," Gail said. "Jihadis understand economy and efficiency as well as any other businessmen. We know now that they have a tie to Tennessee. Tennessee is close enough to the site of the kidnapping that maybe they took the kids to the same place. If we can find that place—"

"We can find the kids," Boxers said.

"And, maybe, the so-called special product," Dawkins said.

"That's a lot of assuming," Venice said.

Jonathan agreed. "Follow the evidence where it takes you, Ven. Let us know what you need from us. How are you on sleep?"

"Better than any of you are," Venice said. "I can keep going."

"I can't," Boxers said. "I know the clock is ticking, but I need a couple of hours of shut-eye. You guys got to sleep on the plane."

"Go take a nap," Jonathan said. "In fact, everybody but Venice take a three-hour break. Dawkins, you can crash on the sofa in my office."

"What happens in three hours?" Dawkins asked.

"By then," Jonathan said, "I will have found a way to talk to Connie Kendall."

"How are you going to do that?" Boxers asked.

Jonathan winked. "I know people," he said.

Chapter Twenty-two

Sandra Grosvenor pressed her lips into a tight line as color flooded her cheeks. "We had a deal," she said.

James Abrenio sat tall in the guest chair opposite her desk, his hands folded atop his crossed legs. His intent was to project neutrality. Peace. But it felt a little like reading a newspaper in the middle of a gang fight. "I thought we did," he said.

"No, James. You *told* me we had a deal. Based on your word, I told the attorney general that we had a deal. Immunity and witness protection. Do you know how many people that involves?"

"Let's be fair, Sandy," Abrenio said. "You can't reasonably hold me accountable for people you spoke to before you should have."

"I did that, counselor, because you told me that it was a sure thing."

"There's no such thing. But none of this is relevant because I am not now, nor was I ever, the decision-maker here."

Grosvenor leaned forward against her desk, clearly preparing angry words, but then she stopped herself.

Abrenio could almost hear her brain churning as she gathered her emotions. Grosvenor's office was a study in contradictions. The permanent parts of the interior—the paneled walls and wainscoting, the polished hardwoods and towering windows—were the stuff of a Hollywood set, designed to project old-school legal authority. As the sitting U.S. attorney, Grosvenor had chosen to furnish the old-school room with decidedly new-school furniture. Abrenio would call it Danish modern. Or, maybe just cold and uncomfortable.

When she'd finished wrestling with her emotions, Grosvenor leaned back again and, in a calm voice, asked, "What happened here, James?"

"My official answer is, I don't know. Connie was never enthralled by the idea of the plea deal, but I thought I had sold her on it. I helped her see that immunity and WitSec were the best options, long-term, for her children. That was late yesterday afternoon. By this morning, she'd changed her mind. I guess she got scared."

"Scared of what?"

Abrenio *piffed*. "Come on, Sandy. Put yourself in her shoes. Her husband is dead, her kids are . . . *separated* from her, and she's staring down the barrel at a really shitty forever. What's *not* to be scared of?"

Grosvenor took her time processing his words. "You said that's your *official* answer. What's your *unofficial* answer?"

"You mean the one for which I have no evidence but only a gut feeling?"

The U.S. attorney did her best to fake a smile. "Yeah, that one."

"I think somebody got to her," Abrenio said. "I think someone told her about her missing kids."

Grosvenor's features hardened. "I seem to remember you having strong feelings that she *should* know."

"Sandy, if you're going to keep slinging accusations my way, this meeting is over. You forget that I don't owe you a thing. You forget that I'm here doing Uncle Sam a favor for a fraction of the fee I could otherwise be making. There will not be another warning. Next shot you fire, I'm just walking away." Abrenio had been planning for this moment, and he could see that his words had hit the way he'd wanted them to.

Grosvenor tented her fingers for a few seconds, and then she spun her ultramodern high-backed ergonomic mesh chair around to face the window behind her. "You make a fair point," she said. "And I apologize. What makes you think that she knows?"

Abrenio had no intention of talking to the back of her chair. He remained silent until she spun back around to face him.

"Hi," he said with a sarcastic finger wave. "She summoned me."

"So? You're her attorney."

"We were scheduled to meet at eleven," Abrenio explained. "I'd spent last night reading over the plea deal, making sure that everything was what it should be, and I was going to review it with her and have her sign it. Then, at seven o'clock, straight up, I woke up to a phone call from the prison telling me that she was insisting on seeing me right away."

"Who was on the phone?"

"I don't know. He gave his name, but after waking

up like that, I was lucky to remember my own. He apologized, then told me that Connie needed to speak with me right away."

"Did he say why?"

"I asked, and he said he was just the messenger. So, I hauled my ass out of bed, showered, and drove out to Murder Mountain. Connie arrived at the interview room at about the same time I did, and she looked terrible."

"What does terrible mean?"

"Haggard," he said. "Like you expect someone to look after they've received news they don't know how to process. She didn't even want to sit. She just said the deal is off. Those were her words. *The deal is off.*"

"Why?" Abrenio asked. "What happened?"

Connie hugged herself, her hands clutching the opposite shoulders. "I just don't want to go through with it. The whole deal."

Abrenio stood and gestured to the other chair. "Please have a seat. Let's talk this through."

"There's nothing to talk about," she said. "I've been stewing over this all night, and I've just changed my mind." She swiped at tears. "It's my life, and it's my decision. Don't forget that I know my rights and my choices."

"Please, Connie," Abrenio coaxed. "Please have a seat. You summoned me all the way in here, so the least you could do is show me the courtesy of a little face time."

Keeping her eyes cast to the floor, Connie haltingly walked the three steps to the immovable chair and sat.

He thought it was interesting that the thought of inconveniencing him seemed to get through to her. It was equally interesting that she sat on the very front edge, as if ready to bolt at the slightest provocation.

"As your attorney," he said, "I owe you total honesty. Blunt honesty. So, here it is, Connie. I think you're lying to me. And here's why. We were scheduled to see each other anyway in just a couple of hours. You could have blown me off then. Instead, here we are."

Connie stared, unblinking, at a spot on the table that appeared to be about five inches in front of her lawyer. The way the muscles of her jaw churned, she might have been chewing gum.

He continued. "The natural thing for you to say here is that you didn't want me to waste any more of my time, but if that were truly the case, that would have been the message. But it wasn't. You brought me out, anyway. Do you want to know what I think?"

That got her attention. She rolled her gaze to meet his.

"I think you have something to tell me and you're trying to screw up the courage to do it."

Tears welled in her lids and spilled onto her cheeks. This time, she made no effort to stop them or to wipe them away. They splashed onto the stainless steel surface of the table.

Abrenio watched her in silence for the better part of a minute. In that time, she only looked away a couple of times. He felt that she was trying to tell him something, perhaps trying to communicate telepathically. And he suspected that he already knew what the message was.

"Are you afraid of talking to me?" he asked.

Her head twitched. Just a little. He read the movement as a yes.

"Did someone get to you? Deliver news to you that scared you?"

Another twitch.

"A visitor?"

Connie stared.

He leaned in much closer. "You didn't move there," *he whispered. "Does that mean no?"*

Twitch.

"Was it another inmate?"

Nothing.

Abrenio scowled. Not a visitor and not an inmate. Who else was there? He felt his eyes grow wide. "Was it a guard?"

This time, the twitch was a full-fledged nod, and her lip quivered. He reached across the table and opened his hand for hers. She presented them both.

"Is it about your boys?" Abrenio asked.

She mouthed "yes," but there was no sound.

"Did a guard threaten them?"

Connie turned nearly backward in her chair as she looked back at the door.

"You're safe in here," Abrenio said. "What you say with me stays with me." His stomach flipped a little as he heard his own words. This was not his playground. He had no idea what kind of recording equipment they might have in place. Just because he didn't repeat what she told him didn't mean that others weren't listening.

"The guard didn't actually threaten them," she whispered. "He delivered a message from someone else. He seemed very uncomfortable delivering it. I'd say he looked scared."

"Who was it?"

"I won't tell you that," she said.

"Why?"

"You lied to me, didn't you?" Connie's face looked startled, as if the question had just popped into her head.

Abrenio waited for the rest.

"You knew that Ryder and Geoff were kidnapped," she said. "You've known it for some time. I knew you were holding something back last time we talked."

Obfuscation made no sense at this point. "Yes," he said. "Well, no. I knew that they'd gone missing. I suspected that they'd been kidnapped, but I didn't know that. I still don't know that."

Connie's sadness dissolved to anger, but she kept her voice low. "You've put them in danger. They could be killed."

"No," Abrenio said. "That's bullshit. I'll stipulate that they're in danger, but I didn't put them there. I'll even cop to withholding information that I probably should have shared with you, but in the absence of hard evidence, the plea deal was and is the best option for your family."

He let that sink in for a few seconds.

"The message you got. Was it from Armand Cortez? Is he the one who nabbed your kids?"

Another panicky look over her shoulder. "Oh, my God," she said. "How did my life come to this?"

"Focus. If it was Cortez, then that's all the more reason to go ahead with the plea deal."

Connie brought her hands to her face as if to squeeze away the fear. "No," she said. "It's far worse than that."

* * *

As Abrenio replayed to Grosvenor the details of his jailhouse confab with Connie Kendall, he decided to leave out the part about the chemical weapons. His client was in deep enough legal waters without having to worry about that, too. "What do you plan to do to find and protect the children now?"

"Did she give you the note?"

Abrenio shook his head. "The note instructed her to destroy it. She tore it up and flushed it down the toilet."

"And she refused to identify the guard?"

"How big a list is there to choose from?" Abrenio replied. "Only a couple of them have the authority to interact with her."

"When did this meeting happen?" Grosvenor asked. "With the guard, I mean."

"In the wee hours," Abrenio said. "Just check the surveillance footage and you'll have your man."

"Did she tell you exactly what the note said about her children?"

"I didn't press for a quote," Abrenio said. That wasn't entirely true, but he didn't want to open the door to her involvement with the weapons shipments. "But the gist was that they'd taken the children as collateral to keep Connie from revealing secrets about what they were doing on behalf of their clients."

Grosvenor blew a dismissive puff of air. "Clients, huh? That's a rather generous term for a cartel mule."

Abrenio didn't rise to the bait, but he squirmed at the thought of allowing her to assume the untruth that Cortez was the man who ordered the kidnappings and killings. Not that the C-Squared hadn't ordered its share of both over the years.

"This is an emergency, Sandy, yet you don't seem too moved by it. You've got to recover her children."

She spun in her chair again to face once more out the window. "It would help if you had seen the note," she said. "It would help if we had the name of the guard who presented it to her, or if we had even a single piece of evidence that what you say is true actually happened."

"Dammit, Sandy, will you at least do me the courtesy of looking at me while we speak?"

When she returned, she looked annoyed. Or, maybe she looked bored.

"I don't understand your resistance to protecting two minor children. If you can find them and vouch for their security, Connie Kendall will give you everything you want."

"Will she, James?" She tented her fingers again, a gesture that he was coming to despise. "Or will that deal be another launching spot for a promise she doesn't intend to keep? Do you know what I think?" She leaned way forward, elbows on the Lucite desktop, fingers still tented. "I think this is one big delaying tactic. I think she's buying time for Armand Cortez to pull some miracle out of his behind."

Abrenio hadn't seen this side of Sandy Grosvenor before. Could it be that she really didn't care? Was it possible to prosecute so many people, build so many cases to prove guilt (and, inevitably, to conceal innocence), that the humanity didn't matter anymore?

"Suppose you're wrong, Sandy? Suppose the evidence is there, but you can't see it, in part because you're choosing not even to try? Suppose Connie Kendall is telling the truth, and those children truly are in harm's way. They're *children*, Sandy."

Her features remained hard as stone. "Then they're safe, aren't they?" she said. "Your client isn't saying a word. And I am going to do everything in my power to send her to the death chamber."

It was the viciousness more than anything that startled him. "No one is safe, Sandy. Not in the hands of—"

His mind flashed back to something Grosvenor had said earlier in their discussion. "Did you say you told the attorney general that Connie was going to sign the plea deal?"

"I did."

His stomach flipped. "Did you tell her personally, or did you tell her through an aide?"

"Through her personal assistant," Grosvenor said. "The attorney general is a busy—"

"Jesus, Sandy. Don't you realize what you have done?" He rose to his feet, one hand to his mouth, the other to his ear, a gesture of burgeoning panic. "You've killed those boys."

"Oh, for God's sake, James. Don't be so melodramatic."

He was done. This was a lost cause. Geoffrey and Ryder Kendall were in serious, mortal danger, and he had to figure out what to do about it. Maybe if he shared what Connie knew about shipments of chemical weapons into the country, he could whet the U.S. attorney's appetite for compromise. For help.

That would take time.

He didn't have time.

Those boys didn't have time.

All he needed in addition to a slowed clock was an idea.

"I'm out," he said. He pivoted and headed for her door.

"Out of what?" Grosvenor said, rising out of her own chair. "Where are you going?"

He didn't bother to answer. He didn't think she deserved one.

The Albert V. Bryan United States Courthouse in Alexandria, Virginia, was an imposing structure, standing on an urban island on Courthouse Square. This section of Old Town was nearly two hundred years younger than the kitschy and oh-so-precious colonial structures that lined the Potomac River on the Virginia side, and though the architects of the business development did their best to pull off a look of colonial charm, the odds were stacked against them when the buildings were ten stories tall.

Like all the other hundreds of federal buildings within a few miles of Washington, DC, this one teemed with security, in addition to the steady stream of armed cops and federal agents who poured in and out on their way to testify in the courtrooms housed inside.

That swarm of law enforcement officers (and the lobby's magnetometers) kept Jonathan and his team outside instead of inside, spread out to keep an eye on the rental Ford Escape that a lawyer named James Abrenio had been driving since his arrival in town from Michigan a few days ago. Somehow, Venice had been able to dig up the fact that he was the lawyer of record for Connie Kendall and that he wasn't local.

Abrenio had chosen to park underground, which made surveillance more of a challenge than Jonathan wanted it to be. People were smart to be paranoid in so densely populated an area, even more so given the proximity to the courthouse and other federal goings on. They were likewise smart to be wary of strangers they see hanging around in underground parking garages. The challenge for the Security Solutions team was to see without being seen and then move in on their subject quickly enough to cut off any escape, yet not so quickly as to trigger his defenses.

They didn't want to hurt him—quite the opposite, in fact—but he had no way of knowing that. The take-down would require finesse, which is why he'd assigned Boxers to park the Batmobile in as dark a spot as he could find, as close to Dawkins's rental as possible, with Gail sitting next to him.

Out on the street, Jonathan and Dawkins watched the courthouse exits from opposing sides of the building, while in Fisherman's Cove, Mother Hen watched the video feeds from inside the building. As she'd explained it to Jonathan, she only had limited access to the feeds on the courtroom levels, but she had unrestricted views of who was coming and going. He hoped that her access to facial recognition software would take some of the pressure off of them to scan every face they saw.

They'd been in place for well over half an hour—maybe forty-five minutes—having picked up Abrenio's rental about fifteen miles outside Alexandria. The company from which the Michigan lawyer had rented his car had installed GPS trackers in all its fleet vehicles. Once Venice had found the vehicle make, model, and VIN, she'd been able to track his progress at every turn until he entered the garage. From there, they just had to park and wait.

Jonathan could think of two or three good reasons for Abrenio to make the drive all the way in from West Virginia to meet in the courthouse, but none of them mattered. What did matter was that they knew where he was, and he'd soon have no choice but to listen to what they had to say.

The radio bud popped in Jonathan's ear, which meant it popped in everyone else's ears, too. "Scorpion, Mother Hen," Venice said. "Your target is leaving the building via the doors on the western side. He's passing through the security barriers now. He should be visible to you in about a minute."

"I copy," Jonathan said. He'd set his radio to VOX to keep his hands free. "That's my side. Big Guy and Gunslinger, you know what to do?"

"On our way," Boxers said.

"Thor, you hang back fifty yards or so until he's fully committed to the parking lot, then close the distance."

"Copy."

"One other thing," Venice said. "I don't know how meaningful this is, but it feels important to me. One of the employees of the prison where Connie Kendall is being held just turned up dead. His name was Sid Hoffman. Pretty senior among the correctional officers. A lieutenant, I think."

Jonathan felt the bloom of dread. "Any word on cause of death?"

"Nothing definitive," she said. "But the police are treating it as a homicide."

"If it walks like a duck and quacks like a duck . . ." Boxers said.

"Okay, team," Jonathan groaned. "This shit's about to get interesting."

Chapter Twenty-three

It had been sunny when James Abrenio had arrived at the courthouse, so he'd decided to leave his overcoat in the car. Now that the sun had slipped behind the clouds, the sudden drop in temperature gave him a chill as he exited the western side of the building. Two months ago, when the temperatures had hovered in the eighties, Courthouse Square would have been packed with people sitting on benches, sipping coffee and eating ice cream. Now, the benches were all but empty, except for one guy in the distance who was just now rising to his feet.

Abrenio had been lucky to find a spot in the garage only two levels down. He entered via the driveway and turned to his right to descend the concrete steps.

Now that he was free of Sandra Grosvenor's office, he wasn't sure what lay ahead for him. What the hell had he been thinking to say yes to this thankless assignment? He'd allowed his ego to get the best of him. How often, after all, does a private citizen get to help in taking down a major drug ring?

"Let no good deed go unpunished," he said aloud as he reached the second basement level.

The first challenge to finding your car in an underground garage was to remember which direction to turn when you cleared the door. He'd left his Escape to the right of the door, about ten slots down.

Busy morning, he thought. It looked like the entire level was full now, where there had been dozens of open slots only an hour or so ago.

The second challenge was to remember what the ass end of a strange car looked like. The front and sides were easy to spot in a crowd, but not so much the back. It helped in his case that his rental was red.

Abrenio was twenty feet away when he pulled the fob from the pocket of his suit pants and unlocked the doors with the push of a button.

"James!"

He jumped. The sound had come from behind and to his left. He turned to see an attractive woman of indeterminate age approaching with a slight limp. She wore casual clothes—khaki pants with lots of pockets with a forest green shirt that also had lots of pockets, along with a black jacket whose zippered front flapped open.

"James Abrenio!"

He took a protective step backward. "Do I know you?"

She offered a warm smile and said, "Not yet, but we're about to spend some time chatting." She raised her right hand to display the small gold badge that she'd palmed. "Special Agent Gerarda Culp. FBI."

His stomach fluttered.

"And I'm Special Agent Contata," said a much larger voice from the vicinity of his rental. He pivoted that way to behold the largest human being he had ever seen. Gigantor likewise displayed a badge. "We need to talk."

Somehow these two did not feel like federal agents to Abrenio. They felt menacing. "Have I done something wrong?" he asked.

"I don't know, have you?" the big man countered.

Abrenio's instinct was to run, but as they closed the distance, that option evaporated. "What do you want to talk about?"

"Do you mind stepping over to our vehicle?" the lady agent said, gesturing to someplace behind her enormous friend.

"Yes, I do mind," Abrenio said. "Whatever you have to say, you can say right here, out in the open."

"Does it have to be difficult?" the big agent said. "Does it have to get violent?"

This definitely did not feel right. He'd attended a training class on self-defense tactics for professionals, and the takeaway from that was very clear. You never get in the car with a stranger. Hard stop.

But was there a law enforcement exception?

He'd be foolish to fight, foolish to attempt to run. Another strategy was to yell as loudly as he could to draw as much attention as possible. Witnesses could only play to his benefit.

As if on cue, the stairwell door opened. The newcomer was dressed in the same style as the others, and he looked vaguely familiar.

"You really don't have a play here, James," the man

said. He likewise produced a badge. "Special Agent Bonner." It was the guy he'd seen rising from the bench in Courthouse Square.

Abrenio felt his options dwindling to nothing. "I don't believe that you're FBI," he said. "Let me see more than a badge. Let me see your creds wallet." Anybody with access to a novelty shop could find a lookalike FBI badge, but the full credentials, complete with watermarks and a picture, were hard to fake.

"We want to talk to you about Connie Kendall," Bonner, said.

Abrenio felt his knees wobble. These were the people who sent the note to Connie.

"James?" It was the lady again, Culp. "Would it help if we told you that we're on your side? And would it help if we told you that we have proof that Ryder and Geoff Kendall were kidnapped?"

"I-I don't know what you're talking about," Abrenio tried, but he heard the pitifulness of his own efforts.

"B-bullshit," the mountainous main said, mocking his stammer.

There was no way for these people to know these things without themselves being the perpetrators. "I'm just the lawyer," he said.

"Then protect the interests of your client," Culp said. She stepped closer, and her smile broadened. "Connie Kendall possesses information that could save the lives of thousands of people, potentially. Or cost an equal number of lives. And I'm not sure she even knows that she possesses it."

The stairwell door opened again, this time revealing a third man with the same tactical sartorial style. "Yeah," the man said. "I'm one, too."

Agent Contata, the huge man who had closed the distance between them by half, said, "Hey, Abrenio. Look at me."

The lawyer craned his neck to look in the other man's eyes.

Contata said, "You need to trust us."

Agent Bonner added, "We can explain everything to you, but not out here. We want to drive around a little and talk. If you don't want to buy what we're selling, we'll drop you back here, and you'll have to live with a lot of deaths on your conscience."

"Starting with those two boys," the big man said.

"And how am I going to do all of this?"

The huge agent said, "You'll start by giving us what we need to know to rescue Ryder and Geoff."

The newest guy to arrive—the one who hadn't bothered to give his name—took a step forward. "Hey," he said. "Be honest with yourself. Do you really see a choice here?"

Venice missed Derek every day. Every single day. He'd lived as a hacker nerd, and he'd died a hero. She wanted to blame Jonathan for bringing violence to the mansion that night, but she knew that was unfair. The reality was that in the end, Jonathan had saved her life.

She felt empty. Derek had understood the world of ones and zeroes in a way that no one in her life could ever duplicate. For those brief months when he was in her life, he had introduced her to newness in every aspect of living, from the bedroom to exotic foods to some of the secret capabilities of the National Security Agency, his employer.

Can a relationship have a *legacy* after such a short period? Venice thought so. She felt him in her life even in his absence. He was there in her professional life, too, manifested in the tools and access codes he had left behind, allowing her to witness and eavesdrop at unprecedented levels. The facial recognition programs alone had changed everything. She'd learned through Derek that once a face is chosen, it can be followed wherever it goes.

From automatic teller machines to gas station security feeds, cameras were always active. Through software deployed by the NSA to *not* spy on American citizens (*cough cough*), the intelligence community could scour the millions of images obtained every second from the tens of millions of security cameras in the United States alone. When the identified subject was spotted, a cyberbell would ring, and the target's location would be noted. Because even the speed of light has limits, the system suffered from an unavoidable built-in delay that could range from minutes to hours— mostly hours, especially since Venice needed to keep her profile low and well-scrubbed—but at least this stuff was possible.

Sitting in her office in the firehouse, Venice had loaded the program with the verified images of the Kadyrov brothers. Even though they were identical twins, few twins were truly identical. If the images were clear enough from the security cameras, the software could detect the differences that the human eye would miss.

While the software churned and worked its magic, she turned her attention to finding out whatever she could about the Kadyrovs. She had to start somewhere, so she targeted the community surrounding Blanton, Tennessee, the area where the Ferguson family was killed. This was where her skills as a hacker came into play. The trick to hacking was to think like the people whose lives you were trying to spy on.

Every community was wired these days, and local chat spaces had replaced the barbershop and church vestibule as the place to gossip. Venice figured that good-looking twins with foreign accents were likely to attract attention.

A search on "Kadyrov" produced nothing beyond the Homeland Security alerts she'd expected. They were not tied to Blanton.

Venice decided that they would have to be beyond stupid to use their real names, so that seemed to be a dead end. But dead ends didn't mean impossible searches. She just needed to shift her approach. And her targets, too.

When most people thought of social media, they thought of the big names, the Facebooks and Twitters. In Venice's experience, those major platforms were of only moderate use in searches like this one. Not only were they well moderated for the most part, they were also filled with fluff. Thoughts that were deemed by major corporations to be dangerous—read, contradictory to what the corporate executives believed—were deleted outright. That left only approved political screeds and cat pictures. They were precisely the wrong places to turn to dig up the kind of dirt that she was looking for.

She wanted the outlaw sites, the underground sites, where savvy gossipers could talk smack about their neighbors with impunity. Every community had them.

The challenge was to find them and then determine the right search parameters.

She got lucky, hitting a smudge of pay dirt within the first half hour. On a site named Fences Make Great Neighbors, she found a brief thread with the subject line "Tall Dark Foreigners on Hawks Mtn Road."

> **HootinHollerin:** Hottie alert! Hottie alert! Any1 know anything about the hot dark twins on hawks mtn?
> **Blinkinblues:** If its who ur thinking of kinda rude.
> **HootinHollerin:** Big eyes. Hair I'd kill for. Makin me wet
> **Blinkinblues:** That's them. I said hi. Told me to eff off.
> **Hootinhollerin:** ROFL!!! Effing is just I been thinkin of!
> **Blinkinblues:** LOLOLOL!!!

"That's the future of America," Venice mumbled. In her mind, everyone who posted that kind of chatter was thirteen or less. How proud their parents must be. At least Blinkinblues looked for personality. For sure, though, the description of the twins fit the Kadyrov brothers.

And she had a new search parameter: Hawk's Mountain Road.

Venice pulled up the public real estate database and searched for Hawk's Mountain Road in Blanton, Tennessee. There wasn't much to it. Maybe two miles long, it defined the eastern edge of three properties and the western edge of two. All five of those properties were huge, with the smallest coming in at thirty-four acres.

She scrolled to the sales records, and she knew she'd found the right place. Of the five properties along Hawk's Mountain Road, only one of them had changed hands in the past five years. Eighteen months ago, the fifty-seven acres at 27998 Hawk's Mountain Road were purchased by Sundial Properties, LLC, for $945,450. Venice would do the research later, but she harbored no doubt that that the company was a shell.

Pleased with herself, Venice leaned back in her Aeron chair and folded her arms. She was 95 percent at where she wanted to be. The gushings of a fawning teenager weren't enough for her to commit all the resources that Digger would bring to the address she identified for him.

Again, there was a way. She just needed to find it.

Leaning back into her computer, she returned to the underground social media sites, this time concentrating on Hawk's Mountain Road. The trick here was to count not just on the search terms but also on the spelling permutations for each of them. First, there was the common internet-ization of the English language, and that was fairly instinctive for Venice. Far more difficult were the spelling attempts made by posters who had no idea that they were getting things wrong.

Apparently, with the exception of Hootinhollerin and her friend, the Kadyrovs kept a pretty low profile. That made sense to Venice. When your purpose in life was to kill innocent people, staying under everyone's radar seemed like the way to go.

After forty-five minutes of ideas that led to fruitless searches, she rose from her chair and wandered to the

War Room next door, where she raided the little fridge for a bottle of sparkling water. "What are you missing?" she asked the empty room. Sometimes, by speaking her thoughts aloud, ideas broke through.

"They've got to eat. They've got to buy soap and whatever you need to make VX. That had to come from someplace."

Probably not Amazon, she thought. One did not just place an order for the paraphernalia to support one's sulfonated organophosphorous compounds, whatever the heck that meant. But really, how were they getting deliveries of . . . stuff?

If they used a trucking service, she could dial into the records of the trucking company to find at least a thread to pull on.

For all she knew, they used helicopters—

"Wait." She froze in place, trying to squeeze something out of her brain that she knew she'd seen. Buried somewhere in all the posts she'd read, there was a reference to a helicopter. Something annoying. Somebody annoyed.

Bringing her unopened Perrier with her, she darted back to her office and rolled her chair back under the keyboard.

Five minutes later, she had what she'd been looking for. She was reaching for the phone to call Digger with an update when her computer dinged. The results from the facial recognition software were beginning to come in.

She navigated to the site to take a look. "Oh, Lordy," she moaned. Dozens of images had already come in, and more were loading every second. Venice wasn't familiar enough with the software yet to know how to effectively sort the images—or if that was even possible—so she was stuck scrolling through them one at a time.

Her initial impression was that Khasan Kadyrov got out and around more than his brother did, and even he did not wander very far. The vast majority of the images came from streetside security cameras, the kind that were designed to keep an eye on parking lots and ATMs but were always recording. Khasan was a loner, and he had a penchant for 7-Eleven coffee and pastries. His interactions with clerks appeared businesslike, if not friendly. He drove an old-model Chevy pickup truck that he would probably describe as green but that probably hadn't borne a recognizable hue in years.

It occurred to Venice as she was scrolling through image after image how little anonymity was left for Americans these days. Did people really understand that their likeness was recorded dozens of times a day or how easy it was to tap into their webcams and smart phones? Everything everybody did these days left an electronic footprint, and the only thing that kept every move from being observed by strangers was the will of the strangers not to take a peek.

Venice felt her mind wandering as she catalogued photo after photo, until one in particular brought her back into focus. Brothers Aslan and Khasan together in a little town called Winston, West Virginia, meeting with two other people in a park that was within the view and focal length of a hardware store parking lot.

The meeting didn't look like a friendly one. The four of them stood abnormally close, which to Venice meant that they were speaking in reduced tones. Aslan looked over his shoulder several times, as if nervous that someone might approach. She scrolled in to get a closer look at the others. The one with his back to the camera was merely a profile as he clearly listened to what Khasan was saying. Venice didn't think there were enough features visible for a successful run through the facial recognition software, but she gave it a shot, anyway. He appeared to have a distinctive port wine stain over his left eye, so maybe that would increase the chances.

Then she ran the other stranger, and the results were nearly immediate. Timur Yamadayev. When a name popped up that fast, it was ordinarily for good reason.

In this case, for *very* good reason.

Chapter Twenty-four

No lawyer in the history of lawyering looked more like a lawyer than this James Abrenio guy. With his tailored suit and perfectly knotted tie against his pressed and spotless white shirt, he was exactly the image that any defendant would be pleased to see in his or her corner. He seemed hesitant about getting into the Batmobile, but not terrified. Jonathan wasn't sure why he found that so interesting. Perhaps Abrenio likewise understood that a clock was quickly ticking down to zero.

They entered the Batmobile through the back door. Dawkins made his way to the third row of backseats, while Jonathan and Gail sat next to each other on the second row. Abrenio sat alone in the first row of backseats, facing the rear, and Boxers drove.

Once they were out of the garage and on the open roadway, Jonathan decided to get right to it. "We need to speak with your client. Connie Kendall."

Abrenio laughed through a scowl. "And I need pigs to fly. Mine will happen first."

"Nothing she says to us can or will be used against her," Jonathan said.

"You don't have that authority, Agent Bonner. In fact, I just left the office of the lady who *does* have that authority, and she's light years away from granting immunity."

"Unless Connie cooperates," Gail said.

Abrenio's jaw locked.

"Which she can't do," Jonathan said, "because her children have been taken hostage. Am I close?"

Color rose in Abrenio's cheeks, but he said nothing. He was waiting for the rest, unwilling to overcommit. Jonathan liked this guy, liked the way he played his hand. He had to be unnerved, yet he still was protecting the interests of his client.

Jonathan changed tacks. "Okay, maybe asking for an audience with Connie was too big an ask. Instead, how 'bout I ask you to talk to her for us?"

"Agent Bonner," Abrenio said, crossing his legs. Jonathan read it as faux calmness. "As long as you keep speaking in riddles, you'll get nothing from me. Can we begin by stipulating that none of you are FBI agents?"

Jonathan let his smile sneak through. "Assume what you like, Counselor, but I'm not yet prepared to take that step. Be assured, however, that I am on the side of Connie's children. My team and I are going to rescue them."

Abrenio cocked his head to the side. Jonathan always thought of that as a puppy-dog head tilt. "You know where they are?"

"Not exactly," Jonathan confessed. "But we think that Connie does, even if she doesn't realize it yet."

"You need to give me more than that," Abrenio said.

"We know that Connie was running more than just drugs for the cartels," Jonathan said. "In fact, we know that it was more her husband who was running them than she, but he's dead and she's left holding the bag. We believe that if we can find the so-called *special product* that she and her husband delivered, then we will find her boys. But tick-tock."

Jonathan could tell from Abrenio's demeanor that his theory had scored a direct hit. "What's ticking?" he asked.

"Every clock you can think of," Jonathan replied. "They've been testing their special product. Killed some people. That means they're on the verge of deploying it. Once it's deployed, Connie and her children become irrelevant."

Abrenio's eyes widened as he considered what Jonathan was telling him.

"The opposite is also true," Gail said. This was the way they'd planned the confrontation. Jonathan would present the reality, and then Gail would present the glimmer of hope. "Once we rescue Geoff and Ryder, Quinto Alvarez loses all of his leverage over the Kendall family."

Abrenio recoiled at the sound of Alvarez's name.

"What?" Gail said. "You look surprised. Yes, we know about the Jungle Tigers' involvement in the special product. His involvement with the *nerve agent*. We even know that Armand Cortez is unaware and that some guy named Lupo is the go-between."

While she gave that a few seconds to sink in, Jonathan watched closely for some indication of what he was thinking. Abrenio would have made a good poker player. His face showed surprise, but little else.

Gail continued, "And none of this that we know could possibly be used in court, so relax. We share this with you to let you know that you have nothing to hide and everything to gain by helping us find out where her deliveries were made, particularly in rural Tennessee."

Jonathan's phone buzzed in his pocket. He'd have ignored it if more people knew the number, but he knew it would be Venice and that she wouldn't interrupt without good reason. He turned away from Abrenio as he clicked the connection on. "I can't say much on my end," he said.

"You don't need to," Venice said. "I know where they are. I can give you an address."

Jonathan cut his eyes to Abrenio, who still seemed engaged with what Gail was saying to him. "I'll get back to you," he said to Venice, and he clicked off.

"Agent Contata," Jonathan said a little too loudly to get Boxers' attention. "Pull over, please. We've taken up enough of Mr. Abrenio's time."

Boxers said, "Yep."

Gail looked confused, but she knew better than to ask questions right now. They had to go another half block or so before Big Guy could steer the Batmobile into the parking lot of a '60s-era strip mall. It was anchored by a national pharmacy chain.

"Sorry for the inconvenience," Jonathan said to Abrenio as they came to a stop. "Turns out we don't need your help after all."

"You know where the Kendall boys are?" Abrenio seemed genuinely jazzed.

Jonathan offered a thin smile, then opened the door. "Have a good day, Counselor."

Abrenio didn't move.

"Don't make me drag you out," Boxers said.

"No need." Abrenio said. "One question, and please be honest with me."

"If I answer, I will tell the truth," Jonathan said. "How's that?"

"It'll have to do. My question is, have you told the truth? Other than, say, who you really are?"

Jonathan definitely liked this guy. "Yes, we have. And I'll go a step further, just in case you were wondering. Assume for a moment that we truly are the federal agents we pretend to be. I swear to you that no one in our chain of command knows what we know. There's still a great deal of value in bringing the chemical agent element to the attention of the U.S. attorney."

Abrenio grinned. "I'm glad to hear that," he said.

"But you have to hurry," Gail said. "For Connie's sake."

"Why is that?"

"Does the name Sid Hoffman mean anything to you?"

"Should it?"

Jonathan explained, "Sid Hoffman is a guard up on Murder Mountain. A senior one. Lieutenant, I think. Or, I should say, *was* a senior guard. He was found murdered a couple of hours ago."

"They're getting desperate," Gail said. "We're concerned that the next day or two might get very bloody."

Jonathan got out of the Batmobile first to make it easier for Abrenio to exit. As the lawyer hit the ground and turned to leave, Jonathan offered his hand. "One more thing," he said.

Abrenio accepted the hand offered to him by Agent Bonner, or whoever he really was. "What's that?"

Bonner's grip grew tighter. "I promise you that we are the best thing to happen to your client in a long, long time."

Abrenio knew there was more, so he waited for it.

"Please understand that we could also become the worst thing in the history of forever to happen to you." This man's eyes were a shade of blue that Abrenio had never seen before, and they burned with a nuclear intensity. "I don't mean that as a threat. I mean it as a promise."

James felt the skin pucker across his shoulders and down his back.

"This meeting never happened," Bonner said. "You never met us. From this point on, you handle the details with your client however you see fit. In a few hours, you'll get a text from an unknown, untraceable number. Stay close to your phone."

Through the whole ordeal, this was the first flash of real fear. "My phone number is private," he said. "No one knows it unless I give it to them."

Bonner smiled. "It's kind of cute that you think that. If the text says 'Alpha,' you'll know that we have the boys and that they are safe. If the text reads 'Bravo,' then you'll know we don't know where they are after all."

James cleared his throat. "What about the rest?" he asked. "You know. The . . . other option."

"Which option is that?" Bonner asked.

"You know," James squirmed. Was he really going to make him say the words? "What if you find the boys but . . . something happens to them?"

Bonner stood a little taller as he drew a sharp breath and held it for a couple of seconds. Then he let it go and said, "Have a good day, Mr. Abrenio. Here's hoping that you never see me again. If you do, prepare yourself for a long and difficult conversation." With that, the man climbed back into the Suburban, this time into the shotgun seat. The door had barely latched before the vehicle was headed out of the parking lot.

James watched after them for a few seconds, trying to make all the pieces fit, and then he scanned the surrounding streets and buildings to get his bearings. He hadn't been paying attention to their route as they were driving along, but they must have filled the time with just a series of turns because he was only a few blocks away from the courthouse and his car. As he walked back, he placed a call to Murder Mountain.

He needed to speak with Connie Kendall again.

After that, he called Sandy Grosvenor. "I'm going to have good news for you," he told her after waiting two blocks of walking for her to come on the line. "But you're going to have to be patient."

"What does patient mean?" She was pissed and made no effort to hide it.

"Forty-eight hours at the most," he told her. "Hopefully less." The red hand icon on the crossing light changed to the white silhouette of a man walking, but he waited to let the approaching car make a turn in front of him.

"What's changed?" Grosvenor asked.

"I can't tell you that," James replied. "Not yet, anyway."

"Don't play games with me, James."

"I don't play games, Sandy."

"I've already told you—"

"Please shut up," James snapped. He'd had it with Grosvenor's attitude. "If things break my way even a little, I'm going to hand you the Holy Grail. If not, then you'll have only lost a couple of days."

"That's too long—"

"I'm done with you for now." He clicked off and laughed out loud. "Damn," he said. "That felt better than it probably should have."

Boxers took a few minutes to change out the license plates and registration again. When he was done and Dawkins had moved back up to the second row of seats, they called Venice and put her on the speaker. "Okay, Mother Hen, what do you have?"

Venice took a few minutes to fill them in on what she'd discovered. She started with the hot young foreigners, but a nighttime helicopter landing on the property seemed to make it unarguable.

"Check your GPS," Mother Hen said. "You need to get started for Hawk's Mountain Road in Blanton, Tennessee."

"Is that where the Kendall boys are?" Jonathan asked. The air inside the Batmobile had turned electric.

"I can't say that for sure," she said. "But it's got to be where the VX is. There are also images of the Kadyrov twins meeting with a man named Timur Yamadayev and another man who I can't quite see."

"Yamadayev is Daud Masaev's number one in the U.S.," Dawkins said. "That's definitely a tie to the VX. Tell me about this other man. What did he look like?"

"I already told you," Venice said. "They were standing four-square. He was the one with his back to the camera. Average height and weight, but he was wearing a jacket, so more detail is hard to define."

"You didn't see anything at all?"

"There's one frame," Venice explained, "a partial profile. He appears to have a port wine stain on his face—"

"Oh, shit!" Everyone in the Batmobile spoke as one.

Jonathan shot a panicked look to Dawkins. "The other doctor?"

"What other doctor?" Venice asked.

Jonathan replied, "A monster. A torturer." When possible, he tried to spare her the goriest details.

"The GPS says it'll take seven hours to get there," Venice said.

"What do you bet I can do it in six?" Boxers said.

When they clicked off, Jonathan tried not to reimagine that awful torture video recast with children.

"Now I'm hoping the Kendall boys *aren't* there," Gail said.

"And I'm more certain than ever that they are," Jonathan said.

Chapter Twenty-five

A while ago—hours?—Officer Al had opened the hatch and thrown down the blankets from the bed. They'd barely hit the ground before the hatch slammed shut again.

If Ryder kept his knees up close to his chest and the blanket wrapped around him as tightly as it would go, he could get warm enough to stop shivering. The trick was to have the edges pulled down tight enough to cover his feet and to not let any gaps open up. Even the smallest opening created a draft. He didn't know how long they'd been down in this place, but he knew it had to have been at least a day. Probably more. For most of it, Geoff had been pressed up tight against him. Neither of them had said anything in a long time.

If Geoff was mad at him, that was fine. He'd earned that. Ryder knew now that it had been stupid to try to get away—knew now that Geoff had been right all along—and he felt terrible about it. He'd apologized five or six times already, and Geoff had told him it was all right, but Ryder knew better. There was nothing all right about any of this, and for no better reason than being impatient, he'd made it all worse. They were down here in this shithole because of that. Geoff had begged him not to try to run, but he'd done it, anyway.

If they ever got out of this—no, they were *going* to get out of this. *When* they got out of this, Ryder was going to do something great and good. He didn't know what it would be, but it would be big and important. For the whole time that he'd been down here, he'd been bargaining with God. *When* he was delivered from this place, he was going to be the best damn kid in the world. Ever.

He thought he might have fallen asleep a couple of times, but he couldn't be sure. He'd never been in a place that was so dark that your eyes never adjusted. It was always like black ink on black velvet. He didn't even know if his eyes were open or closed, so it was hard to know if he was awake or asleep.

Geoff was asleep, for sure, unless he snored while he was awake. On a different day, in a different place, Ryder would have poked him and told him to shut the hell up. Now, though, today, in this place, he kind of liked the sound. It helped him forget a little.

He knew that Officer Al and Officer Kim were still here because he could hear their footsteps and the sound of furniture scooting around. He could also smell food cooking. Baked beans, maybe? He didn't think even for a second that they were going to share their food.

The guards talked a lot, but Ryder couldn't make out the words. They'd laughed a few times, but they'd also sounded like they were mad. The words had the quick, punchy rhythm of an argument.

Ryder hadn't been paying attention all that closely in the beginning, but he was pretty sure that each of the arguments—three of them in total, he thought—had come after a phone had rung, the muffled default tune that came with every smart phone. It was amazing what you could notice when there was nothing else to do but listen.

Ryder was shocked at how calm he felt. He'd done his crying, and he was still doing his praying, and if he thought too hard about where he was—in an underground room where people might never find them if Al and Kim went away—he could get his heart rate to spike. But for right now, he felt sort of at peace. What was going to happen was going to happen.

The phone rang again, and this time he held his breath to see if he could hear this end of the conversation.

The phone call didn't last very long, but this time the argument afterward was a big one. The two men shouted at each other. Ryder held his breath to listen and squeezed his eyes tightly shut, as if that could improve his hearing.

He thought he heard the word *kill*, but he couldn't swear to it. Maybe it was just the word he dreaded the most. There was lots of moving around this time, and something heavy dragged across the floor.

Before, when the arguments happened, they were over and done with quickly, but this one went on and on. He had no way to know how many minutes, but more than a few. A half hour, maybe?

"What's going on?" Geoff asked. He sounded groggy.

"I don't know," Ryder whispered. "Keep your voice down. They just got another phone call, and they started shouting. Something's happening."

"To us?"

"I don't know. I hope not."

"What do you think it is?"

"*Shh*. I can't—"

Quick footsteps overhead grew louder and then stopped closer than any of the others had been. The hatch made a loud *thunk*, and light poured into the space from the living room. The light brought a wash of warmth with it.

"—stupid idea," Officer Al was saying. "What's the sense of leaving that kind of evidence?"

"Hello, boys," Officer Kim said. He was dressed like a doctor, wearing a green suit with a V-neck just like they wore in medical shows. The shirt matched the pants, and his mask hung down on his chest like a little bib. "We're going to make a movie together."

Boxers couldn't quite close the deal at six hours, but he did make to Blanton, Tennessee, in six and a quarter. The GPS coordinates from Venice took them directly to Hawk's Mountain Road. They arrived at dusk, and Big Guy pulled the Batmobile off the rutted road into a tangle of bushes. If the satellite images were correct, the chances of anyone passing or noticing them at this spot were well south of slim. As the crow flies, they were less than a half mile from the Kadyrovs' house.

Presently, the field team sat in the first two rows of seats, concentrating on the video screen in the dashboard. From the driver's seat, Boxers worked the controls for Roxie, the latest in his obsessive purchases of aerial drones. In helping to design the specs for Batmobile 2.0, he'd made sure that Roxie's signal could be watched directly from the car's built-in color screen, thus bypassing the need to gather outside around a tiny laptop.

The property featured four structures, at least one of which appeared to be a barn and another that appeared to be a shed—or maybe a smaller barn. A small house sat nestled between those two buildings. It had the look of a playhouse, or maybe a guest house. Two windows on either side of a center door.

A much larger house sat about seventy-five yards downhill from the barn, the nearest of the other structures, this one surrounded by two layers of security fencing. An old pickup sat out front and looked the worse for wear. As Boxers cycled in and out of the thermal imagery view, the engine block printed as cool. Significant heat plumes from two chimneys told them that somebody was home, but it wasn't yet dark enough to expect lights to be turned on.

"Do you think they're in there?" Gail asked.

"Let's go take a peek," Boxers said.

"Not yet," Jonathan said. "Let's watch from here a little more. Get the lay of the land. We have no idea what we don't know." He wasn't sure what he was looking for, but he'd had his ass handed to him more times than he could count by walking unprepared into an unknown situation. "Whatever's happening in there has been going on for a long time. A few more minutes won't make that much difference."

"Said the hangman," Dawkins quipped. No one laughed.

Roxie flew a three-sixty around the main house. "Only two doors," Jonathan observed. "Windows are all closed."

"There's the source of their electricity," Boxers

said, pointing to a generator in a lean-to open shed on the red side—the right-hand side—of the main house.

Gail shot a forefinger to the screen. "Someone's arriving." A small SUV with its headlights on pulled off Hawk's Mountain Road into what looked like a span of woods.

Jonathan cranked his head around to see if he could see the action in real time through the back window. He couldn't. "Did anybody see that driveway when we were coming in?"

"I wasn't looking for it," Boxers said. "But no."

As they watched the screen, a man exited what looked to be an earthen berm to the left of the roadway and walked to the driver's window. They talked for half a minute, and then the man returned to his berm. A gate pivoted open.

"And that, lady and gentlemen," Jonathan said, "is why we take our time on thorough recon."

"The next Roxie is going to have a directional microphone," Boxers announced. "We'll get our movies with sound."

"Follow the truck," Jonathan said. "See if it's anybody we recognize."

Boxers fiddled with the exposure, making the image as bright as possible in the deepening dusk. As the image shifted, Jonathan could see now that the SUV was a Honda. Whether through a zoom lens or an altitude change, the image looked to be taken from only a few feet away.

The driver sat for a frustratingly long time after he'd pulled to a stop.

"Is he talking on the phone?" Gail asked.

"Looks like he might be," Jonathan said. The angle

and tinting of the glass made it difficult to discern details, but the shadow of the driver could very well have been talking on the phone.

When the driver's door finally opened, Jonathan found himself holding his breath in anticipation. "Be sure to snap singles in case he moves through the frame too fast."

"It's digital, Boss," Big Guy said. "Every frame is a single if I want it to be."

Jonathan blushed.

"Don't feel stupid," Boxers said. "Sometimes you just get tired of not hearing your own voice."

Jonathan flipped him off.

The driver stepped out of his door, then reached back inside and produced a drink cup with a straw in it. When he stood and turned, his features were clearly visible.

"Holy shit!" Dawkins exclaimed. "That's him! That's Timur Yamadayev."

That settled it. This was the place, and it was time to take it down.

"Can you get a peek through the windows now?" Jonathan asked.

"Is a wild bear Catholic?" Boxers moved the controls while never taking his eyes off the screen. The image dipped to nearly ground level and zoomed up to the glass. "For those who are concerned," Big Guy said, "Roxie is still thirty feet from the building."

Yeah, Jonathan didn't say. *We're all concerned as hell for the health of the toy.*

The window they'd chosen didn't show much. It was on the black side of the building—the back—and it revealed only a darkened space.

"Go around to the white side," Jonathan said. The front.

"He just went through the door," Boxers said. "A little risky to bring Roxie into everybody's eye line."

"I promise I'll buy you a new one if this one breaks," Jonathan said in a tone that was normally reserved for small children.

"Don't forget that you don't bounce as good as you used to," Big Guy grumbled.

The image shifted.

Roxie eased in closer. She cruised past the green pickup and the black Honda on the way to the front window. The lights were on inside now. The curtains were drawn, but they weren't very thick and they weren't pulled completely closed. There was enough of a gap to see glimpses of people as they moved around.

"I see two adults," Dawkins said.

"I don't recognize them," Jonathan said. "I thought we were going to find twins."

"What the hell is that one wearing?" Gail asked.

"Oh, holy shit," Boxers said.

"Surgical suit," Dawkins said.

"That's one of the Kendall boys!" Gail proclaimed. He was being dragged across the floor by his arm.

Jonathan felt his heart rate double. "Suit up, people."

"We don't have time for that," Boxers said.

"We've got to do this right, Big Guy," Jonathan insisted. "Night vision, speed, and violence. Three extra minutes." As he spoke, he exited the Batmobile and walked around back to the lift gate.

Chapter Twenty-six

Officer Kim offered his hand to help Ryder clear the hatchway, but he turned it down, choosing instead to put his hands on the floor and press himself up. When his waist was clear, he brought his leg up and stood. Then he turned around and helped Geoff up and out of the hole.

The look of dread in his little brother's face frightened him. Startled, he turned back toward the kitchen and saw that the place had been set up like a television studio. The big wooden table had been moved more to the center of the room and was surrounded by odd-looking lights on top of tall poles. Three cameras had been set up on tripods, and they were all pointed toward the table.

"What is this?" Ryder asked. His stomach was beginning to cramp.

"I told you," Kim said with a big smile. "We're going to make a movie."

"What about?" Geoff asked. He'd moved in very close to his brother. Ryder could feel his heartbeat.

"We need to have an official record," Officer Al explained. He smiled, but the smile wasn't right. "Nobody's going to hurt you."

"I don't believe you," Ryder said.

Officer Kim took a step forward and seemed to inflate. "Don't call us liars," he said. "I don't like it when people call me a liar."

Ryder couldn't take a step back without going back into the pit, so he sidestepped one pace to his left. "I-I wasn't calling you a liar," he stammered.

"Well, what do you call it?"

"He's scared," Geoff said. "He says stupid stuff when he's scared."

Ryder shot him a look, but it went ignored.

"We do this one thing," Officer Al said, "and things get a lot easier for you." There was that smile again. "I promise."

Officer Al reached behind his back and produced two pairs of handcuffs.

"We're going to be doing a little bit of theater," he said. "Our bosses can't know that we have you wandering around the camp freely, so I need you to let us put these on you."

Ryder circled away, with Geoff still glued to his side. This wasn't right.

"I know it sounds scary," the cop said. "I'd be scared, too, if I were you. I get it. But I promise it won't take long. Just long enough for a short video, and then we'll all be done. We might even have a pizza for you here somewhere."

That smile. It might as well have been on a mannequin. All mouth but nothing in the eyes. The eyes were just black and dead.

"We can just hold our arms behind our backs," Ryder suggested. "We can pretend."

"Or we can dislocate your elbows and pretend they're fine," Officer Kim said. By contrast, his smile seemed very real.

"We have to do this, boys," Officer Al said. "We really do. Please don't make it be a bad thing."

Shit, shit, shit. Ryder needed to do something. They needed to get out of here. They needed to run. *How'd that work for you last time?*

Officer Al went to Geoff first. "Let me see your left hand," he said.

Geoff looked to Ryder. *What do I do?*

Ryder had nothing. He stared through clouded vision as his little brother held out his skinny arm and the cop put one of the bracelets on. He did it softly, almost gently. The ratchets seemed unusually loud as they clicked shut. He didn't shut them tightly, though.

"Is that okay?" Officer Al asked. "Not too tight?"

"It's fine," Geoff said.

Officer Al held out the second set. "You're next, Ryder," he said. "Left hand."

Even as he raised his arm, Ryder couldn't believe he was doing it. He found himself watching the open bracelet that was still dangling from his brother's arm. Maybe they were just cuffing one hand? He liked that thought. When his left wrist was cuffed, he brought it up to his face to take a closer look. The cuff was shiny.

"Now, we need to finish," Officer Al said. "Put your arms behind your back."

It was as if someone else was controlling his body. He knew this was a stupid idea. How many times had Dad talked to him about stranger danger? You never let yourself get tied up. You let yourself be killed before you let that happen. It's easier to talk about than it is to do. He brought his right hand around to his back.

The touch of the cold bracelet made him jump. Then, after the ratchet was closed, both the left and the right were squeezed down tight. "Ow!" he said. "That's too tight."

Everybody jumped—even the cops—as the door opened and a man Ryder had never seen before entered the room. The others seemed afraid of him, which made Ryder *really* afraid of him.

"Damn you both!" the man boomed. "This is as far as you've gotten? I ordered this thing to be done by now."

Officer Kim said, "One of us is less committed to the cause than the other." He focused his words at Officer Al. The newcomer seemed angered by this.

"I'm concerned that we're making a mistake," Officer Al said. "This video is a mistake. Killing children on video? That can't be anything but bad for—"

Geoff jumped at the same instant as Ryder. They collided, and Geoff damn near fell back into the hole.

"You promised!" Geoff yelled. He started to run, but the new guy stepped into this path and grabbed him in the middle.

"What have you been doing?" the new guy shouted.

Officer Kim wrapped a beefy arm around Ryder's chest and then swept his legs out from under him. That grip kept him from hitting the floor hard, but he hit, nonetheless. His cuffed hands drove into the small of his back and cinched another click tighter.

Kim sat on Ryder's stomach, making it impossible to breathe, facing toward his feet. Another pair of handcuffs appeared and Ryder felt them close around his ankles. The chain on these was shorter than before. His big toes touched each other.

"Ry!" Geoff yelled.

"I'm right here, Geoffy," he tried to say, but he couldn't get sound to come out with all the weight on his belly. When Officer Kim stood, Ryder closed his eyes and clenched his jaw. "Don't fight them," he said. "Don't make them hurt you." There it was, he thought. He'd just decided they were going to die.

With the weight lifted, he could turn his head. Geoff lay on his stomach, six feet away, legs together, arms cuffed at the small of his back.

"I love you, Geoffy," Ryder said.

"I love you, too, Ry-Ry. Are they going to kill us?"

Ryder knew what the right thing was to say. He was the big brother. It was his responsibility to make everything as right as it could be. Little kids Geoff's age shouldn't have to deal with this kind of stuff. But he wasn't going to let his last words be a lie.

"Yes," he said.

Geoff's lips pursed together and trembled as a tear spilled from his temple onto the floor. "Is it going to hurt?"

A lump of emotion the size of a tennis ball materialized in Ryder's throat. "I hope not," he said.

"A-are we going to be brave?"

Ryder didn't even know what the question meant, but it ripped into his chest, causing him to cough out a sob. "I'm going to try," he croaked.

Seconds later, he was startled by the ripping sound of duct tape, and a strip of it was pressed against his lips. Officer Al did the same on Geoff. He didn't just tape a patch on him, though. He wrapped it twice all the way around his head before tearing it and pressing the tail of the tape into place.

Across the room, in the kitchen, bright lights erupted to life. Ryder maneuvered to his right side and craned his neck so he could see what was happening.

Officer Kim sat on a tall stool like the kind of bar stool guitar players like to sit on. His surgical mask was up around his face now, so only his eyes were showing, and they were covered with sunglasses. He was facing a camera that was located about ten feet in front of him. Officer Al walked over and stood next to the camera, then held up a big piece of cardboard with words on it.

"Betrayal has consequences," Kim said, looking into the lens. "I wish what you are about to see did not have to be done, but you need to understand that your word is your bond. When you betray your word, it affects people. It affects you, but more than that, it affects your loved ones. You know, of course, that the penalty for betrayal is death. For some who live in danger all the time, I've heard that death is thought of as a welcome relief. No one will welcome this."

Officer Kim paused for a few seconds, staring into the camera.

"Cut," he said. Then he turned back toward the boys. "Let's get their clothes off."

Jonathan led the team through the woods as they approached the concealed guard shed. They'd left the Batmobile at the top of the hill, engine and lights off. Out in the country, mechanical noises traveled farther and drew more attention than they did in the city. Absent good intel on what was going on inside the cabin, he didn't want the sound of an engine to force something bad to happen.

They were all kitted out in black, NVGs in place. All but Boxers had decided to leave their rucksacks in the vehicle, but otherwise, Jonathan had insisted on what he called *full soldier*. Ballistic helmets and vests with plates inserted. He brought his M27 carbine along because it was *always* along, but he expected his suppressed MP7 4.6-millimeter personal defense weapon to do most of the work tonight.

The others carried identical gear, except for Big Guy, who toted a 7.62-millimeter HK 417 portable cannon. Dawkins carried the collapsible twelve-foot pompier ladder they would use to scale the fence.

"Hold here," Jonathan whispered into his radio as they closed in on the guard shack. He didn't want them stacking up at the door, especially since he didn't know what kind of surveillance equipment had been deployed.

He switched on his infrared laser sight. The intense, thin green beam reached out far into the woods.

"Let me circle around and cover your approach," Boxers said.

Jonathan didn't reply because even if he'd said no, it was still going to happen. He paused where he stood and scanned and listened. Autumn was the toughest time of year to make a stealthy approach through the woods. Everything was dry and crunchy, and the tree branches held few leaves to muffle the sound.

"I'm in place," Big Guy whispered, and the beam of his laser sight settled on the guard shack door.

There were several ways to take this down. Jonathan actually considered knocking but figured that that would put everyone on edge. Instead, he just eased up to the door and turned the knob. The door scraped and squealed as he pushed it open. As the wash of light bloomed, he lifted his NVGs out of the way. With his IR laser now rendered useless, he raised his weapon to his shoulder to engage the red dot optical sight.

The inside looked like most similar structures he'd seen. Two desks sat nose-to-nose, and a tiny television displayed grainy images from a table off to the side. Coffee cups and dirty paper plates littered every surface. Directly across from the door, two AR-platform rifles occupied a rack that could have held eight times that many.

A voice called from a back room in a language Jonathan didn't recognize. Eastern European, he guessed. A smart roll of the dice would say Chechen. Jonathan waited.

The voice spoke again ahead of a toilet flush. Ten seconds later, a door opened and a man in his late twenties exited the bathroom, still blousing his shirt just so around his belt. He continued to speak to the floor until he rocked his gaze up and he saw Jonathan. His whole body shifted, like a dog on point.

"Don't be stupid," Jonathan said. He settled his red dot on the center of the guard's breastbone. From over Jonathan's left shoulder, a visible laser beam lit up the guard's forehead. "You don't have to get hurt. How many people are inside the cabin?"

The guard's eyes darted everywhere but at Jonathan's face. He was weighing his options. Jonathan figured it would take only a few seconds for the guy to realize that he didn't have any.

When the guard shifted his eyes toward the gun rack, Jonathan followed his gaze, only to realize half a second later that he'd been suckered. The guard whipped his hand toward a sidearm that was concealed under his shirt. Jonathan dropped to his right knee and fired three rounds in less than a second, nailing the guard in the heart, killing him before his knees had a chance to buckle.

"Nice shootin'," Big Guy's voice said in his ear. "I was half a pound of trigger-pull away from taking him out myself."

"I'm clearing the rest of the building," Jonathan said. With the extended stock of his MP7 tucked into his shoulder, he swept the weapon left to right as he advanced toward the door whose opening was clogged by the guard's body on the floor. The door panel itself was pushed flat against the wall, and it had been pierced by the three bullets that had killed the guard.

"We're clear," Jonathan said. "Thor, bring up the ladder."

"Hey, Scorpion," Boxers said over the air. "We need to pick up the pace." Big Guy dropped his 417 to let it hang against its sling and lifted his NVG array. The screen of his smart phone illuminated his face in the darkness. "All y'all will want to see this. Move fast."

As they gathered around him, Boxers bent at the waist and held the screen out for everyone to see. Before leaving the Batmobile, he'd programmed Roxie to hover six feet off the ground, about twenty feet from the front window, where it would continue to spy on the activities inside.

"Is he talking into a camera?" Gail asked.

"Look behind him, at the table," Boxers said. "They've got it lit like daylight."

"Oh, holy shit," Jonathan said. He pointed to a spot on the screen. "Can you zoom into there?"

Boxers manipulated the screen with his fingers, and it filled with the image of a deployed roll of surgical instruments.

"Where are the boys?" Dawkins asked.

Boxers zoomed back to the original image size. "I don't see them," he said. "But we know they're there." He darkened the screen and slipped the phone back into his pocket. "Now," he said.

Jonathan recognized the tone and the body language. "No shortcuts, Big Guy," Jonathan cautioned. "If we die, those kids get no help at all."

"Then hurry the hell up."

Jonathan looked to Dawkins as he flipped his NVGs back into place. "Throw the ladder."

Pompier ladders were specifically designed to scale obstacles. Essentially a long pole with a hook on one end, it featured rungs attached to either side of the pole. When extended, this one from the Batmobile was twelve feet long, and the spring-loaded rungs deployed automatically. Dawkins snagged the top of the fence gate with the hook, then braced the base against the gravel drive. To be climbable—for the rungs not to roll precariously—the ladder had to be positioned as close to vertical as possible. Jonathan was impressed that Dawkins knew how to do that.

With the ladder in place, Jonathan surveyed his crew. Weapons, night vision, assorted other gear all looked right. "Thumbs up if you're ready."

Thumbs.

"Questions?"

Boxers was already on his way up the ladder. The way it creaked under his weight, Jonathan wondered if there'd be any ladder left for the rest of them, but he kept his mouth shut. One of the tricks to managing Big Guy was knowing when not to poke the bear.

Chapter Twenty-seven

When Ryder saw the gleaming edge of the knife in Officer Kim's hand, he screamed, but the tape over his mouth stopped the sound.

"Easy, dickhead," Kim said. "Does this look like a good time to go flopping around?"

Ryder craned his chin down to his chest as the cop lifted him by the collar of his sweatshirt and slipped the blade through the neck hole. Holding the fabric tight, he sliced it all the way down the front of Ryder's body, exposing the flesh of his chest and belly like a boat creating a wake in the water. The blade hung up on the sweatshirt's waistband, causing Officer Kim to cuss under his breath.

"All the way off or just expose the stomach?" Officer Al asked. Ryder looked over and saw that Geoff had been turned onto his back, and his shirt had been opened the same way.

"This will do," Kim said. He grabbed Ryder by the front of his pants, behind his belt buckle, and by his hair and lifted him off the floor. "Carry them to the table."

Ryder was oddly aware and surprised that the belt digging into the small of his back hurt more than the fist in his hair. He couldn't turn his head to see if Geoff was being carried, too, but he heard footsteps on his left.

The lights became much brighter. Kim grunted as he lifted Ryder to chest height, and then dumped him on the table, right on top of his cuffed wrists. A second later, Geoff landed next to him, a foot or two away. He looked even more terrified than Ryder felt.

Remember, Ryder said silently, hoping that somehow his brother could hear him, *we're gonna try to be brave.*

"Turn the camera on again," Officer Kim said as he bloused open the remainder of Ryder's sweatshirt and tucked the edges underneath him, between his cuffed hands and the small of his back. He did the same to Geoff.

"We're on," the most recent arrival said from behind the camera.

"Meet my friends Ryder and Geoffrey," Officer Kim said. He was pulling on some rubber gloves. "I'm sorry to say that they must pay for their mother's mistake."

What mistake? What was happening?

"In these days of modern medicine, we've come to believe that surviving surgery is dependent upon effective anesthesia. That's just not true. For many years . . ."

For the first time, Ryder saw the scalpel in Kim's hand. It gleamed in the reflected glare of the bright lights.

". . . astonishing ability to sustain pain."

Ryder screamed again, his terror muffled by the tape

around his mouth. He bucked his body to get away, but Kim put a gloved hand on the center of his chest. "Remember what I told you about moving around too much."

Jonathan and Boxers stood on either side of the front door while Gail watched through the window. Dawkins had moved to the red side, where, when the balloon went up in just a minute or two, he'd put bullets through the generator to kill the power.

Jonathan tested the thumb latch on the door panel and whispered a curse when he found it didn't move. "Front door is locked," he whispered over the air.

"Git," Boxers said. He nudged Jonathan out of the way and pressed a GPC—general purpose charge—into place over the lock assembly. He pressed the detonator into place and stepped back. "Charge is ready."

"I know y'all know this," Jonathan said, "but be sure you see your targets. And watch your background. Gunslinger, are you ready?"

"Affirmative."

"Big Guy?"

"Yep."

"Thor?"

"All set."

"Okay," Jonathan said. "On zero. Three, two . . ."

"Ordinarily, we would use a paralytic drug at this stage to keep the patient from inadvertently killing himself with wild gyrations." Officer Kim had moved to a position on Ryder's right.

The scalpel came closer, held in a special, delicate way. With his other hand, Kim stretched the skin of Ryder's stomach taut. "Hold still now, Ry-Ry. You're going to feel—"

In an instant, the world came apart in a jumble of noise. First, there was a string of gunfire, then an explosion shook everything as the lights went out. In that tiny fraction of a second, after a huge *boom*, the darkness was beyond dark. Dark like down in the hole.

Then, the shouting started.

Jonathan turned away and shut his eyes as the GPC blasted a nearly perfect round hole in the wall where the lock assembly had been. The door flew inward, and it was time to move. Jonathan led with Gail in the number two slot and Big Guy bringing up the rear.

"Kendalls, stay down!" he yelled. "Don't move!"

It was a gift to know exactly where his targets were. As soon as he cleared the entryway, he pivoted left and fired two quick rounds through Timur Yamadayev's forehead. Someone else—Boxers, he thought—hit the taller captor, the one in regular clothes, but he didn't go down. Instead, he grabbed Geoff by his shackled ankles and pulled him toward the edge of the table, as if to pull him onto the ground. But he was working blind and making a mess of it, mostly just spinning the kid in place.

On the other side of the table, the captor in the surgical mask knew exactly what he was doing. He'd lifted Ryder by the underside of his jaw and was slashing at the boy's chest with the scalpel blade. In his peripheral vision, Jonathan saw Big Guy dart that way.

He turned his attention back to the attacker manhandling Geoff, the younger brother.

Jonathan moved in on the man, lifted him by his collar, and shot him through the temple, the spray of brains luminescent in the glow of his night vision. On the other side of the table, a man screamed, and there was the unmistakable sound of bones snapping.

The surgeon's hand—the one that used to hold the scalpel—was backwards now at the end of his arm. Jonathan cringed as he watched Boxers hyperextend the arm and slam his fist onto the exposed elbow, bending it back on itself.

Ryder was writhing on the floor at Boxers' feet, trying to get away. Geoff was still on the table, frozen. "Kendall boys!" Jonathan yelled. "We are here to rescue you! You are out of danger!"

He'd put a hand on Geoff's chest in hopes of reassuring him but got exactly the opposite result. The kid panicked. He bucked and screamed, the words unintelligible.

Across the table, Boxers shoved the doctor hard, sending him backpedaling in the dark until he fell on his mangled arm.

"Settle down, Geoff," Jonathan said softly, but the boy was beyond terrified, beyond understanding.

"Gunslinger, Thor, get the kids out of here, please."

He more sensed than watched his team swing into action, his attention focused on Boxers.

"Fight back, you piece of shit," Big Guy said as he moved in on the doctor. "What, can't you hold your own when they come a little bigger?" He stomped his heel down onto the surgeon's remaining hand—his left—and more bones broke. The man screamed again.

Boxers laughed. "What's that?" he said. "I can't hear you." He stomped again on the same hand.

"Big Guy," Jonathan said over the air, and then he reached to his radio and switched back to PTT mode, push to talk. "Big Guy," he said again.

"Not now, Scorpion," he said. "I'm busy." He drew his KA-BAR knife from its sheath on his vest. "What do you say, doc? I can carve on people, too."

"Big Guy, listen to me. We're not about this."

Boxers lifted the surgeon from the floor by his jaw, the same grip that had been used on Ryder Kendall. "No, *you're* not about this," he said. "For human waste like this, I am *all about* this." He slashed his knife across the surgeon's eyes.

"God *damn* it!" Jonathan shouted. "Stop."

Boxers tossed his victim back onto the floor. "I can do this all night."

The man howled. He was terrified. From the way he moved, Jonathan could tell that he was trying to protect himself, but nothing worked. Everything was broken.

"Hurts, doesn't it, you piece of shit."

This was wrong. Boxers was in a frenzy, spun up beyond control. Jonathan had seen him like this only once before, and it had caused an early separation from the Army for both of them.

Jonathan raised his MP7 to shoot the suffering man, but as the IR laser beam settled on the surgeon's head, Boxers whirled and grabbed the rifle's foregrip, pushing it off aim.

"Stay out of this, Dig," he growled. "If you can't take it, get the hell out."

Jonathan had never been on the wrong end of Big

Guy's menace before. The temperature of his bloodstream dropped twenty degrees.

Jonathan lifted his NVGs out of the way and stared up at Big Guy's silhouette. "Who the *hell* do you think you're talking to?"

Boxers said nothing, didn't move. His chest heaved, and his breathing came in loud gulps.

"Get your hands off my firearm," Jonathan said.

Control returned over the course of fifteen or twenty seconds. Jonathan felt Big Guy's fist release his gun.

As Jonathan rocked his NVGs back over his eyes, Boxers lifted his own out of the way. "I, uh, I'm sorry, Boss. I don't . . ." His voice trailed away.

"Go find the rest of the team," Jonathan said. "Help settle those boys down, and see if they need medical."

"Look, Scorp . . ."

"We're fine, Big Guy," he said. "Really. Get out of here, and let me finish this."

Boxers rested a hand on Jonathan's shoulder and gave it a squeeze. It was as close to a hug as Big Guy could manage. They'd talk about this later—hopefully over some single malt—but for now, it was over.

Jonathan turned back to the suffering man on the floor. Blood from his eyes had transformed his face into a gleaming wet mess. Jonathan had never been able to abide torture. Even in his violent line of work, there had to be rules, lines never to be crossed. For him, torture was the most vivid line of all.

Not that there wasn't satisfaction to be gleaned from watching the suffering of a monster who had caused so much suffering for others.

"Please help me," the doctor said. Blood spattered from his mouth on the hard consonants.

Jonathan stooped to his haunches, adjusting his weaponry so it wouldn't poke him. "Was it worth it?" he asked. "Whatever this was about, was it worth all of this?"

The man only moaned.

"So, what's the target?" Jonathan asked. "We know about the VX and the Mexican connection, but the target is one detail we don't know. What can you tell me about that?"

"Screw you," the man said.

For a second or two, Jonathan had to fight a nearly overwhelming urge to punch his broken bones again. "Bad time to cop an attitude, dickhead," he said.

The surgeon spat a wad of blood.

"Tell you what," Jonathan said. "If you answer my question, I'll put a bullet through your head and make all of this end quickly. If you sit there just looking ugly as shit, I'll walk away and let the suffering go on. You'll be blind and crippled while you starve to death or get eaten up by gangrene. Hell, I'll even leave the door open so maybe you can *literally* get eaten up by something. There are cougars up in these parts, aren't there?"

"I don't give a shit what you do," the man said.

Jonathan smiled. There was no humor in it. "A soldier to the end, huh?"

The man spat another wad.

"Okay, then," Jonathan said. "Have it your way." He grunted as he pressed himself back up to standing. "I'll leave you alone with your pain."

As Jonathan started toward the door, he had every intention of staying true to his word. In the end, though, he couldn't do it. Suffering was suffering, and torture was torture. He turned, raised his MP7 to his shoulder, and settled the laser on what was left of the doctor's right eye.

"Get that gate open," Jonathan said into his radio as he stepped out into the yard. "We've made a lot of noise, and I want to get on the road. Break, break. Mother Hen, Scorpion. Scene is secure. Three tangos sleeping."

"I copy, Scorpion," she said. "I can't believe what they were about to do to those poor children." Jonathan had forgotten that Venice could monitor Roxie's video signal. "Big Guy, if you get your drone to fly higher, I can keep an eye out for approaching vehicles."

"Roger that," Boxers said. Ten seconds later, Roxie's rotor blades spun faster and louder, and its silhouette disappeared into the night.

The Kendall boys lay in the grass in the darkness, where Gail and Dawkins were trying to comfort them. They'd settled down considerably from a few minutes ago, but they were still trussed up and terrified. The tape had been removed from their mouths, but not much else had changed. "Goggles up," Jonathan said as he approached, and he pulled a white-light Mini Maglite from its loop on his vest. "Good evening, boys," he said. "Sorry we took so long." He kept his tone light, not wanting to trigger another panic attack or a pity party.

Jonathan tapped Dawkins on the top of his helmet to get his attention. "Take security," he said.

Dawkins arose, brushed himself off, and rearranged

his weapons slings. While everyone else was engaged in focused work, it was always a good idea for one person's sole job to be keeping an eye out for approaching hazards. Tonight, that was Dawkins's job.

Jonathan directed the beam of his light to the older boy's chest, where he was bleeding from a half dozen lacerations. "You're Ryder, right?"

The boy nodded.

Jonathan shifted to the other one. "And you're Geoffrey?"

Another nod.

"Good," Jonathan said with a smile he hoped they could see. "I'd hate to think we made all this mess while rescuing the wrong kids." He leaned in to get a closer look at Ryder's chest. All but one appeared to be purely superficial, maybe requiring a few stitches, maybe not. One of the slashes was concerning, though. It was at the boy's diaphragm, where the belly meets the chest, and a glob of subcutaneous fat had avulsed through the laceration.

"I need to get a closer look at this," he said. "I'll try not to hurt you."

Ryder jerked back and brought his knees up in a defensive posture.

Jonathan sat taller and presented his hands in surrender. "Okay," he said. "I won't touch. Are you having any trouble breathing?"

The boy shook his head no.

"Could you speak to me, please?" Jonathan said. "It's one of the ways I can tell how badly hurt you are."

"I can breathe fine," he said.

"Count to ten for me," Jonathan instructed. "Forward and back."

Ryder did as he was told.

Jonathan turned to Geoff. "Your turn."

Likewise.

"What does that do?" Geoff asked.

"What, counting? That tells me that you can hear, understand, respond, and speak in complete thoughts. If you'd said, 'one, two, six, *L, M, N, O, R*,' I'd have been worried." He winked.

Geoff smiled.

Jonathan's earbud popped, and Boxers' voice said, "Charge is set on the gate."

"Stand by," Jonathan said. "There's going to be another explosion," he said to the kids. "You won't get hurt, but Gunslinger and I are going to cover your ears. Close your eyes."

Jonathan and Gail each straddled a kid, knees in the dirt, backs facing the gate. Their own earpieces would protect their eardrums from the overpressure, so they cupped their palms over the boys' ears. "We're all set," he said into the radio.

"Fire in the hole. Fire in the hole. Fire in the hole."

The explosion was a fraction of the size of the previous one. Jonathan guessed that Big Guy had just used a couple of loops of detonating cord.

"What did you do?" Ryder asked.

"We opened the gate," Jonathan replied. "With style."

"My wrists hurt," Geoff said. "Can you get these handcuffs off?"

"When my big friend brings our vehicle around, we can get them off," Jonathan said. "We have keys inside."

"Are you the police?" Ryder asked.

"FBI," Jonathan said. He hated lying to the kids, but the truth was too complicated. And, frankly, none of their business.

"What about those other guys?" Geoff asked. It wasn't clear if he was speaking to Jonathan or Ryder. "The guys in their underwear?"

Jonathan and Gail exchanged confused glances. "Sweetie, I'm afraid we don't know what you're talking about," Gail said.

Ryder pointed up the hill with his forehead. "There were two creepy guys up there the other day who were hanging out in nothing but their underwear."

"Are they there all the time?" Jonathan asked.

"We only saw them once," Ryder said. "They went in and out of the house on the hill."

"Which one?"

"The one on the left."

"Officer Kim hated it when we saw them," Geoff said. "He got really, really mad. My wrists really hurt."

Headlights approached from the woods. "Is that you approaching the gate, Big Guy?"

"It is, and everything's bulletproof, so fire at will." A beat. "Don't actually shoot."

Jonathan smiled. Karma could be a bitch, and some words should not be allowed simply to hang out there.

Jonathan said, "Be advised that PC-one's wounds do not appear to be life-threatening. He doesn't want them handled, but I'm hoping someone can talk him into letting you dress and bandage them." He looked straight at Ryder as he made his report.

"Break. Mother Hen, how are we looking from above?"

"Not a soul is moving, except for you guys."

"I copy."

The Batmobile closed to within a few yards of the kids, stopping when they were in the brightest wash of the headlights.

Jonathan stood and gave Gail a hand getting to her feet. "Slinger," he said in a low tone, "I want you to take care of freeing these kids and packaging them for transport out of here. Get them inside the vehicle, and give them some water and food. Let them get warm, and talk to them."

"You going up the hill to investigate the outbuildings?" she asked.

"Yeah. I'm going to take Big Guy with me and leave Thor here with you."

She gave a half-hearted thumbs-up. He knew she didn't like to get left out of the cool stuff.

"The clock's ticking," he said. "You're a hell of a lot better at the touchy-feely stuff, and Big Guy sucks at it. He'll scare them to death."

"I get it," she said. She pivoted toward Dawkins. "Thor," she called, pulling his gaze. "You and I are going to get Ryder and Geoff ready to get out of here and get warm."

Boxers was just climbing down from the Batmobile when Jonathan snagged him by his arm. "Come with me, Big Guy," he said. "You and I are going for a walk."

At the summit of the hill, before committing to the next step, Jonathan made Boxers cycle through plain light, IR, and UV lenses as Roxie flew a low circle around each of the three buildings. Nothing moved.

Still, they advanced as if bad guys were lying in wait for them. Rules were rules for a reason, and when you tempted fate as regularly as Jonathan did with his team, every cut corner was an unnecessary liability. The willingness to do things the right way every time was what separated professionals from wannabes.

The plastic boxes with self-contained breathing apparatuses on the exterior wall pretty much cut to the chase, as far as Jonathan was concerned. Then, a peek inside at the ventilated workstations and laboratory equipment sealed his decision. A scary facility under any circumstances, the green hues of IR illumination through NVGs made it look even worse. "We're not going in there," he said.

"I knew there was a reason I liked you," Boxers said.

"We'll let Wolverine know, and she can handle the investigation and cleanup."

"Chem weps scare the piss out of me," Big Guy said. This from a man who rarely confessed to being frightened of *anything*.

The next building was the smallest of the three, and it revealed itself to be nothing more than a run-of-the-mill storage shed.

"This last one looks interesting," Boxers observed.

Jonathan moved to the window in the nearest side—the green or left-hand side—and took a look. The gingham curtains told Jonathan that someone had once cared about this place, but their sun-brittleness told him that that time had passed years ago. He shone his light through the glass and illuminated what might have been a dorm room. Twin beds defined the outer perimeter, and a folding card table dominated the middle. Clothes and assorted junk lay scattered everywhere.

"Nobody's home," Jonathan said. "Let's go in."

Boxers moved to the front door, stepped back, and then fired the sole of his boot into the door, which exploded inward.

"Was it locked?" Jonathan asked.

"I have no idea," Big Guy said. "It's not now."

Jonathan scanned the mess with his light. "Any theories?"

"They should have bathed more often," Boxers said. "Smells like a fart in here."

That was exactly what it smelled like. Body odor combined with odd spices and old sweat. "Why would they live in this tiny place all the way up here when they have that whole cabin down the hill?"

"Maybe they got thrown out to make room for the kids," Big Guy guessed. As good a theory as any. "There's nothing in here, Boss."

Jonathan didn't answer. Instead, his attention was drawn to the papers strewn across the top of the table. A dozen or more laser-printed pages had been carefully stacked in one corner of the tabletop. That stack of papers was the only neat thing in the whole room. That meant it was important.

His earbud popped. "Scorpion, Mother Hen. There's activity on Hawk's Mountain Road. A vehicle approaching. A truck of some sort. A pickup."

Jonathan shot a look to Boxers, who already had his screen out of his pocket. He adjusted the image with his thumbs. "Not a cop," he said. "Unless he's in an unmarked vehicle."

Big Guy watched some more, and Jonathan watched

him watch. When Boxers' shoulders relaxed, Jonathan breathed again. "Just somebody passing through."

Still, it was a reminder that there was a penalty for dawdling. Jonathan scooped up the pile of stacked papers. He turned his light off and brought his NVGs back down. "Gunslinger, Scorpion. We're done here. Coming down."

Chapter Twenty-eight

Ryder and Geoff wouldn't let go of each other's hands. They sat in the first row of backseats, which had been turned around to face front. They fell asleep, or at least Jonathan thought they did, and the fear of awakening them kept everyone else from saying anything.

Ryder had allowed Gail to put antibiotic cream on his cuts and tape them with gauze. They didn't say much, and Jonathan didn't ask any questions. He had no idea what they'd been through, and he knew just enough about psychology to know that an improperly asked question could do more harm than good. Plus, he really didn't want to hear the answers.

Jonathan was keenly aware that the last time the boys were in a vehicle on their way to shelter, they'd witnessed two murders and then their nightmare had begun. There was no way to avoid the déjà vu element here. He hoped they'd simply stay asleep and make the drive go faster.

It was no longer possible for Ryder and Geoff to be taken to Resurrection House. The kids knew too much about the team's identities. They didn't know names, but they'd seen faces, and Fisherman's Cove was too small a town to guarantee that they would not cross paths.

"Where are you taking us?" Ryder asked at a whisper.

"I'm not asleep," Geoff said.

"Okay, where are we going?" Louder this time.

Jonathan left the talking to Gail. "To a place called Shenandoah Station," she said. "You've been there before."

"The Ballentines?" the boy asked. "We didn't like it there."

"No, not the Ballentines."

Jesus, Jonathan thought. *If these kids ever figure out the body count associated with their adventure, they'll never be right in the head.*

Gail said, "You weren't at this place very long. It's where you were last. Right before . . . Well, right before."

"Where the priest came?"

"Exactly."

"Hey, are they okay?"

Jonathan felt the air get heavier. Thicker.

"No, sweetie," Gail said. "He died. The driver, too, I'm afraid."

"Were Officer Al and Officer Kim really cops?" Geoff asked.

"No, they weren't."

A beat. "I'm glad you killed them," Geoff said.

Ryder added, "I wish I'd have been able to do it."

Yeah, there was some serious shrink time in their future.

It was after two when the Batmobile pulled up to the front door of Shenandoah Station. Soren Lightwater was on the front porch waiting for them. An electric space heater glowed at her feet, and she held a heavy wool blanket around her as she moved back and forth in the porch swing. She stood as the Suburban pulled to a stop.

"Everybody wait here," Jonathan said, and he stepped out into the cold.

"A priest called me," Soren said as he approached. She offered her hand.

He took it. "Thank you for agreeing to take the boys," he said.

"It's what we do. I'm glad you found them."

Jonathan shifted and cleared his throat. "Listen, about the other day."

She silenced him with a raised hand. "Don't," she said. "You were only partially wrong. Bobby Z no longer works here. Shenandoah Station will no longer be a stop of the Cartel Railroad. I can't believe that happened."

"And as far as I'm concerned, it never did," Jonathan said. "All of that ends here tonight, with this conversation."

Soren looked doubtful. "Why do I sense that there's more?"

Jonathan smiled. "It must be late," he said. "My poker face isn't working for me."

She waited for the rest.

"I'll give it to you straight. The long and short of it is, not only did your drug transgressions never happen, my team and I were never here."

"I don't understand."

He chuckled. "I bet you don't. It's better if you don't try."

"How am I going to explain the arrival of two brothers?"

"You'll be hearing from some folks in the morning who will share all the details. Trust me, there will be no trouble to you for any of this."

Soren's deep scowl lines stood out in high relief in the wash of the headlights.

"You're not really with the FBI, are you?"

Jonathan danced his eyebrows. "Thank you again," he said. Without turning away from Soren, he waved at the Batmobile. It was time to transfer the children. "They've been through a lot," he said. "Way, way more than most adults could handle. Keep that in mind."

He heard the Suburban's door open and feet hit the ground.

"How do you want to be introduced?" he whispered.

"I'll take care of that," she said. Her face blossomed into a bright smile. "You must be Ryder and Geoffrey," she said. "I've heard so much about you. I missed you when you were here last time."

The boys looked dead on their feet, the dictionary definition of exhausted.

Soren stooped to their eye level. "Oh, you poor things. Let's get you inside and warm you up."

Soren stood and, in what appeared to be a well-practiced maneuver, eased the boys away from Gail and past Jonathan without looking and without a word. She never glanced back, and neither did the boys as she escorted them up the three steps, across the porch, and through the front door.

"Wow," Jonathan said. "That was fast. Probably best for all."

When he looked to Gail, he was not surprised to see tears balanced on her lids. He reached out, and she took his hand. "A hug from them would have been nice," she said.

"That seemed to go well," Boxers said as Jonathan and Gail climbed back into the Suburban and took their seats.

"They've been through too much," Gail said.

"At least they're alive to recover," Jonathan said.

Boxers maneuvered the Batmobile onto the road, and they were on their way.

"Hey, guys?" Dawkins said. "I've been going through these documents you took from the Kadyrovs' cabin. I didn't think it was appropriate to talk while the boys were here. Do you have any idea what you got?"

"Just a glance," Jonathan said.

"These are subway schedules for the Washington Metro system." Originally started in the late 1970s, the Washington Metropolitan Area Transit Authority's subway system ferried hundreds of thousands of commuters every morning and afternoon to, from, and through the city and its suburbs in Virginia and Maryland. "I think we found their target."

"That's a big system," Jonathan said. "Must be close to a hundred stations. Anything in the stack of papers to indicate which one?"

"Not that I've been able to find."

"What about a timeline?" Boxers asked.

"No." Dawkins shuffled through the pages. "At least not yet. There are some handwritten notes in the margins, but I can't read the language they're written in. I guess my Chechen isn't all that it used to be."

"You speak Chechen?" Jonathan asked.

"I was being ironical."

"We need to read Wolverine in on this," Boxers said. "She's got about thirty-five thousand sets of eyes she can bring to the mix."

"And tell her what?" Gail challenged. "That we think documents we seized illegally during a break-in *might* show that an attack *might* be coming at an *unknown* time to one of a hundred subway stations? What's she supposed to do with that?"

"How about your outfit?" Jonathan asked Dawkins.

"What, the DEA?" Dawkins sounded horrified. "Not in this lifetime. I wouldn't do well in prison."

"We don't have anything to give any agency, Dig," Gail said. "There's no meat on the bones."

"So, what do you suggest?" Big Guy asked. "Other than staying off the Metro system for a while?"

Jonathan thought it through. It no longer made sense to head back to Fisherman's Cove, exhaustion notwithstanding. "Head into the District," he said. "We'll crash for the night."

"The morning commute in DC starts at five a.m.," Dawkins said.

"If they hit at five, then we miss it," Jonathan said. "There are limits on top of our limits here. I'm not going to go off half-cocked and get all of us hurt."

"What can we even do?" Gail asked. "I mean, as a practical matter, I'm assuming that disarming a chemical weapons bomb is outside of even your expertise."

Outside of his expertise was the polite way of expressing the truth of it, which was that he had no earthly clue.

Gail continued, "And we can't walk around the city in Level A suits."

"Isn't it obvious?" Big Guy said. "We have to stop them *before* they plant their devices. Stopping people is definitely in our wheelhouse."

"I've got to wake up Mother Hen," Jonathan said. "She's got to flog the shit out of her facial recognition toys. If she can find them, at least we can have a shot at a step two."

"But how?" Dawkins asked. "Say it's a hundred stations. Four of us. Even if we can locate them, they're not going to stick around and be caught. How do we not be too late?"

"Whatever we try will be a long shot," Boxers said, "but we can narrow things down. For example, I think it's a high-probability guess that they'll want to target rush hour, right?"

Jonathan had no problem with the logic.

Big Guy continued, "So, building on that logic, it makes sense that they'd want the largest number of victims."

"As terrorists so often do," Gail said.

"Exactly. So, we can write off any of the suburban stations. At any given moment, the highest concentrations of people are going to be inside the city, not outside of it."

Jonathan took his phone out of his pocket and pulled up the map of the Metro system. It was the same map that was posted in every car on every train. Some said the map with its graphic display of the various train lines—Red, Green, Orange, Blue, Yellow, and Silver—looked like a crippled spider. To Jonathan, it looked like someone dropped colorful spaghetti.

"We're spitballing here, so we'll stipulate that the highest concentration of people is key. So, the stations where you can transfer from one line to the next would make the most sense. Agreed?"

"Sure," Gail said.

"Right," Jonathan said. "And we'll also stipulate that Virginia and Maryland are out. That leaves transfer stations within the city itself."

"That's pretty much every stop," Dawkins said. "Orange, Blue, and Silver all run on the same tracks, and so do Green and Yellow."

By now, Gail had produced her phone, as well. "Don't discount the tourists," she said. "In fact, I think tourists are the key, so long as we're taking wild guesses. You talk about the five a.m. commute, but none of the DC attractions are open at that time. The tourists are all in bed. I think we're looking at the afternoon commute. Most people will be commuting home, and the museums will have just closed."

"I think you're right," Dawkins said. "It's been a while since I did that god-awful commute, but the afternoons do tend to be worse than the mornings. So long as the trains don't break down. As if that doesn't happen every day."

"All right," Boxers said. "It's my turn to guess wild-assedly. Look for the transfer stations that have the most available lines *and* are near something worth looking at. Fort Totten won't be ground zero."

"Okay, Big Guy," Jonathan said. "You're the one

who lives downtown. Where would you plant a device for maximum effect?"

Boxers chuckled. "Is this me as a terrorist or me as me? Personally, I'd like to nuke both ends of Pennsylvania Avenue and get a fresh start."

Jonathan let the moment pass.

"There's really only three options," Gail said. "Metro Center, Gallery Place, or L'Enfant Plaza."

"Unless there's a convention in town, it won't be Gallery Place," Boxers said. "You have the maps. L'Enfant Plaza has all five lines, right?"

"Correct," Jonathan said.

"And it's in the middle of most of the tourist shit," Boxers said. "That's our station."

"Just like that?" Dawkins said. "Declare it to be so, and it is?"

"Welcome to the private sector, Special Agent Dawkins," Jonathan said. "We're flying without a net here, and we're doing it without authorization from anyone. If we miss, we miss. It's happened before, and it undoubtedly will happen again."

"We'll revisit all of this," Gail said. "And we'll get Mother Hen to work some her magic, but we have a place to start."

"And the plan will be?" Dawkins pressed.

"To stop them," Jonathan said.

"Who's to say they'll stay together?" Boxers asked. "There are two of them."

"There are at *least* two of them," Gail added.

Jonathan smiled. "Words cannot express how proud I am that my team of crack operators—the ultimate professionals—can count accurately all the way to two."

He switched away from the internet and opened the telephone app.

"Venice's not going to like being woke up at this hour," Boxers said.

"Oh, she won't mind," Jonathan said. As if saying it could make it true.

Chapter Twenty-nine

They crashed in Boxers' home on Swann Street in Northwest Washington. Twenty years ago, the neighborhood had been a shithole filled with whores and drug dealers. Now, you couldn't touch a house for less than a million dollars, and a million would be a steal. Jonathan had been here before, but the others had not, and he enjoyed seeing their reactions to the place. Nobody expected Big Guy to be a collector of fine art and antiques.

What amused Jonathan was the relative scale of the house versus its occupant. The Federal-style townhouse was over a century old. At the time of its construction, no architect could have anticipated an occupant of Big Guy's dimensions. While the ceilings were high to manage the summer heat, the rooms themselves and the archways leading to them all seemed too small. Every step Boxers took seemed to test the structural integrity of the floor joists.

The sleeping arrangements had been sparse. Big Guy took his own room, of course, and Gail got the spare bedroom, leaving Dawkins and Jonathan to share space on the living room floor. Not that it mattered for the two hours that they'd allotted themselves for shut-eye.

Big Guy awoke first, came downstairs fully dressed, and headed for the kitchen, where he put on a pot of coffee and scrambled a dozen eggs. He even set the kitchen table for all four of them.

"I can do more than just kill people and break things," Big Guy said when Gail expressed her surprise that he was so gracious.

"Yeah, but which do you prefer?" Jonathan teased, earning himself a one-fingered wave.

By eight o'clock, they were ready to roll. But with nowhere to roll to.

"Nothing on the news this morning about an attack," Dawkins said. "That's got to be good, right?"

"Better than bad," Jonathan agreed.

Boxers had converted the basement level of his house into an office and play space. Beginning straight up at 0800, the four of them sat in black leather lounge chairs staring at a sixty-inch flat-screen television, where they hooked into a videoconference with Venice.

"Good morning, Mother Hen," Jonathan said as Venice settled into her seat in the War Room.

She sipped her coffee. "I suppose," she said. "How are you all?"

"Anxious for this to be done," Gail said.

"Be careful what you wish for," Venice said.

Jonathan asked, "Have the Kadyrov brothers shown up anywhere in the last few hours?"

"First of all," she said, "you'd think that in these

days of heightened awareness for terrorist threats and the like that the second largest transportation system in the United States would have a reliable network of security cameras, wouldn't you?"

Jonathan said "I certainly would" because it was the right thing to say and Venice was clearly at the beginning of a roll.

"Well, you'd be wrong," she said. "Half of the cameras are offline, and half of the ones still in service have lenses so filthy that you can barely see through them."

"This is coming around to an answer, right?" Boxers asked.

"Do not press me this morning, Big Guy," she threatened. "I am not in the mood."

"Yet the question remains," Boxers mumbled.

"Your microphone is better than you apparently believe it is," Venice said.

Jonathan spread his arms, as if declaring a base runner safe. Time to let that go.

"But to answer your question," Venice said, "I've caught snippets of them in various places downtown over the past twenty-four hours. For example, I know they had a late lunch yesterday from a food truck in Farragut Square. And it might give you a chill to know that each of them is carrying a blue backpack, the kind college kids take to classes with them."

"Food trucks have security video feeds?" Dawkins asked.

"No, but the Army Navy Club across the street does," Venice said. "From there, they headed north."

"Farragut has two Metro stations," Gail said. "North

and West. The park is immediately adjacent to Farragut West."

"We should check that out," Dawkins said.

"That was yesterday," Jonathan said.

"They could have planted it then."

"Be too risky," Boxers said. "Someone would find it. At least they'd have to assume that. Maybe they were just casing the location."

"Maybe they were just eating lunch," Jonathan said. "Ven, do you have any evidence that they went into the station?"

"No, that's one of the unreliable camera systems."

"Which happens to be closest to the White House," Gail said.

Venice said, "They did go into Farragut North, though. I think I was able to capture their fare card. If that's the case, then they got off at Bethesda."

"You said you *think* you captured their fare card," Jonathan said.

"It's an imprecise science," she said. "I could see them go through the turnstile on the security video, and then I was able to see which card numbers went through at the same time. The presumption is that the time stamps on the video and the turnstiles are synced up." She rolled her eyes. "It also assumes that no one else was using a different turnstile at the same time. As I said, it's imprecise."

"Bethesda?" Jonathan said.

"There's a lot of shopping and restaurants there," Dawkins said.

"Walter Reed is there, too," Boxers said, referring to the Walter Reed National Military Medical Center, formerly known as the National Naval Medical Center.

Something tightened in Jonathan's gut. "Oh, shit. That'd be a hell of a target."

"I've already thought of that," Venice said. "Three things. First, the closest stop to Walter Reed is actually for NIH, National Institutes for Health. Second, there's no evidence of them being there. And third, how would they get in even if they did get there? It's a military facility."

She was right. They needed to stick with their original guesswork. Every place in the DC area had terrific potential as a target. "So, have we seen anything of the brothers after they got off the Metro in Bethesda?"

"By then it was getting pretty dark," Venice said. "Street cameras aren't all that useful, and the vast majority of the business cameras are either not tied into a network or subscribe to a service I can't tap into."

"Is there a service you can't tap into?" Jonathan teased.

"I'm sure there must be," she replied with a smile.

Gail said, "So, what do we do now? If we're right that they're going to target rush hour, this afternoon is a long time from now."

"I say we alert the FBI and let them take the lead on this," Dawkins said.

"We can't do that," Venice said.

"And we've already discussed it," Gail said.

"I'm less sure about that than I used to be," Jonathan said. "The stakes are just too high. We at least need to share what we know. Wolverine can figure it out from there."

"Think this through, Dig," Boxers said. "There's a lot of underlying intel that we can't share."

"Wolverine has never demanded that we share

means and methods," Jonathan said. "I don't expect her to start now."

"Have you ever stood between her and thousands of people dying?" Dawkins asked.

"Listen, Thor," Jonathan said. "You don't know what you don't know." He looked into the camera, and by extension at Venice. "Contact our special friend. Tell Wolfie that we need to meet at Location Bravo as soon as she can make it. Make sure that everyone knows how important it is."

The Cathedral of Saint Matthew the Apostle dominated its section of Rhode Island Avenue in Northwest Washington—more or less equidistant from the Farragut North and DuPont Circle Metro stations. The seat of the Archdiocese of Washington had recently undergone an extensive renovation, during which FBI Director Irene Rivers had managed to reengineer Our Lady's Chapel, to the left of the nave, to be one of the most acoustically secure spots in North America. Jamming signals emitted from behind the elaborate mosaic work made electronic eavesdropping impossible, and when Wolverine was present, her security detail kept curious eyes away.

In a city that was awash in SCIFs—secure compartmented information facilities—this was the only one that was unknown to but a handful of people, all of them within the Bureau, plus a tiny few outsiders, all of whom worked for Security Solutions.

Jonathan arrived at the church early, not because being first was important, but because the ticking clock in his head was pounding ever harder. He didn't wait in Our Lady's Chapel, though. He didn't want to bring undo attention to himself, and he likewise didn't want to spin up Irene's security detail when they arrived. Instead, he slid into one of the pews in the sanctuary and had a chat with God. Raised as a Catholic in a household run by a career criminal, Jonathan considered his relationship with the Church to be a rocky one, but he'd survived too many close calls that should have killed him not to think that God had a plan for him and looked out for him.

This morning, he prayed to be right in his guesswork—or totally wrong about the whole plan to attack with nerve agent. Either way was fine. He prayed that God would help him make the right decisions with his team and help all of them stay out of the way of stupid decisions.

He'd taken a position near the rear of the sanctuary, where he would be more likely to see or hear the doors open when Wolverine arrived. He was thrilled when her team came through the doors ten minutes early. Irene Rivers looked to be somewhere between annoyed and angry as she allowed herself to be led and followed by her detail as they walked directly to Our Lady's Chapel. She held a thin manila envelope in her right hand as she walked, and it occurred to Jonathan that he could not remember the last time he saw her empty-handed.

He rose from his pew and fell in line behind the rear guard of her detail.

Sensing the presence—and probably a threat—the guard turned and braced to intercept Jonathan. Then his features relaxed a little.

"Remember me?" Jonathan said. "I'm like a bad penny. I'm the reason your boss is here."

The guy turned, and Wolverine was already waving Jonathan forward. "Thank you, guys," she said to her detail. "He's fine."

As Jonathan passed, her detail turned away from the chapel to look out into the sanctuary, doing their best impersonations of wooden soldiers.

Irene took a seat in front of the beckoning statue of Mary, who was reaching out to worshippers with one hand while showing the way to Heaven with the other.

"It's a busy day, Digger," she said, getting right to it. "What has Father Dom in such a lather?"

"Your day's likely to get a lot longer," Jonathan said.

"Oh, Lord, what did you do?"

"Such respect I get," Jonathan said through a smile. "I haven't done anything yet. Well, today." Over the course of ten minutes, he caught her up on the details of rescuing the Kendall boys.

"Well, that's wonderful news," Irene said when he was done.

"Your tone makes it sound less than wonderful," Jonathan said.

"Connie Kendall rescinded her agreement to accept immunity in return for testifying against the Cortez cartel," Irene said. She pushed an errant strand of pale red hair away from her eye. "Apparently, someone told her that her children had been kidnapped, and she clammed up. I wonder who did that?" The question was an accusation.

"You really don't know?" Jonathan said. "It wasn't me, that's for sure. It was a guard."

Irene scowled. "And you know this how?"

Jonathan folded his arms and crossed his legs, intentional body language to tell her she'd reached the edge of the intel real estate that she could visit. "One day, Wolfie, when you're done with official Washington, you're going to have to come and play with the cool kids."

"Tomorrow is sounding good to me," she quipped, and she turned her attention to her file folder. Some body language of her own.

"I haven't yet gotten to the reason I'm here," Jonathan said. "How about the courtesy of a little eye contact?"

She made a show of closing the folder and putting it on her lap. Then she pasted a clownish smile on her face. "Is this sufficient?"

"God, you're pretty when you're bitchy," Jonathan said.

Her eyes darkened. "I dare you to say that again."

He moved along. "Okay, here's the thing. Armand Cortez had nothing to do with kidnapping those boys. It turns out he actually liked the kids and fully expected Connie to spill her guts to you guys."

Irene's face was a mask of confusion. "Who kidnapped them, then?"

Jonathan smirked. "Remember the Jungle Tigers cartel?"

"I thought you destroyed them."

"I couldn't destroy what I couldn't see," Jonathan said. "A thug named Quinto Alvarez survived, apparently, and he's working to bring them back to their former greatness, and they're funding it with nerve agent."

Her jaw went slack. "*Nerve agent* is a big term," she said. "What do you mean?"

"I mean the big stuff. VX."

"Oh, shit," Irene spat. Then she nodded at the statue of Mary. "Sorry." Then she muttered, "I never did believe that we got all of that junk out of Mexico." Her scowl returned. "Wait, what does this have to do with Connie Kendall and her children?"

"Apparently, her husband, Craig, was the mule used to distribute the nerve gas to their customers in America."

"They had customers in the U.S. for nerve gas? Who?"

"Chechens."

Irene closed her eyes and brought a hand to her head. "Oh, God, no. Those guys are ruthless."

"Tell me about it," Jonathan said. "The place we rescued the Kendall boys from was one of the cells they were using to stockpile the VX and assemble the devices."

Irene's shoulders sagged. "Oh, shit. Shit, shit, shit. And Holy Mother, even you have to be saying the same thing. Digger, please tell me that these cell members are among the bodies you tell me that I will find in Blanton, Tennessee."

"Some, but not all," Jonathan said. "Again, I can't get rid of what I can't see. Two of them had already left by the time we got there. They left behind a ton of shit they hadn't yet used."

A thought bloomed in Irene's head. "Blanton, Tennessee," she said. "Dead cows?"

"And three dead people," Jonathan said.

"Okay, now I'm connecting the dots," Irene said.

"Why did it not occur to me that you had something to do with that?"

Jonathan considered correcting the record—that he had no hand in that particular aspect—but what was the point? He explained, "The Chechens who got away are twins, Khasan and Aslan Kadyrov. Both are on the watch lists, both came into the country through Texas."

"Of course they did," Irene said. "How do you know this when I don't?"

"Because you follow rules," he said with a grin. "Rules have never been my strong suit. Now, here's the bad part."

"Oh, holy crap, you haven't gotten to the bad part yet?"

"They're going to hit one of the main Metro stations at rush hour."

"Today?"

"We think so."

Irene shifted in her chair so she could drill him with her gaze. "You *think* so? What the hell does that mean?"

"It means that I don't know for sure. They left their place yesterday, and we know that they were roaming around DC yesterday. It makes no sense for them to draw this kind of thing out too long."

As the shock passed, skepticism fell in behind. "How do you know they're going to hit the Metro system?"

"Because we found papers related to the system in their house. They were the only elements in the whole place that were carefully stacked."

She stared, as if deciding whether to have him committed.

"And it makes the most sense," he added. Hearing the words articulated made him realize how stupid they sounded. He watched as Irene's jaw muscles flexed and unflexed.

"Dammit, Digger, what am I supposed to do with this?"

He shrugged. "I don't know," he said. "Maybe I just wanted to share the wealth. Can you get the transit authority to shut down the system?"

"No!" Irene cringed at the tenor of her own voice. "Even if the threat were definite and known, that would be a tall order. But on a rumor? On intuition? Absolutely not."

"Raise awareness levels?" he suggested.

"That's not possible," she said. "After a decade of Condition Orange—after a decade of crying wolf twenty-four seven—nobody listens to threat levels. We can't even get people to evacuate their below-sea-level homes in front of a Cat Five storm."

Jonathan felt deflated. "At least you can't accuse me of keeping you in the dark."

"This time," Irene corrected. "This *one* time you bring me into the light. I don't even have anything to bring to a court for a warrant."

It felt as if the meeting was about to end, but Jonathan felt uncomfortable about that. He steeled himself with a huge breath. "There's one more thing you need to know."

"Oh, God, please make it stop."

"We can follow them."

"Who?"

"The Kadyrov brothers."

"What do you mean, you can *follow* them?"

Jonathan quibbled, "*Follow* is the wrong word. We can track them."

Irene exuded skepticism. "How?"

"Promise me you won't ask for details."

"Is this about breaking more rules?"

"Oh, hell, yes. Mother Hen has stumbled upon some kick-ass facial recognition software. When they pass in front of a camera—even a passive camera—we can snap their photo, and then track them on a timeline."

"Any idea how many laws you're breaking there?"

"Not a hard number, no. I can share their picture, if you'd like, but I can't share the technology we used to get it."

"No," she said. She was beyond dismissive in her tone. "What would I do with it? I need warrants and court orders to do what you do on a whim. I don't want to be left holding your smoking gun."

"I don't get it, Wolfie." Jonathan's patience had eroded to nothing. "I'm telling you that this thing is going to happen. If not today, then tomorrow or the next day. What I'm hearing from you is a willingness to just let it happen."

"I have no choice, Dig." She had tears in her eyes, something he didn't think he'd ever seen before. "Among the stuff I hate about this godforsaken job, do you know what is the worst? The fact that we are not prepared to prevent crime. No police agency can do that. We *investigate* crimes after they happen and do our best to put the perpetrators away. We're janitors, Dig, not operators, and it tears at me every single day."

Jonathan had never seen this side of Irene before. It unnerved him a little.

"Do you have any idea how much I wish my Bureau

could do what you do? Do you know what a burden that goddamn Constitution is? But guys with long hair and buckles on their shoes decided a long time ago that we would be a nation of laws and that even the worst of the worst have rights. Overall, it's a pretty great system, don't you think?"

Jonathan didn't answer what he knew had to be a rhetorical question.

"So, here we are, where we've been so many times in the past. I will cover for your carnage in Tennessee, as I covered for your carnage at the foster home, and I pray that you figure out a way to stop the sons of bitches before they can attack my neighbors. If you can, then I'll cover for you again. If you can't well, just step out of the way and let me do my cleanup job."

Chapter Thirty

While the L'Enfant Plaza Metro Station fit the bill for best terror target and it was the closest station to art galleries and the Smithsonian's National Air and Space Museum, the station itself sat in the middle of the ugliest office buildings in Washington. Jonathan wondered sometimes if the architects were Soviet-era refugees from Eastern Europe. Canyons of flat façades and rectangular windows. A national chain had recently opened a hotel atop the station, but the designers of the public spaces favored dainty and uncomfortable over comfort or utility.

Jonathan had no idea how long his team would have to hang around.

In a gesture that was equal parts defiance and efficiency, they took the Metro to L'Enfant Plaza. The area afforded limited local parking, and where it was available, six-foot height restrictions applied within the garages, a little tight for the Batmobile. It was going to be a long day. Or several days.

They emerged to sunlight on Seventh Street and Maryland Avenues, Southwest, a little after 3:45 P.M.

Kitted out in 5.11 Tactical pants and shirts, sidearms in the open and badges clipped to their belts, they looked like the federal agents they were pretending to be. Each carried an equipment bag with a vest and short-barreled rifle inside.

Jonathan wore his Colt 1911 high on his right hip and four spare mags on his left. His radio rested behind his holster. He reached around and pressed the key to activate the wireless bud in his ear. He flipped the switch to VOX. "Mother Hen, do you copy?"

"Loud and clear," she said. "Nice to have you back."

The Metro system had been built long before anyone thought of digital communication as it existed today, and as such, the tunnels were black holes for radio traffic.

"Any updates on our friends?"

"A possible," she said, "but nothing firm. They might or might not have had a late lunch at McDonald's in Bethesda."

"What's the nearest Metro station?"

"Friendship Heights."

"Are cameras working there or not?"

"Or not," she said.

"Murphy rides again," Jonathan said. "Okay, well, we're here at L'Enfant Plaza. Let us know everything when you know it." He reached behind and turned his radio back to PTT.

"What are we doin', Boss?" Boxers asked. "This is not what we do. Our mission is accomplished. The Kendall boys are whole and healthy."

"Let's walk and talk," Jonathan said. He pointed across 7th Street, Southwest, and led the way toward a little patch of green called Hancock Park. Red metal chairs sat around red metal tables at random intervals, designed to be as uncomfortable as possible. Four millennials in expensive business casual suits cut off their conversation and stood as the team from Security Solutions approached.

"Pigs in a blanket," one of them said.

"Fry 'em like bacon," said another through her lip ring as she walked away.

"Eat shit and die," Boxers replied.

"Spreading love and cheer wherever you go," Jonathan said. They assumed the kids' places around one of the little tables.

"Are you ignoring Big Guy's question?" Gail asked. "What *are* we doing? What is our plan? Every time it comes up, you divert to something else."

Jonathan held up his hands. "What do you want me to say? It's obvious, isn't it? We react."

"We're not cops, Dig," Boxers said. "You want us to do what the *real* cops aren't willing to do."

"Since when do you back away from danger?" Jonathan challenged.

"Don't even *think* of playing a coward card with me," Big Guy said. "There are a million different ways that this can go wrong. Let's start with the fact that it's the middle of the day and we're out in the open. Covert is our thing, not hey-look-at-me."

"You have to look at the flip side," Dawkins said. "How do you live with yourself if you do nothing?"

"No lectures from the new guy, okay?" Boxers said. "But how do I *live* with it? The same way that the FB-friggin'-I will live with it. We've already done our job."

"No," Gail said. "We haven't. We have knowledge

and the ability to save many lives. Harry is right. We can't do nothing. *I* can't sit by."

Dawkins leaned into the table. "I've got another wrinkle," he said. "Friendship Heights is on the Red Line. The Red Line doesn't come here to L'Enfant. To get here, they'll have to change trains in Metro Center, which is also a pretty tasty target. Maybe we're in the wrong place."

"Or maybe they'll split up," Boxers said.

"Or maybe a thousand other things," Jonathan said. "We can second-guess without end." He scratched the sides of his head with both hands, his tell for frustration. "Look, what's going to happen is going to happen, and it's going to unfold the way it unfolds. The best we can do—"

"Scorpion, Scorpion, Mother Hen."

"This sounds hopeful," Jonathan said. He flipped the switch to VOX. "Go ahead."

"I don't have visuals," she said, "but the fare cards I flagged yesterday have just entered Friendship Heights."

"Stand by," Jonathan said. He flipped the radio switch back to PTT. "I don't spend a lot of time riding the subway. If I recall, once they're in the system, they'll be lost to us until they leave their final station stop."

Dawkins nodded aggressively. "Exactly. They can do whatever transfers they want without using the cards again. But to get out, they have to swipe their cards when they leave the station."

Jonathan keyed his mic again. "Mother Hen, we're going to be über-dependent on the facial recognition from now on. I don't know what kind of fine-tuning you can do, but for the time being, I don't care about anything that happens outside the Metro system."

"Got it," she said.

Jonathan said, "To be clear, they're going to have to transfer to get to us. If they transfer at Metro Center, they'll be on Blue or Orange Lines. But if they wait to transfer at Gallery Place, they'll get to L'Enfant Plaza on the Yellow or Green."

"Don't forget Silver," Dawkins said off the air.

"Oh, yeah," Jonathan said on the air. "And don't forget Silver."

"It'd been easier just to say watch every line," Venice said. Jonathan could hear the smile in her voice.

Jonathan opened up his equipment bag and pulled out his vest and rifle. "How long ago did they board the train?" he asked.

"Um . . . four minutes ago. According to Metro's website, it's a seventeen-minute ride to Metro Center, then five minutes to L'Enfant Plaza. Total of thirty-seven minutes, if everything's running on time."

"Oh, I'm confident that they'll be on time," Jonathan said with a wry chuckle. "This will be the one day out of the whole year when everything will run on time." He looked to his crew. "Time go to work. Any questions?"

They had all started kitting up as well. "Would you have answers if we did?" Boxers quipped.

As they rose from the chairs and headed back into the station, Jonathan said, "Once we're inside, we need to split up, but we stay on the upper level. The trains come in on different levels, but they can only exit from the upper level."

"How many entrances?" Gail asked.

"Four," Dawkins said. "This one, plus the Plaza Mall, Seventh and C, and D Street."

The architects who designed the Metro system got the aesthetics right. Reminiscent of the best of the Paris Underground, the L'Enfant Plaza station featured soaring ceilings and side platforms. The acoustics were always loud, but Jonathan figured that tourists had to be impressed by what they saw, especially if they were coming from the claustrophobic New York subway platforms.

But even the largest spaces have choke points, and here those points were the turnstiles and ticket machines. Now that the museums were closing and the workday was ending, the crush of people—the crush of targets—was huge. It was as if someone had opened a human spigot. Commuters showed little patience with hesitant tourists and no interest in lessening their confusion.

Their cop costumes allowed them to bypass the normal entryway to the platforms and gain access through a swinging gate that normally was reserved for people in wheelchairs.

"Everybody go to VOX," Jonathan said. "Mother Hen, radio check."

"You're scratchy, but I can hear you," she said. She sounded scratchy, too. She ran through a radio check for each of them.

Jonathan had one last chat with his team. They spoke face-to-face, but he also wanted it out on the air for Venice to hear. "You know what these guys look like. We know that they'll be carrying blue backpacks. Station yourselves near the turnstiles and watch. If you see one or both of them, sing out and the rest will come running."

"Or just shoot the sons of bitches," Boxers said.

"Just be damn sure who you're shooting," Jonathan said. He wasn't sure whether or not Big Guy was kidding, so he opted to believe he was being serious. "Watch your background. A dead bad guy isn't a good thing if the good guy behind him gets hit with the same bullet."

"Hmm," Boxers said, feigning interest. "Don't hurt the innocent. Interesting safety tip. Thanks for sharing."

"You know," Gail said, "if these guys hit this place and we somehow don't see them, we're going to be among the victims."

"Seven minutes to Metro Center if they're running on time," Venice said.

"Split up, people," Jonathan ordered. "We're going to do this. We're going to stop them."

They left Gail to cover Maryland Avenue and 7th Street—the spot they'd been standing at—and wandered off to the three other compass points. Jonathan planted himself at the ticket station closest to the 7th and C Streets exit. As he looked in toward the swirling crowd, he marveled at how little he could actually see. It was a wall of people. Their movement looked more peristaltic than deliberate. He couldn't imagine the chaos—the carnage of trampled people—if a panic ignited in here.

He noticed with no small degree of sadness, regretting the way life used to be, that despite his vest and firearms, he was virtually invisible to the commuters and tourists. The constant threat of terrorism—particularly in city centers such as this—had become that commonplace.

But a Metro Transit cop did notice.

Jonathan noted that he was being eyeballed by the guy a full thirty seconds before the cop started his way, talking into his radio as he approached. Even as the cop got closer, Jonathan wasn't sure whether his uniform was black or navy blue.

"Afternoon," the cop said. The name WEISER was stitched into his vest. "Mind if I ask you for some I.D.?"

In Jonathan's ear, Venice said, "Three minutes to Metro Center."

"Sure," Jonathan said. He pulled his creds case from his back pocket and fingered it open with one hand. "Special Agent Neil Bonner."

Weiser barely glanced at it. "What's up?" he asked. "Are you expecting trouble?"

"We're not sure," Jonathan said.

"Be careful, Boss," Boxers said in his earbud. "Don't overcommit."

Jonathan wasn't sure about the next step. He could use the additional set of eyes—as many additional sets as he could get—but Officer Weiser hadn't yet seen his twenty-fifth birthday and wouldn't have authority to be of meaningful help.

"We've got a pair of fugitives we're looking for, and we think they might be on one of the incoming trains." Jonathan liked the lie, so he sold it by sharing a picture of the twins from his phone. "We think they'll be carrying blue backpacks."

"Are the backpacks a problem?" Weiser asked.

"I hope not," Jonathan said. "That's the identifier I have. That's how I'll know it's them."

"Two minutes to Metro Center."

"Have you shared this with my command staff?" Weiser asked.

Jonathan forced a laugh. "Yeah, right. Right after my afternoon with Director Rivers, I called up your chief to give him a heads-up."

Weiser laughed, too. "Yours is not to reason why, right?"

"Exactly."

"Want me to pass the word to the others on my shift? We can keep an eye out, too."

"How many on duty here in the station?"

Weiser said, "Right now? Me and two others. Well, one other, really, cause one of them's driving the desk in the office."

It was a tempting offer.

"Don't do it, Scorpion," Boxers said.

Jonathan said, "Sure, we could use the extra eyes. Tell your counterpart to look for twins with backpacks."

"I can't detain somebody for being a twin," Weiser said. "Hell, I'm a twin."

"Break, break," Venice said. "I have a positive hit from a camera on at least one of the twins getting off the Red Line at Metro Center."

"What else do you have?" Jonathan asked. For Weiser's sake, he pointed to the bud in his ear.

"That's all of it," Venice said. "For now."

"I copy," Jonathan said. The clock was ticking down to nothing now. The target would either be Metro Center or here. If he'd guessed wrong, then there you go. A lot of people would die, and the perpetrators would get away with it—at least until Wolverine could take care of her *custodial duties*.

Jonathan stepped away from Weiser without saying anything more. Yes, it was probably rude, but he had work to do. "Mother Hen said it's a five-minute ride from Metro Center to here. That means any one of the trains that arrive in the next ten minutes."

Behind him, he could hear Weiser saying something about twins into his radio.

According to the electronic sign near the tracks, on the far side of the escalator from where Jonathan stood, the next Blue Line train would arrive in two minutes, and the next Orange Line would arrive in three. Then there'd be a Silver in five. Any one of them could have the Kadyrov brothers on board. Ditto the trains that were arriving downstairs.

People swarmed the tracks, awaiting their turn to climb aboard, even as others were trying to detrain.

This whole plan suddenly seemed like a very bad idea. Hopeless.

"Mother Hen?" Jonathan asked.

"Still nothing. They still have not used their fare cards to leave a station."

From behind, commuters continued to swarm in. Some headed to the Blue, Orange, and Silver tracks straight ahead, and others flowed down the escalators to the Green and Yellow lines. The suspended sign announced the current status of the incoming Blue Line train as ARR—arriving.

Even from this far away—call it fifty yards—Jonathan could feel the pulse of the air pressure as the eight-car train cleared the tunnel and slowed to a stop.

"Mother Hen, do you have good images from this station?"

"Better than most," she said. "More cameras working than not."

The doors of the train opened, and people surged

forward. "It's like watching a worm shit people," Boxers said.

"And every one of them is wearing a backpack," Gail observed.

The wall of people targeting Jonathan's turnstile moved like a tsunami, everyone jockeying for position to get their fare card into the slot before the guy behind them could beat them to the punch.

So many faces, so many backpacks.

But the backpacks didn't matter, did they? If the Kadyrov brothers got this far—got as far as the exit turnstile—they wouldn't have the backpacks with them. They would have dropped them somewhere in the station.

"Scorpion, Gunslinger. This is a lot of people."

"Hang in there," Jonathan said. "It's the best we've got. Thor?"

"I feel like a rock in a stream," he said.

As more people flowed into the station, Jonathan realized that the exodus had slowed to a trickle. People entered at their own schedule and pace but left in clumps.

As the Blue Line train left, Jonathan felt a sense of hopelessness. The brothers could have been tying their shoes right in front of him and not have been noticed. Maybe if he fired a shot in the air, he could start a stampede and clear the station that way.

And maim hundreds in the process.

The suspended sign announced that the Orange line was now arriving, and the scene from the Blue Line repeated itself. The train—with nine cars this time— glided to a stop, and the doors opened. People swarmed. It was all barely controlled—

"I've got them," Venice said. "They just got off the train."

Jonathan's heart rate doubled. "Where are they? Which car?"

"I don't have that level of detail. They're moving with the crowd. I don't know which direction. I don't have my bearings. I can't orient the directions."

"Weiser!" Jonathan shouted. "They're here."

"How do you—"

"I *know*, okay? Get your guys—"

Venice said, "They dumped a backpack behind a short wall."

"Just one?"

"Yes. They still have the other. They're still walking together."

Jonathan grabbed Weiser by the collar of his vest. "There's a backpack with a bomb behind a short wall. I don't even know what that means. It's chemical agent, not explosives. You need to evacuate the station."

"Jesus, I don't have that kind—"

Jonathan saw the Kadyrovs. They were walking together, showing no signs of urgency or stress.

Jonathan let go of the cop. "I see them. They're headed toward me."

"Headed your way," Boxers said.

This was it. Finally, it would be over.

But the brothers buttonhooked to their left, Jonathan's right, as they passed the escalator to the bottom level and started down.

"Shit, they're going below," Jonathan said. He took off at a run to catch them. People jammed the escalator—both sides—so he opted for the stairs. They were likewise packed. "Federal officer!" he said, pushing commuters aside. "Make a hole."

In his ear, he heard someone trying to say something, but the signal couldn't get through. Not down here.

At the bottom now, Jonathan was in the thick of the commuter soup.

"You almost made me fall, dickhead." Jonathan cranked his head to see a twenty-something with a congressional aide badge clipped to the pocket of his suit coat. "Goddamn cops. No wonder—"

Jonathan pushed him aside.

The Kadyrov brothers were here. Somewhere. According to the electronic signs, the next train would be an eight-car Yellow Line train and it would be arriving in two minutes.

This was nuts. It shouldn't be this hard. Jonathan needed a better vantage point. He darted to one of the stone benches designed for tired travelers and stood on the seat.

There!

They'd made their way to the far end of the track— whether the front or the rear of the train, Jonathan didn't know. They were surrounded by others, and they didn't seem to care.

And the second backpack was gone.

For all Jonathan knew, they'd put it directly under the bench he was standing on. Both bombs were set. All these people.

"Mother Hen, Scorpion. They need to evacuate this station."

Static. He had no idea if the message went through.

One minute till the next train.

Shit, shit, shit.

Jonathan mumbled, "Desperate measures, desperate times." He brought his M27 to his shoulder, took a deep breath, and yelled, "Kadyrov! Don't move!"

The assembled crowd yelled, but the brothers seemed almost ready for it. At the sound of their names, they pivoted on their own axis, drew pistols, and fired. Jonathan heard three shots, and a lady near him fell.

Jonathan was able to squeeze off one shot—an enormous, ear-shattering boom underground like this—before the panic consumed everything. He thought for sure that he hit one of the brothers, but the other was untouched.

People screamed. Some ran, some stayed still, but everybody was either pushing or being pushed. Jonathan had no shot to take. He couldn't even see his targets anymore.

And the train was approaching.

Lights in the floor flashed to announce the subway's arrival, and Jonathan could see the headlights approaching from inside the tunnel.

Jonathan had to get to the brothers before they could get on that train. He did not want to have a shootout in such a crowded space.

He pressed through the crowd, working his way back toward the Kadyrovs and the approaching subway train.

A woman screamed up ahead. It was the kind of scream that spelled more than fear. It was pure terror. "No!" she yelled. "Please, please, no!"

As the approaching Yellow Line train emerged from the tunnel, Jonathan got his first glimpse of a dead

Kadyrov on the floor, and then he saw a live Kadyrov using a teenager as a shield. He had his arm around her throat and a pistol to her head as an older woman—presumably her mother—begged him to let her go.

The instant Kadyrov saw Jonathan, he leveled the pistol at Jonathan and snapped off a shot. Essentially unaimed, the bullet passed frighteningly close. Jonathan dove behind one of the enormous concrete pillars that kept the main level of the station off of the lower level.

The train slowed just like the others had, but then it seemed to change its mind. From coasting speed, it launched off like a rocket, sending people inside the cars sprawling and increasing the panic on the platform.

An ear-splitting evacuation alarm sealed the rest of that deal. Within thirty seconds, the platform was empty.

Jonathan couldn't just cower here. Kadyrov was a man who wouldn't hesitate to kill thousands. A hostage wouldn't bother him a bit.

"Mr. FBI man!" Kadyrov yelled. "Do you want this girl to die? Can you live with that on your conscience?"

The mother pleaded, "Please let her go. Take me, instead. Please."

"How about I take you, too?"

Jonathan heard the modulation in the sound of Kadyrov's voice. He was moving, trying to get a better position. Jonathan shifted around his pillar.

"Are you Khasan or Aslan?" Jonathan yelled. He dared a peek around the curve of the pillar and saw that Kadyrov was using the girl dangling from his arm to protect the left side of his body and had the mother backing in unison to shield his right—the side that held the gun. It was a Glock, and he was trained well enough to keep his finger outside the trigger guard. It never ended well for hostage takers who accidentally blew the brains out of their hostages.

"You know my name!" Kadyrov said. "Then you know that I am not afraid of dying. Or of killing."

"You've got no play here," Jonathan said. "You can let your nerve toys do their thing, but who are you going to kill? Other than yourself, of course?" As he spoke, Jonathan slid to his belly on the floor, doing his best to preserve the protection of the pillar.

"I'll take out who I take out," Kadyrov said. "Maybe just us."

Lying on his right side, Jonathan shifted his rifle to his left shoulder and scanned for a target to shoot. Center of mass was out—any kill shot was out for right now, but with a little time and a touch of opportunity, you never knew.

If Kadyrov was willing to die from his own poison, he'd have activated his bomb by now. At least, that's what Jonathan told himself.

Over the squeal of the evacuation alarm, Jonathan heard Boxers yell, "Hey, Scorpion, how ya doin'?"

It was the fraction of an instant Jonathan needed. The sound of Big Guy's voice clearly startled Kadyrov, who whipped his head around to the source. In so doing, he lifted the teen's feet up off the ground high enough to expose his own ankle. Jonathan shot it.

Kadyrov lost his grip on the girl, and she dropped at his feet, exposing his entire torso. Jonathan shot him four times, and God only knew how many times Boxers shot him. Big Guy glided down the stairs with his HK 417 still pressed to his shoulder. Without looking at Jonathan, he said, "You okay, Boss? Need a Band-Aid or anything?"

"I'm fine, thanks."

"Glad to hear it. I believe this man is as dead as any dead man I've ever seen. How's his brother?"

"At least as dead."

"Okey-dokey," Boxers said. "Can we go home now?"

Chapter Thirty-one

James Abrenio stood as Connie Kendall entered the interview room. He waited until her shackles were removed and the guard was gone before he said, "Ryder and Geoff are fine. They've been rescued, and their captors are dead."

Her reaction startled him. As she brought her hands to her face, her knees buckled. He rushed forward and got his arms around her before she went all the way to the floor. "Easy, easy, easy," he said. "This is good news."

Connie put her arms around his shoulders, pressed her face into his shirt, and sobbed. James shot a nervous look toward the door, fearful of how the guard might react if he saw this kind of personal contact. Then he realized that he didn't care. He repositioned his arms and hugged her in return.

They stood like that for the better part of a minute as the emotion poured out of her, soaking his shirt. He thought he understood, but he wasn't sure. She'd lost her husband, thought she'd lost her children, and now the glimmer of good news broke everything loose inside. He decided to hold her until she pushed away.

Finally, she did. "I-I'm sorry," she said.

He helped her to a bolted-down chair.

"That came from nowhere. I'm so sorry."

"You've been through a lot," James said. He took the seat opposite hers.

Connie laughed and pointed. "Oh, my God," she said. "Your shirt."

He pulled it away from his chest and gave it a look. "It's just water and snot," he said. "I'm sure it'll wash out."

"Tell me about my boys," Connie said.

"That's pretty much all of it," James said. "They were rescued by a team from the FBI. Their kidnappers did not survive the encounter."

"Are Geoff and Ryder okay?"

"Entirely unhurt," James said. "They've been taken to a facility in Virginia, and last I heard, they were sleeping."

"What about emotionally?"

James hedged. "I don't know how to answer that. I'm certain that you'll be able to contact them soon."

"How did that happen? Who found them? How?"

James laughed and pumped the air with his hands. "Whoa, whoa, whoa. All in good time. I don't even know all of those details yet. I just know—I have *verified*—that they are safe and sound."

"Who's protecting them?"

"I've got that covered," James said. "Let me show you something." He lifted his soft leather briefcase from the floor and put it on its side on the table. "When

I spoke with the U.S. attorney yesterday and withdrew your agreement for immunity, she was not a happy camper. In fact, she essentially threw me out of her office and told me to tell you to get used to the idea of never seeing freedom again."

As he spoke, he saw a dreadful cloud form over Connie's features. He was ruining the moment.

"Wait, wait," he said. "There's a happy ending." He pulled a manila folder out of his briefcase and flipped it open. "What I have here is a new immunity agreement. Full and complete immunity from prosecution. Release from prison and house arrest until your cooperation is complete, and then you're free and clear."

Dread transformed to delight. "What does house arrest mean?"

"Just what it sounds like. Well, not your current house, and there's a witness protection element to it, but it means you can live with your children."

She covered her mouth with her hands. "Effective when?"

"Soon," James said. "As early as tomorrow, no longer than three or four days."

Connie thrust her hands onto her head, her fingers disappearing into the tangle of her hair.

"I-I don't understand. What changed? Other than Ryder and Geoff being safe?"

"I convinced them that you have a lot more to offer now than you did yesterday. Turns out that you are the key to uncovering a Chechen terrorist ring. And you can help identify the supply chain for a flow of chemical weapons into the United States."

Her expression of happiness dimmed. "The cartels

are not going to just sit by and let me testify. They're going to come after me."

"Uncle Sam is making a big offer, Connie. You can't expect it to be free of charge. Would it help to know that the Marshals have never lost a WitSec participant?" He opened the immunity offer to the back page and handed her a pen from his suitcoat pocket. "The sooner you sign, the sooner you'll see your boys."

"Can I take a few minutes to read it?"

"Of course," James said through a smile. "Just don't even try to change a word of it."

The shootout in the Washington Metro system made national news. It seemed that Khasan and Aslan Kadyrov were wanted for the murders of three men in Blanton, Tennessee, in an argument over a methamphetamine lab they were running out of an outbuilding. They were tracked to Washington, and when the FBI moved in to make an arrest, the brothers opened fire and were killed.

Some stills released from Metro's security cameras showed the final confrontation. The agents' faces were blurred, however.

According to a Justice Department spokesman who got face time almost every week on the news networks, the rumors of backpacks filled with chemical weapons proved to be false. Yes, the Kadyrov brothers had backpacks that they discarded, but they contained only drug paraphernalia. The backpacks were treated as hazardous materials, nonetheless.

"Can you mute that, please?" Jonathan asked. The

Security Solutions team sat around the teak table in the War Room.

Venice clicked the remote, and the screen went silent.

"You know that's all a lie, right?" Jonathan asked. "A buddy of mine down at Blue Grass Army Depot in Kentucky told me Uncle Sam disarmed those two devices and shipped the active ingredients out to them. Drug paraphernalia, my ass."

"What, you want us to take credit?" Gail asked.

"Of course not," Jonathan said. "But nothing about that report was true, other than the dead bodies. They make lying look so easy."

"Here's the best part," Boxers said. "If a reporter gets too close to the truth, they'll be labeled conspiracy theorists. I think the system works perfectly."

"Did you notice the blurred faces?" Venice asked. "Yours in particular?"

"I did," Jonathan said. "That was good work. Thank you."

"That wasn't my good work," Venice said. "That was Derek's good work. He was able to program the NSA facial recognition program to automatically recognize and blur your features. Boxers' and Gail's, too. Even mine, for whatever reason. Until someone recognizes the change and fixes it, you never have to worry about being inadvertently photographed."

Jonathan saw the pain in her face as she remembered Derek. "He was a good man," he said. "I should have been nicer to him."

"What's the deal with Harry Dawkins now?" Venice asked. "Is he joining the team or not?"

"For now, he wants to have his cake and eat it, too. He's only a few years away from a government pension But he says he'll try to be here if we need him."

"I want to say something," Gail said. "For the record. We did the right thing going after the Kadyrovs. We had a responsibility to act on the special information we had."

Jonathan and Boxers exchanged looks. "Okaaay . . ."

"Just promise me we'll never do something like that again."

ACKNOWLEDGMENTS

There's an old trope among authors that writing is a solitary, lonely business. In my experience, that's really not true. Sure, when I'm deep in my head writing a story, I need to have a quiet room and I prefer not to be disturbed, but that's pretty much the way it is with any job, isn't it? I'm fortunate to be surrounded with a supportive team of friends, family, and fellow professionals who make what I do a delightful experience.

The star of my team is likewise the star of my life. Without my lovely bride, Joy, nothing would be worth anything. I love her more every day.

On the technical side of things, I owe thanks to a lot of people. Rick McMahan, Jeff Gonzales, and Steve Tarani show great patience as my weapons experts, as does Robbie Reidsma of Heckler and Koch. Chris Thomas is my go-to for aircraft-related expertise. Thanks, guys.

Craig and Connie Kendall have been friends of mine for decades, and they're genuinely wonderful people. So wonderful, in fact, that they donated generously to the RiteCare Scottish Rite Childhood Language Program to have characters named after them. As they say, this book is a work of fiction, and any similarity between characters and real people is purely accidental.

While on the topic of Freemasonry, many thanks to all my brothers for being a constant source of support and friendship.

James Abrenio . . . I told you I'd do it!

Thanks, also, to the Rumpus Writers. I deeply value the company and critical abilities of Art Taylor, Donna Andrews, Ellen Crosby, and Alan Orloff.

My team at Kensington continues to work overtime to make me look better than I am. My editor and lead whip-cracker, Michaela Hamilton, is the best in the business. We've walked a lot of miles together, and I've enjoyed every step. A thousand thanks to my publisher, Lynn Cully, and to Steve Zacharius, the man in the corner office. Thanks, too, to Vida Engstrand in the publicity department, who, together with Lauren Jernigan, Ann Pryor, and the rest of team, make it possible for my work to somehow rise above the noise of the book industry. And, of course, there's Alexandra Nicholajsen, my real-life Venice, who helps me tame the ones and zeroes of cyberspace.

Finally, thanks to my friend and agent, Anne Hawkins of John Hawkins and Associates in New York, for making this ride a really fun one.

Exciting news for thriller fans!
John Gilstrap is about to launch a brand-new
thriller series.
Introducing a bold new leader in a dangerous world . . .

CRIMSON PHOENIX

Coming soon from Kensington Publishing Corp.

Keep reading to enjoy a sample excerpt.

Chapter One

Phones shouldn't ring after 8 P.M. Anything after five, even, was always bad news. Now, at ten-fifteen, a voice asked, "Is this Victoria Emerson, U.S. representative for Idaho's Fourth Congressional District?"

The question came before she could say hello. "Who is this?" she asked.

"Please respond to my question." The voice was male, and his tone was urgent.

"Yes, it is," she said. "Now who is this?"

"Major Joseph McCrea," the voice replied. "Dragon Fire is active. This is not a drill."

Victoria's heart skipped, leaving her light-headed for an instant. "Dragon Fire?" she asked. She heard the tremble in her voice, and it angered her. "Not Dragon *Shield*. Dragon *Fire*?" The difference meant everything.

"Yes, Ma'am, Dragon *Fire*. I will arrive in five minutes to transport you to safety."

It was too much to comprehend. The United States was at *war*. DEFCON One. Release of nuclear weapons imminent. "I-I don't know that I can be ready that quickly."

"Ma'am, I have orders," McCrae said. "I'm taking you to safety. You do not have a vote in this. Five minutes." The line clicked to silence.

Victoria stared at the handset. Could this really be happening?

The kids.

"Lucas!" she yelled. "Caleb! Out here, right now." As she spoke, she beelined across the living room and took the stairs two at a time to the second floor of their split-level Arlington rental. "Lucas and Caleb, now!"

Their rooms lay to the left at the top of the stairs, and the doors were close enough that she could throw them open simultaneously, prompting them both to snap their laptops closed in a weird unison.

"Mom!" they said together.

"How about a knock?" Caleb added. Barely fourteen and the oldest by two years, he'd settled comfortably into his teenage self-righteousness.

"Both of you," she said. "Grab your go-bags and be ready in three minutes."

Caleb rolled his eyes. "I've got a math test tomorrow. Can't I skip this one?"

As if math were the reason he so quickly slapped his screen shut. "No," she said. Her tone left no room for discussion. "We do these things for a reason."

She shifted her focus to the room on the left, to Lucas's room. He was already up and on his way to his closet. He enjoyed the bug-out drills. "You heard me Luke?"

"I'm doing it now," he said. "Where are we going this time?"

"Three minutes," Victoria repeated.

Though her heart raced and her head swam with fear, there was a certain calm in knowing exactly what to do. She'd gotten the idea of bug-out drills from Stan Hastings, a colleague from Maryland's Fifth District, who convinced her that as the world grew steadily more dangerous, there was an ever-increasing chance that the time would come when elected officials would need to leave their urban homes in a hurry. In a day when politicians were assaulted in restaurants and on the streets, was it that much of a stretch to imagine a time when they'd be attacked in their homes?

"Nobody ever died from an abundance of safety," Stan had told her.

And now it was paying off. Victoria darted to her closet, where a jungle-camouflaged backpack sat in the corner. The contents of her pack were identical to that of each of the boys', with obvious accommodations for gender and size. It contained a complete change of clothes, toiletries, a liter of water, and an assortment of energy bars. And, if they had to hunt for food or defend themselves, each pack contained a Ruger 10/22 Takedown Lite rifle along with one hundred rounds of .22 Long Rifle ammunition.

Fully loaded, the packs weighed about twenty-five pounds, borderline too heavy for Luke over long periods, but if he started to wear out, she and Caleb could redistribute some of his stuff to their own packs. God forbid Luke be given a lighter load to begin with. "I'm as strong as he is" versus "Why can't he carry his fair share?"

If it came to that, Victoria had every confidence that they'd work it out somehow.

When she returned to the hallway, the boys were there. Luke looked genuinely ready to go. Long-sleeve shirt, jeans, hiking boots. Caleb wore a T-shirt, shorts, and flip-flops. It was his silent thumb in her eye.

"Caleb Morris Emerson," she said in the tone that still inspired fear. "Put the correct clothes on and be ready to go."

"Why? All we do is drive around and—"

She sharpened her look, and he backed away.

"Okay, *fine.*" Caleb stormed back into his room. Coat hangers clattered against the walls of his closet, boots thumped against the floor.

"Are you okay, Mom?" Luke asked. "You seem . . . nervous."

What could she say? *I* am *nervous, baby. The world is about to end . . .*

The house shook from a heavy hand pounding on the front door.

"Jesus!" Luke blurted.

"Watch your mouth," Victoria snapped. "Caleb, now! Come with me, Luke." She tried to keep her stride even and calm as she descended the stairs and crossed the living room.

The pounding repeated, this time more staccato.

"I'm coming!" Victoria yelled.

"Don't answer it!" Caleb yelled from above. "It's dark out. You don't know who it might be." When he wasn't totally consumed by being a pain in the ass, her eldest took his man-of-the-house role very seriously.

"You just hurry up and get down here!"

Victoria pulled the door open to reveal an Army major in a crisply pressed jungle camouflage uniform. He carried a holstered pistol on his hip. Behind him, three other soldiers flanked the walkway to her front door, their backs turned as they scanned the neighborhood for threats.

"Good evening, ma'am," the major said.

"Not hardly," she replied. "Is this really real?"

"Ma'am, given your position, I imagine that you know more than I do. I have my orders, and you are them."

Caleb arrived in the doorway. "Who the hell is this?"

"My name is Major McCrae," the soldier said. "Ma'am, we have to leave right now." He reached out to grab her arm, and she pulled away.

"How dare you touch me," she said.

"Hey, asshole," Caleb said. "What are you—"

"Quiet, son," McCrea said. "Ma'am, I already told you. You don't have a say in what follows. I would love for you to walk with me, but if I have to carry you, that's what I will do."

"You can't talk to my mom like that," Caleb said. "She's a member of Congress."

"Caleb, hush," Victoria snapped.

"But you're his boss!"

Victoria held up a hand to calm her son. "Caleb, we're going with the major."

Luke looked as frightened as Caleb looked angry. "Mom?"

McCrea said, "Just you, Ma'am. Not the boys."

"Bullshit," she said. "I'm not leaving them."

"Ma'am, you know the rules. I am authorized only—"

"Major McCrea," Victoria said. "I understand that you have your orders, but if you try to separate me from my kids, one of us—you or me—is going to wake up dead in the morning. Do not try me on this point, sir."

She saw her words impact the major. No one in Congress had greater respect than she for the American military, and one of the reasons why the system had worked as well as it had over these two and a half centuries was that even the highest-ranking officers understood the importance of civilian oversight and control.

He blinked.

"Very well, then," McCrea said. "All of you. But we have to move now."

Victoria put an arm around each of her boys and ushered them out the door and into the humid July air. "You heard the major," she said. "Time to go."

"Go where?" Caleb protested. "This isn't how a bug-out drill works. Who is this guy?"

"I'll explain in the car," Victoria said. "We have to go."

Once they were all out on the front stoop, Victoria closed the door behind them. Then she pulled up short. "Dammit," she said. "I forgot my keys."

"Keep going," McCrea said. "I'll personally replace anything that might get stolen." He used a gentle touch on her backpack to keep the parade moving out into the yard.

"Are you really going to do that?" Luke asked. "Replace anything that gets stolen?"

"No," McCrea said. "What's in the rucksacks?"

"Survival gear," Victoria said, and she recited the list.

"Any electronic gear in them?" McCrea asked. "Phones, tablets, e-readers, laptops?"

The boys stared, clearly a silent yes.

McCrae made a beckoning motion with his hand. "Hand them over. All of it. Cell phones, too."

"Why do you need them?" Victoria asked.

"Because my orders tell me to confiscate them. And, ma'am, you can bet that 'I have orders' will be my standard answer to every question you might have. I'm not making this stuff up as I go along."

"What are you going to do with our stuff?" Caleb asked. He hadn't moved.

"What's your name, son?"

Caleb told him.

"Well, Caleb, here's the thing," McCrea said. "You can take them out carefully and hand them over, or I can have my troops take *all* of your stuff and leave it behind."

Caleb looked wounded. "Mom?"

Victoria did not like this man, and she particularly did not like his manner. No one had the right to speak to her or her children that way. "Do what he says."

"But Mom—"

"Now, Caleb. You, too, Luke. Take out all of your electronics and hand them over to the major."

Victoria unslung her pack and set the example for her boys. When Caleb complied, Luke followed suit, handing over more gear than Victoria even knew they carried.

McCrea said, "Thank you. Now we need to get going."

Soldiers formed a security corridor that dead-ended at a black Suburban idling at the curb. They all carried rifles, but they didn't seem anxious to use them. In fact, they mostly looked terrified.

As they reached the curb, Caleb pulled up short. "No," he said. "This isn't the way it works, Mom. This has *never* been the way it works. We go in our own car because that's where the extra provisions are."

Victoria pulled on his arm. "Not this time, Caleb."

"Stop!" Caleb yelled. He was far louder than he needed to be, and Victoria knew this was his way of getting the most attention. "Tell me what is going on! I am not getting into a car with a guy in a uniform who *says* he's a general or a major or whatever. Jesus, Mom, you've trained us not to do that very thing."

This was going to spin out of control. Neighbors would soon be peeking out windows, and maybe they were already calling the police.

Victoria shot her hand out like a striking snake and cupped Caleb's neck at the spot where his spine joined his skull, and she pulled him close. "Do not shout," she said. She looked to the men who surrounded her, then dropped her voice even lower. "The reason this is different is because this time it's not a drill."

She felt him stiffen as his skin became hot. "W-what are you telling me?"

"I'm telling you to get in the car," she said. "We can talk all you want in there. But not out here." She let go.

To her left, Lucas stood very still. A shadow engulfed his face, but his glistening eyes shined through. "Mom, I'm scared," he said.

"We're all scared," she said, cupping the back of his head and urging him toward the Suburban.

Victoria looked to McCrea, but he was stone-faced. Next to him, a young soldier looked close to tears. "You should get home to your family," Victoria said to him.

The soldier stiffened and shifted his eyes to the ground.

McCrea added more pressure to her back. "Inside, Ma'am," he said. "It's not a short drive."

It wasn't until she was seated inside the Suburban and they were moving that she realized the driver was also in an Army uniform.

"Mom, you said we'd talk about what's happening once we were in the car," Caleb reminded her. "We're there now."

Her head was spinning way beyond answers to a fourteen-year-old. She ignored him. "Major McCrea," she said.

He turned and looked at her from the shotgun seat.

"Why are the roads clear? Why haven't our phones squealed with an emergency alert?"

"I'm not the policy person, Congressman. Congresswoman?"

"Ma'am is fine," she said. If this were a different day, she'd have asked to be called Victoria, but not tonight. She was senior to every military officer in the country, and they needed to know that.

She was tempted to press for an answer when a piece fell into place for her. The NCA—National Command Authority—wanted the elements of the federal government ensconced in safety before the possible retaliatory strike could be launched. They couldn't alert the media or the general public without alerting the enemy.

"Oh, my God," she said. "We're launching the first strike, aren't we?" She directed her words to the back of McCrea's head, but she was surprised to hear them spoken out loud.

"Mom?" Luke said through a choked voice. "What are you talking about?"

"Are we going to war?" Caleb asked. He looked even more frightened, but he couldn't possibly understand the ramifications of war.

"I think we might, sweetie," she said.

"You're a congresswoman," Caleb protested. "Don't they have to get your permission first? We studied that."

"Only for a declared war," she answered. "The president has wide discretion short of that." *And we gave her that power*, she thought. The United States had not fired a bullet in a declared war since Japan's surrender in 1945, but it had nonetheless sent thousands of its sons and daughters to die in conflicts all around the world.

Victoria was only in her third two-year term in the House of Representatives, having won each time by huge margins in her district, but she was as aware as any news junkie of the growing troubles between the United States and Iran and Russia, with Israel being the focus of it all, but she was nowhere near the top secret inside scoop on impending war.

"What about Adam?" Luke asked.

Victoria's stomach flipped. The oldest of her three boys, sixteen-year-old Adam, was Victoria's firstborn troublemaker, and he had refused to make the trip from Idaho to the Washington 'burbs. He chose instead to enroll in the Junior N. Van Noy Military Academy in Preston.

"Major, I need to contact my son," she said.

McCrea shot a look to the driver but said nothing.

"Major McCrea, did you hear me?"

"I heard you," he said.

"I need to call him."

"That can't happen," McCrea said. "Operational security is paramount."

"But my *son* is in jeopardy."

Again, McCrea said nothing.

"Major, I need your phone."

"Ma'am, I can't allow you to use the phone. I can't allow you to use flares, smoke signals, or loud screams. The rules for Dragon Fire are very clear on this."

Victoria leaned forward in her seat, grabbed a handful of McCrea's uniform shirt. "I'm not *asking*, Major, I'm telling you—"

McCrea whirled in his seat, taking her on face-to-face. "That your son is in danger!" he shouted. "Yes, I get that. So is mine. And his two sisters and my wife. Three hundred fifty *million* American sons and daughters are in danger, *Representative* Emerson. You have a free pass to a safe bunker, Ma'am, but you're one of the lucky eleven hundred. Countless sons and daughters are about to die. I pray to God that yours and mine are not among them."

Victoria started to say something, but McCrea wasn't done.

"I think there's a very good chance that I won't see tomorrow, Ma'am, and I don't think there's a chance in hell that I'll see next weekend. But I have orders to deliver you to safety, and that is what I am going to do. I have orders to maintain strict electronic silence on this, and I'm going to do that, too. If I'm remembered by anyone for anything I've done, it will be that my last act on Earth was to obey my orders. Are we clear on this?"

The heat in McCrae's eyes was blistering. His words infuriated her, but less for the delivery than for the reality of their meaning. America was going to war.

And millions were likely to die.